Drawn Back

By Keith Tittle

This book is dedicated to my mother, Donna Doyle, who passed along her love for novels, and her desire to write them. I trust this would have made the grade, Mom.

My deepest thanks to my family, to Denny Bershaw, and to the others in my life who have inspired and supported me through the creative process; to my Muse, who restored my passion for writing; and finally, to Mark "Crusher of Hopes and Dreams" Lewis, for volunteering his invaluable editing services.

–1–

August 4, 1929

Footsteps and angry whispers.

Carl's eyelids fluttered open involuntarily at the sounds, but his eyes registered only shadows ... vague, indistinct, shapes.

There should have been more pain. That's how he knew he was dying. It had been excruciating at first, but now he lay sprawled awkwardly across the floor like one of his daughter Julia's old rag dolls, beyond the pain. Beyond caring.

He was dimly aware of the slow rasp of his own breathing, and of the hands that gripped him, roughly. But when the final moment came, Carl didn't feel much of anything at all.

He'd become little more than a silent, detached, spectator at his own execution.

January 18, 1991

Patrick O'Connell zipped his light jacket up before stepping onto the sidewalk outside of Cramer Hall. The January air in Portland felt crisp, but it was far from the bitter cold of his winters at the University of Wisconsin. He walked at a leisurely pace, watching with amusement as a parka-clad student scurried by like an Inuit in an Arctic storm.

Then he checked his watch and saw that he had only five minutes until his appointment with Miss Wirth. Turning east, Patrick hurried across Broadway to the administrative offices in the University Services Building.

When he'd joined Portland State's history department, the university had arranged for a small apartment near the campus. But the space had proved too small for a lifetime's collection of books and records, so Patrick posted a notice on the staff bulletin board saying that he was in the market for a house to rent.

Within a day, Miss Wirth had contacted him to say that she had just the house he was looking for. They'd arranged to meet in front of the University Services Building, where she worked as an administrative assistant, so that she could give him a tour. What they hadn't arranged, Patrick realized as he came to the building entrance, was a method to recognize each other.

"Professor O'Connell?"

He turned to see a petite young woman—bundled up in a heavy coat and gloves—hurrying along the sidewalk.

"I thought that might be you. I'm Rachel Wirth. Hopefully, you haven't been waiting too long," she said. "I had to drop off a file at the English Department, and it took a little longer than I'd expected."

"Just got here myself," Patrick assured her. Rachel smiled in relief as she directed him to her car, a newer BMW sedan parked along the curb.

"Nice car," he observed as he settled into the comfortable leather seat. "Admins must get paid more here than at the University of Wisconsin."

"Hardly!" she said with a laugh as she maneuvered into afternoon traffic. "This was a gift from my Grandma, Julia. She spoils me a little."

A few minutes later they merged onto the 405 freeway, heading north. Rachel signaled for the inside lane.

"I was surprised to hear you were looking for a house to rent already," she said, casually. "The apartment the University arranged for you must be cramping your wild bachelor lifestyle."

Patrick looked over in time to catch her grin. "Careful," he said with a smile, "that's how reputations get ruined."

"Or enhanced."

He laughed in spite of himself. "I'm pretty much a recluse these days. Just give me a good book and some jazz on the stereo and I'm happy."

Rachel glanced at him. "Oh, we're going to have to work on that," she assured him.

They took the Vaughn Street off-ramp, just before the Fremont Bridge. Ahead, a large white structure at the very base of the West Hills dominated the neighborhood. Atop the building, towering letters proclaimed it to be Montgomery Park.

Rachel must have seen him looking at the sign. "That's the old Montgomery Ward building. Someone remodeled it for office space and changed the name a couple of years ago. It'll always be *Monkey Wards* to my dad, though."

"I thought my father was the only one who used that line," Patrick said with a laugh. He looked at the street ahead. "This may be a little farther from the campus than I'd hoped. What's the commute like?"

"You're just a couple of blocks from a bus stop, or a twenty minute bike ride."

"At my age, that sounds too much like exercise."

"And you're *so* old," she agreed with mock seriousness.

The car headed west along Thurman. Stately elm trees formed an archway of branches across the road, and vintage apartment buildings, immaculately maintained, lined the right side of the street. On the other side, equally-aged storefronts advertised ethnic delights and funky chic.

As they continued on, the apartments and stores gave way to tidy wood-framed houses. Patrick guessed that most had been built before the thirties, although some might have dated back to the turn of the century. They crossed a steeply-inclined bridge, probably as old as the neighborhood itself. Below, a narrow, heavily wooded ravine stretched off to the south.

"One of the entrances to Forest Park," Rachel explained, clearly enjoying her role as tour guide. "There's miles of trails that wind all through these hills."

Patrick nodded. "The largest woodland city park in the country."

"Sounds like somebody's been reading the Chamber of Commerce brochures."

"I didn't want to come out here and look like a complete tourist," he admitted with a laugh.

Thurman continued to climb, following slow, serpentine curves along the side of the hill. Above, tendrils of cloud danced with the smoke that rose from nearby chimneys, caught in the tangled branches of ancient trees. In the distance, the Willamette River threaded its way through the valley to disappear into gray winter mists.

"Here we are," Rachel announced, pulling the BMW over to the curb.

As they climbed out into the brisk afternoon air, Patrick took a moment to study the house in front of him. Built along the northern edge of the street, the house stood two storeys high, but probably no more than thirty feet deep from front door to back wall, ingeniously allowing it to take advantage of its narrow sliver of a lot. The hill dropped away sharply behind the building, affording a spectacular view of the river basin below.

Provided that he could afford the rent, Patrick doubted that he'd find a more perfect location.

"Coming, Professor?" Rachel called from across the street. She stood beside a gate set into a low rock wall. Beyond the wall, the hillside rose in terraced levels to a house unlike any he'd ever seen. The first storey had been built of stone, large quarried pieces of rock giving the structure the feel of a mountain lodge. Above that, wood framing carried the house up until it reached a half-timbered gable and steeply pitched roof.

Rachel grinned at him, crooking a finger, and playfully beckoned him to join her. As he approached she opened the gate.

"I think there's been a mistake," Patrick said as they walked up the wide steps. "There's no way I could rent a house like this."

"I know it doesn't look like much from the outside," Rachel laughed, "but I think you'll love it if you give it a chance."

She unlocked the heavy front door and stepped aside, ushering him in.

The interior exuded an understated charm and lack of pretense that caught Patrick by surprise. The finishing touches—like the oak paneling and recessed ceilings— were clearly expensive, but they were neither gaudy nor impractical. The house had been built as a home, not a showcase.

"Make yourself comfortable while I go put the tea kettle on," Rachel said, guiding him to the parlor.

The room felt like a museum display capturing life in a typical 1920's American home. The vintage Mission-style furniture had been arranged to take full advantage of the view; the landscaped hillside, the trees lining the street, and the river stretching off into the unseen distance.

"Look who I found lurking in the kitchen," Rachel said brightly from behind.

Patrick turned as she came into the room carrying a silver tea service, followed by an elderly, elegant woman dressed in a Kate Hepburn-style pants suit. She looked to be in her eighties, but carried herself with an energy that made her seem much younger. The woman glided across the room—there could be no other description for the way she moved—and greeted him with a warm smile.

"Professor O'Connell! It's a pleasure to see you again."

Patrick was startled by the familiarity of her greeting, but he recovered in time to extend his hand.

"A pleasure, Mrs. ... Wirth?" The sentence ended as a question, Patrick completely uncertain as to the identity of the person now firmly clutching his hand like an old friend.

Rachel, standing to one side, seemed to be thoroughly enjoying his discomfort.

"Professor O'Connell," she said at last, "this is my grandmother, Julia Wirth. Grandma, this is Professor Patrick O'Connell."

"Rachel, I obviously know this young man." Julia caught Patrick's eye and winked as she released his hand at last. She directed him to the sofa nearest the window, then took a seat in one of the high-backed armchairs near the fireplace

"But he," she added with a look of disappointment, "clearly doesn't remember me."

He was about to apologize when he saw the same mischievous gleam in Julia's eyes that he had seen when her granddaughter teased him.

"It's all right, professor," Mrs. Wirth said with a laugh as she accepted a cup of tea from Rachel. "I would have been very surprised if you had remembered. We met only briefly at President Lattimer's faculty mixer."

"Grandma is a major contributor to the university," Rachel explained as she brought Patrick his tea.

"I would hardly refer to us as *major* contributors, although the Senator and I always tried to be supportive. And my donations do get me invited to all the best parties. Now, professor ..."

"Please, call me Patrick, Mrs. Wirth."

"And you must call me Julia," she replied with a warm smile. "So tell me, Patrick, what do you think of our house?"

Before Patrick could answer, Rachel jumped in. "Oh, I don't think the professor likes it at all. He told me he could *never* live in a house like this."

"That's not what ..."

"Is that true, Professor?" Julia asked, eyebrow arched in mock indignation.

"No, it's just that ..." he began again, then gave up with a laugh when he saw their amused expressions. He resigned himself to being the straight man to their comedy team. They were Siamese twins born sixty years apart, and joined at the sense of humor.

"Well, Patrick," Julia said as she rose from her chair, "despite your shocking lack of architectural appreciation, I insist that you allow me to take you on a tour."

"I'd be honored," he told her, standing as well. Julia took his arm and led him from the parlor, Rachel trailing close behind.

"The house was built in 1910 as an anniversary present for my mother," Julia explained, pausing in the entryway. "We lived at the bottom of the hill at the time, just on the other side of Balch Creek, and Mama and Papa went for walks up into the Heights nearly every evening.

Mama loved to look at all of the beautiful homes and dream.

"One evening, they walked farther along the hill than normal, and Papa stopped in front of this house. 'What do you think of this one?' he asked. Mama, of course, thought it was wonderful. Then he took her hand in his and she felt something cool press into her palm. It was the key to the front door.

"I still have that key," she added, in soft voice.

Patrick smiled at the image. He'd always been a sucker for stories like that, an unabashed romantic.

They moved on into the dining room, large enough to accommodate a party of twenty with ease. Patrick's eyes were immediately drawn to the high ceiling, where plaster detailing divided the surface into three foot square panels, joined at each corner by small diamond-shaped sections. Within the center of each panel, a four-leafed clover design had been fashioned.

"That's called quatrefoil," Julia said, following his gaze. "Papa thought clovers would bless the house with good luck."

"Was he right?" He regretted the question when he saw a brief sadness pass across Julia's face.

"Not entirely," she answered, simply, as she guided them into the kitchen.

The white wooden cupboards reminded Patrick of the Midwestern farm kitchen at his grandparent's house in Iowa. At the far end of the room a small breakfast nook, with a simple wooden table and four straight-back chairs, overlooked the back yard.

The only jarring elements in the kitchen were the hideous avocado colored stove and refrigerator, obvious remnants of the seventies.

Fortunately, there were no more anachronisms as the tour continued. The woodwork and cabinetry throughout the house spoke of a genuine pride in craftsmanship. All of the furniture had been beautifully fashioned of oak, in the same Mission style as the pieces in the parlor.

"Every stick of it came from my father's factory down the hill," Julia told him with obvious pride. "He handcrafted much of it himself."

As they climbed the stairs to the second floor, Patrick found himself drawn to a large oval portrait of a young woman. The photograph had been hand-tinted to capture the brown of her eyes and the auburn in her hair. Typical of the period, the woman's face held no expression. Still, Patrick thought he could see the beginnings of an irrepressible smile at the corners of her mouth.

Julia, he knew at once.

"Would you like us to leave the two of you alone?" Rachel teased, standing on the step below him.

"Don't be jealous, dear," Julia said. "You can't fault a history professor for showing a little interest in an old relic."

"Grandma, I would hardly call you a relic," Rachel laughed.

"We are none of us what we used to be, are we?" Julia looked to Patrick, smiling slyly before continuing upstairs.

There were four bedrooms on the second floor, not overly-large but comfortable. Two of the rooms faced the back of the property, the garden and the tree-lined hills.

The other two—Julia's and her brother's rooms, in their youth—looked out over Thurman Street and the Willamette River, far below.

"My window on the world," Julia called it.

"It's an amazing view, and an amazing house. I don't know how you can leave it."

Julia looked at him in surprise. "Patrick, I haven't lived here in almost sixty years, not since I married Mr. Wirth. No, the house is quite empty and in need of looking after."

"But, all of the furnishings. I thought ..."

"I could never bring myself to part with them, or the house. I'll feel so much more comfortable knowing that you'll be here to truly appreciate and care for things."

"As much as I would love to, I doubt that I could begin to cover the rent on a house like this."

"The *rent*?" Julia turned to her granddaughter.

"I forgot to tell him," Rachel said, wearing a guilty smirk, "at least, at first. And then when I saw the look on his face out front ..."

Now it was Patrick's turn to be confused. "Would someone like to tell me what's going on?"

"Patrick, dear, I never intended to rent this house to you," Julia said, casting a half-hearted scowl in Rachel's direction before smiling up at him. "I want to *pay* you to stay here."

Over the next few weeks, January sleet and ice gave way grudgingly to February rain. Layers of gray clouds, coming in from the Pacific Ocean, pushed up over the

West Hills and spilled out over Portland in a thick, rain-saturated blanket.

There were times, Patrick had to admit, that the incessant rain got on his last nerve. But on a lazy Sunday morning—sitting by a toasty fire, with Cannonball Adderley's *Willow Weep For Me* playing softly on the stereo—the rain pattering against the library windows seemed almost a luxury.

The decision to accept Julia's offer to serve as caretaker hadn't been a particularly difficult one for Patrick to arrive at, and for reasons far more compelling than the money he would save on his expenses. There was something about the house itself that captivated him; certain buildings echoed with history as they aged, but Julia's home practically resonated with it.

Julia had offered him five hundred dollars a month to live there. Since he didn't really need the extra income, he'd offered instead to do the job in return for the roof over his head.

"Old houses need lots of love and attention," Julia had insisted. "I'll see a return on my investment eventually."

He briefly considered attempting to renegotiate their arrangement again that afternoon, when Julia and Rachel came for their weekly tea, but as his grandfather had always pointed out, "There's not much to be gained by beating a dead horse."

Julia stretched her legs out, bringing her feet closer to the warmth of the fire. "One of the curses of growing old," she sighed. "I always seem to be cold, especially this time of year."

Patrick had arranged two chairs in the library near the hearth, with the tea service set up on a table between them. The weekly teas had been her idea. "Visiting privileges," she'd called them. Rachel usually joined them, but this afternoon her grandmother had her running errands, joking that she'd wanted Patrick all to herself.

"This room was always my favorite growing up," Julia said, looking about the book-lined room with a smile. "Rachel's as well. She used to line all of her stuffed animals up by the window and read to them as if she were the teacher and they the class."

"I can't help but notice that the two of you are a lot alike."

Julia considered his observation for a moment.

"We are, aren't we?" she conceded at last, a touch of amusement visible in her eyes. "My son implies that it's more of a curse than a blessing. He says she's entirely too strong-willed for her own good."

"Something no one would ever accuse you of, I'm sure."

"Well, just between the two of us, I've always had an independent streak a mile wide, much to my late husband's dismay."

"How did you and the Senator meet?"

"A friend of mine introduced us, just after my father died. There were some complications with the estate. Ed had just opened his law office here, and I hired him to attend to the legal issues."

"Love at first sight?"

"Hardly," she chuckled. "Ed was a wonderful man, but I certainly don't remember a bolt from the heavens when we met."

"Does that sort of thing *ever* really happen, outside of the movies?" Patrick asked with a smile.

Julia cocked her head to one side, looking at him seriously. "Oh, it happens all right. Not often. Perhaps once in a lifetime, but when it does ..." She paused, then grinned. "It did not, however, happen with me when I met the Senator. It's a good thing he was persistent, or I might have wound up an old maid."

Patrick laughed. "I doubt that very much, Julia."

"I suppose you're right," she admitted, looking to the fire. Her voice took on a softer, more somber tone. "Going through life alone isn't a very appealing prospect, is it?" She turned to him with a wry smile. "Speaking of which, I think I should warn you that Rachel is becoming quite fond of you."

He shifted a little in his seat, uncomfortably. He'd picked up on Rachel's interest, as well, and had no idea how to deal with it.

"I have to warn you," Julia told him, "if she inherited anything from her grandfather, it was his determination."

"I'll try to remember that."

"Patrick, dear," she said, reaching over to give his hand an affectionate pat, "I doubt very much that she's going to give you the opportunity to let it slip your mind."

"What about you, Julia? Have you always been the persistent type who got what she wanted out of life?"

Her smile grew thoughtful. "I learned a long time ago that fate rarely hands you precisely what you want, and when it does, it's never exactly how you would have scripted it."

Patrick nodded. "The story of my life. What I haven't been able to master is the knack of handling that with your obvious grace."

Julia grinned.

"Grace, my ... Aunt Fannie! Frankly, I don't know how Ed put up with my impatience when I was younger. Eventually, though, I realized something important."

She leaned forward, suddenly as serious as he'd ever seen her.

"You have to have faith that things will work out the way that they're meant to. Perhaps not the way you would have wanted, but the way they were meant to be, just the same."

Patrick kept his doubts to himself.

An hour later, Julia was napping in her chair beside the fire. Patrick carried the tea service into the kitchen and had just begun to wash out the cups when the doorbell rang.

He opened the front door to find Rachel, her coat dripping with rain and her hair in a wet tangle of curls.

"Haven't you ever heard of an umbrella?" he asked as he ushered her inside.

"You are new around here, aren't you? Real Portlanders don't use those things." She noticed that he was still looking at her.

"*What?*" she asked, looking a little self-conscious.

"I was just thinking that bedraggled looks good on you."

"Careful, Professor," she said with a smile. "Grandma Julia's going to think she has competition."

She walked down the hall to the library, leaving Patrick with the disquieting feeling that he'd just opened a door he might not be quite ready to walk through.

You have to have faith, Patrick. Things will work out.

Julia's voice echoed softly around him, gently distorted like a carnival mirror of sound. He turned to see her standing behind him, holding out her hand.

Patrick reached out, and a shock of energy ran through him. He couldn't move, couldn't break free, his hand glowing with a cold blue fire that crept inexorably up to his shoulder, then on until it enveloped his entire body.

The way they were meant to be. Julia faded from sight, like Alice's Cheshire Cat.

A second surge of energy flowed through Patrick He felt himself lift like flotsam riding the crest of a wave, drifting toward ... another voice now, coming from somewhere in front of him. The words were indistinct but the tone sounded angry, or frightened.

Or both.

Patrick found himself on the upstairs landing of Julia's house. The lamp on the table by the front door shone below, its light faint and wavering. In its washed-out glow, two men slowly appeared, like an old movie projected onto wisps of smoke. They were little more than indistinct shadows, without detail and focus. One figure stood. The other lay in a twisted heap near the foot of the stairs. Patrick had enough experience with bodies during the war to know a corpse when he saw one.

A psychology professor once explained to Patrick that the difference between dreams and nightmares lay in the level of emotional response. Dreams were where the mind went to play, a series of images that ran like an interactive movie.

Nightmares, on the other hand, just scared hell out of you.

Patrick had plenty of experience with both. He rarely remembered more than a few details about his dreams the next day. His nightmares resonated long after he woke, filled with smoke and blood, fighting at Quang Tri and Dong Ha, the deaths of friends and faceless enemies.

Thank God those nightmares came far less often than they once had.

Long after snapping awake in his bed, Patrick could still see the image of the two men in the entryway long after he'd opened his eyes. For reasons he couldn't begin to explain, he knew instinctively that what he'd experienced last night hadn't been a dream *or* a nightmare.

Someone had died at the bottom of that staircase.

Patrick took a seat in the room nearest the entrance of the Cheerful Tortoise, watching as the restaurant filled with Portland State students. The Tortoise was a downtown institution, nearly as old as the college itself.

He ordered a Pabst Blue Ribbon and a half-order of nachos, then settled in to wait for Rachel. Julia would have been the more logical person to ask his questions of, but Patrick couldn't risk opening old wounds—or inviting uncomfortable questions—so he'd called Rachel and asked if she'd like to get together for a beer after work. She'd agreed eagerly.

While he waited, Patrick ran through the list of reasons why he should be avoiding Rachel. After all, her interest in him made him more than a little uncomfortable. And he had just come through divorce, battered and bloodied, and determined never to open himself up to that kind of pain again. Certainly not with such a young woman who was—and this was the best part—the granddaughter of the woman who was both his landlord and a major benefactor to the college he worked for.

Still, when Patrick spotted her hurrying over to his table he couldn't help but appreciate how attractive she made jeans and a sweater look.

As soon as she was seated, Rachel ordered a Budweiser and a Giant Tortoise Burrito. When the server insisted on seeing her identification to confirm that she was, in fact, old enough to drink, Rachel simply grinned at Patrick's discomfort and handed over her driver's license.

Then she cheerfully attacked his nachos while they launched into conversation that felt very much like first date banter. They talked music and movies and Rachel's job with the university. She asked about his classes, about Wisconsin; about everything—he couldn't help noticing— except his personal life before Portland.

There comes a point, however, when casual conversation moves in more meaningful directions or peters out completely. They had already reached that point by the time Rachel's dinner arrived. Neither of them willing to push on into new territory, they ate in silence for a few minutes.

"How is Julia?" Patrick asked at last.

Rachel smiled. "As happy as I've seen her in years. She said to give you her best."

"You told her we were getting together?"

"I tell my grandmother everything. Anyway, she's been wondering when you were finally going to ask me out." She paused, took a sip of her beer, then added, "Frankly, I've been wondering that myself."

Patrick felt himself tense. *From pleasant to uncomfortable in nothing flat.*

"Breathe, Professor. I was just teasing you. God, you're almost too easy. So, over the phone you said something about putting together a family history as a surprise for my grandmother?"

"It's kind of a hobby of mine," he said, happy to change the subject. "I thought it might be a nice way of thanking her for giving me a place to stay. I hoped you could assist me a little. You know, fill me in on a few names and dates."

"I don't know how much help I can be. Dad's not exactly into all of this genealogy stuff. He's definitely more of a here-and-now kind of guy. So, unless I go to Grandma Julia ..."

"You're not real good at undercover work, are you?"

"Care to rephrase that question, Professor?" she asked with a smirk.

"Behave," he laughed. "I just meant that the idea is to surprise Julia, remember? Besides, you don't need to do much digging. I'm only looking for a place to start my research."

"Like what?"

"Well, the date people died is usually the best place to begin. Local papers generally put some details in the obituary, and I'll work my way back from there."

"And reading about dead people is a hobby of yours?" She wrinkled up her nose, eyeing him with amusement. "That *is* fun. Any particular dead person you're interested in?"

"Well, I was thinking about starting with Julia's father. He died sometime before the Depression, right?"

"How am I supposed to find out the specific date? I'm not wandering through some old cemetery in the rain so that you can get your jollies."

"Afraid of ghosts?"

"And what are *you* afraid of, Professor?" she asked, a sly twinkle in her eye.

"You, frankly."

"Just so we're clear on that." She gave him a satisfied smile.

"Do you have a family bible?" Patrick asked, trying to get the discussion—and his thoughts—back on track.

"Grandma Julia has one in her library. Anybody else you want to know about while I'm in there?"

"What do you know about her brother?"

"Uncle Jacob? She really doesn't talk about him much. Why?"

"Just curious. I'm guessing he was pretty young when he died, since Julia inherited everything."

"Maybe he was the black sheep of the family, ran off with the minister's wife or something like that."

"We'll make a detective out of you yet," he said with a laugh.

"Does that mean you'll get back to me about that *undercover* work you were talking about?"

"You know, that kind of thing is exactly why I'm afraid of you." Seeing her triumphant look, he asked, "Does this mean you're going to help?"

"Well, it'll cost you," she said with mock seriousness, "but I'll do what I can ... for grandma," she added with a smile that could only be described as devious.

The week passed without a word from Rachel. Patrick found himself checking his voicemail more often than usual, resigned to the knowledge that his anxiousness had more to do with Rachel than with any information she might find for him.

Fortunately, there'd been no repeat performances of the vision, no voices in the dark or bodies at the bottom of the stairs. The dreams that *did* come, however, were far more vivid—and disconcerting—even if they were a hell of a lot more pleasant.

When Julia and Rachel came by for their weekly visit the following Sunday, Patrick couldn't help noticing that there seemed to be more subtext to tea time than in a Noel Coward play. Rachel grinned in his direction whenever

Julia's attention was somewhere else, and Patrick spent more than a little of the afternoon actively not noticing.

Julia was far too sharp to miss the playful tension around her, but Patrick couldn't tell from her expression if she quietly disapproved or found the whole charade amusing.

Even with all the subterfuge, or perhaps because of it, he found himself more reluctant than usual to see them to the door. As Rachel moved out onto the front step, Patrick felt her left arm slide lightly across his lower back. He stiffened as her hand dipped briefly into his back pocket. Then a quick squeeze of his butt and she had moved on past, a very smug look in her eyes as they said their goodbyes.

Patrick pulled the folded envelope from his pocket as soon as the door had closed. He looked at the words Rachel had written on the front:

Open this and the price is dinner and a movie this Friday. We're talking date, Professor.

He didn't hesitate for long. Inside the envelope he found that she'd gone beyond his expectations, writing down information going back four generations, but the most interesting entries were at the bottom of the list.

Jacob Lundgren, died April 6, 1919

Sarah Anderson Lundgren, died April 9, 1919

Carl Lundgren, died August 4, 1929

At least he had something to keep him occupied until Friday.

Monday dawned cold, but blessedly dry and clear, drawing large numbers of Portlanders outdoors to stand blinking in the unfamiliar sunlight. Like a spontaneous mass migration, people flocked to the park blocks where street corner vendors seemed to appear from nowhere to dispense hot dogs and burritos from their steaming, brightly colored carts.

Patrick soaked in the quiet celebration on his way to the Oregon Historical Society. As an employee of the university, he enjoyed full access to the society's extensive archives.

He made his way upstairs to the research room and stopped at the first of the two workstations just off the entrance. The woman behind the desk smiled up at him.

"Can I help you?"

He pulled the paper Rachel had given him from his pocket and asked for *The Oregonian* and *Oregon Journal*, April 6th through the 11th, 1919, and August 4th through the 8th, 1929. She jotted the dates down on a notepad.

"I can get those for you, if you'll follow me." She guided him to the far end of the room past tall gunmetal gray cabinets. Each contained drawers labeled with small white tags showing the newspaper or periodical name and their date range. The librarian found the ones he'd requested.

"Have you ever used our machines before?" she asked as she led him through a doorway. Four large Minolta viewers sat against the back wall of the small room.

"Years of practice. It's kind of a prerequisite when you teach history."

"Then I'll leave you to it." She powered the first machine on for him. "Just put the materials on the cart by the doorway when you're finished. You can pay on your way out for any copies you make, fifteen cents apiece."

Patrick threaded the first roll of film through the viewer's plates. The roll held almost one complete month's worth of *The Oregonian*, from March 29 to April 27, 1919.

Based on the date of Jacob's death, and the fact that his mother had also passed just days later, Patrick had a pretty good hunch about what he was going to find.

He located a short obituary for Jacob Daniel Lundgren in the Tuesday, April 8th edition. No cause of death was given, only Jacob's age and the names of his surviving family. It took a search in the *Oregon Journal* to confirm his theory.

The article was brief, just a few short paragraphs;

> *Jacob Lundgren, son of businessman Carl Lundgren, passed away last Sunday at the family's Portland home. The official cause of death was given by the family physician as Influenza. Jacob was twenty four years old.*
>
> *A veteran of the last war, Jacob served with distinction in the Fifth Army Division. Twice wounded, at Meuse-Argonne and Clery-le-Petit, he was invalided out last year. Upon recovery from his injuries, Jacob worked in the family's business, Lundgren Furniture.*

Influenza.

Patrick remembered time spent with his grandmother, a little fireball of a woman who had gone into nursing school during the last year of the Great War, intent on serving in France. But the fighting had all but ended by the time she graduated. She'd felt almost cheated, she had admitted.

Then came the Spanish Influenza. The flooded, mud-mired trenches of Europe had provided a perfect breeding ground for the contagion. When the influenza came home with soldiers of both sides of the war, it touched off a pandemic that, within months, swept around the globe and killed an estimated fifty to one hundred million people.

Farmers who had never been sick in their lives passed away within a day of their first cough, his grandmother had told him, while frail, sickly souls made miraculous recoveries. There seemed neither rhyme nor reason to the disease, only a pervasive sense of inevitability that your family, sooner or later, would be touched by God's Hand.

That Hand had touched the Lundgren's not once, but twice. Three days after Jacob's death, Sarah Lundgren had also died of the disease.

He removed the microfilm from the viewer and popped in another roll—the *Oregon Journal* for August of 1929—determined to see his research through, although some of his initial enthusiasm had drained away.

He started with the day Julia's father had died. On the second page, prominently placed in the right-hand column, he found what'd he'd been looking for.

CIVIC LEADER FOUND DEAD

Tragedy Laid to Fall

BODY FOUND BY SECRETARY

Prominent Portland businessman Carl Lundgren died tragically in his own home on Sunday night or early this morning, police reported.

> *Employees at Lundgren Furniture became concerned when Mr. Lundgren failed to appear at his office as expected. His long-time assistant, Lillian Ruth Langseth, drove to Mr. Lundgren's home. There, through the window, she saw a lifeless body in the entryway.*
>
> *Upon forcing their way into the Thurman Street home, police found the body at the foot of the staircase to be that of Carl Lundgren.*
>
> *According to the coroner, Dr. Earl R. Smith, Mr. Lundgren had been dead about ten hours. Smith stated that the cause of death was likely a broken neck suffered in a fall.*
>
> *Detectives believe that Mr. Lundgren fell down the staircase when he stumbled in the darkness during the night. One of the victim's slippers was found two steps down from the second floor landing, supporting the theory.*
>
> *Mr. Lundgren's daughter Julia, a teacher at nearby Chapman Elementary School, was contacted immediately by the authorities.*

Patrick leaned back in his chair and reread the article, comparing it to his dream. Carl had stumbled in the dark, a detail that seemed like a puzzle piece that wouldn't quite fit. And who was the other man he'd seen? Not a police officer, at least not in uniform. Patrick was sure of that. *Maybe a detective,* he thought, *or the medical examiner.* But that didn't feel quite right, either.

Patrick punched the Print button on the viewer and the machine spat out a copy of the story. There were no additional details in the later papers, except for a brief notice about Carl's funeral, held the following Thursday.

Frustrated, he realized that he still had more questions than answers, and no idea of where to go from there.

Just to cover all of his bases, Patrick spent another two hours compiling everything that he could find about Carl, and Lundgren Furniture. Nothing seemed to bring him any closer to understanding what he'd seen, or why he'd seen it.

At least he could be reasonably sure that he wasn't entirely crazy. Somehow that fact should have felt just a little more reassuring.

–3–

With his research at an apparent dead end, all that remained was to follow through on his end of his deal with Rachel, a prospect both appealing and slightly terrifying. Despite his newly-acquired bachelor status, he hadn't dated anyone but his wife since high school.

In other words, he'd been out of circulation roughly as long as Rachel had been alive.

Jesus, he thought, *let's not focus on that reassuring fact.*

The reservations were for Friday at eight o'clock. Rachel asked him to pick her up around seven so that they would have time for a drink before dinner. He'd been a little surprised, then, when she called just after four that afternoon.

"Is there any way that we could get an earlier reservation?" she asked. "I have some things to take care of in the morning."

"I'll see what I can do," Patrick promised. He called the restaurant, only to find that Jake's was booked up for the entire evening. He let Rachel know the bad news, half expecting her to cancel their dinner completely.

"Maybe if we get there early, a table will open up," Rachel suggested instead. "Why don't you pick me up at six?"

Patrick rang her bell a minute or two after the appointed hour—not that he was at all anxious—and moments later Rachel stood in the doorway, dressed in a silky robe that stopped a few scant inches short of being indecent.

"You're early!" she said, accusingly, looking more nervous about this dinner than Patrick felt, as if that were even possible. Oddly, that had the affect of relaxing him a little.

"You told me six," he pointed out, calmly.

She hurried into the kitchen to check the clock over the stove. "Oh, crap! How did it get so late?"

By now he had stepped into the apartment, closing the door behind himself. She came out to the living room and looked him over.

"I have to admit, Professor, you clean up nicely. Can I get you anything while you're waiting for me to pull myself together?"

"I'm fine," Patrick managed. Rachel half-dressed was a little more than he'd been prepared for. She grinned at him, no doubt sensing his discomfort.

"I'll be right out," she said with a wink. Then she turned and hurried off down the hall.

When at last she was ready to go—wearing a simple blue dress that accentuated both her figure and her amazing legs—Patrick couldn't escape the fact that she was, without a doubt, stunning.

She gave him a nervous smile. "Does my hair look all right? I must have changed it at least five times before you got here."

Any doubts that he'd had about how Rachel viewed their dinner were immediately resolved at that moment; even he knew that no woman put that much effort into their hair just to go out to dinner with a friend.

They managed to find room for two at the bar. Patrick ordered a Jameson's, neat, for himself and a martini for Rachel. This time he masked his embarrassment when the bartender asked Rachel to show her ID, but she'd grinned at him just the same as she handed over her license.

"So, is this where you have all of your first dates take you?" he asked.

"Only the ones I blackmail into asking me out," she laughed. Then she turned serious. "You sure you're okay with this?"

"Let's just say I'm getting adjusted to the idea." He grinned, raising his drink in a toast. "To beautiful women and swift kicks in the butt," he offered.

"And," Rachel added, touching her glass to his, "to men with the wisdom to know when they've been neatly outmaneuvered."

"This is a nice restaurant," Patrick observed, taking in the rich, dark, wood and old photographs on the walls.

"Jake's has been around forever, so I figured it would be right up a history professor's alley. In fact, this is where Grandpa Ed proposed to Grandma Julia. That's why I like coming here. It's like turning back the clock."

"So, how long were your grandparents married?" he asked.

"Practically forever. It would have been fifty-seven years when Grandpa passed."

"Impressive."

He saw her hesitate. A conversational shadow hovered between them. She took a sip of her drink while she carefully avoided eye contact.

"There's something you want to ask me, isn't there?" he asked. He caught the look on Rachel's face, the shock that he'd been able to read her so well.

"I was just ..." She looked down briefly, running her finger nervously along the edge of her plate. Then, the decision made—"I was going to ask how long you were married," she admitted.

"Not as long as I'd expected." Patrick didn't ask how she'd known. He assumed that Julia had made a few calls in her role as the doting grandmother. In truth, he was almost relieved that the subject had finally been broached.

"Can I ask what happened?"

He shrugged.

"I wish I knew," he said. "We were married twenty years and then one day I came home to an empty house."

Rachel just watched him for a few moments. He'd never known anyone who could express so much with a look—often amusement, more often mischief, and at this moment, empathy.

"When I was growing up," she said at last, "Grandma Julia used to tell me that when the right person comes into your life, you can feel the connection at every level. You ever feel that way about your ex?"

"Honestly? No. We'd been dating since our sophomore year in high school, and when I enlisted, I guess everyone, including us, just kind of assumed we'd marry after I got back from Vietnam. So we did."

"Were you the same person when you came back?"

Patrick drank the last of his whiskey and stared at the empty glass for a moment.

"I'm not sure either one of us was," he said finally. "What about you? Have you ever found that connection with anyone?"

"I stopped looking for that a long time ago. That's way too much pressure to put on any relationship. It kind of becomes the elephant in the corner, you know? I figure if it's going to happen, it'll happen."

"Wise beyond your years."

She grinned. "I am, aren't I? Speaking of years, I forgot to ask if all my detective work paid off. How goes the research project?"

"Well, I haven't had much time to work on it, but I've made a little progress."

Rachel watched him in patient silence, clearly not intending to let it go at that. He'd expected as much.

"Your great uncle, Jacob, was a soldier in the Fifth Infantry Division during the First World War. Oddly enough, that's the same division I served in during Vietnam. He was wounded twice in France, seriously enough to be sent home."

"Is that why he died so young?"

"No, he died of influenza, the same epidemic that took your great-grandmother a few days later."

"God, that's *horrible*. No wonder Grandma doesn't talk about them very often. What about her father? Did you find out anything more about him?"

"Carl came to Portland from Tacoma, where he'd worked for the railroad building passenger cars. He opened up a small furniture repair shop, producing some custom-made pieces on the side for a few well-heeled clients, and pretty soon he was in the furniture manufacturing business."

Rachel nodded. "Grandma said that he made a lot of the furniture for the Lewis and Clark Exposition—benches, tables, things like that—even got some national attention. Then his business went crazy. How did he die? Or do I really want to know?"

"He was killed in a fall in 1929," Patrick said, hoping that she would let him leave it at that. In fact, Rachel seemed happy to accept his answer at face value. Perhaps she'd had enough grim details for one evening.

"Where do you go from here?" she asked after a few moments.

"I don't think there's much point in continuing, do you? Given the circumstances, I really doubt that Julia is going to want to relive that part of her life."

Rachel considered that and smiled, that mischievous glint in her eye once more. "Well, at least it wasn't a total waste of time. I got the leverage I needed to get you off your butt and take me out. Now, what should we do after dinner?"

"I thought you needed to get home early."

"Oh, yeah, I forgot." Rachel crinkled up her nose. "Home it is," she said with a sigh.

Patrick waited awkwardly as Rachel unlocked the door to her apartment. He wasn't sure what he wanted to happen next. No, that wasn't true; he knew *exactly* what he wanted to happen. He just didn't know if he was ready to take that step, any more than he knew whether the woman looking at him from the doorway even wanted him to.

They stood there for a moment, their mutual nervousness almost palpable.

"I have to say," Patrick managed at last, "that this evening has been the nicest blackmail payment I've ever paid. I'm just sorry that it had to end so early."

Rachel smiled. "Can I tell you a secret? That whole thing about having to get up early tomorrow ... I made that up."

"Why?"

"In case our date went a little farther than I was ready for."

She stepped forward and gently pressed her lips against his, holding the kiss a moment or two before pulling back.

"Now, I think that *you* may be the one who isn't ready," she added, softly.

He looked at her. "Rachel, this would be so simple for me ..."

"If it weren't so complicated, right Professor?" She kissed him again, lingering a little longer this time. Then she stepped into her apartment and closed the door behind her.

Patrick was wide awake at five o'clock the next morning, despite having spent a restless night. He forced himself to leave the warmth of his bed for the purifying exertion of a weight lifting session in the next room, a morning ritual that he'd maintained since the Army.

Pushing himself a little harder than usual, his muscles protested and his upper body glistened with a heavy sheen of sweat. Satisfied, he lifted himself off of the bench and padded down the hall to take a long, hot shower.

As he toweled off, Patrick took stock of himself in the mirror. The image in the glass was encouraging; only a few hints of gray showed in his dark hair and—even though he'd never been fanatical about exercise—years of weights, occasional jogging, and just enough Taekwondo to keep his skills from totally deteriorating, had kept him fairly lean. He had to admit he'd held up pretty well compared to a lot of guys his age.

Compared to men Rachel's age, on the other hand ...

"Stop being so damned insecure," Patrick said to his reflection as he hung his wet towel up on the rack to dry.

An hour later the breakfast dishes had been cleared away, and a load of laundry churned in the washing machine downstairs. Patrick poured the last of the coffee into his cup and looked out the kitchen window. It promised to be a beautiful morning. The cloudless sunrise made the steep hillside along the southwest edge of the property fairly glow. He contemplated spending the day outside, making a mental list of the things he needed to accomplish before spring.

Just then the doorbell rang, a rare event since he'd moved in, and all the more so this early in the morning. Setting his coffee cup down on the counter, Patrick hurried to the entryway.

"Good morning!" Rachel greeted him brightly as he opened the door. She stepped inside and planted a quick kiss on his cheek. Bundled up for a cold February morning, she wore jeans and hiking boots, with a gray

Portland State sweatshirt visible beneath her partially unzipped ski jacket.

She grinned at him as she pulled her gloves off. "You know, you don't look particularly well rested for a guy who got home early last night."

"I didn't sleep too well. For some reason I had a lot of pent-up energy."

"Poor baby," Rachel teased. "I was out like a light as soon as my head hit the pillow. I don't suppose you have any coffee?

"I'll gladly make more," Patrick told her, leading the way back into the kitchen.

"So," he said as he cleared the grounds from the earlier pot and prepared another filter. "To what do I owe this unexpected visit?

"Well, it occurred to me that I kind of cheated myself out of some time with you on our date ..." She paused, watching him pour water into the coffee maker.

"And?"

"And it looks like it's going to be an incredible day," she said, coming back to the conversation, "much too nice to let you sit with your nose in some dry old book in front of the fire."

He laughed. "For your information, I am capable of a little more exertion than that. As a matter of fact, I was planning on getting a head start on the spring clean up in the yard."

"Yard work! How can you waste the first nice weather of the year on yard work?"

"I suppose you have a better idea?"

"Much better. Do you have a pair of warm hiking boots?"

"I'm from Wisconsin," he reminded her. "I have it all; boots, woolen socks, long underwear ..." Rachel raised her eyebrows, shooting him a sly grin. "If you don't stop making faces like that, I'm going to think your intentions are less than honorable," he warned her with a laugh.

"Hey, you're the one who brought underwear into the conversation! Before you dig yourself in any deeper, Nanook, why don't you go get ready? You and I are heading out into nature this morning."

"What about your coffee?" His finger hovered over the Brew switch.

"It'll wait. I have a feeling we'll need something hot by the time we get back."

Fifteen minutes later Patrick was walking alongside Rachel as she led him up Thurman Street.

"Where are you taking me?" he asked. They were moving away from the city, into a part of the neighborhood that he hadn't visited before.

"I decided that it was about time you found out just how incredible your new back yard is."

About five hundred yards from the house, Thurman curved to the right before ending at a locked gate. Beyond the gate, the lane continued on under a new name: Leif Erikson Drive. Here and there, patches of weathered asphalt gave a clear indication that the road had been paved at some time in the distant past.

"I usually stick to the Wildwood Trail," Rachel said, her breath a lacy mist in the cold air as she pointed up into the forest of Douglas firs and broad leaf maples to their left, "but that gets a little messy during the winter. Leif Erikson stays passable pretty much all year long."

"This doesn't look like any trail that I've ever been on," Patrick noted.

"Actually, it's just a road the city closed to cars a couple of decades ago."

"How far does it run?" Patrick had already begun to consider the mountain biking opportunities. It had been a long time since he'd put his bike through its paces.

"Eleven miles, from Thurman out to Germantown Road. But don't worry," she added with a grin, "I won't make you walk the whole way ... this time."

He laughed. "Are you questioning my fitness?"

"Well, it's not like I've had any way to gauge your stamina yet, right?" The look in her eyes was pure mischief.

Patrick stopped walking and reached for her arm. As she turned to him he pulled her close and leaned in. This time there was nothing tentative about their kiss. When they finally came up for air, she rested her forehead against Patrick's chest for a moment.

"We are definitely going to have to do more of that," she said at last, looking up at him with a warm smile. "But first, we should probably talk."

Taking his hand firmly in hers, Rachel started walking again, setting a slower pace this time. Patrick said nothing, sensing that she needed a chance to work through her thoughts. The sound of their boots on the loose gravel was all that broke the silence.

"That was a very nice kiss," she said finally, her eyes still focused on the road before them, "but we both know that you're not entirely comfortable with what's going on, are you?"

"No, not entirely," he admitted. "First of all, there's the difference in our ages ..."

Rachel came to a stop and looked up at him. "You think I have some weird father-fixation, don't you?"

"I didn't say that."

"But the thought crossed your mind, didn't it?" He nodded, reluctantly. "Of course it did. Why else would someone like me have any interest in an old guy twice my age, right?"

Patrick gave her a guilty smile. "I guess I deserved that."

"Damned right you did!" Rachel's tone carried more than a hint of exasperation. "Let me tell you something, for the record. I have never before had the slightest interest in any man who was more than a couple years older than me. You're the first, Patrick.

"And wipe that smug grin off your face," she added, unable to suppress a laugh. "You're not all that, you know.

"The point is, I feel more in synch with you than I've ever felt with anyone else. I'm happy around you, and I don't think a connection like that comes along very often. So don't expect me to walk away from it just because there's a few years age difference."

Seventeen years, he thought, but wisely kept it to himself.

"So, what else you got?" she demanded, that mischievous look in place once more.

"Well, there's Julia. I'm not sure how she's going to feel about me dating her favorite granddaughter."

Rachel's smile faded. "I think I know what you mean. That's got me a little worried, too, but not for the same reason. Grandma Julia knows how I feel about you. In fact, you might as well know that she's been pushing for me to ask you out for awhile now, saying that if I wait for you to make a move, I could be an old woman like her.

"What worries me is what might happen if things don't work out with us. I've never seen Grandma happier than she has been since you showed up. You may be more important to her than you are to me right now, and I don't want to be the reason you leave."

"You won't be." Patrick promised, pulling her close.

After a minute she stepped back from his embrace and looked into his eyes.

"So, Professor," she said, sounding as though she were struggling to keep her tone light, "I vote we just let things play out the way they play out. When you're ready to take another step, let me know. No expectations, and no pressure."

With that, Rachel moved close again. She put a gloved hand behind his neck to pull him down so that she could kiss him deeply. When she broke off, her eyes held an unmistakable confidence.

"No pressure, huh?" Patrick managed with a laugh.

She smiled. "That wasn't pressure. That was just good salesmanship."

When the doorbell rang Sunday afternoon, the tea service had already been set up near the fireplace in the library.

Before Patrick could even help Julia with her coat he found himself in a warm, lingering hug from Rachel. He glanced over to see the older woman looking up at him with a huge grin.

"It's about time," Julia said as her granddaughter finally released him. "I was beginning to wonder if you two would *ever* get in gear."

"You don't mind?"

"Patrick, dear, if I have to lose your affection to another woman, I'd rather it be to my granddaughter. Might as well keep things in the family, right?" she added with a wink.

"Julia, you could never lose my affection," Patrick said as he bent down to kiss her cheek.

After hanging their coats in the closet, he followed them down the hallway to the library. Julia took the chair closest to the fire while Patrick poured their tea. Rachel wandered over to the stereo and began thumbing her way through his extensive record collection.

"Do you mind if I put on some music?" she asked, glancing back over her shoulder.

"Not at all," he told her, although he doubted that she'd find much of interest. His tastes ran mostly to classic jazz, with just enough 60's and 70's rock mixed in to mark his age.

"What do you think, Grandma? Bix Biederbecke, Chick Webb, or Art Tatum?"

"Whatever you pick is fine," Julia said, grinning at the surprised look on Patrick's face. A moment later the sound of Chick Webb's big band flowed from the speakers, a very young Ella Fitzgerald joyously belting out the vocals.

Rachel rejoined them, foregoing the open chair in favor of a spot on the thick Oriental rug, where she leaned back to rest against Patrick's leg.

"You know jazz," he observed, trying not to focus on the warmth of her body.

"Grandma practically raised me on the stuff."

"Mea culpa," Julia admitted, smiling. "But in my defense, I *was* one of the original jazz babies. A foreman at Papa's factory gave me some of Louis Armstrong's Hot Five records, and I was hooked."

"You own original Hot Five recordings?" She nodded, bringing an appreciative whistle from Patrick. "They must be worth a fortune!"

"You should see the rest of Grandma's collection," Rachel said. "It puts yours to shame."

"Believe me, I'd love to. I've picked up a couple of rare pressings here and there, but on a professor's salary, my opportunities have been pretty limited."

The song ended and *You Showed Me the Way* started up. Patrick reached down and began to lightly stroke Rachel's neck as he watched the flames dance up from the fire. He only realized what he was doing when she laid her head back against his knee with a quiet sigh.

Julia looked at him and winked, her eyes shining with approval.

Over the next week Rachel seemed content to give Patrick the space he needed to think things through. Not too surprisingly, the absence of Rachel only caused him to think about her more, which he suspected had been her intent all along.

Friday evening, he took her out to dinner and then to a small jazz club that he'd heard about, Jazz de Opus, on the edge of Chinatown. They made themselves comfortable on one of the soft couches in the lounge and ordered a bottle of Sangiovese. As the waitress walked away Rachel snuggled up against Patrick and pulled his arm around her, resting her head on his shoulder.

"Tired?" he teased.

"Nope. Just very relaxed."

He turned and kissed the top of her head gently. She leaned back and looked at him with a coy smile.

"That was entirely too fatherly. Care to try again?" she asked, moving forward to press her lips to his. They only separated when they heard the waitress clear her throat as she set their wine on the table.

Patrick saw her give them a bemused look as she filled the glasses.

"Well, that was awkward," he said with a chuckle when they were alone once more.

"But very promising." Rachel smiled sweetly as she raised her glass. "To progress."

"I'll gladly drink to that."

They settled back into the soft cushions and sipped their wine, enjoying the Coltrane album playing over the club's speakers.

"So," Patrick asked at last, "what are we doing tomorrow night?"

Rachel looked at him in amusement. "I wasn't aware that *we* were doing anything. Are you beginning to take me for granted already?"

"I was just expressing a little wishful thinking."

"Well, sorry to disappoint, but tomorrow I have plans to go out with some old girlfriends from high school."

"*Old* being a relative term, obviously," he pointed out, earning himself a punch in the arm. "Hey! Be careful there. At my age, I bruise easily."

"Maybe you *are* too old for me," Rachel said with a hint of irritation.

Patrick pulled her into another kiss in answer. She pretended to resist at first, slowly pulling away, but he gently caught her lower lip between his teeth and held it until she plunged back with passion, moaning softly.

When they finally separated, Rachel whispered, "Maybe not."

She leaned forward, resting her forehead against his chin, and took a deep breath as she collected herself. Then she pulled back and smiled at Patrick.

"You keep that up, and I may be forced to take things to the next level whether you're ready for it or not."

"I'm getting there," he promised. "When I'm ready, you'll be the first to know."

Sunday morning, Patrick was considering starting a second pot of coffee when the phone rang. He answered, knowing that he would find Rachel on the other end of the line.

"Good morning, Professor!" she said, cheerfully. "What are you up to this morning?"

"Waiting for you to come over and help me with some yard work while the good weather holds."

"Gee, that sounds exciting."

"It's all about the company," he laughed. "How soon can you get here?"

"Half an hour. But you better have coffee waiting for me."

True to her word, Rachel showed up on his doorstep thirty minutes later, dressed to work in jeans and her old P.S.U. sweatshirt. He handed a travel mug full of hot coffee to her and led the way to the back yard, where he'd already assembled the tools they'd need.

"You weren't kidding, were you? What's the plan?"

"I figured we'd spend about two hours getting as much weeding done as we can. Then I'll fix some lunch. After that, you can go pick Julia up for tea this afternoon."

She grinned. "Man, you really *do* have this all figured out. What would you have done if I hadn't called this morning?"

"Pretty much the same thing. I just wouldn't have enjoyed myself nearly as much."

He handed a pair of gloves and a trowel to Rachel, then put her to work in the flower bed by the back steps while he started in at the far corner of the house. He figured that, with luck, they'd meet somewhere in the middle. Progress, however, was slower than he'd hoped. The weather had warmed up just enough to let the ground thaw a bit, but it still took a lot of effort to loosen the roots of the weeds that carpeted the long-neglected bed.

They'd been at the job for twenty minutes or so when he heard Rachel call out, "Hey! Look what I found!"

Wiping his grimy hands on his jeans, he headed over to where she knelt by the steps, pointing to the freshly cleared ground.

"I pulled a bunch of weeds out and that brick kind of flipped up on its side. Look what was under it."

There—pressed into the brick's impression in the ground—was a very old key. It looked to be in pretty good shape, rusty in places but intact. He picked it up and gently brushed the loose dirt from its surface.

"Nice find. Didn't Julia say that she had the original key for the house?" Rachel nodded. "I wonder if she'd like to add this to her collection?"

"You know," Rachel said, kissing him on the cheek, "you can be the most thoughtful guy, sometimes."

He smiled at the compliment.

"I do what I can."

By noon they were both cold and hungry, and ready to call it a day as far as work was concerned. Patrick gathered up all of the tools and carried them to the shed in the far corner of the back yard, while Rachel headed into the house. It took about fifteen minutes to put everything away before he followed her inside.

He took off his dirty boots, placing them with Rachel's in the small mud room just off the back door, and stepped into the warm kitchen to find a steaming cup of coffee waiting for him on the nearest counter. His bathrobe lay across one of the kitchen chairs, a folded piece of paper set on top. But it was what was on the floor that caught his attention; Rachel's jeans and sweatshirt lay in a conspicuous heap by the door to the basement.

Patrick eyed the pile warily as he picked up the paper and flipped it open.

Lose the clothes and put on the robe, the note said. *I'll throw everything in the washer after my shower.*

He looked down at his dirt-covered pants, then at the trail they'd already tracked into the house, and realized that it wouldn't be a good idea to go all the way upstairs to change. Still, the idea of stripping down to his skivvies with Rachel in the house was more than a little disconcerting.

Patrick quickly peeled off his sweaty outer layer of clothes, adding them to Rachel's pile. Then he pulled on the robe and—making sure that the sash was secure—headed upstairs to his bedroom.

The bathroom door at the end of the hall was closed, and he could hear the sound of the shower running. He hurried into his room to grab something to wear.

There were three separate piles of laundry on his floor—darks, whites and permanent press—that hadn't been there that morning. Without a doubt, the baby blue bra and panty set on top of the permanent press pile had been added recently. Patrick stared at the lingerie like a deer caught in high-beams at night.

Then he heard the shower being turned off. He pulled himself together, threw his robe onto the bed, and pulled on a pair of sweat pants and a loose t-shirt.

By the time Rachel wandered into the kitchen—dressed in Patrick's robe and carrying an armful of clothes—a large pot of soup was on the stove, reheating, and Patrick was in the process of preparing grilled cheese sandwiches.

"That smells wonderful," she said as she made her way to the basement door, "but hold off on those sandwiches. You need a shower."

He glanced up as she disappeared downstairs, relieved that the robe she was wearing was large enough to leave plenty to the imagination. He just wished that his imagination wasn't so well-developed.

He was about to head upstairs to clean up when Rachel returned for the clothes they'd left on the floor. She bent to retrieve the pile, causing the front of her robe to open a little. It wasn't enough to reveal anything, just enough to make him forget to breathe for a moment. Then, clothes in hand, she stood, smiled sweetly at him, and headed back down to the laundry room.

Suddenly, a shower sounded very good.

"You have a way with soup," Rachel said as she gathered their bowls and plates from the table and carried them to the sink. Patrick grabbed their glasses and followed. "The sandwiches were good, too, but we've got to get you to use Tillamook cheddar instead of that Wisconsin stuff."

"Sacrilege!" he exclaimed in mock indignation. Actually, he'd tried the local cheddar and had to admit it was pretty damned good, but he wouldn't admit that to Rachel. She had the upper hand in far too many areas already.

"So, now that you've cooked for me, I suppose I'll have to return the favor."

He grinned. "That depends. Are you any good in the kitchen?"

"I'll tell you what ... why don't I come over on Friday and make dinner? You can decide for yourself."

"That sounds like a plan."

Together they made short work of the kitchen duties. As Patrick wiped his hands on the dish towel, Rachel found a bottle of Pinot in the wine rack.

She handed the bottle to him. "Why don't you open this and take it into the other room while I rotate laundry?"

"Yes, ma'am," he said with a grin. "Just remember that you still have to go get Julia soon."

He carried the uncorked wine into the library, where he half-filled the two glasses he'd brought along. Then he lit the fire already laid out on the hearth in anticipation of Julia's tea. Finally, he put his favorite Charlie Christian record on the turntable. In a moment, the slow rhythm of *As Long As I Live* filled the room.

He settled in on the window seat and turned his attention to the scattered clouds that had begun to gather to the east. After two week's respite, the forecast called for heavy rain by mid week.

"Nice choice in music."

He looked up as Rachel entered, watching as the bottom of the robe opened just enough to offer tantalizing views of her legs as she walked.

"Uh, Rachel," he managed, trying to keep his voice even. "Don't you think it's time you got dressed?"

"Can't. My clothes are still in the dryer." She gave him an innocent smile. "Besides, this is much more comfortable."

"For one of us."

"Awww, I'm sorry." She tossed one of the pillows off of the loveseat his way. "Why don't you position this strategically while I get our wine?"

He had just enough time to put the pillow in his lap before Rachel handed his glass to him. Then she nestled in between his legs, wiggling across the window seat until her back was against his chest. Apparently satisfied with the fit, she took Patrick's free left hand and guided his arm around her waist.

"You're not playing fair," he said quietly. "You promised no pressure."

"I lied," she admitted, stroking the back of his hand. "But you can relax. I'm not trying to seduce you, Professor. After all, I have to go get Grandma soon. This is just ... cuddling."

So they cuddled, content to listen to the fire crackling on the hearth and watch the river traffic on the Willamette far below. When the album ended, neither of them made any move to put more music on.

Finally, and with obvious reluctance, Rachel eased out of his embrace and headed off to attend to the laundry.

When she reappeared ten minutes later, the robe had been replaced by her jeans and sweatshirt.

"I'll be back with Grandma in a little while," she said, sitting down beside him at the window. "Oh, and I went ahead and got everything ready for tea, so all you'll have to do is put the water on."

Patrick pulled her close and kissed her, softly at first and then with considerably more heat. When at last she pushed him away her cheeks were flushed.

"*Now* who's not playing fair? I have to go."

He followed her to the door. Outside, a brisk east wind made the tree branches dance along the hillside. Patrick grabbed a warmer jacket out of the entryway closet and held it open while Rachel slid her arms into the sleeves.

"Thank you, sir." She tilted her head up so that he could kiss her one last time. "This has been nice," she added, simply.

"It has," he admitted. "The nicest day I've had in a very long time."

Late that evening, rain pattered softly against the kitchen window, sliding down the glass to congregate in small dark pools at the bottom of the frame. The east wind had continued to marshal the clouds over the city until the moon and stars had dimmed into obscurity. The old house—wrapped in a gray shroud of drizzle and mist—seemed as isolated as a remote mountain cabin.

It felt, in a word, lonely.

Patrick washed the last of his dinner dishes, setting the plate in the drain board alongside the cups and saucers from that afternoon's tea.

Now what the hell do I do? he wondered, wiping the dampness from his hands. The lectures for both Monday's and Tuesday's classes were good to go. All of the quarterly grades were up to date. And next quarter's curriculum was essentially just a slight refinement on the class he'd taught on nineteenth century American imperialism back in Madison. Patrick had discovered a 1922 edition of James Ford Rhodes' *The McKinley and Roosevelt Administrations* in Julia's library that might offer some additional insight on the subject, but even the thought of delving into an old history book failed to arouse much interest.

He spotted the bottle of Pinot that he and Rachel had opened earlier that day. As he poured a glass, he noticed the old key they'd rescued from the flower bed sitting on the window sill.

A little water—along with some judicious rubbing—and the dirt came away, leaving only a bit of rust to show for its years under the brick. He smiled and headed down to the basement, in search of the jar of naval jelly he'd spotted when he'd first moved in.

Restoration seemed to be the theme of the day.

–4–

August 4, 1929

Brian Daly knelt on the back step and reached through the railing, feeling blindly with his right hand along the border of the flower bed. The third from the front, he'd been told. Brian tipped the brick up on its side and found the cold metal key lying beneath. With a grin, he stood and made his way up the stairs to unlock the door. Then he returned the key to its hiding place.

Quietly, ever so quietly, Brian eased the back door open. The house was silent as the grave. Still he hesitated on the brink, a wee voice in his head telling him to turn and run.

It wasn't that he didn't recognize the advice as sound—more often than not, that damnable voice had proven right—but the realities of life usually dictated a bold course. *No real money to be made being timid and safe, not these days.* And as much as Maggie might harp on him for what she called his "activities," it was nothing compared to the hell she gave him when the icebox was empty and the bills went unpaid.

Well Maggie, my love, he thought, as he eased through the doorway and into Lundgren's darkened kitchen, *after tonight we'll be living like the fockin' kings of old. At least for a while.*

Brian moved quietly through the room, his eyes adjusting to the darkness. The place was neat as a pin, not a dish on the counters nor a pot in the sink. It seemed unnatural to Brian's way of thinking. A kitchen should look lived in, with a few dirty plates or the odd pan or two lying about to recall the glories of the meal gone by.

But Lundgren would have none of that, he realized with irritation. No, everything would have to be clean and tidy and in its proper spot, just as it always had to be at the factory. The memory of it appeared in Brian's head and along with it flowed cold anger; Lundgren pacing about the shop floor at the end of shift like a fockin' lord, sharp eyes missing nothing. There could be no sawdust nor wood scraps around the tables, not a thing out of place. And God help a man if the odd tool came up missing from time to time.

Well, I'll be sure to tidy up after myself tonight. Can't be having anyone knowing I've come to visit, can we?

He stopped at the dining room door and pushed it open. The door swung back silently on well-oiled hinges. The room beyond, lit only by pale moonlight through the windows, looked just as it had been described to him, with its table large enough for the grandest of banquets, and the tall oak sideboard practically groaning under the weight of all that fine silver.

The thought of those riches made Brian's palms itch under his gloves. For a moment, his resolve faltered as old temptations took hold. But his instructions had been clear. "Touch nothing, take nothing," Lewis had said. His very manner had suggested it would be a deadly mistake to disobey.

Brian cast one last covetous look at the sideboard and moved on.

He paused at the entryway, looking into the parlor where the moonlight struggled against the heavy curtains at the windows. To his left, a long hallway led to the old man's study. Brian could just make out part of the study door from where he stood. No light shone along the threshold.

Reassured, Brian pulled the pistol from his coat pocket and crept over to the foot of the stairs. The tricky part, this. There was always the risk of a creaking step, even in the best built houses. A familiar noise like that could bring a sleeping man awake in an instant.

He was glad of the pistol and the comfort it brought him. He'd been ordered not to bring a weapon, informed in no uncertain terms that the old man's death was to look like an accident and nothing more. But Brian knew Lundgren as well as any and better than most. Old or no, the man could be as strong as a bear. Best to have a little insurance, orders be damned.

He started his slow, cautious climb to the second floor. By the fourth step he could hear Lundgren's steady breathing coming from one of the bedrooms above. He continued to listen to the sound as he climbed, alert to any change.

Halfway up the stairs he froze in place, his left foot hovering over the next step. The room above had gone quiet. Brian gripped the pistol a little tighter and waited, peering into the darkness.

After a few eternal moments, he heard the rustle of bed covers and Lundgren began to snore, softly at first, then louder until Brian was sure it could be heard by the neighbors with ease.

He grinned in the darkness and moved faster now, two steps at once and all in time with the steady rumbling from the bedroom ahead. *No fear of creaking stairs with that noise*, he thought.

When he reached the upper landing, he stopped and slid the pistol back into his coat pocket. Then he knelt on the last step and removed his gloves. From the other side of his coat, he pulled heavy fishing line and two strips of cloth. Setting to work in earnest, he wrapped the thick cloth around the right-hand baluster at the top of the stairs, about three inches up the post. Then he laid the fishing line on top of the material, pulling it snug before tying it off. Keeping the line as taut as possible, he edged across the step to repeat the process on the opposite post.

Brian tested the tension, assuring himself that it would do the trick. Then he moved down a couple of steps to admire his handiwork. The line was all but invisible in the darkness, and the cloth wrapped around the posts—a clever little trick to keep the line from biting into the wood—would only be seen if someone thought to look for it.

Satisfied, he reached back into his coat and retrieved the gloves, pulling them on before working his way down to the entryway.

At the bottom of the stairs he turned to his left and entered the parlor. He moved more quickly now that the trap had been set, his mind going over the rough drawing he had been shown of the layout of the room. The radio would be against the wall just to his left. Beyond that, he knew, there should be a floor lamp. The shapes were obvious even in the darkness. Brian moved to the lamp and pulled the chain.

The sudden light assaulted his eyes, and it was all he could do to keep from cursing aloud as he shielded his face and blinked away the stars.

"Oh, there's a clever lad," he muttered, darkly. Maggie would have laughed if she'd been here to see that. He pushed his wife from his mind and focused once more on the task at hand, a task that dear Maggie most certainly would not approve of.

Once his eyes had adjusted to the light, he stepped over to the radio. It was a grand thing, four feet tall and maybe two and a half across, and all done up in a fine wooden cabinet. The radio's dial was centered in the front, just above two golden knobs.

Brian turned the knob on the left and grinned as he heard the hum of the tubes. The sound of an orchestra came through the set's speakers, faintly at first, then growing in strength as the tubes within warmed up.

In the few seconds the radio took to reach its full volume, he had already left the parlor to hide in the comforting darkness of the dining room. He leaned against the wall, waiting, listening as the music played in the room across the hall. His hand moved back to the pistol in his coat pocket almost of its own accord.

Any moment now, he told himself, but the old man's damnable snores could still be heard above the music. Each second that ticked by carried the seeds of doubt. He considered going back into the parlor and turning up the volume but that meant leaving the comfort of the darkness, something he couldn't quite bring himself to do.

Make a decision, man, he scolded himself. *It's take a chance or nothing at all.*

At last, the tension became too great and he crept into the entryway. One step forward, then another, and one more. He was halfway to the parlor when he heard the old man snort abruptly. Still as a statue, Brian waited for the sounds to guide his next step. In the seconds that followed, the sweet dance music coming from the radio echoed through the otherwise silent house.

Then a floorboard creaked somewhere above Brian. He jumped, cursing himself for his nervousness as he beat a hasty retreat back into the shadows. Heart pounding, he settled in to wait once more.

He could hear the old man moving around now, slow steps toward the bedroom door, then the soft creak of hinges.

"Julia?" Lundgren called from the landing. "Is that you?"

Brian could almost see the man standing at the railing, looking down to the light from the parlor as he waited for a reply that would never come.

A puzzler, that, isn't it? Brian thought to himself. *Lights on and the radio playing, nice as you please. And there's the beauty of it, for how often does Death announce itself so openly?*

"Daughter, is that you?" Brian heard concern in the Norwegian's voice, but still no wariness.

Then the shuffle of feet on the landing above. He held his breath as the old bastard moved to the stairs. *Don't look down now. Keep your eyes on that light below, and your mind on the music.*

Suddenly Lundgren cried out. Brian heard a heavy crash as the old man's body hit the stairs hard. Something snapped—wood, or bone, or both—as he tumbled out of control down the long staircase, landing with a meaty thud on the entryway floor.

The sickening finality of the sound stood out in stark contrast to the dance music still playing in the parlor beyond.

Brian peeked out and saw the body, face down in an awkward sprawl. He approached slowly, pocketing the pistol, more confident with each step that he had no further need of insurance. The body lay unmoving,

Lundgren's left leg and arm twisted at impossible angles, his head turned to the stairs.

But the old man was still alive, his breathing shallow and rasping. For how long, Brian had no way of knowing.

"Well, we can't have that now, can we?" Brian whispered. Shaking, he reached down and took a firm grip of Lundgren's chin with his left hand, the back of the Norwegian's head with the right. A knee placed between the shoulder blades and a quick, violent twist ... The neck gave a satisfying snap.

Brian continued to kneel there as Lundgren's last gurgling breath escaped. The right leg twitched, his body unwilling to concede to the inevitable. Then that, too, came to a rest.

The realization of what Brian had just done took hold then and chilled him. As much as he played at being a villain, he'd never killed a man, never listened to the hollow rattle of someone's last living breath.

He hurried to the radio, impatient to turn off the damned music that still echoed through the house. All he wanted to do was finish the job and curl up in a bottle until the memory of this night went away, or at least, the sharp edges had dulled a bit.

One of Lundgren's slippers lay on the steps. Beside it, three of the thick railing balusters had been broken in Lundgren's fall. Brian passed them quickly on his way back to the top of the stairs, pulling his pocketknife out as he climbed.

He sat on the top step and looked back down at the body.

"To hell wi' ya," he growled at the corpse, unnerved. "Ya brought this down on y'rself, ya self-righteous bastard."

He reached out and cut the line from one post with shaking hands.

"I warned ya when I got sacked there'd be a reckoning."

The other side of the line separated against the sharp blade.

"I just didn't know I'd find someone who'd pay me for the privilege."

He shoved both the line and the strips of cloth into the jacket pocket from which they'd come before moving back down the stairs. Then he stopped to look once more at the man he'd just murdered. *Time for the packet.* Brian pulled the thick, sealed envelope from his inside coat pocket.

"A little present I'm to leave behind," he explained to the dead Norwegian, "compliments of the fella who sent me. I'll just be leaving this on your desk, shall I?"

Brian started to step around the corpse, then froze in place, his body tingling as if he were in the middle of an electrical storm.

A bluish light came from the upstairs landing, faint and wavering. The glow seeped into every corner like a cold, unnatural fog, touching everything and illuminating nothing. Then, as he watched in terror, the light began to fall back upon itself, slowly gathering to take the shape of a man. The figure hovered at the railing, a featureless face turned toward Brian.

"Jesus, Mary and Joseph!" he whimpered, unconsciously crossing himself. As he backed away he tripped over Lundgren and fell heavily to the floor. The envelope slipped from his hand, skidding unnoticed across the entryway.

Brian scrambled quickly to his feet and made for the front door, clawing to get a grip on the knob. Desperately, he pulled on it and ran out into the darkness, away from the house, and his crime, and whatever it was that he'd just seen.

Patrick's head ached, and a pervasive chill racked his body. Every muscle throbbed, almost as though they'd been pulled to their limit and snapped back like rubber bands. He half-staggered, half-crawled, down the hall to the bathroom, barely making it to the toilet before he vomited and collapsed on the cold tile floor.

Five minutes ticked by, maybe more, before the worst of the symptoms passed. He struggled to his feet and managed the distance between the bathroom and his bedroom, feeling a little stronger with each step. By the time he reached his bed the only residual effect of his experience was the dull aching in his muscles and joints.

Sleep no longer an option, Patrick pulled on a pair of sweat pants and a heavy flannel shirt. Then he went downstairs to make a pot of coffee and ride out the rest of the night.

When the pale dawn touched the hill just behind the house, bare trees casting lacy shadows against the retaining wall, Patrick still sat at the kitchen table. He'd wrapped a blanket around his shoulders to ward off the

February chill. The cup of coffee in front of him had grown cold again.

After the chaos of Vietnam, he had worked hard to convince himself that life played itself out in predictable patterns, that logic—applied through the proper academic filter of science or history or mathematics—could answer every question. He'd found comfort in that. But no logic he knew of could explain what he'd been through that night. All of his years of study had left him with only a quote from Hamlet to mock his convictions.

> *There are more things in heaven and earth, Horatio, Than are dreamt of in your philosophy.*

Last night had been a variation of Patrick's previous experience, the key elements all there but in sharper definition and greater depth. The two men on the landing, this time as solid and real as the kitchen table in front of him. The killer stood over the body of Julia's father, pulling a thick packet from the inside pocket of his worn, sweat-stained coat.

"A little present," he'd said with a grim smile. "Compliments of the fella who sent me."

A moment later, his expression had changed into one of absolute terror. Stumbling backward over Lundgren's twisted body, the packet had slipped from his hand, disappearing beneath the coat rack by the front door, which stood open in the wake of the man's panicked flight.

Then Patrick had been pulled back as suddenly as he'd arrived—the scene before him dissolving and spinning away—until it felt as though he'd slammed down into his mattress, his body reacting like a heroin addict in withdrawal.

Fucking H. G. Wells. How did you manage to miss that little detail in The Time Machine?

Sitting in the cold morning light, Patrick's eyes were drawn to the *Collected Works of William Shakespeare* lying open beside his cold coffee, and the words of Hamlet's ghost.

Murder most foul, as in the best it is;

But this most foul, strange and unnatural.

–5–

"Doctor Templeton?" Patrick called as he pushed the door from the outer office open slowly.

The figure seated behind the cluttered desk certainly looked the part of an academic, with his unruly gray hair, tie knotted sloppily, and tweed sport coat appearing faintly rumpled. Patrick would have bet a month's salary he'd find leather patches at the elbows, and a pipe tucked into one of the pockets.

He guessed Templeton to be in his late sixties. His face showed his age far more readily than did his salt-and-pepper hair. The years had etched their lines in his coffee-brown skin. There were creases in the brow from decades of concentration, and crinkles around the eyes, no doubt from a lifetime of grinning just as he did when he looked up to see Patrick standing in the doorway.

"A visitor!" the doctor exclaimed with delight. He rose from his chair with surprising energy and rounded the desk to shake hands with his guest. "Max Templeton. I know, it sounds like a character from a romance novel, doesn't it?" he added with a chuckle.

"Patrick O'Connell." He grinned involuntarily as Templeton enthusiastically pumped his hand. "I was hoping to have a minute of your time,"

"Absolutely! Have a seat. Any distraction that pulls me away from the drudgery of grading papers is welcome." He waved his hand at the mound of essays hiding the blotter atop his desk. "Of course, I could always pass these off onto a grad student, but I find as I get older I'm looking for more ways to prove my usefulness, not fewer."

Patrick looked around Templeton's office—much larger than his own Spartan office—and wondered if the room's size was a product of the doctor's tenure, or a reflection of the Physics Department's status at the university.

"Now then," his host said gently as he settled back into his chair, "what can I do for you, Professor O'Connell?"

"Please, call me Patrick." Then he realized that Templeton had referred to him as *professor*. "Have we already met?"

"Not officially. I arrived late to the new faculty reception last fall, but you were pointed out to me. I believe you were referred to as our 'Wisconsin refugee.' I trust you've acclimated yourself to the university?"

"And the city. Madison is a wonderful place to live—most of the year—but I'll take the winters here."

"Happy to trade snow for rain, are you?" Doctor Templeton laughed. "You'd probably get some arguments from the locals this time of year."

"Only because they haven't experienced the joys of ten below zero."

"Point taken." Templeton studied him for a moment, curiosity obvious in his eyes. "You still haven't mentioned the reason for your visit, Patrick. We don't get many visitors from the History Department up here."

"What can you tell me about time?" Patrick asked.

Templeton grinned at his guest. "There's an old joke about an exchange student from Eastern Europe who is taking English classes at the local college. One day, as he's hurrying to his class, he realizes that he's left his watch on the table beside his bed. He stops the first person he meets, a physics professor, and asks, 'Excuse please, what is time?'

"The professor looks at him nervously and says, 'Wouldn't that be a more appropriate question for a professor of philosophy?'"

"Serves me right for posing such a ridiculously vague question," Patrick admitted with a laugh. "May I be more specific?"

"Let's hope so." Templeton shot him an amused, encouraging smile.

"What I'm really interested in is time *travel*. I was wondering if it's scientifically possible for someone to be transported from one point of time to another."

Templeton set his tea cup down onto his saucer and studied his guest, an odd expression on his face.

"An interesting question," the doctor said after a few moments. "Until very recently, nearly every reputable physicist would have given you a resounding '*No*,' and ushered you to the door. We even developed the Paradox Argument to prove the impossibility of time travel."

"The Paradox Argument?"

"A nice, unassailable bit of logic. Let's say a man travels back in time and accidentally kills his paternal grandfather as a child. As a result, the traveler's father is never born. Neither, therefore, will be the time traveler himself."

"But," Patrick said, following the scenario to its logical conclusion, "if the time traveler is never born, it's impossible for him to travel back in time to kill his grandfather."

"Precisely."

"You said that *until recently* physicists would have told me that time travel wasn't possible. What's changed?"

"Well, the Paradox Argument notwithstanding, a few stubborn people kept digging and proved that, mathematically at least, time travel is indeed possible. This forced the physics community to accept movement between timelines. Unfortunately, the Paradox argument had become so firmly imbedded in any discussion of the subject that it became something of a millstone around our necks.

"Fortunately, theories are rarely in short supply in the field of physics. Tell me," Templeton asked, "are you familiar with the term *multiverse*? It was coined by the philosopher William James around the turn of the century, although the word's use in this context can be traced, largely, to the science fiction of author Michael Moorcock."

Patrick shook his head.

"Well, multiverses, or Quantum Universes, as they are sometimes called, are essentially alternate timelines. Using our example, when the time traveler kills his grandfather, he's altered history as he knew it. According to the Multiverse Theory, at that instant an alternate timeline is created. There are now two Portlands, two Earths, two universes. The consequences of his grandfather's death are played out in the new universe, while the traveler's own timeline continues on unchanged."

Patrick's logical mind struggled with the concept. "Where does this new universe exist?"

"We're a little vague on that point. Some believe parallel to our own, others that it overlays our reality, occupying the same space but in a separate dimension."

"Uh-huh," Patrick muttered, skeptically. "And how can matter replicate itself instantaneously?"

"The details are a little sketchy there, as well."

Patrick looked at the professor and shook his head. "You don't really buy into this theory, do you?"

Templeton smiled. "Not really. I think it's merely a creative response to a fundamentally flawed argument."

"Meaning?"

Dr. Templeton leaned back in his chair and clasped his hands together in front of him. His smile took on a decidedly guileful look.

"I think perhaps I should ask a question or two of my own before divulging any more trade secrets." He leaned forward. "What's behind this interest in theoretical physics?"

"Curiosity?"

"You don't seem the type. Besides," the doctor added with a grin, "historians are notoriously plagued with constipation of the past."

The description was so apt that Patrick couldn't help but laugh.

"I know one or two particularly crusty professors in my department that fit that description perfectly. However, I'd like to think I keep an open mind. Yesterday, I overheard a couple of my students talking about a lecture you gave on this subject. I thought perhaps you might have a few of the answers that I've been looking for."

"And what's prompting these questions of yours?"

"I'd rather not say. At least at this time."

"Interesting choice of words." Templeton smiled. "However, I think that an intellectual discussion such as this requires a certain amount of frankness and honesty from both parties, don't you?"

Patrick hesitated. In the world of academia, privately shared information—even of a personal nature—seldom stayed private for long among educators. After all, what good is knowledge if you can't use it to enlighten others? Stories circulating among colleagues that Patrick thought he had witnessed a sixty year old murder would hardly enhance his professional standing at the university. And he had Julia to consider as well. She was well known at the university. The last thing he wanted to do was cause her—or Rachel—any embarrassment.

Patrick weighed his misgivings against his need for answers that would help him make some sense of what had been happening.

"Can we could keep what I'm about to tell you strictly between ourselves?" he asked at last.

Templeton nodded.

"I recently started living in an old house in northwest Portland. One night I had an experience that I couldn't quite explain. Now, I'm pretty sure I know what happened. What I was hoping you could do is tell me *how* it happened."

He leaned forward in his seat. "You see, somehow, for a few moments, I was back in the year 1929."

He watched Templeton closely, trying to gauge his reaction. Strangely, he saw no disbelief, nor amusement. On the contrary, Templeton looked back at him with intense interest.

"I would very much like to hear the details of your experience."

To Patrick's surprise, the events of that first night began to flow out of him—a little tentatively at first, then in a great flood of detail.

Templeton took notes on a legal pad while he listened in silence. When Patrick had finished, the doctor sat back and studied the jottings on his pad. After a minute or two, Patrick got the impression the physicist had forgotten he was even there.

"Doctor Templeton?"

Templeton snapped out of his thoughts, looking at his guest as though for the first time.

"Forgive me. The problem with a scientific mind. It doesn't take much for us to go charging off into calculations and theory." He tapped his pencil against the pad. "How can you be certain this wasn't a dream?"

"The house has been owned by the same family since it was built. I asked a few questions of the granddaughter, then went through the newspaper archives. I found this."

Patrick handed a copy of *The Oregonian* article about Carl Lundgren's death to Templeton. The doctor looked at the paper for a moment, then pulled the top drawer of his desk open and extracted a pair of reading glasses. With a quick glance at Patrick that seemed to say *It's hell getting old*, Templeton turned his attention to the article once more.

"Well," he said when he'd finished, "I agree that seems to elevate your experience beyond the level of mere dreams, but I'm not sure it supports your conviction that you've somehow made a trip back through time."

"Not one trip," Patrick said. "Two. Just a few nights ago it happened again. The same physical sensations, the same scene at the bottom of the stairs, but with much greater clarity. The man I saw standing over the body had just murdered Carl Lundgren. I heard him talking about it, trying to justify what he'd done. He'd been paid to do it."

Templeton leaned forward. "Did he say by whom, or why?"

"No, but he had an envelope that the person who'd hired him said he was supposed to leave behind."

Templeton studied the article once more. "There's nothing here about an envelope," he pointed out. "Didn't he leave it?"

"He left it, but I don't think it was quite the way he'd intended." Patrick smiled. "He dropped the envelope and ran out the door when he saw me at the top of the stairs."

"You mean when he saw *something* at the top of the stairs."

"No, I mean when he saw *me*. I'm sure of it, and it scared hell out of him. He hauled ass into the night, leaving the front door wide open."

Templeton considered this for a moment. He looked back at his notes, then to the article, and finally back to Patrick. "Then what did you do?"

"Nothing. I snapped back, my own time, my own bed."

"Are you sure you didn't do anything else? Didn't touch anything, didn't go after the man?"

"No, I was only in 1929 for a few minutes before I was pulled back. Why?"

Instead of answering, the doctor got up and walked over to the window. Dark clouds hung in the sky outside, and heavy raindrops pattered against the glass. Templeton looked down at the park blocks below in silence, hands behind his back, fingers nervously twitching.

Finally he turned to face Patrick.

"Physicists developed the Multiverse Theory to resolve the paradox issue, but *I* think the assumption that someone traveling into the past introduces a new element into the timeline ignores the possibility that the traveler has always been a part of that timeline. "

"I'm not sure that I follow."

"Through some phenomenon—perhaps a form of wormhole—the years 1929 and 1991 became linked, past, present, and future. Over sixty years ago, you interrupted a murderer before he could complete his task. The ripples that flowed out from that event have been felt ever since.

"And," the professor added, "I suspect that you played a much more significant role than you realize. You said that when the murderer fled into the night, the front door stood wide open. How was Carl Lundgren's death discovered, according to the paper?"

"His secretary came to his house the next morning, and saw the body through the window."

Templeton nodded. "That implies that the front door was closed. According to the article, the police had to break into the house, which means the door must also have been locked. But you said the murderer left it standing open when he ran. Do you think he would have taken a chance and returned to close it?"

"No, but that doesn't mean that *I* closed the door," Patrick argued. "Don't forget, there's still the person who paid to have Lundgren killed."

"True, but you're forgetting the envelope. Whatever it contained must have been of significance, and yet there's no mention of it in the newspaper. It would seem someone removed it before the police arrived. I hardly think that would have been the person who wanted the envelope left there in the first place, do you?

"No," Templeton said, "I think you, yourself, removed the envelope and closed the door behind you. What you did after that, well ..." His eyes twinkled with amusement. "I suppose time will tell."

Patrick sat in stunned silence for a moment.

"Let's say that you're right," he managed at last. "Let's say, for the sake of argument, that I am going to be pulled back through the portal again. Would I be able to come back, or is it possible that I could become trapped in 1929?"

For the first time, the doctor looked troubled. "So far this 'portal,' as you call it, has worked in both directions, so the *possibility* of return clearly exists. Whether you'll return the next time, or return to this period ..."

He left the rest unspoken.

There was a soft knock at the office door and Templeton's assistant stepped into the room. She looked from the doctor to Patrick, then back to Templeton with an apologetic smile.

"I'm sorry to bother you, but Mr. Broadfoot is waiting for his appointment."

"I believe we've just finished, Mrs. Meier. Please tell Reuben that I'll be with him in a moment."

She nodded and disappeared back into the outer office, closing the door behind her. Patrick stood, reluctantly, and reached out to shake the older man's hand.

"Thank you for your time, Doctor."

Templeton returned the handshake. "You'll tell me how our theory works out, won't you?"

Patrick managed a weak smile and moved to the door. He was just about to open it when Templeton stopped him.

"This man who was killed, Carl Lundgren, wouldn't by any chance be the father of Mrs. Julia Lundgren Wirth, would he?"

Patrick didn't answer, didn't even turn around to look back, but his body language must have spoken volumes.

"Under the circumstances, I can appreciate your request for confidentiality."

By four o'clock Templeton had wrapped up the meeting with his student, eager to return to far more important matters. He picked up the legal pad next to his blotter and perused the notes he'd taken earlier.

Phenomenal. This had been precisely why he'd pursued a career in physics in the first place. He had been the only one in the department who had shown more than a passing interest in time travel theory, had, in fact, committed an inordinate amount of his career—at least in the opinion of most of his colleagues—to the subject. And

Professor O'Connell selected him to confide in based upon an overhead conversation between two undergrads.

Simply phenomenal.

Whether this was Fate, or merely one of the great coincidences of the universe, this was too important to keep to himself, regardless of his promise of confidentiality.

Templeton reached for the phone on his desk and dialed the only person he knew would understand.

Patrick pulled the heavy drapes in the library closed, hiding the windows and muffling the patter of the rain outside. According to the forecast, Portland was in for high winds and heavy rain through the night, and into the early hours of Saturday.

The storm was the least of Patrick's worries.

The only light in the library came from the fire on the hearth. The warm glow rippled across every surface and brought shadows alive as the flames danced and leapt in the stone fireplace. He nudged another log into position and settled into his chair, absently reaching for the glass of Bordeaux on the small table beside him. He sipped the wine without really tasting it, the fire in front of him little more than a distraction.

The fresh log began to smoke and hiss. Dried bits of moss and loose bark flared briefly before burning away. Long fingers of yellow and red flame caressed the wood, crawling over its surface until the fire caught hold all along the pine cordwood.

He heard Rachel moving around in the kitchen. She had followed through on her promise to make dinner—a very impressive chicken curry over ginger rice, followed by a delicious chocolate rum mousse—and refused his offers to help or to clean up afterward. Instead, she'd handed him his glass of wine, ushered him to the library door, and put him to work building the fire.

"Go process, or whatever it is you need to do," she'd told him with a gentle smile. "I'd like a little company after dinner."

It was a subtle reminder that he had been largely absent for several days, his mind a very long way away.

Somehow, he could no longer convince himself of the absurdity of Templeton's proposition. He was part the house's history. And if Templeton's theory held true, the only way that Patrick could have tampered with the envelope the killer had dropped would be to physically manifest in 1929. That implied the possibility that he could be harmed, perhaps even killed, before he could find his way back to the present.

If I come back at all.

The anticipation he felt reminded him of waiting for his unit to be called back up to the line during the war; never knowing when it might happen, or whether they'd be coming back. Only that going was inevitable. The oppressive weight of that reality drove some guys crazy. Others became so hardened that they let nothing, and no one, get too close. After all, you can't be afraid of losing everything if you've convinced yourself that you care about nothing.

Patrick closed his eyes, listening to the sound of Rachel moving around in the kitchen. *Too late for that*, he realized.

When at last she joined him, Rachel ignored the chair Patrick had moved next to his own, preferring to sit on the floor facing the fire. She nudged her way back between his legs and rested her chin on her knees, content to simply watch the flames.

Patrick reached out and stroked her hair gently.

"Feels nice," she murmured, her eyes now closed as she relaxed and gave herself over to his touch. After a few moments she pulled away slightly and turned to look up at him. "Can I ask you a question?"

He just smiled and nodded.

"Is your ex the reason you're afraid to let me all the way in?"

"Jackie? No. Not at all."

"Then what's the problem, Professor?" she asked, a hint of her usual humor creeping in to her tone.

"It's complicated. Or maybe I'm just making it complicated, I don't know." He reached out to run his fingertips lightly along her cheek, then leaned over and kissed her.

"Very nice," she whispered. "We'll have to try that again when I can stay longer."

"You're leaving?"

"You didn't hear a word I said when I got here, did you?" He grinned, and she rolled her eyes in exasperation. "God! What am I going to do with you?"

"Stay the night," he said, pulling her closer. "Maybe we can come up with some creative ideas."

"*Tonight*?" she said with obvious exasperation. "You decide to make your move *tonight*?"

"What's wrong with tonight?"

"You'd know if you'd ever pay attention. Grandma asked me to come and stay with her, which means ..." she said as she pulled herself to her feet, "that I should probably get going."

"You can always sneak back later."

"Tempting, Professor, but she usually keeps me up for hours, talking." She smiled down at him. "There will be other nights, though. You can count on it."

Patrick walked her to the door where they lingered over their goodbyes. Finally, reluctantly, Rachel nudged him away and opened the door.

Outside, the rain fell in heavy curtains. Caught by the gusts of wind buffeting the west hills, the storm blew in every direction at once. Rachel declined Patrick's offer of an umbrella—"Wouldn't do any good tonight, anyway," she pointed out—and pulled her coat a little tighter around her.

"Oh, I almost forgot!" she said. "Grandma wants to take the two of us out for St. Patrick's Day lunch tomorrow, if the weather will cooperate. In honor of her favorite Irishman."

Patrick laughed. "Tell Julia that her favorite Irishman would be honored."

He kissed Rachel deeply, then turned her around to face the elements.

"Now go," he ordered, with more firmness than he felt. "You're letting out all the heat."

The storm had faded while he slept.

Patrick thought that the sudden quiet, after hours of rain and wind, had been the reason he'd woken up. Then he heard soft footsteps out in the hallway, and the creaking of his door as it opened. Fully awake, his body tensed as long-dormant instincts kicked in.

Then he caught a familiar scent on the cool night air.

Resisting the urge to smile, he watched through half-lidded eyes as Rachel made her way quietly across the room to his bedside. She paused near the foot of his bed, her nervousness almost palpable. After what felt like an eternity, she reached down and took hold of the bottom of her sweater dress, easing it above her thighs. Then, crossing her arms in front of her, she pulled the dress slowly up and over her head.

Patrick stopped breathing for a second. The glimpses she'd offered him before—dressed in her robe the night he'd arrived to take her to dinner, or in his own robe the day they'd worked in the yard— hadn't prepared him for this. His eyes traced her body, along her leg to her hip, to the gentle curve of her waist. He lingered there for the briefest of moments before continuing up to the swell of her breasts, then on to the line of Rachel's shoulder as it flowed gracefully up to her neck, disappearing beneath a tangle of dark curls.

Clad only in a white, lacy, bra and panties that fairly glowed in the pale light shining through his bedroom window, Rachel conveyed a sense of both innocence and seductiveness he'd never dreamed possible.

She turned away to lay her dress across the foot of the bed, then reached back and unhooked her bra. He watched it slide from her shoulders, and as she stood in profile her firm, tear-shaped breast came into view, nipple erect from the chilly caress of the night air.

Please, God, don't let me forget this moment, he prayed, as she hooked her thumbs into the waistband of her panties and pushed them down over her hips. Bending slightly, she shimmied into complete nakedness. Then she hurried around to the far side of the bed.

Patrick felt the covers lift gently from his body just long enough for Rachel to crawl between the sheets. Seconds ticked by; long, agonizing seconds while he anticipated her touch. He wanted desperately to reach over and pull her to him. Somehow, though, he managed to continue feigning sleep.

This was her moment, her initiative, and he couldn't bring himself to steal that from her.

Finally, her cool, naked form came to rest against his. She slid her hand tentatively across his bare chest, chuckling softly to herself as her fingers played with the thin forest of hair she'd found there before continuing her journey down his body.

"You're awake, you faker," she whispered a moment later. "Or part of you is, at least."

"Guess you need to work on your ninja skills a little more."

"Why didn't you say something?"

"This was more fun. Besides, I was enjoying the show. Thoroughly. Waiting for you was the hardest thing I've ever done."

"Good. Now you know how I've felt."

With one hand she tugged at his shorts under the covers.

"Need some help?" he offered as he lifted his hips obligingly.

"I think I can manage," she assured him, disappearing from view beneath the sheets. "They *do* seem to be snagged on something, though," she added a moment later, her voice muffled by the covers.

Successful at last, Rachel worked her way back up slowly. She allowed the hard tips of her breasts to just graze his legs, his hips, then his stomach as she slid along his body. He reached down, caressing her gently with both hands, and was rewarded with a soft moan before she leaned forward and pressed her body firmly against his.

She nuzzled her cheek against his neck with a sigh. Patrick wrapped his arms around her and ran his hands along her back, down to her soft, perfect bottom, then up again, committing every inch of her body to memory.

They lay like that for a few wonderful minutes before she lifted herself up and brought her face close to his. Her curly auburn hair cascaded down around their faces like a veil. Rachel brushed her lips gently against his, her breath warm and sweet, but when he tipped his chin up to kiss her fully she leaned back, a devious smile on her face.

"Oh no, Professor," she teased, pulling herself up—reluctantly, he thought—until she was straddling his waist. "You've had your chances. Tonight, I make the rules."

With that she rocked her hips back and forth, sliding herself against him, gently at first, then more firmly as she increased the tortuous pleasure. This time it was his turn to moan.

"You like that?" she asked, the answer obvious.

Before he could even respond, she lifted up until the only contact between them was where her knees and legs rested against his sides. Instinctively, he reached for her waist to pull her back, but she quickly captured his hands, linking her fingers between his to keep him at bay.

He thrust his hips up to meet her, only to feel her squeeze her legs tighter against him so that her body rose right along with his.

"God," he whispered in amused frustration, "why do I put up with you?"

"Because you *love* me," Rachel answered without hesitation. She paused for a few moments to let her words sink in. Then she released his left hand and reached between them to guide him home.

"I love you, too," she added, softly. Letting go of his other hand, she lowered herself slowly onto him with a quiet, ragged sigh.

In near silence, Rachel set a languid pace. Her body lifted and fell gently, as though the connections between them—both physical and emotional—were too important to cede to lust. This moment had been a very long time in the making, and needed to be savored for as long as possible.

Patrick closed his eyes and gave himself over to the sensations, reveling in the softness of her skin, the curves of her body, as he fell into rhythm with her.

At last she reached a wave too strong to ride out. Rachel gasped and pressed herself hard against him, her movements more urgent, more insistent. Her hips finally stopped bucking as she fought to catch her breath.

Patrick eased her onto her back, rolling with her. He brushed the damp hair away from her face and smiled down at her. Given what had just happened between them, the look of shyness he saw in her warm, brown eyes almost made him laugh. Instead, he reached up and caressed her check, lovingly. Rachel closed her eyes and leaned into his touch, kissing his thumb softly as it neared her lips.

"You are the most beautiful woman," he whispered as he began to move with her again.

She opened her eyes at that and pulled him close, kissing him deeply, meeting his passion, urging him on.

Patrick woke to the peal of thunder. The house trembled as the sound rumbled directly overhead, the winds blowing even harder than before. A white-hot flash of lightening, followed almost instantly by another thunderclap, threatened to shake the house from its foundation.

He rolled over to find himself alone, the indentation in the pillow beside him—and the faint, lingering scent of Rachel—the only proof that her visit hadn't been a dream.

"Because you *love* me ..."

He lay in the darkness and wondered at how matter-of-fact she'd managed to make those words sound. In one whispered sentence she'd made them real. Somehow, that felt right. And scary as hell at the same time.

Well, I'm wide awake now.

With a sigh he slipped out of bed and started for the kitchen to warm up some milk. He wasn't sure if it really induced sleep, but as his mother always insisted on making it for him as a child, the placebo effect probably counted for something.

He'd almost made it downstairs when he heard glass shattering somewhere above. He scrambled back up to check the bedroom windows, sure that the wind—carrying some piece of debris—had broken a pane.

He found nothing at first. All of the windows on the second floor were intact, the sounds of the storm still muffled behind the curtains. He'd almost convinced himself that he'd imagined the sound when he noticed the door to the attic rattling a little in its frame. He opened the door and felt cold, damp air rushing down the narrow stairway.

Patrick hurried back to his bedroom and grabbed the flashlight he kept in the nightstand. Then he started up the stairs once more.

Shortly after moving in, he'd taken a thorough look around the house and property. In a house as rich in history as Julia's, he'd hoped to find the attic stuffed to the rafters with vintage clothes and furniture. Instead, he'd found the attic empty.

At least the lack of clutter, though unromantic, made it easier for Patrick to find where the wind was coming in. The beam from his flashlight reflected off of shards of glass on the rain-soaked wooden floor, just below the broken octagonal window at the western end of room.

The wind and the glass weren't as much of a problem, of course, as the water that would eventually damage the ceiling in the room below.

Patrick ran downstairs to the kitchen to grab two small plastic shopping bags from the drawer next to the sink, and the broom and dustpan from beside the refrigerator. Then, on his way back up to the attic, he gathered a couple of bath towels. Properly armed, he headed off to battle the storm.

Lining one plastic bag with the other, he stuffed about half of one of the large towels inside. Then he eased the bag through the broken pane. Once outside the narrow opening, the towel mushroomed out just enough to keep the wind from pushing the makeshift barrier back inside the attic.

Preventing it from falling out the other side was another matter, but he had already spotted a couple of nails sticking out of the framing of the attic's unfinished walls. He looped the handles of the shopping bags over the nails in hopes that the anchor, along with the weight of the towel, would hold through the night.

Satisfied that the wind and rain were no longer getting inside—and more than a little proud of himself for coming up with such an ingenious solution so quickly—Patrick swept up as much of the glass as he could spot in the dim light.

Confident that he'd gotten most of the shards, he tossed the second towel down onto the floor and braced himself with one hand while he moved the towel around with his foot to dry the wooden planking. As he shifted his position, his hand brushed against something on the rafter.

He shone his light on the object and found a small box, probably hidden away decades ago, or perhaps merely put up there to get it out of the way while the attic was being cleaned out and then forgotten.

From its size, he guessed it might be an old cigar box, the kind that children had been using as treasure chests for generations. Resisting the temptation to investigate— plenty of time for that later, he realized—he picked up the sodden towel from the floor and, with one last check on his improvised windbreak, headed back down stairs to study the contents of his discovery in better light.

When he was a kid, Patrick spent most of his summers on his grandparents' farm in Iowa. He'd had a great time tagging along behind his grandfather—after whom he'd been named—as he'd tended to the cows and chickens, or tinkered with the farm equipment. But, most of all, Patrick loved running through rows of tall feed corn, and building forts in the grove of ash trees not far from the farmhouse.

One day, when he was probably nine or ten, he stumbled across a dented metal box—rusty and caked with dirt—partially buried near the roots of one of the oldest trees in the grove. Convinced that he'd discovered an ancient treasure, he'd plucked the box free from its hole and carried it back to the house.

While his grandmother hovered nearby, muttering dire warnings of lockjaw, his grandfather placed the box down on top of his newspaper in the middle of the kitchen table. Together they studied his find, offering up guesses as to what might be inside. As Patrick's imagination ran inevitably to tales of jewels and cash, even his grandmother began to show some interest.

Rust held the hinges immobile until oil was liberally applied. Patrick's grandfather carefully worked the cover loose and had begun to raise the lid when he stopped and looked at his grandson.

"Are you *sure* you want me to open this?" he'd asked. "Dreaming and knowing are two different things. As long as the lid stays closed, the possibilities are endless.

"Do you understand what I mean, boy?"

Patrick had nodded. "I'd rather know," he said to his grandfather. Together they pried the lid open, exposing the contents to the light of day for the first time in decades.

Three tarnished coins, all dated 1883, lay on top. Beneath the money was a small notebook. The pages inside had mostly been nibbled away by time and mildew. They could almost make out the name on the cover, but only the first part, Jasper, was really legible.

Tucked inside the book—and in surprisingly good condition, considering—was a sepia-colored photograph of the very farmhouse that Patrick and his grandparents were sitting in. A team of horses stood hitched to a wagon in front of the big wrap-around porch. Beneath the wagon—taking full advantage of the shade—lay a small white dog, one ear cocked as it studied the photographer, a moment of curiosity captured for all eternity.

There hadn't been anything else in the box. Patrick couldn't remember if he'd been disappointed by how little they'd found—he probably had been—but he did remember the many nights he'd spent that summer lying in the dark thinking about Jasper, and the dog, and how they'd all somehow become connected when he'd found that old, rusty time capsule.

When he'd gotten home, Patrick's father helped him make a shadow box to display the coins. The photograph of the house he'd given to his grandparents. It sat in a place of honor on their mantle for nearly twenty years until first Grandpa, and then Grandma, had passed. Only then had the picture been reunited with the coins once more.

Patrick looked over at the two frames, standing side by side on his dresser, before turning his attention back to the cigar box he'd set on the nightstand.

With the dust wiped away, the details on the cover became clear. The brand name, *Gold Standard*, was embossed above a bronzed, muscular arm holding a set of scales. A large gold nugget sat on one side, improbably balanced against a perfectly rolled cigar on the other.

As he slid his thumbnail gently under the edge of the box lid, he remembered his grandfather's words once more.

"As long as the lid stays closed, the possibilities are endless."

It didn't stop me before, he thought with a grin, *and it's certainly not going to stop me now*. He opened the box with care.

The first thing Patrick saw was a postcard, with six small portraits of attractive young women flanking an artist's rendering of a grand hotel. He recognized the hotel as the Multnomah. The building still stood in downtown Portland, although he was pretty sure it had been converted into office space.

The caption on the postcard read,

> *Pretty girls*
> *Pretty girls everywhere*
> *But PORTLAND BELLES are claimed most fair*

Someone had written the name *Mae*, in delicate and precise script, just below one of the girl's pictures and, on the back of the card, the words *To Jacob, with affection*, in the same flowing hand.

Beneath the postcard were letters to Julia's brother, all in distinctly feminine handwriting, though not all in the same penmanship. Patrick smiled as a much clearer image of Jacob Lundgren began to form in his mind.

Under the letters lay dance cards, souvenir postcards from trips to Seattle and Los Angeles, and a brochure advertising the 1905 Lewis and Clark Exposition in Portland.

At the very bottom, he found two small tin infantry men and an officer on horseback. They were likely the first treasures that Jacob had stored away, a permanent reminder of his childhood. And beside them lay a silver locket on a chain.

He pressed the button on the top and the catch released, the cover flipping open in his hand. Inside, an inscription had been added in the most delicate engraving imaginable:

With love,

Julia

On the opposite side of the locket sat a photograph of Julia as a young woman, perhaps in her early twenties. The resemblance to Rachel was uncanny. *But what would a picture of Julia at that age be doing in with her brother's things in the first place? She couldn't have been more than fourteen or fifteen when Jacob had died.*

More than a little confused, Patrick carefully replaced the artifacts and closed the lid.

He was up early the next morning, as usual, despite the long night. He checked first on the attic, relieved to see that his makeshift patch job had held through the storm. Then he fixed a quick breakfast before venturing out into the yard.

The storm passed during the night, and St. Patrick's Day dawned with clear blue skies. A number of branches were scattered around the back yard, nothing more, and the house had escaped unscathed except for the broken window.

He worked for a few hours picking up the largest of the branches and piling them along the east side of the property. Satisfied that he'd at least made a good dent, Patrick wiped the grime from his hands before going up to shower and get ready for his lunch date with Rachel and Julia.

As soon as the women arrived, a little after noon, Rachel disappeared into the kitchen to start a pot of tea. Julia wandered into the parlor, arm in arm with Patrick. In deference to the holiday, she wore a dark green pants suit. A small jade shamrock pendant hung around her neck.

Settling in at the far end of the sofa, she patted the seat beside her, grinning up at Patrick with a gleam in her eye.

"I've come to know that look," he said with a laugh as he joined her on the couch. "Whenever you or your granddaughter gives me that look I'm in serious trouble."

"I have no idea to what you're referring." She pouted unconvincingly for just a moment before her smile returned. "I had a phone call from an old friend the other day. Doctor Templeton tells me that you came to see him."

Patrick tried not to react.

"Don't worry." She gave his knee a motherly pat. "Maxwell was just concerned about you."

"I'm sure he was," Patrick said softly. *That must have been some discussion,* he imagined, *undoubtedly laced with unpleasant terms like delusional and unbalanced.*

"It isn't what you're thinking," she assured him, as though she'd been reading his thoughts. "It's just that he knows you're going through a very difficult time, and he's worried about how well you're holding up."

"How much did he tell you?"

"Oh, everything, I'm sure. About 1929, and my father ... and the man who killed him."

Something in her tone caught his attention. "You already knew that he'd been murdered, didn't you?"

"Practically from the beginning," she admitted, watching his reaction.

"But, I went through the newspapers. The police declared it an accident. What made you decide they were wrong?"

Julia grasped his hand firmly between her own.

"Let's just say that I didn't invite you into our lives to take pity on a poor history professor."

The silence that followed seemed to last for an eternity. But then time was clearly a concept Patrick didn't understand as well as he'd once thought. A thousand questions collided with each other in his mind until he settled on the only one that really mattered.

"Does Rachel know?"

Julia shook her head. "No. I think this is the only secret I've ever kept from her. I wasn't sure how she'd react, I suppose, and I couldn't bear the possibility that she'd think I'd gone a little funny, you know?"

"I can understand that."

Julia looked hard into his eyes and gave his hand another squeeze.

"Of course you can. Anyway, even if Rachel *had* believed me, and I suppose she might have, my son would probably have assumed the worst and packed me off to a home for the permanently addled. We couldn't have that, could we?"

"Couldn't have *what*?" Rachel asked as she stepped through the doorway with the tea service.

Julia never missed a beat.

"I was telling Patrick that we couldn't have him going out today without wearing something green." Smiling, she reached into her jacket pocket and pulled out a small, but expensive looking, shamrock pin. Its emerald leaves appeared to be set in sterling silver. Her hands trembled slightly as she pinned it to his shirt.

"A present for my favorite Irishman."

"Thank you," Patrick said, embarrassed, feeling as though he should say something more. *An Irishman lost for words, and on St. Patrick's Day. The first sign of the Apocalypse.* Then he remembered Jacob's cigar box upstairs on his nightstand.

"As a matter of fact, I have something for you, too."

He stood and walked to the doorway, pausing to give Rachel a quick kiss as he hurried past to retrieve Jacob's letters and mementos. Hopefully, Julia could explain the mystery of how her locket had managed to find its way in with the other treasures.

As Patrick reached out to open his bedroom door, however, it felt as though his fingers had passed through a spider's web of electricity. He tried to pull his hand away but his muscles refused to respond. The vague feeling of something on his skin gave way to a tingling that grew more intense and painful as it spread up his arm and into his shoulder, then across his neck and face.

The air around him seemed to congeal into a pulsing, invisible mass. When he opened his mouth and cried out against the pain, his voice came back to him, distorted and dull. Patrick struggled against his rising panic. At some level he understood what was happening. He'd expected this.

But not the pain. Why so much pain this time?

Because you're resisting. Stop fighting.

The energy surged around him, his body almost floating in the viscous pool of transparent electricity. He forced himself to relax and at once the pain faded, although the energy still flicked at his skin like angry ants.

A faint, bluish light enveloped him like neon cellophane. He had a nagging, uncomfortable feeling that the glow emanated from within his own body.

The world faded into a shapeless mass around him. He felt as much as heard a muffled thud rolling toward him through the dense atmosphere. Then the sound reached him again, a little sharper, a little less distorted than before. And then a third time, and a fourth. Each time louder and crisper than the last, until it resolved itself into distinct elements; the sound of something heavy falling, the splintering of wood, a final distant thump as motion became stillness. The same sound over and over, coming to him in waves like ripples on a pond, radiating out from the spot where a stone has landed.

Then a new sound, clear and close.

"To hell wi' ya," a voice thick with an Irish accent growled from somewhere to his left. "I warned ya when I got sacked there'd be a reckoning. I just didn't know I'd find someone who'd pay me for the privilege."

Slowly, inexorably, the wave carried Patrick toward the voice. The upstairs landing burst into view as though he'd emerged from a tunnel. The center of his vision cleared while the edges remained stretched and distorted. Paralyzed, Patrick watched the scene play out before him once more.

In the light of the table lamp near the front door, Patrick saw Carl Lundgren, lying dead at the foot of the stairs. The husky man who had killed him stood over the body. He reached into his shabby coat and pulled out the thick envelope.

"A little present I'm to leave behind, compliments of the fella who sent me. I'll just be leaving this on your desk, shall I?"

The energy around Patrick flared up, his body shimmering with a strange, intense, blue light that made the shadows around him dance like moonlight reflected on a slow-moving stream.

Below, the Irishman turned toward him, the unearthly light reflected in his terrified eyes. He stumbled backward, tripping over Carl's body. The envelope flew from his hand and slid out of sight beneath the hall table. Then, with an agility that belied his size, the murderer leapt to his feet and rushed for the door.

Patrick felt the floor beneath his feet as the wave receded, and with it the paralysis that held him. He gripped the handrail for support, struggling to stand on rubbery legs.

On the landing below, the front door stood open. Carl Lundgren's killer was long gone. Patrick couldn't hope to catch up, not with the floor rolling beneath him like a ship's deck.

Somehow he managed to negotiate the stairs without falling. Edging past Carl's body, he used the wall to help maintain his balance as he reached the entryway and pushed the door shut. Then, his back against it, he slid down slowly until he came to rest on the cold parquet floor.

Not going anywhere anytime soon.

Every muscle ached and protested even the slightest movement. He leaned his head back and closed his eyes, trying to focus on relaxing. First his neck, then his shoulders ... the simple meditation techniques he'd learned over the years through his martial arts studies kicked in. The tension slipped away from his body and his rabbiting heart rate slowed to something approaching normal.

Several minutes passed before he felt ready to move again. It took some doing but he managed to get to his feet, though he still clung to the door for support.

And then he heard footsteps moving up the walkway toward the house.

He looked at the narrow windows on either side of the entryway. No time to get clear without being seen, so he pushed himself up against the door and prayed that whoever it was outside wasn't planning on coming in.

The footsteps stopped just the other side of the door. Patrick waited for a knock or the sound of a key in the lock.

Seconds passed, then he heard a faint scuffing to his left. They were at the window now, probably peering in. Carl Lundgren's dead, vacant eyes looked back from the foot of the stairs.

Patrick heard a soft grunt from the other side of the pane, then footsteps again, fading slowly down the walkway to the street below. He risked a glance through the window but saw no one. Patrick looked down at the twisted, broken body of Julia's father.

"I don't know who you pissed off, but they obviously wanted to make damned sure you were dead." He smiled grimly at the corpse. "What the hell have you gotten me into?"

Carl stared back in stubborn silence.

Patrick spotted the corner of the packet the Irishman had dropped, jutting out from under the hall table. When he picked it up, he saw that the front of the envelope was stamped *Bank of Kenton* in crimson ink in the upper left-hand corner, along with an address on Denver Avenue in Kenton, Oregon. He turned the envelope over and found it unsealed. Inside were what appeared to be legal documents.

As he began to unfold them, five bundles of twenty dollar bills—each bound by a Bank of Kenton strap—fell to the floor.

Patrick stared at the money for a minute and wondered how he could still manage to be surprised by anything after what had happened to him already. Then he turned his attention to the paperwork in his hand.

The documents—drawn up by a Portland law firm, Bishop and Goldmark—detailed the sale of Lundgren Furniture to a company called Peregrine Industries, for a total of one hundred eighty-five thousand dollars. Flipping quickly to the last page of the contract, Patrick found Carl Lundgren's signature already inked on the dotted line.

He looked over at Carl.

"Well, I think we can take a guess at *why*, can't we? You wouldn't sell the company, so they found someone to remove you from the equation. And this," he picked the money up from the floor, "is supposed to be the down payment that proves you agreed to the deal."

He folded the contract carefully around the bundles of money and slid it back into the envelope. Then he headed upstairs.

If he really was here to stay, at least for awhile, Dockers and a polo shirt would hardly help him blend into his surroundings. In Carl's closet he found four neatly pressed suits that looked as though they might just fit. He selected a single-breasted coat made of light brown wool, and a matching pair of slacks. *Or would that be trousers? Or pants?* It would probably be the little things that made him stand out, he realized, the wrong word or oddly turned phrase.

Patrick put the suit on, along with a starched white dress shirt he'd found hanging next to it. The clothes fit reasonably well. Just a little tight across the shoulders, and a little long in the sleeves.

He located a brown tie hanging inside the closet. The fabric was much lighter than the neckwear Patrick was used to, almost as thin as a woman's scarf, but with effort he managed a passable Windsor knot.

Carl's shoes were another matter. The oxfords were at least a size too small, and pinched Patrick's feet both in width and length, but he didn't really have much choice.

As he squeezed his foot into the shoe, he considered his options. The smart thing to do would be to find a place where he could stay for a few days while he figured out his next step. Of course that would take money, but at least there wouldn't be any problems there.

He picked up the packet from the top of the dresser and looked inside. Five bundles of twenties, a thousand dollars per bundle. Five thousand dollars in 1929 should be more than enough to cover a hotel, a new wardrobe, shoes that fit, and perhaps even some answers.

Patrick pulled three twenties out and slipped the cash into his pants pocket. He tucked the rest away in his inside coat pocket and checked out his image in the mirror over the dresser. The bulge in the pocket was too noticeable with the coat buttoned, so he left it undone.

Then, in the mirror's reflection, he noticed his own clothes at the foot of the bed.

He rolled them into a bundle that would be a little easier to tuck away, and looked around for a secure hiding place. Carl's room was out of the question, he realized at once. The man was so organized and fastidious that anything Patrick introduced would seem out of place. No doubt every room in the house would be the same. Except perhaps ...

The attic looked exactly the way Patrick had hoped to find it when he'd first explored the house; filled from floor to rafters with old furniture, steamer trunks, and wooden boxes. He navigated through the maze of heirlooms, making his way to the small window at the far end of the room.

The faint glow from the moon outside provided just enough light for him to find Jacob's cigar box tucked away in the rafters. If no one would discover the cigar box for another sixty years, he reasoned, taking his bundled clothes and carefully placing them alongside, then this was as safe a hiding spot as he could hope to find.

Downstairs once more, Patrick stepped carefully around Carl's body as he moved to the front door. Passing the mirror above the hall table, Patrick took a long look at his reflection.

Something was missing, and he immediately realized what it was. He took one of Carl's hats down from a nearby hook and placed the hat—camel-colored wool felt with a black band and narrow brim—on his head, tilting it slightly down in front. At least he didn't *look* like a walking anachronism, he decided. Still, he was bound to slip up somewhere, say the wrong thing at the wrong time.

Maybe I can pass if I talked like a character in a Dashiell Hammett novel. Patrick smiled at the thought. *Or pass myself off as a Midwesterner in Portland on business.*

The more he thought about it, the better the idea sounded. His knowledge of history should prevent him from making any serious gaffes, and in an era without the advantages of mass media, who would be likely to question the occasional anomaly?

Satisfied that he had at least an outline of a plan, Patrick stepped out into the world of Langston Hughes, F. Scott Fitzgerald, and Ernest Hemingway.

But not before he closed and locked the door behind him.

–6–

The walk from Carl's house to the commercial district of northwest Portland took twice as long as it might normally have. The shoes were partly to blame, of course—Patrick's feet felt like they were being methodically squeezed in a vise, and he was pretty sure he'd begun to develop a blister of majestic proportions on his right heel—but his sense of wonder helped push the pain away.

The world had a surreal edge to it, as though God had shifted everything an inch to the right when no one was looking. The night was clear but dark, the moon only a thin sliver in the cloudless sky. Patrick could just see the Willamette River through a gap in the trees, a black ribbon disappearing to the north, spanned only by a railroad bridge. The graceful suspension bridge to St. Johns that Patrick had become so accustomed to seeing didn't yet exist.

The lights of Portland glowed softly in the valley. Small pockets of incandescence marked little communities to the east and north that would eventually overflow their boundaries, until they all blended together into one.

Closer at hand, the large and elegant houses along the south side of Thurman Street seemed largely unchanged, but on the north side a young forest—elm, and oak, and thick undergrowth—stood where smaller homes would eventually perch along the edge of the hillside. Pale moonlight glinted off the steel rails of a streetcar line that snaked its way down Thurman.

Patrick turned south before he hit the main thoroughfare of 23rd Avenue. He'd read of a few speakeasies operating in the area known as Slabtown during Prohibition, just the kind of place that an Irishman who'd had the fear of God put in him might hole up in. This was no time for a chance encounter.

Instead, he decided to follow 24th all the way south to Burnside Street. From there, he would continue on into downtown Portland. There should be plenty of hotels to choose from once he got to the city's business district, a distance of probably two and a half to three miles.

Very doable, he thought, *provided my feet hold out.*

He'd just passed Kearney Street when he came across a brick firehouse; Engine 17, according to the large red and gold sign above the door. The station sat mid-block, a two-storey building with twin engine bays on either side of the entrance. The left bay stood open, revealing a fire truck that gleamed even in the indirect light coming from the open door behind it. The historian in Patrick couldn't resist taking a closer look. He walked up the short driveway, stopping just outside the bay.

"She *is* a beauty, isn't she?"

Patrick spun toward the sound, the unmistakable lilt of Erin clear in the voice coming from the shadows to his right. For a moment his nerves convinced him that the Irishman had found him. In the darkness of the courtyard beyond the engine house, he caught the glow of a cigarette and the outline of a man several inches taller than the killer he'd seen at Lundgren's.

The other man chuckled as he stepped into the light, letting Patrick see the black fireman's uniform and silver bars that marked him as a captain.

"Didn't mean to give you such a start." His grin belied the sentiment more than a little. "Are you interested in fire engines, then?"

Patrick turned his attention back to the shining red truck in the bay. Not large by the standards of his own time, the engine was nonetheless impressive, the whole affair a spectacular combination of gleaming brass and polished crimson paint.

"Not overly," he admitted, "But, as you say, she is a beauty. How old is she?"

"The department brought her in last year. She's a '27 LaFrance, a full one hundred thirty horsepower."

If not for the obvious pride in the man's voice, Patrick might have found it difficult not to laugh. His '68 Camero boasted two hundred ten horsepower, and probably weighed less than a quarter of the weight of the fire truck in front of him.

"That's impressive," Patrick managed.

"Can I interest you in a cup of coffee, Mister ..."

"O'Connell. Patrick O'Connell." The two men shook hands.

"James O'Halloron. Now, about that coffee?"

Patrick nodded with a grin and followed the captain back through the bay and into the company's narrow dining hall. The room was empty, save for a lanky young man working away on an enormous stack of dirty dishes.

"That would be Billy," O'Halloron said as he reached for a pair of large potholders next to the cast iron stove at the far end of the room. The young man managed a weary smile and returned to his duties. O'Halloron lifted an enormous coffee pot from the burner and filled two mugs, sitting on the nearby counter, with the hot black liquid.

"Billy was lucky enough to be fingered for kitchen duty," the captain said as he handed a steaming mug to

Patrick and guided him to a seat at the long wooden table that ran practically the length of the room. "Of course, that means the rest of us have had to suffer."

Billy turned from the sink, wiping his hands on his stained apron. "I didn't hear you complaining when you went back for another helping tonight, Cap."

O'Halloron ignored the comment. He winked at Patrick and raised his mug. "Drink up, Mr. O'Connell. Billy may be mediocre with meat and potatoes, but he's absolute shite with coffee."

Patrick grinned and took a drink of the worst coffee he'd had since 'Nam, and that was saying something. It didn't slip his attention that Billy was watching him closely, so he managed a smile and took a second sip. Only when the young man turned back to the dishes in the sink with a smug look did Patrick allow himself a grimace, bringing an appreciative chuckle from the captain.

"So," O'Halloron leaned forward, his hands wrapped around his cup, "what has a Midwest boy wandering the Nob Hill neighborhood at this time of night?" Noticing the startled expression on Patrick's face, he broke into a sly smile. "My parents live just outside of Chicago. I'm only three years in Portland myself."

"I guessed Chicago the moment I heard your accent," Patrick said with a grin.

"Well, at least I've the decency to sound like an Irishman. For an O'Connell, there's an appalling lack of God's own music in your voice."

"I'm afraid my family is too long removed from County Tyrone, Captain."

"Jim, please."

"Jim it is, then. And please, call me Patrick."

"All right, Patrick." The captain's expression turned serious. "Now that we've settled that matter, perhaps you can answer my earlier question. Why are you walking the back streets of Nob Hill so late in the evening?"

Patrick noticed Billy's progress with the dishes had come to a complete standstill as the young man listened in. O'Halloron waited patiently.

"I got off the train from Chicago this evening and decided to stretch my legs, see a bit of the town before I find a hotel. I was thinking of staying at the Benson or the Multnomah," Patrick added, tossing out the names of a couple of hotels he knew had been around as far back as 1929, "unless you can point me to something closer."

"Well, I might know of a place not too far from here," Jim said. "You probably won't find the room as grand as the ones in those other places you mentioned, but it's clean, and the prices are reasonable. And the food is first-rate. The truth is," he added with a grin, "that's usually where I go whenever Billy draws kitchen duty."

"That's not why you spend so much time there," the young fireman at the sink said without turning from his chores. O'Halloron chuckled.

"Billy, I'm going to walk Mr. O'Connell down to the Campbell. Do be so kind as to stop by for me if the alarm rings, won't you?"

"Don't we always, Cap?"

Patrick followed Jim back through the bay and out to the street. They turned south and ambled more than walked with any sense of purpose. The captain looked like a man who was worrying something over in his mind. They were almost to Hoyt Street before O'Halloron spoke.

"You puzzle me," he said, his voice contemplative.

"How so?"

"Everything about you—from your clothes to your manners—says gentleman. But I have a sense that there's more to you than that." He looked over at Patrick. "You remind me of a couple of fellas I knew back in Chicago. Soft-spoken, like you, but they could be stone cold killers when they had to. be. They worked the rackets for Moran's Northsiders, running whiskey … and a few of the other vices.

"Not that I'm saying you're one of them," O'Halloron added, quickly. They'd turned east along Hoyt when the captain stopped and turned to him. "No, I trust my instincts, and they tell me that you're a decent enough fella, but that still doesn't explain why you've lied to me."

"Have I lied?

"You have. And badly, too, if you're telling me that you just got off the train from Chicago. There's hardly a wrinkle in that suit of yours, so unless you *stood* the entire way …"

Patrick couldn't help but laugh. "You should have been a detective instead of a fireman, Jim."

"It doesn't take a detective to see through this one. You've either grossly underestimated my intelligence, and what man could do that who's come to know me?" the captain said with a wink, "or you're a very bad liar. Frankly, I don't think lying is a skill you've practiced much.

"Either way, I'll need some answers about your business here before I'll vouch for you with my friends."

"Fair enough," Patrick said after a moment's consideration. "I'll tell you as much as I can, and then I'll leave the rest up to you."

O'Halloron nodded.

"What I am is complicated, but I can promise you that no one on either side of the law has any interest at all in my presence here." The captain seemed to relax a little at that.

"As for why I'm here," Patrick continued after a moment, "a young woman is in danger but she doesn't realize it yet. I'm going to do anything ..." He paused to let that sink in. "Anything, to protect her."

Silence hung between them for a moment. Then O'Halloron clapped a heavy hand on Patrick's shoulder and grinned.

"Let's go find you a room then, shall we?"

Patrick recognized the Campbell Hotel at once. The large brick building, converted to apartments and offices, would still be a commanding presence on 23rd Avenue in his own time.

Jim led the way down Hoyt to a small side door. He knocked twice, paused, then rapped three more times, and Patrick heard a bolt slide back. The door opened a few inches. He could just make out a large man standing in the darkness, his features obscured by shadows.

"*Jesus Christ*, Jim." The man's deep voice held equal parts exasperation and amusement. "Every time you show up in that damned uniform of yours, I swear I age a good ten years. Come in, both of you."

For a moment, Patrick thought that they were the only customers in the speakeasy, but as his eyes adjusted to the dim light, he realized that there were several people seated around the large room, tucked here and there behind the wooden pillars and potted plants.

"So, what can I do for you two?" The man who had let them in had taken up his post behind the long oak bar.

"I'm hoping you can help us with a couple of things, Mac," O'Halloron said.

"Knowing you, I can guess part of it already." The bartender placed two large tumblers in front of them. He brought up a half-full bottle of Jameson's Irish Whiskey from behind the counter and poured healthy shots for each of them.

"Mac," O'Halloron chuckled as he raised his glass, "you're a grand man, for a Scot."

"I'll let that pass for now." The bartender turned to Patrick with a grin. "Maybe I'd better introduce myself. Hell could freeze before O'Halloron here remembers his manners. Larry McKenzie." he said, extending his hand.

"Patrick O'Connell. A pleasure to meet you."

"I'm sure it would be if you're socializing with the likes of the captain here." McKenzie looked over as O'Halloron laughed heartily at the insult. "Now, Jim, I believe you said that you needed my help with a *couple* of things."

"Mr. O'Connell here needs a room, and I told him that you might have something to fit the bill, providing he's not too fussy about the company he keeps."

"The fact that he's sitting next to you would seem to argue otherwise, wouldn't it? How long will you be staying, Patrick?"

"I'm not really sure. I have some business to take care of, and no idea how long it will take."

O'Halloron grew quiet as Patrick talked, taking a sudden interest in the napkin beneath his empty glass. McKenzie glanced at his friend.

"Something you're not telling me, Jim?" All traces of playfulness faded from his voice. The big Irishman raised his head, looking from McKenzie to Patrick and back again with a practiced look of feigned innocence.

"I'll tell you what," Patrick said with a smile, "why don't you direct me to the men's room and I'll leave the two of you to discuss this in private."

"Past the stairs and through the door, then a quick left," McKenzie directed.

Patrick slid from his bar stool and wandered off in that direction, happy to take his time so that O'Halloron and McKenzie could work things out between them. Hopefully, the captain's gift for blarney would serve them both well. McKenzie seemed like the type who could be trusted. Of course, all bets would probably be off if O'Halloron shared his suspicions about Patrick's ties with the gangs back in Chicago. Then again, his friend ran a speakeasy, so maybe he wouldn't have a problem with having a racketeer under his roof.

He studied his reflection in the mirror. The man peering back looked a lot more like an exhausted history professor than any gangster he'd seen in the old movies.

But if I can't look like a gangster, Patrick realized, *I can at least spend money like one.* He pulled five more twenties from the envelope and tucked them into his front pocket before making his way back to the bar.

McKenzie and O'Halloron stopped in mid-conversation when they saw him approach. The Irishman wore a faint smirk on his face. McKenzie's expression was far more difficult to read.

"I want no trouble," the innkeeper said, cutting straight to the chase. "My sister-in-law runs this hotel; it's all she and my nephew have in the world, and I'm here to protect her interests. But Jim thinks you can be trusted, and I guess that's good enough for me. You'll have your room. For tonight, at least."

"Thank you." Patrick pulled out his money and laid the five twenties on the bar. McKenzie's eyes grew wide, and even O'Halloron seemed momentarily stunned at the sight of all that cash.

"That'd cover the better part of a month," McKenzie managed at last.

"Less than that, I'm sure, if you add in my meals and Captain O'Halloron's bar tab," Patrick said with a grin, drawing a laugh from both of them. "Anyway, I prefer to pay in advance. If I have to leave suddenly, this would be one less thing that I'd need to worry about."

"Can't argue with that," O'Halloron pointed out. "Better take the money, Mac, before he changes his mind and takes his business elsewhere."

McKenzie shrugged and picked up the twenties.

"Happy to have you with us, Patrick. Now, do I need to send someone for your trunk?"

Before he could answer, O'Halloron laid his hand on Patrick's shoulder. "My friend is traveling light this trip,

Mac, so I suspect that he'll be needing some things come the morrow. Can you see to it?"

The innkeeper nodded. "I'm sure we can arrange something."

"Thank you, Mr. McKenzie," Patrick said, feeling a sense of relief.

"Please, call me Mac. We can take you to your room whenever you're ready, and I'll have someone here about your clothes first thing in the morning."

"Can we make it second thing, Mac? I've come a long way and I think I might want to sleep in a bit tomorrow."

The glowing tip of Leon Brent's cigarette cut through the darkness in the study. The only other light came from the street lamps below, leaving him largely in shadows.

He was alone, the family long since in bed. His wife hadn't asked where he'd been when he got home, or what he'd been doing. She preferred ignorance to unpleasant truths, and this night's truth was more unpleasant than even she could imagine.

In his mind, he pictured Lundgren sprawled out at the foot of the stairs, looking toward the window with dead eyes.

Such a shame the old man had to die. If only he hadn't been so fucking unreasonable about letting go of the company.

Of course there were still details to attend to, loose ends to tie up. But those things would wait until the morning. All he wanted to do tonight was savor the moment.

He was close to success. He could feel it.

The pale morning sun wormed its way through one of the larger holes in the stained window shade, falling squarely across Brian's haggard face. He cursed and rolled over, burying his head in the pillow, but there was nothing for it. He was awake, and the image of an avenging angel haloed in light came swarming back into his mind. There'd be no more rest this morning.

I killed Lundgren. Took my own two hands and snapped the old man's fockin' neck.

Whatever he'd expected to feel when the deed was done, all he'd woken up with was the certain knowledge that he'd fallen as far as a man could fall. There could be no absolution for the crime of murder. Brian had known that from the moment the old man had taken his last rattling breath.

That's why he'd imagined the angel, he knew. His mind had forced him to see what his soul already understood.

Until that moment, Brian had never thought of himself as a truly bad man, though he'd have to admit there were many as would take exception to that. A stray tool might find its way to the pawn shop, certainly, and a fella or two had been relieved of the burden of carrying a heavy wallet, but the little things a man might be forced to do to keep the wolves at bay were as nothing to murder.

It had taken the better part of a bottle last night to ease the guilt and earn a bit of sleep, and he now had the throbbing head to attest to that. He groaned and cursed again, then slowly pulled himself from under the covers to sit on the edge of the bed. His head pounded in protest.

Standing on uncertain legs, he made his way down the short hall to the bathroom. Like the other rooms of the apartment—and the building itself—the bath was shabby and in a general state of disrepair. But it was clean; he had to give his Maggie that much.

Turning the tap on, he waited until the brown water ran clear before splashing his face with shaking hands. His reflection looked back from the mirror through red, puffy eyes. Water trickled down through whiskers already showing gray at thirty-five. He grimaced.

You killed a man last night, and this is the face of the monster you've become.

He'd half-hoped the angel had been real. Even as he ran down the hill from Lundgren's he'd prayed for a quick end, the sound of wings behind him in the night and the swift judgment of a fiery sword, all no less than he deserved. Still, he'd not stopped running until he had reached Slabtown, had he?

Brian moved back to the bedroom to change out of the grimy clothes he'd worn to bed. As he pulled on clean trousers, the aroma of coffee and bacon reached out to him from the kitchen. There'd be eggs then as well, and potatoes frying in the pan. In a mood or no, whether he was deserving or no, Maggie saw to her man.

Dressed, he traveled the few steps from the bedroom to the main room and sat wearily at the table. His wife worked at the potatoes in the small kitchenette, poking and turning them in the cast iron skillet irritably.

She'd been a beauty when he'd met her, a fiery redhead of eighteen with a passion that more than matched her temper. And in her eyes he had seen the possibilities of children, and a home, and the comfort of a fine woman at the end of the day. So he'd set out to win her heart, and much to his own surprise—and the dismay of all the other lads flitting about her—he'd succeeded.

Then, like the thief Brian now knew himself to be, he'd stolen both her youth and her dreams. While Maggie was still as fair as any woman her age—at least in his eyes—the flame of passion had been extinguished, replaced only by anger and sadness in turn.

Yet another crime for which I'll receive no absolution.

At least God, in his infinite wisdom, had seen fit to keep the marriage childless. Though Maggie may have longed for a wee one, Brian knew in his heart of hearts that he would be as great a failure as a father as he had been as a husband.

Maggie none too gently set a plate of food in front of him, along with a steaming cup of black coffee.

"Thank you, my love," he said, his voice barely a mumble. She ignored him and turned her back to him once more as she prepared a plate for herself. Then, in silence, she took her seat on the other side of the table. He couldn't bear to look at her, focusing instead on the food in front of him. Maggie was a fine cook, but this morning Brian ate as much for atonement as for nourishment.

Still she said nothing, and the silence became more than he could stand. When he looked up, the sadness he saw reflected in his wife's eyes tore at his conscience.

"I'm sorry, Maggie." He could think of nothing else to say, though he knew well enough that the words no longer held any meaning for her. She'd heard them far too many times. She stared back at him for several moments, then nodded toward the living room behind her husband.

"An envelope came for you this morning," she said, her voice conveying no emotion.

He turned to look. The envelope sat on the table beside his armchair.

"What's in it, then?"

"And how would I know that?" There was anger in her voice now, no mistaking. "You've made it perfectly clear that I've no business nosing into your affairs."

"What I do, woman, I do for *you*," he snapped, realizing as he did so that this could not end well.

"Brian Daly, you could work in the sewers all day and come home stinking of shite, and I'd be proud to tell everyone that you do it for me. But dealings with shadowy people who leave notes behind the milk bottles? That I'll have none of."

"You'll damn well spend the money they pay me, though, won't you?" he growled.

He knew it had been the wrong thing to say, knew it even before he saw the pained look in Maggie's eyes. There were never any tears, not with her, not anymore, but the eyes gave glimpses of what lay behind the walls she'd built. Brian had hurt her again, this wound perhaps as deep as any he'd ever caused, and he cursed himself once again for the man that he'd become.

Maggie pushed her plate away and took her leave down the hallway to the bedroom. All without a word. The silence she left in her wake roared in Brian's ears.

He knew he should go to her, beg her forgiveness, but not once did he seriously consider doing so. He lacked the courage—had always lacked the courage—to do the right thing. He smiled grimly at that, knowing that he was afraid to go to Maggie when just last night ...

Last night I took the old man's life.

He shuffled slowly to the living room, settling into his battered chair as he picked the envelope up from the table, holding it out as though it were an evil, living thing. It didn't have enough weight to it to contain the balance of his blood money. He pried open the flap of the packet and pulled out the note, a childlike scrawl written on cheap, stained paper.

A time and a location, nothing else. Seven words, two of them misspelled. An educated man's obvious attempt to appear uneducated. Brian crumpled the paper in disgust and dropped the ball into the wastebasket on the other side of his chair.

"All right then, we'll meet," he muttered. "And we'll have done with this, once and for all."

Someone was knocking.

Patrick opened his eyes and looked to the clock on his nightstand, but the clock wasn't there. Neither was the nightstand, the dresser, or anything else that he expected to see.

Christ, he thought, *it wasn't a dream.*

The events of the previous evening—the murder, and meeting Jim O'Halloron and McKenzie—rushed back. He remembered saying his goodnights, then making his way up to his room. The last thing he recalled was sitting down on the narrow bed to remove his shoes. He must have hit the wall of exhaustion then, because now he was curled up on top of the covers, still dressed in the clothes he'd appropriated from Carl.

"Mr. O'Connell?" a small voice called from the other side of the door.

"Hold on a minute."

Patrick struggled to sit up, every muscle protesting. He made his way across the small hotel room and opened the door part way, looking down at the young boy waiting for him in the hallway.

"Can I help you?" he asked, vaguely aware of how shabby he must look in another man's rumpled suit.

"My uncle said to tell you that Momma's going to stop serving breakfast in a half hour." The boy sounded very serious and formal. "And he also said to tell you ..." His voice drifted into awkward silence.

"Tell me what?" Patrick gave Mac's nephew a reassuring smile.

"That the royal dresser will be here to measure you for your wardrobe at ten." The boy grinned, then scurried off toward the staircase.

Twenty minutes later Patrick sat at a table in the otherwise empty dining room, contemplating the large helping of eggs, ham, and diced potatoes before him.

"You'd better tuck in," Mac said, settling onto a chair across the table. "You look like you could use a good meal."

Patrick took his first bite, savoring the delicious home-cooked flavor. Mac sipped at an enormous mug of black coffee while he watched his guest work steadily through the small mountain of food.

"I'd say you were fairly hungry," the Scot observed at last. Patrick had finally begun to show signs of slowing, although it may have been because his plate was nearly empty.

"You have no idea. Your sister-in-law is an amazing cook."

"I'll be happy to pass along the compliment, although I suspect the clean dish will be clue enough. How long has it been since you've eaten?"

Patrick grinned.

"Honestly, it feels like years." He laid his fork across his plate. "Now, I have a question for you. Do you always show such an interest in your guests, or am I a special case?"

"Let's say you've piqued my curiosity. Enough to give my old friends down at the precinct a call to check on you."

"The *precinct*? Why, Mac! There's more to you than O'Halloron let on. And what did you find out?"

"Just what Jim assured me I'd find. You don't appear to be on any wanted lists, here or in the Midwest."

"You sound disappointed."

Mac smiled. "Not really. I'm not even surprised, to tell the truth. I'm an ex cop. I've spent enough time dealing with criminals to trust my instincts on these things. You're no racketeer, regardless of what you led Jim to believe."

"Actually, he jumped to that conclusion without any help from me."

"But you didn't try very hard to convince him otherwise, did you?"

"True. Do I need to find another hotel, Mac?"

"Why don't you tell me what's really going on, then we'll see," Mac replied, poker face once again firmly in place.

"How much did Jim tell you last night?"

"Just that there's a woman in some kind of trouble and you're here to help." He paused while the waiter came by to refill their coffee cups and clear Patrick's dishes away. When the young man had disappeared back into the kitchen—leaving them alone in the dining room once again—Mac added quietly, "That may be the truth as far as it goes, but I suspect there's more to the story."

Patrick nodded. "Someone wanted her father to sell his business. When he refused, they decided he'd be easier to deal with if he were dead. I got here too late to prevent that."

"Go to the police."

"There's no point. They arranged the death to look like an accident, and I don't have any proof otherwise. It's not even a matter of my word against theirs, because I still don't know who *they* are."

"I see your problem," Mac said. For a few moments he sat in thought, holding his coffee cup in front of him with both hands and staring into the black liquid abyss.

"So," he said at last, "now that the father is gone, you're thinking they might go after the daughter next. Have you told the girl?"

"She's never even met me." Her brother served in my division during the war, and I feel I owe it to his family to help." Technically, both statements were true. Patrick wanted to avoid lying to Mac if he could. "So, what do you say? Do I stay, or do I go?"

"You can stay," Mac said, after a moment, "if you'll agree to two things. First, you have to promise me that none of this trouble comes back to the Campbell. As I said last night, this hotel is all that my sister-in-law and her son have, and I won't let anything happen to it, or them."

"Fair enough. And the second stipulation?"

Mac grinned sheepishly as he rubbed a calloused knuckle across the stubble on his chin.

"Once a cop, always a cop, I guess," he said. "You keep me informed on what you find, and I'll help you in any way I can. It can't hurt to have someone with connections in your corner."

The "royal dresser" Mac's nephew had mentioned turned out to be a salesman from the men's department at one of the downtown stores, Lipman and Wolfe. The dapper young man took Patrick's measurements, enthusiastically making recommendations regarding materials and styles while Mac looked on in amusement.

In the end, Patrick put in an order for four suits, along with the other requisite accessories. The salesman seemed more than happy to accept fifty dollars as a down-payment, along with an additional ten for his trouble. The store would call later with the final total, Patrick was assured, and the clothes should be delivered no later than the next morning.

"So, what are your plans for the rest of the afternoon?" Mac asked after Patrick had put Lundgren's suit back on. Mrs. McKenzie had thoughtfully pressed out the wrinkles while he'd gone through his fitting, "so that you won't give the hotel a bad name," Mac had explained with a grin.

"I thought I'd take a look around town, get the lay of things." Patrick started to slide his foot into one of Lundgren's shoes and immediately realized an important item he'd forgotten to order.

"I don't suppose there's a shoe store nearby?" he asked as he gingerly squeezed his foot into the leather vise.

"A bit tight, are they?"

"I grabbed them in a hurry," Patrick told him honestly, hoping the explanation wouldn't require more ... well, explanation. "I guess I should have found a better fit."

"Murtaugh's Shoes, at 23rd and Overton. Tell Chester that I sent you."

"Will he give me a good deal?"

"Chester?" Mac laughed. "Not a chance, but at least he won't overcharge you like he does most out-of-towners."

The night before, Portland had seemed slightly surreal; viewed through the darkness, the similarities to the city Patrick would know sixty years hence seemed to outweigh the differences. But in the light of day, he felt like an extra on an elaborate Hollywood soundstage.

Every detail fascinated him, from the clothes people wore to the cars they drove, and the newspapers they purchased at the corner newsstand. Patrick spent twenty minutes looking through issues of magazines with titles like *McClure's, Science and Invention,* and *Liberty,* periodicals he'd only seen on microfilm or gathering dust on the shelves of antique stores.

He wandered along 23rd until he came to Murtaugh's. The shoes on display in the window looked well-made. Then again, so did the instruments of torture he currently wore.

"How can I be of service?" The voice was deep and good natured, and emanated from a stocky man who had suddenly risen like a jack-in-the-box from behind the counter.

"You must be Mr. Murtaugh," Patrick said. "Mr. McKenzie at the Campbell said that you were the only man to see about some shoes."

Murtaugh's smile warmed several degrees. "That was good of him. It's entirely true, of course, but nice of Mac to say so, just the same."

Patrick grinned. "He also said that I could count on you not to overcharge me like you do the rest of the out-of-towners who wander in."

Murtaugh let out a booming laugh that threatened to shake the shelves around them.

"So," he managed at last, "I take it you're a friend of his. I suppose there goes my profit for the day."

Patrick sat down in a chair and began prying Carl Lundgren's shoes from his feet. "Mr. Murtaugh," he said, grimacing as the last one stubbornly released its painful grip, "just find me two or three pair that actually fit, and you'll be happy I walked through your door."

−7−

Brian made his way through the dark tunnels, with only his flashlight and a better-than-average understanding of Portland's underground to guide him. He took no real comfort from either.

The tunnels underneath Portland were built years earlier to move goods from the river to storage rooms beneath the saloons and hotels that lined the waterfront. When Oregon banned alcohol in 1916, a full three years before the rest of the country went dry, the bars in this part of town had moved underground practically overnight. Ships from Canada carried double cargos, the legitimate items the stevedores unloaded during the daylight hours, and the good stuff that went into the passageways after dark.

Brian had worked the tunnels in the early dry days, before racketeers began giving preference to those who didn't try to liberate a bottle or two for their efforts. After that, Brian had come to the tunnels as a customer only, but come he had, nonetheless.

Just months earlier, the city had torn down the dilapidated warehouses and wharfs along the Willamette River to make way for a new seawall. In the process, the engineers had sealed the waterfront entrances to the underground network.

Even so, smaller sections still linked businesses near the river front, providing a haven for opium, prostitution, and assorted other activities that polite Portland society would prefer to pretend didn't exist.

Brian had entered this particular set of tunnels through a boarded up store off of Front Street, just as he had two weeks earlier. He moved through the darkness, counting the passages as he went. A side passage opened to his left, the muffled sounds of drunken laughter and jazz music drifting in on the damp air. His flashlight beam caught another opening, this one on the right. The light danced across broken shards of brown and green glass.

He shivered and crossed himself as he hurried past the side tunnel. Rumor had it that liquor wasn't the only kind of spirit you came across down there.

Brian heard a faint rustling sound in the darkness behind him. Rats … the filthy little buggers. Occasionally he'd shine his light back the way he'd come and see the beam reflecting in a dozen tiny red eyes. After a while he stopped looking.

Continuing on, he found the small archway along the left wall, so low that he practically had to crawl to get through. Once through the opening, the passage expanded enough for him to walk upright. The room he found himself in was maybe twelve feet across and sixteen long. A naked light bulb glowed from the ceiling, its glare almost impossibly bright after the darkness of the tunnels. At the far end of the room a rickety-looking staircase led up to … actually, he wasn't exactly sure where it led up to, because he had no idea where he was, but standing at the foot of the staircase was the man he'd been summoned by: "Black Dan" Lewis.

Lewis was one of a handful of men who ran the rackets in Portland. Booze, dope, gambling, and prostitution; if it was illegal and profitable, Lewis had his hand in. Working for him was often lucrative. Crossing him … well, few tried it more than once.

Being a man of some scruples and strong survival instincts, Brian had done his best to avoid doing either since he'd lost his job moving booze.

That's why it came as a great surprise when Lewis had summoned him here two weeks earlier. Word had it that Brian harbored a grudge against Carl Lundgren, he'd said, and might be interested in being paid to take his revenge. Brian had asked how much he might expect to be paid. Five hundred dollars, he'd been told, half in advance, and the other half when the job had been completed.

Brian hadn't asked what the job entailed. He hadn't needed to, with a sum like that.

Along with the money, he'd received very specific instructions as to how and when he should go about the task. He was given a thick packet to be left, unopened, on the old man's desk. He'd pocketed the instructions and the envelope without question. Lewis seemed to accept his lack of curiosity as a matter of course.

That had been the only time they had met, until now.

Brian walked out into the room, emerging warily from the tunnel like a mouse from its hole. Lewis—the cat—grinned as his guest stepped into the light.

"There you are! I was beginning to give you up as lost." Brian started to mumble an apology, but Lewis waved it off. "Don't matter. I knew you'd come as long as I had your money."

He pulled a bundle of cash from his overcoat and tossed it onto the ground a couple of feet in front of Brian. "It's all there. You've earned every cent. The police have already written the old man's death off as an accident."

"Just did what you asked." Brian slowly stooped to pick up the money, watching the other man warily all the while.

"Almost," Lewis said, the friendliness in his voice dimming a little. "There's the matter of the envelope I gave you. The one that was supposed to go on Lundgren's desk. Don't seem to have made it there, what I hear."

Brian straightened up, the money forgotten in his hand.

"I left it at the house. Swear to God, I left it there."

Lewis smiled again, thin-lipped and dangerous. "You sure? There, on the old man's desk in his office?"

"Well, not on the desk. But I know I left it where it could be found. Bet one of those cops pinched it. You know how they can be."

Lewis nodded as though he knew all too well how they could be.

"Don't matter," the racketeer said again, his voice friendly once more. "Just would have been cleaner if they'd found the packet."

"Cleaner?"

"Now we may have to handle the daughter in a different way. Too bad. I hear she's all right," he finished with an evil grin.

"Look, I done the old man, but I can't do no girl."

"Course not. I wouldn't dream of asking you to."

A heavy hand grabbed Brian's shoulder from behind, forcing him around. He felt a sudden, searing pain as the blade went in, driving deep into his belly and then up with enough force to lift him off of his feet for a moment. His attacker's other arm pulled him in close.

"Why would we ask you to handle the girl," the words were soft in Brian's ear, the voice familiar somehow, "when you can't even deliver a fucking package?"

The blade slid out of Brian's body for a moment before it plunged in again, but this time he felt no pain as he slipped from the man's embrace and fell to the ground, only dimly aware of someone stepping over his body.

Dan Lewis looked down at Daly, watching as the big Irishman lay dying. The whole process had gone more smoothly than he'd anticipated.

"Now what?" he asked Leon Brent casually.

"Now I see if I can find what that fucking mick did with my envelope."

"I have people I can send. No need for you to do it."

"Some things are better attended to personally. Besides, the fewer people we involve, the fewer loose ends like Daly we'll need to attend to."

"There's a point," Dan conceded. The fact that there would be fewer people to share the profits with didn't escape his attention, either. "Grab the money and let's go."

Brent crouched down beside the fallen Irishman. Dan could just see a hint of the thick bundle of cash under the dead man's body.

"Come here and give me a hand."

Dan grunted and reluctantly knelt down beside Daly. As he reached out to push the body aside, his breath caught at the intensely sharp pain in his chest. Stunned, he looked down at the handle of a knife jutting out from just above his top coat button.

He tried to speak, to breathe, but couldn't. The knife had gone in deep, and he was dimly aware that he was dying.

The pain faded quickly. His heart managed a few feeble beats, then stopped.

Leon looked down at the two men lying on the hard stone floor. A falling out among thieves, that's what the police would call it when the bodies were finally discovered. Two men, two knives, a wad of cash and one bloody mess.

Shame to leave the money, he thought, *but that's the cost of doing business. And it's a small enough price to pay to make sure that no one can follow the trail back to me.*

–8–

Besaw's Café stood on the corner of 23rd and Savier, just blocks away from Lundgren Furniture. The diner was busy, its tables occupied by a mix of shopkeepers, sales girls, and factory workers, scrambling to grab a bite to eat before their lunch break ended.

Patrick found an empty stool at the counter. A smiling, round-faced waitress scurried over with a cup and saucer in one hand, a menu in the other.

Meat loaf for thirty-five cents, pie ala mode for fifteen, coffee for a nickel; at these prices Patrick could live like a king on the money that the murderer had left behind. No wonder Mac's eyes had gone as wide as saucers when he'd paid a hundred in advance for room and board.

While he ate, Patrick turned his thoughts once more to finding the Irishman. He'd seen the man only briefly, but there hadn't been anything unusual that would make him stand out in a crowd. Half of the customers in the restaurant fit his general description.

Patrick had one thing working in his favor, however; he knew the killer had been fired by Carl, probably recently. With luck, someone at the company might be able to point him in the right direction.

If I can give them a reason to talk to me in the first place, that is, he thought, dourly.

Lundgren Furniture sat at the corner of NW 16th and Vaughn Street. The production end was housed in a large wood-framed structure that might have been built around the turn of the century. Along the west end of the block, a newer-looking building—with the stucco walls and low-pitched, terra cotta tiled roof that Patrick always associated with 1920s architecture—held the administrative offices.

Both buildings were locked up, presenting an eerie pocket of silence in an otherwise bustling area of northwest Portland. Someone had posted a sign on the doors to the offices, a hand-written notice stating simply that Lundgren Furniture would be closed until further notice. Visitors to the factory would apparently have to wait for the afternoon newspapers to find out that Carl was dead.

Lost in thought, Patrick almost missed the sound of footsteps behind him.

"I'm sorry, mister, but the offices is closed today."

The deep voice held a trace of a southern accent. Patrick turned to see a large, ebony-skinned man dressed in coveralls watching him from the bottom of the steps to the factory office. He appeared to be in his late forties or early fifties, gray sprinkled liberally through his close-cropped hair. The sawdust on his clothes marked him as one of the factory workers.

"So I see." Patrick moved back down the steps, holding his hand out as he reached the sidewalk. "Patrick O'Connell."

The employee looked a little disconcerted by the friendly overture. "Otis Loring," he said at last. He returned the handshake tentatively, but made no eye contact as he did so.

"Tell me, Otis, why is the factory closed on a Monday afternoon?"

"Mr. Lundgren had an accident this morning, They say ..." the big man paused, his voice catching. "They say he's dead."

"I'm sorry. I understand that he was a very good man."

Otis looked up at that, and in his eyes Patrick saw intelligence and passion.

"Mr. Lundgren was the finest man ever lived." His voice was raw with emotion. "Give me a chance to do something with my life. Made me a foreman when most of the crew wouldn't even work with a colored man, and made them like it, too. I'll never forget that."

"He obviously put a lot of trust in you," Patrick said. That brought a grateful smile. "Tell me, do you know anyone who wanted to hurt Mr. Lundgren, anybody who might have had it in for him?"

"What do you mean, have it in for him? You mean you think Mr. Lundgren was *murdered*? I don't believe it. Who would do something like that?"

"That's what I want to find out," Patrick said. "I got word someone hired a man who used to work here—an Irishman about my height, maybe a little shorter—to kill Mr. Lundgren. Do you know anyone like that, anyone who might have had a grudge against him?"

Otis eyed Patrick suspiciously. "You a police officer?"

"No. I served in the war with Carl's son, Jacob," he said, falling back on the convenient lie. "I feel that I owe it to Jacob to help. Obviously I got here too late to save his father, but I'm going to make sure nothing happens to Julia, if I can help it."

Otis nodded, as though the concept of a debt of honor made perfect sense.

"You say this Irishman used to work here? About your height?" Otis ran a beefy hand through his course hair. "Sounds like Brian Daly, maybe. He fits that description well enough. Don't seem like the type who could kill someone, though."

"What did he have against Mr. Lundgren?"

"About three weeks back he got caught stealing tools. Mr. Lundgren called him up to the office and sacked him on the spot. Daly was angry enough to spit nails. He was yelling that Mr. Lundgren would get his, promised there'd be hell to pay. I didn't think much of it at the time. Truth is, Daly is always sayin' things like that when he gets mad."

Patrick could feel the hair on the back of his neck rise to attention.

"Do you know where this Daly lives?"

Otis nodded. "Mr. Lundgren had me deliver his last paycheck. Lives in the Rosemont Apartments, a few blocks over on 16th and Lovejoy."

"What about an apartment number?"

"Can't say," he answered, his tone flat. "They don't allow coloreds in that building for no reason. I just give the check to the old man watching the door."

"I appreciate your help." Patrick reached out to shake the foreman's hand once more. "I'm staying at the Campbell Hotel. If you think of anything else, that's where you can find me. And, listen, until I know who and what I'm up against, it's probably best if you don't talk to anyone else about this."

Otis looked down at their clasped hands, then back up. He no longer seemed to feel the need to avoid eye contact.

"You really think Miss Julia could be in trouble?"

"I really do."

"Then you let me know what I can do to help," he said, firmly. "You just let me know."

The waiting is the worst of it, Leon thought.

The old man sat in that chair of his on the stoop, smoking one cigarette after another and monitoring the comings and goings of tenants and visitors alike, making it damned difficult to get upstairs and search Daly's apartment for the contract and money.

Leon had to find that envelope. Too many things could go wrong if someone else got to it first.

The old man finally stood up slowly and shambled into the building, leaving the entrance unattended for the first time in over an hour.

About damned time. Leon hurried over to the stoop and made his way up the creaking stairs to the third floor.

After a quick reconnaissance of the Rosemont, Patrick headed over to the little diner across the street. Sitting at a table by the window, he ordered a cup of coffee and a piece of pie, then settled in to watch for the man his gut told him had killed Carl Lundgren.

Forty-five minutes later he was still watching.

The Rosemont was an older tenement in a neighborhood of late nineteenth-century homes and more modern, slightly more upscale apartments. The paint—a dark, almost brownish red the color of dried blood—had weathered and flaked away around the entryway and windows. Clothes dangled from rust-speckled fire escapes, or hung drying in the afternoon sun from lines stretched between the tenement and the neighboring buildings.

The only ways in or out of the Rosemont were a door at the front and the fire escapes; two on either side of the tenement, and two more opening onto a half-alley behind the building.

There had been very little activity so far. The elderly man who served — officially or unofficially — as the doorman for the building had helped a couple of women carry their groceries up the stairs, and given a stern lecture to a young boy who had burst headlong through the wooden doors. Then, as the child ran off up the street, the gray-haired sentinel had struggled to his feet and disappeared inside.

A moment or two later, a man — slightly hunched over and wearing a long black overcoat — had hurried up the stairs and gone inside. Even from a distance Patrick could tell that he was too tall to be the guy he was looking for. Besides, he moved with a slight limp that Patrick was sure the Irishman hadn't had.

Patrick grew more and more antsy with each passing minute. He wasn't cut out for surveillance.

If Daly isn't the one I'm looking for, I'm wasting valuable time, he decided. *Besides, if I wait here any longer, I'm going to overdose on caffeine.*

He paid his bill and walked out into the afternoon sun, making his way across 16th Avenue toward the Rosemont. With each step he felt more confident that he was making the right decision. If Daly wasn't the man he wanted then it was back to square one, but eliminating a possibility was still a step forward, wasn't it?

Besides, it has to be Daly. The description, the threats; everything fits together too neatly.

By the time Patrick arrived at the stoop, the elderly man had returned once more to his cane-backed throne at the top of the steps, a smoldering cigarette held between his bony, nicotine-stained fingers. Close up, he looked even more ancient than he'd seemed from across the street, his skin a mass of tiny wrinkles that flowed into pronounced furrows at the corners of his eyes and mouth. He peered down at Patrick from beneath the frayed bill of a dark blue workman's cap, his gaze neither suspicious nor overly friendly.

On the lapel of his well-worn jacket he sported a small metal pin; a red, five cornered shape that Patrick immediately recognized as a corps badge.

"Cuba, or the Philippines?" he asked, nodding toward the pin. The Spanish American War was only a guess, but an educated one, given the man's age.

The old guy looked a little startled. He glanced down at the pin on his lapel as though he'd forgotten he was wearing it.

"Cuba," he said cautiously. "First Division, Second Infantry."

"See much action?"

That drew a smile. "I was at San Juan Heights and Santiago, so I had just enough action for my tastes."

"I know what you mean. I saw enough for a lifetime in the last war."

The old man laughed, humorlessly. "There won't *ever* be a last war, son. You here to visit someone?"

"I'm looking for Brian Daly. I understand he lives here."

"You a cop?"

"No, but he's in some trouble. I'm hoping I can head things off before he digs himself in any deeper."

"Trouble, huh? Well, that sounds like Brian all right. What is it that you want?"

"I just want to talk to him. Someone's setting Daly and a friend of mine up for a pretty serious fall. Truth is, I don't give a damn about Daly, but I do care about my friend. Unfortunately, I can't help her without keeping Daly out of more trouble."

The old man studied Patrick. After a few moments, he said, "I haven't seen Brian since he left this morning. Can't say if he's come back or not."

"Could we find out for sure?"

"Don't see why not." He rose slowly from the rickety chair. "If Brian isn't home, then maybe his wife, Maggie, can tell us when he'll be back."

The old man's clothes hung awkwardly from his painfully thin frame as they climbed the creaking wooden stairs to the upper floors. They left the stairway on the third floor, and made their way to an apartment near the far end of the hall. The old man gave a tentative knock, so soft that Patrick wondered if anyone could have heard it.

"Maggie? Maggie, darling, it's Elmer."

There was no answer, but Patrick thought he heard someone whispering from the other side of the door. The old man knocked a second time.

"Maggie? Please open the door, honey."

Patrick heard a muffled cry. He looked to the old man—to confirm he hadn't been alone in hearing the noise—just as a shrill scream ripped through the quiet hallway. It died as suddenly as it had begun.

"Don't just stand there, boy," the old man said, urgently. "Get that goddamned door open."

The wood was stronger than it appeared, but Patrick's second kick splintered the frame and the door flew back with a crash. Inside, Daly's apartment was in complete disarray; cushions ripped and torn, cupboard doors open with their contents strewn about the floor. Just outside of the tiny kitchenette lay a young woman. Her eyes stared blankly at the bloody carving knife on the floor in front of her. A pool of crimson flowed from the gaping wound in her throat.

"Oh, *goddammit*, Maggie!" the old man wailed, hurrying to the dying woman's side.

Patrick looked wildly around the apartment, his eyes falling on the open window just as he heard the sound of someone on the fire escape outside. He raced to the window and saw a man—dressed in a familiar black overcoat—scrambling to get to the ground and the gap running between the buildings. Patrick followed him out onto the escape.

"Get that son of a bitch!" Elmer called out angrily as Patrick hurried down the ladder. Below, he heard the sound of gravel crunching and glanced over to see the killer hurrying away. Despite his limp, which seemed more pronounced now than before, the man moved with surprising speed.

Jumping from the upper rungs of the last ladder, Patrick landed hard on his feet, staggering to keep upright.

By the time he regained his balance there was no one else in sight. He ran between the buildings, out to Lovejoy Street, but he was already too late. For the second time in two days, he'd watched while a murderer escaped.

Leon risked a quick peak around the corner of the building he'd taken refuge behind, hoping for a better look at the man who had chased him from the tenement.

When the door had crashed open as he hit the fire escape, his first thought had been that the police must have found Daly's body in the tunnels and had come to let the wife know. But the man standing at the end of the alley was no beat cop. Judging by the clothes he wore, he was no detective either. The style might be a couple of years out of fashion, but even from half a block away Brent could tell an expensive suit when he saw one. So, if the guy wasn't the law—and he clearly wasn't a tenant in that dive of an apartment building—who the hell was he, and why did he pick that moment to show up at Daly's place?

Still a little breathless, Leon watched as his pursuer looked up and down Lovejoy before finally disappearing back around the corner toward the front entrance of the Rosemont apartments.

Satisfied that he was in the clear, Leon headed back to where he'd parked the Packard. He left the black woolen overcoat behind, its blood-soaked sleeve, along with the gloves he'd been wearing, carefully tucked underneath. The police would find them soon enough, but there'd be nothing that could tie them back to Leon.

There shouldn't be anything to connect Daly to him, either, but the close call he'd just had made him wonder. It was just a matter of time before the bodies in the tunnel turned up. If Lewis had been discreet—as he'd promised to be—then the matter should end there, a classic falling out among thieves. But if Lewis had opened his mouth about the plan, then there was at least an outside chance that someone would come looking for Leon.

He knew about vendettas from his Chicago days. It was time to get his wife and kids out of town, just to be on the safe side, and find some way to wrap this Lundgren business up quickly.

When Patrick returned to the Rosemont, Elmer was back on the stoop. He held a smoldering cigarette in his shaking, blood-stained hand.

"The bastard got away," the old man said. There was no sense of accusation or disappointment in his tone, just the acknowledgment of an obvious truth. "Well, you tried, and I thank you for that."

Patrick couldn't manage anything but a nod. Two murders, two killers, and he felt as though he were farther from the truth than when he'd arrived.

"Listen, son," Elmer said, his voice surprisingly steady, "I just called this in to the police, and they're on their way. Do you want to be here when they arrive?"

That would be interesting, Patrick realized. *No identification, no convincing reason for coming to see Brian Daly, and I'm carrying a wad of cash that would choke a small horse.*

"Not particularly. The only description I could give them is that the guy was maybe six foot, with dark hair, a limp, and wearing a black overcoat. Not much to go on."

"Then you best be on your way. I'll tell them what they need to know."

"I appreciate it." He started down the steps, then turned back to Elmer. "My name is Patrick, Patrick O'Connell. I'm staying at the Campbell Hotel for a few days. I need to find Brian more than ever, now. If he shows up, will you let me know?"

Elmer offered up a grim smile. "After what happened to Maggie? You're damned right I'll let you know, on one condition. I get whatever's left of him when you're done."

The sound of evening traffic drifted in through Patrick's hotel room window. He lay on his bed and stared up at the ceiling, unable to clear his mind of the image of Maggie Daly lying in a pool of her own blood, unable to shake the guilt of causing the young woman's death.

Patrick had returned to the Campbell that afternoon to find his new suits draped neatly across his bed, the rest of his Lipman and Wolf purchases—wrapped in brown paper—stacked nearby. The shoes he'd purchased at Murtaugh's were waiting for him as well, the boxes set just inside the door. Twenty minutes later, the clothes had been transferred into what his grandmother had always referred to as a chifferobe, the shoes neatly arranged underneath. Patrick was fresh out of distractions.

Restless, he'd watched the street life along 23rd from his window for awhile. His earlier fascination with the world he'd only been able to read about before had been replaced by the gnawing fear that he wasn't up to the role he'd been forced into.

In the end all he could manage was to lay sprawled on the bed, staring off into space and praying for sleep to provide some relief from the storm clouds gathering in his mind.

It was late evening when someone knocked at his door, softly at first, then more insistently when he elected to ignore it.

"Patrick," he heard from the other side of the door, "I'd like to talk to you."

"Not a good time, Mac."

"Good a time as any," the innkeeper answered, sounding determined.

Mac waited patiently until Patrick had stepped back into the room to let him in. He carried a towel-wrapped bundle—suspiciously bottle-shaped—in one hand, and a folded up newspaper in the other.

"Didn't see you come down for supper," Mac observed as he settled onto the cane-back chair by the window.

"I didn't have much of an appetite tonight."

Mac nodded. "I figured it was something like that. Still, I had my sister-in-law put together a tray for you, just in case. My nephew should be bringing it up in a little bit. In the meantime," he added, "I thought this might help."

He removed the towel to reveal a bottle of Jameson's. He poured a generous amount into one of the drinking glasses on the table beside him, handing the whiskey to Patrick. Then he poured a second—albeit smaller—drink for himself.

Patrick eyed the amber liquid; he'd never been much of a drinker, but at the moment he had to admit that it looked pretty damned good. He raised the glass and took a long swallow, savoring the warmth as it flowed through his body.

Mac just watched him for a moment, his own drink untouched. Finally, he said, "You know, I found that story you told me at breakfast a little hard to believe. I mean, a deep, dark murder conspiracy sounds a bit melodramatic for our little city. Then I ran across this."

He opened up the newspaper he'd brought with him and laid it on the bed. Patrick looked down, quickly spotting the same story about Carl's death that he'd seen on microfilm at the Historical Society.

"They're after Lundgren Furniture, aren't they? And this Julia Lundgren, she's the girl that you're trying to help."

Patrick smiled grimly and took another swallow of whiskey.

"Help?" he said, as the warmth flowed through him. "Mac, so far I've done a hell of a lot more harm than good."

"How do you figure?"

"An innocent woman died today because of me." It was a relief to admit that out loud, but it did nothing to ease the guilt he felt.

Strangely, Mac seemed to take this revelation in stride. He simply leaned over and poured a little more whiskey into Patrick's nearly empty glass.

"The way I heard it, you probably came closer to saving Maggie than to getting her killed." He smiled grimly at the look of surprise that must have appeared on Patrick's face. "I used to patrol this neighborhood when I was a beat cop. Elmer has been sitting out on that stoop for as long as I can remember.

"What I want to know is, how did you happen to be there in the first place? Granted, there isn't much that I would put past Brian Daly, but he wouldn't have been the first person I thought of when it came to murder."

Patrick stared into his glass, wishing he could tell Mac everything.

"My information said the guy hired to kill Carl was a former employee at the factory," he said at last, "an Irishman about my size. Someone at the factory mentioned that Daly made some threats when Carl fired him recently. It seemed like it might be worth following up on."

"Well, your instincts were apparently good."

"And look how well it turned out for Daly's wife," Patrick muttered bitterly as he drained the remainder of his whiskey.

"Elmer said it wasn't a pretty sight."

"I've seen worse." Patrick reached over for the bottle, pouring more whiskey into his glass. "But that was wartime, Mac. We all knew what the risks were. But Maggie Daly was just … collateral damage."

Mac gave him a puzzled look, the phrase obviously foreign to him.

"An innocent, caught in the crossfire. In the wrong place at the wrong time. And if I hadn't shown up when I did …"

"Maggie would still be dead." Mac took the glass from Patrick's hand and set it on the bedside table. "Her killer came prepared for blood. Use your head, son. Why do you think he was wearing an overcoat and gloves in August?"

"How did you ..."

"The boys found them in a pile just around the corner, on 17th, Maggie's blood all over them. Whoever this guy is, he's not planning on leaving any loose threads. That's why Maggie died, not because you showed up at the wrong moment."

Patrick caught a strange look on Mac's face. He was sure something had just gone unspoken. Before he could ask, however, they heard a quiet knock from the hallway. Mac opened the door to the young boy who had come to tell Patrick about breakfast that morning. He stood outside, holding a linen-covered tray. Mac ushered his nephew in and directed him to set the meal on the small table beside the bed.

"My nephew, Jimmy," Mac said. "Jimmy, this is Mr. O'Connell."

"It's very nice to meet you, Jimmy." Patrick reached into his pocket and pulled out a silver dollar. "This is for bringing my dinner up."

The boy's eyes were almost as big around as the coin he now held.

"Thank you, Mr. O'Connell," he said, barely able to suppress his excitement.

"You're very welcome."

Mac watched the exchange in amusement. "Now, run back down to help your momma," he said at last, ushering his nephew out the door. When he'd closed the door once more, he turned to Patrick with a stern look on his face.

"You are going to spoil that child, tipping him more than the cost of the whole supper."

"I lost my head," Patrick admitted with a smile. It felt good to smile. "Thanks for the reassurance about what happened today, Mac, but I still feel like an armchair detective who's in way over his head."

"Don't kid yourself. You *are* in over your head. But at least you don't have to figure this out all by yourself anymore.

Patrick gave him a puzzled look. "Meaning?"

"Meaning, I'm going to help you as much as I can."

"Once a cop, always a cop?"

"Something like that. Let's just say that I don't like the idea of someone getting away with one murder, let alone ..." Mac's voice trailed off once more.

"Is there something you're not telling me?"

Mac nodded. "After Maggie's death, the boys put out an all points for Brian. Acting on a tip, they found his body in one of the tunnels downtown, near the waterfront. Apparently, he'd had a falling out with one of our local crime bosses—a lovely piece of work named "Black Dan" Lewis—and they somehow managed to fatally stab each other when no one was there to see what happened. Very neat and tidy, except for the fact that neither Lewis nor Daly was ever known as a knife man."

"What are the police doing about it?"

"Not a damned thing. The way they have it figured, Lewis and Daly killed each other, and someone from Lewis's gang murdered Maggie in retaliation. Oh, they'll make an effort to figure out who killed her, but I'm guessing they'll be looking under the wrong rock. My gut tells me that whoever is attempting to grab Lundgren's company is operating outside of Lewis's organization."

"And without Brian, we've lost our best lead."

"Well, that might be painting the picture a little too black." Mac said, reassuringly. "The Brian Dalys of the world don't attract much attention, but someone as prominent as Dan Lewis ... well, there's usually someone who notices who they've talked to, or where they've gone. If shutting Lewis up covers the killer's tracks, it was probably a private arrangement between them. But there's still a chance they met somewhere public to set this whole thing up. Find where they met, and maybe we find someone who can give us a description of your murderer.

"I'll make some calls and see what I can learn." He stood and rewrapped the towel around the bottle. "In the meantime, you need some food in your stomach and a good night's sleep. Just put the tray out in the hall when you're done, and I'll send Jimmy around to collect it in the morning."

"I'll do that," Patrick said, following him to the door. "And thank you. It's a relief to know that I'm no longer wandering through this maze by myself."

The innkeeper smiled. "There's still a chance you may get lost, even with me along, but at least you're guaranteed that the company will be first-rate."

The next morning, there were just a handful of customers in the dining room when Patrick made it downstairs for breakfast. He started to sit at the counter but Mac shook his head, nodding toward one of the open tables farthest from the kitchen.

As soon as he was settled, the waitress—a curvaceous little blonde who introduced herself as Elizabeth—arrived with coffee and took his order. Moments later, Mac sat down across from him.

"You get any sleep?"

"Some, but it took awhile. Maybe I should have had you leave the bottle last night."

"Listen to the voice of experience; whiskey doesn't help you sleep after something like that, and it doesn't make the nightmares go away."

"What does?"

"Nothing I've found," Mac admitted, "except time. But nailing the bastard who killed Maggie can't hurt. And to that end ..." He slid a piece of paper across the table to Patrick. A single word—*Cicero's*—had been scrawled on it in pencil.

"What's this?"

"Cicero's is a restaurant—or a nightclub—depending on which door you go through. It's the favorite watering hole for half the politicians in the city. It's also where Lewis held court for the past three years. According to my friends, if someone wanted to ask him for a favor, that's where they would have gone."

"Sounds like we should pay a visit."

"Not *we*. You. Not to worry, I'll be there if you should need me. But I'm not so far removed from the force that I wouldn't attract some attention, and that won't help either one of us."

"Do you have a plan, or am I supposed to make it up as I go along?"

"Oh, I always have a plan." Mac grinned. "But first I have a question. Have you ever done any acting?"

They spent the rest of the day matching all of the known facts against Mac's strategy, searching for weaknesses and risks, and identifying the key players. Patrick had to admit the plan was comforting in its simplicity

Lewis's lieutenant, and most likely to move to the top of the organization, was Carlo Pellizotti.

"He's a violent little shit," Mac explained, "and I do mean little. He only stands about five foot two and doesn't weigh more than a wet cat, but what he lacks in size he more than makes up for in meanness and a willingness to inflict pain. That makes him dangerous, but predictable.

"If you push him—and that's just what you're going to do, by the way—Pellizotti won't do anything personally. No, he'll delegate that privilege. There's always muscle at the entrance to the club, screening everyone coming in, but the guy who enforces the rules is Frankie Abbado. Word is, Lewis kept Frankie close whenever he was meeting with someone at Cicero's, so if anybody can give us a description of our killer, he's the one."

"How do we get Frankie someplace where we can talk to him?"

Mac smiled. "By relying on the predictability of our enemies. Pellizotti isn't going to risk alienating the cream of Portland's crop by roughing you up inside the nightclub. That's what back alleys are for. You get Frankie outside where I'll be waiting."

Patrick shook his head. "Nothing doing, Mac. I can't have him knowing that you're involved in this. Just tell me how to recognize Frankie and I'll handle the rest."

"Look for the bull elephant wearing a tuxedo. I kid you not ... Frankie is about six-five and weighs in at around three hundred fifty pounds." Mac looked at Patrick, probably searching for any signs of concern, then grinned. "That doesn't worry you at *all*, does it?"

"Not really. I just have to leverage his size against him."

"Like the old boxing adage, 'the bigger they are, the harder they fall,' huh?"

"Something like that."

"Then all we have to do is make Pellizotti angry enough to earn yourself a trip to the alley, but not angry enough to have you winding up dead in a shallow grave somewhere in the woods."

The public face of Cicero's was a popular family-style Italian restaurant. Access to the speakeasy was at the back of the restaurant, just past the restrooms, through a recessed doorway.

The back alley that figured so prominently in Mac's plan was really nothing more than a service area running half the length of the block between Cicero's and the Broadway Theater. The alley was probably twelve feet across at the street opening, and closer to twenty immediately behind the nightclub. In addition to the theater exits that opened onto the alley, there were two doors from Cicero's; one from the kitchen and one from the club. It was through this second door that, if all went well, Patrick hoped to be escorted by Frankie.

He looked around for something that might give him a tactical advantage. With his training, he didn't think taking the bouncer down would pose too much of a problem. The real trick would be keeping the big man down long enough to get some answers from him. A black Dodge delivery van parked along the opposite side of the alley from the club gave Patrick the inspiration he was looking for.

He explained how he intended to use the truck to Mac.

"God, are you optimistic," the Scot chuckled.

"Always. Do you think you can make sure that no one drives the damned thing away before I get myself thrown out of the club?"

"Wouldn't be a bit surprised. In the meantime, why don't you head back to the hotel and get ready? And you might want to stand a little closer to your razor when you shave. You show up looking like that and they're likely to give you the bum's rush before you even get inside the club."

Patrick rubbed the stubble on his chin, realizing that the last time he'd shaved had been the morning he'd made his time jump. That would put it at about seventy two hours, give or take six decades.

"Stop by Parnell's Barbershop, at 21st and Kearney," Mac directed. "Tell Willie that I need him to make a respectable gentleman of you. At least on the *outside*."

From the slowly rotating barber pole outside, to the black and white linoleum tiles on the floor, the barbershop was exactly what Patrick had hoped it would be. Bottles and tins of various shapes and sizes adorned the shelves, their labels advertising products like Wildroot Hair Tonic and Brilliantine. Some names were more familiar, like Brylcreem—"A little dab'll do ya," or so the television commercials that Patrick grew up with would have had him believe.

Once he got over the initial nervousness of having someone holding a straight razor to his throat, Patrick found the experience of an old-fashioned shave—the hot towel wrapped around his face, the swishing sound of the blade sliding back and forth across the razor strop, and the gentle, almost surgically precise way that the barber went about his work—one of the few aspects of the time that he wished had survived the decades.

On a whim Patrick spent an additional fifty cents for a bottle of Bay Rum Aromatic Tonic on his way out, images of the slicked-back look of Rudolph Valentino and George Raft coming to mind.

After dinner in the Campbell's dining room, he went upstairs to prepare. He needed to dress as though he belonged in a club that catered to Portland's elite, so he selected a dark gray pinstripe suit and starched linen shirt, a broad purple and black silk tie, and gray socks.

Satisfied with his appearance, he carefully massaged some Bay Rum into his hair, combing it through until he'd achieved the dapper Jazz Age look that he'd been hoping for. One last glance in the mirror and he headed out to catch the streetcar downtown, feeling every bit like an extra in a Cagney movie.

–9–

It was almost eight before Patrick made his way back to Cicero's. He found Mac stationed at the entrance to the alley. The delivery truck was still in place, both tires flat on the passenger side.

"Damnedest thing. Sparkplug wire's gone missing, as well," the Scot said with a grin. "You ready?"

"I'd say that we're about to find out, aren't we?"

Mac nodded, looking Patrick over. "Well, if this doesn't work, at least you'll make a pretty corpse. You remember the layout inside the club?" Patrick nodded. "Good. Then I'll be here waiting here for you when you come out with Frankie."

"Out of sight," Patrick reminded him.

"Out of sight," his friend agreed, "unless things get out of hand."

Judging from the line of people waiting for an open table, Cicero's was as popular a restaurant as it was a speakeasy. Patrick made his way through the would-be diners, moving down a dimly-lit hallway until he came to a recessed doorway. He pressed a buzzer to the right of the heavy oak door and waited, the password provided by one of Mac's detective friends at the ready.

Almost immediately the door opened slightly, the light from inside blocked by a large man in a dark suit.

"May I help you?"

"I'm with Grigsby," Patrick said. The gap opened wider and he stepped through the doorway to find himself in a second hallway, the far end of which was obscured by a heavy curtain. The sound of lively music could just be heard from beyond.

The doorman, dressed in a tuxedo and thick-set as a heavyweight fighter, smiled without warmth. He looked Patrick over as the door closed behind them with a solid click.

"I don't think I've seen you before." Patrick caught only the faintest hint of suspicion in the bouncer's voice. "I'll need to pat you down before you join the party."

Patrick held his arms away from his body, noticing as he did that a second guard, similarly dressed, had appeared from behind the far curtain. The newcomer watched the search with nothing more than mild curiosity, having apparently made up his mind that Patrick posed no threat.

"I apologize, sir," the doorman said with little conviction. "Just a precaution. Nate, show this gentleman in, please."

Patrick lowered his arms and walked to where the second man held the curtain back, revealing yet another door. As the drapery fell in place behind them, Nate rapped twice and the door swung open immediately. Loud jazz music washed over them on a blue haze of cigarette smoke.

"Enjoy," Nate said pleasantly as Patrick stepped past him and into a speakeasy scene right out of *Public Enemy* or *Some Like It Hot*. On a raised stage in the far corner a small, all-black jazz band performed a lively ragtime. Men in expensive suits smoked thick cigars and drank highballs. Women, many waving long cigarette holders around like conductor's batons, sipped champagne and cocktails.

Patrick made his way to the crowded bar, edging himself in between a distinguished-looking older man in formal attire and a very attractive woman, perhaps in her early thirties, wearing a beaded silk dress. She gave him a quick appraisal when he accidentally brushed against her arm, then rewarded him with a bright smile.

"I'm Ruby," she said, extending her hand to him, palm down.

Patrick tried to decide whether he was supposed to shake her hand—which would have been an awkward proposition at that angle—or kiss it. *What would Valentino do*, he mused, then leaned forward to lightly brush his lips across the back of Ruby's hand.

"Patrick," he said with a smile.

"Aren't you the charmer?" She studied him for a moment longer, then turned to the woman sitting to her right. "Watch out for this one, Sally. He looks like a white slaver to me."

Sally looked at Patrick with unfocused eyes before turning her attention back to the cocktail in front of her.

"What about it, Patrick?" Ruby asked in a teasing voice. "Are you here to lure me into a life of lust and debauchery?"

Patrick laughed. *So much for the innocence of days gone by.*

"Some other time, I'm afraid."

"That's too bad," Ruby said with a sigh. "You will let me know if you decide to change your mind, won't you?"

"Ruby, you'll be the first to know," he promised as the bartender stepped up to take his order. "Whiskey for me, and one of whatever the lady here is drinking," Patrick said, indicating his new friend.

"Another Manhattan, Ruby?" the bartender asked. She nodded happily, and he waddled off to grab the cocktail shaker.

"So, Patrick, are you here with someone?" She reached over and ran a crimson-painted fingernail playfully along his sleeve.

"No, but I am looking for someone ... a *specific* someone," he added quickly before Ruby could take advantage of the opening.

She pouted—fetchingly, he had to admit—but the arrival of her Manhattan seemed to brighten her spirits. By the time Patrick had finished paying for their drinks, Ruby had turned her attention to a distinguished, silver-haired gentleman who had sidled in between Sally's stool and her own. Patrick seized the opportunity and surveyed the room.

He spotted Frankie Abbado immediately. It would have been hard not to, really; the bouncer wandered through the room, head and shoulders above the clientele like Mt. Everest rising above the Himalayas.

Patrick watched how the big man carried himself, assessing his target. Mac had put Frankie at three hundred fifty pounds, probably a fair estimate, but he ran more to fat than muscle. His hands looked to be perhaps twice the size of Patrick's, fingers like over-plump sausages and fleshy rolls showing at the wrists. Heavy jowls hung over the edges of his starched white collar, and he moved with an awkward gait.

The bouncer's coat fit as tight as a straight jacket across the shoulders and in the arms, which could only slow the bodyguard down in a pinch.

No doubt the bouncer was strong, but in Frankie's profession, size alone was probably the most reliable weapon when it came to intimidating troublemakers. Mac suspected that it had been years since anyone seriously tested his fighting abilities the way that Patrick was planning to.

In stark contrast to Frankie's lumbering presence, the little man walking in front of the bouncer—matching Mac's description of Carlo Pellizotti right down to the oversized cigar and gaudy diamond cufflinks—moved with precision and energy, conveying an air of tension that had patrons shifting uncomfortably around him. His eyes seemed to take everything in at once as he passed among the customers, shaking a hand here or giving a hearty pat on the back there, a smarmy grin pasted onto his hawk-like countenance.

Patrick's targets identified, he continued his causal reconnaissance of the night club. Other than the wait staff and the two guards watching the main entrance, there didn't appear to be any other employees on the floor, although more muscle would undoubtedly be stationed at the alley doorway as well.

He turned his attention once more to Frankie and Carlo. They now stood no more than ten feet from Patrick's position. Pellizotti chatted with a group of obviously well-heeled customers while Frankie hovered nearby, a disinterested look on his face. Patrick glanced up at the big man's eyes and found little indication that the bouncer was paying much attention to his surroundings, apparently confident that his ability to walk upright was all that was required to do his job.

Mac's source had assured them that Frankie carried a pistol—a Smith & Wesson .38 caliber revolver—but there was no sign of a shoulder holster, and no possibility that the weapon could be tucked into the front of his belt because Frankie's belly hung over the waist of his pants, preventing him from even buttoning up his tuxedo. That meant that the bouncer carried the gun at his back where it would be more inconspicuous, but harder to get at quickly, especially for a man packed into a tux a couple of sizes too small for him.

Pellizotti wrapped up his conversation and walked in Patrick's general direction, with Frankie following behind like a plodding old bull dog.

Show time. Patrick felt the once-familiar adrenaline surge of impending combat course through his body. Running through Mac's plan one last time, he casually stepped to his right, blocking Carlo's path.

"Aren't you Carlo Pellizotti?" Patrick asked, his words slightly slurred, his voice intentionally louder than it needed to be, like a man two drinks over his limit.

Pellizotti stopped and looked up sharply, his gaze wary even as an insincere smile crossed his face. Behind him, Frankie barely managed to come to a halt before he ran over his boss.

Reactions are pathetically slow. Patrick filed the observation away with satisfaction.

"Have we met?" Pellizotti asked. His smile was friendly enough, but there was no warmth in his tone.

"No, but I'm ... I was ... a friend of "Black Dan," so I know all about you." He looked down at Carlo and blinked a couple of times, as though he were trying to clear his vision. "I didn't think that you'd be quite this *short*, though," he added in amusement.

The barb hit its mark, as Mac had known it would. Pellizotti glared at him, fists forming even as the muscles in his neck tightened. Frankie started to move forward, but his boss held out his arm.

"You appear to have had a little too much to drink," he said as he forced himself to unclench his hands, "and I think you need to leave now.

"Besides," he continued, his public smile once more in place for the benefit of the customers who were beginning to notice the confrontation, "you're confused; I've never even heard of this Lewis person."

Patrick laughed loudly, startling Pellizotti and drawing even more attention their way.

"Sure you have. Your old boss, "Black Dan" Lewis. Ran this place, along with most of the booze, gambling and prostitution in the city."

Murmurs rippled along the bar and from table to table. The customers Pellizotti had been chatting with a few moments earlier stood, nonchalantly gathering their things as they looked to leave. It appeared that others would soon join the exodus.

"Hey," Patrick said, leaning forward unsteadily, "with Dan gone, that makes you the big man around here, doesn't it?"

Pellizotti suddenly resembled nothing so much as a coiled snake, eyes as cold and dark as obsidian.

"You've just made a very bad mistake," Pellizotti said in a soft, steely voice. "Frankie."

The bouncer stepped forward, grabbing Patrick's left shoulder.

"Hey, bub, that hurts!" Patrick grimaced, staring up at the bouncer as though he'd just noticed him for the first time. "My god, you're tall ..." He looked back down at Pellizotti and grinned. "You two should dress up like Mutt and Jeff for Halloween. Take first place every time."

The comment brought a murderous glare from the little Italian, and more than a few subdued chuckles from the patrons within earshot.

"Show our ... guest ... out," Pellizotti growled, "and see to it personally that he don't come back."

Frankie spun Patrick around and guided him—none too gently—past the customers at the bar and then through the heavy red velvet curtains draped across an alcove at the far end of the room. Once they were out of sight of the customers, the bouncer pushed Patrick up hard against the far wall, holding him there as he opened a heavy door leading out of the club.

Maintaining his painful grip on Patrick's shoulder, Frankie forced him into the short, dimly-lit hallway beyond the threshold. The door swung shut behind them, completely drowning out the music inside. A few feet away, seated in a chair beside what was undoubtedly the door to the alleyway, yet another tuxedoed guard looked up as they entered. Patrick grinned drunkenly, leaning against the wall as though on unsteady legs.

"Hey, Frankie, what gives?" the muscle asked, amusement clear in his tone. "Need me to take out the garbage?"

"Boss wants me to tend to this one personally," Abbado told him. "Go inside and keep an eye on things until I get back."

The guard moved past them and through the entrance to the noisy club. When the hallway was quiet once more, Frankie reached down and opened the door leading to the alley.

"C'mon, buddy. I'll try to make this as quick and painful as possible," Frankie chuckled, pushing Patrick outside.

Patrick dropped down to the pavement and stumbled forward. As the bouncer followed him through the doorway, things went south for the big man in a hurry.

Taking out an opponent who has a serious size advantage isn't as hard as it might seem, if you've got the proper training. A punch to the throat, delivered with enough force, will crush the windpipe and leave even the biggest man vainly struggling for one last gasp of breath. A blow to the temple can quickly cause unconsciousness, blindness, or even death.

Neither technique, however, lends itself very well to gathering information from the victim afterward. That takes a little more finesse.

As Patrick pretended to stumble out into the alley, he planted his right foot and pivoted around, slamming his fist hard into Frankie—just above the groin—as the bouncer was about to step down. The bouncer instinctively doubled over, lowering his hands to protect his testicles even as he began to fall off-balance.

Patrick's knee was already on its way up, crashing into Frankie's nose with a sickening crunch. The big man bellowed in pain and tried to swing his right hand behind his back, the seams of his too-tight jacket stretched to their limit as he reached for the .38 tucked into the waistband of his pants. A forearm smash to the side of his head toppled Frankie to his hands and knees.

Patrick reached down and snatched the .38 from Abbado's belt. The sight of Patrick behind the pistol took any remaining fight out of Pellizotti's bouncer.

"What, are you gonna kill me?" Frankie groaned, looking back through tear-filled eyes at the man he had seriously underestimated. Blood flowed freely from his broken nose.

"That's up to you. See, I have a few questions to ask, and I think you're just the guy to answer them. But not here. You see that truck over there?" he asked, motioning toward the black Dodge truck parked across the alleyway.

Frankie nodded, scattering droplets of blood across his shirt and jacket.

"Let's go over there where we can talk in private, shall we?"

The bouncer struggled to his feet and began shuffling toward the truck. As they neared the Dodge, Frankie's shoulders tightened and his fists clenched. Patrick drove the edge of his foot into the back of Abbado's leg, just behind his right knee, sending him crashing down to the ground once more.

"Let's not try that again," Patrick advised, calmly. "There are other people I can ask my questions of. Now, crawl the rest of the way."

"You son of a bitch," Frankie growled, but he did as he was told. When he was almost to the Dodge, Abbado looked back over his shoulder.

"Under the truck," Patrick told him.

"What? You got to be kidding! There's no way I'm fitting under there."

"Do the best you can. Head and shoulders first."

"Go screw." Frankie glared back at his tormentor in defiance.

"You know ..." Patrick glanced down at the pistol in his hand, "I could never quite get the hang of using one of these to get people to talk. It's not as easy as you might think," he added, looking back at Abbado. "You have to find just the right place to put a bullet into a guy without hitting a major artery. Half the time they bleed out before I get anything really useful from them.

"Still," he said, smiling cheerfully, "I suppose practice makes perfect, right?"

He had barely leveled the gun at Frankie before the bouncer had wedged himself firmly under the running board of the truck.

"Now, let's get some answers." Patrick crouched to make himself heard. "I'm looking for the man who killed Dan Lewis."

"That's what this is all about? That goddamned potato eater, Daly, *he's* the one who killed the boss and everyone fucking knows it!"

"Language, Frankie, language." Patrick nudged Abbado in the ribs with the muzzle of the gun. "Let me ask you something, did your boss seem like the kind of guy who could be taken by a nickel-and-dimer like Brian Daly? No, they were both set up, and I want the man behind it."

"I don't know who you're talking about," Frankie said after a moment, his voice more subdued than before.

"I think you do. My guess is that Dan met with this guy at the club to discuss some kind of job. He's a couple of inches taller than me, and more broad-shouldered. Walks with a limp. Ring any bells?"

When Frankie didn't say anything, Patrick poked him with the muzzle of the .38 once more.

"Don't fall asleep under there. I asked if that description rings any bells."

"Yeah," Frankie answered, sullenly. "I remember the guy."

"Tell me his name."

"I never caught it."

"Frankie, you're really beginning to piss me off." This time, Patrick pushed the muzzle of the pistol up hard into the bouncer's ribs and held it there.

"I mean it!" Abbado squirmed in vain to relieve the pressure in his side. "I don't know his name, but he's a regular. Comes in two or three times a week. Dan seemed to be pretty chummy with him, like they was old friends."

"What makes you think he's the guy I'm looking for?"

"Last time he came in, he and the boss went into the office to discuss some kind of business. I don't know what," he added, anticipating Patrick's next question. "Anyway, after they met, the boss sent one of the boys to find Brian Daly and bring him around for a talk."

"Why Daly?"

"No fuckin' idea. The only work he ever did for Lewis before that was unloading shipments of booze through the tunnels, but the boss got rid of him quick when the stupid mick kept helping himself to the merchandise."

"What about the guy I'm looking for? Have you seen him again?"

"Not since that night."

Patrick heard a soft sound to his left, like someone quietly clearing their throat, and looked over to see Mac motioning that it was time to go. Patrick nodded, then turned his attention back to Abbado.

"All right, Frankie, is there anything else you think that I should know before I take off?" The question was met with silence. "You sure? Because when I find this guy—and I will find him, you can bet on it—if there's *any* little detail that I think you forgot to share, I'm going to come back for you, and I promise that you will never know what hit you."

"He has a scar," the bouncer said softly.

"What was that?"

"A scar," Frankie repeated, a little louder this time. "Along the left side of his head, near his ear."

"You see, that's exactly the kind of detail that I was talking about. All right, big guy, I'm going to leave now. I suggest you wait here a few minutes, just so that I don't feel like you're trying to follow me."

"Wait! What am I supposed to tell Pellizotti?"

Patrick could hear the anxiety in the bouncer's voice.

"I guess that's up to you," he answered, feeling a little sorry for Abbado. "I'll tell you what I'd say, though. I'd tell that little prick that when you got out into the alley there were three or four guys waiting. Big guys, with guns. Tell your boss they had a message they wanted you to deliver."

"What message?"

"That Pellizotti better watch his back, because what happened to Dan Lewis could happen to him, just as easily."

"What good will that do?" Frankie asked, confused.

"I don't think he'll be in a hurry to get rid of his number one bodyguard if he thinks someone's gunning for him, do you? Now, be a good boy and stay put for the next few minutes."

With that Patrick pocketed the pistol and moved quickly down the alley. Mac grinned as he approached.

"I'll be goddamned," the Scot said, shaking his head.

"What?" Patrick knew he was grinning as well, the inevitable aftereffect of too much adrenaline and a huge sense of relief. He'd pulled off his performance—pretty well too, if he said so himself—and managed to get away in one piece.

"I'll ... be ... goddamned," his friend muttered again as they walked toward 4th Avenue and the streetcar back to the Campbell.

Apparently, there was nothing more to be said.

Leon was just about to bed when the phone rang. At first he thought it might be Evelyn, calling to let him know that she and the kids had arrived safely at her mother's in Boise. Then he realized that it was the private line reserved for his clients and a select few business associates. He stepped into the study. More out of habit than necessity, he pulled the door closed behind him.

"This is Brent," he said, brusquely.

"Mr. Brent, I'm glad you're still up." The voice on the other end sounded strained, and only vaguely familiar. "This is Carlo Pellizotti. We met a couple of times when you came in to Cicero's."

Leon leaned forward in his chair. "I don't remember meeting you," he lied.

"Don't matter. The thing is, you did some work for Dan Lewis ..."

"Dan Lewis is dead," Brent said flatly.

"Right, right, but, the thing is, Dan always relied on you when there were complications or he was away, and, well, now that I ..."

"Now that you've taken over his business interests, you need my help." Leon's tone was intentionally condescending.

If Pellizotti noticed the slight, he chose to ignore it. "See, something's come up, and I need to leave town for a few days. I want you to keep an eye on things while I'm gone."

"I'm an attorney. I don't run nightclubs, and I don't manage organizations like yours."

"No, nothing like that. I got my nephew to handle the day to day operations. I just need you to be available to him if, well ... if there are any legal problems that come up while I'm gone."

"For how long?"

The other end of the line was silent for a few moments. "Long as it takes," Pellizotti said at last.

"I'll need a thousand as a retainer."

"A grand? That's a lot of money."

"And yet, that's my fee. Take it or leave it."

"All right, all right," Pellizotti said. He was clearly unhappy, but apparently unwilling to push the matter.

"Have someone bring the money to my office first thing tomorrow, in cash. How can I reach you if I need to?"

The question brought another pause. Either Pellizotti wanted to keep his new attorney in the dark as much as possible, or he just didn't have any answers.

"I'm not sure yet. I'll be in touch in a few days," he said as he hung up.

Leon replaced the receiver in its cradle, and leaned back in his chair, staring off into the shadows. Judging from the tone of the man's voice, something was seriously wrong. Leon prided himself on being an astute judge of people, but it didn't take much skill to figure out that Pellizotti was running scared. Someone had put the fear of God into him, and according to Lewis, that took some doing.

The timing was too damned coincidental. Leon remembered the man who had interrupted his search of Daly's apartment. He'd assumed that it had been Lewis's organization, looking for a little retribution. Now he had to consider that there might be more to it than that.

His carefully woven tapestry was beginning to unravel.

Now that Patrick had a couple of Prohibition-era gin joints under his belt, he decided he liked the subdued atmosphere of the Campbell much more than the gaudy glitz and noise of Cicero's. Especially when there was thinking to be done.

Mac sat opposite him at a table far from the bar, two shot glasses and a bottle between them. Neither man had done more than sip at their drinks while they dissected the information gathered from Frankie Abbado earlier in the evening.

"It seems like a lot of effort for very little return," Patrick said, frustration clear in his voice.

"Every piece fits into the puzzle somehow. That little scene you played in the alley tonight got us a step closer to finding Maggie's killer. If nothing else, it probably rattled a cage or two. Maybe our guy will get nervous and make a mistake."

"Maybe. But other than the fact that this guy has a scar across his left temple, what did we really learn that we didn't already know?

"Well, the fact that Frankie didn't have a clue who he was, or where Dan knew him from, probably means that our guy isn't involved in the rackets. Not directly, at least."

"He could have been lying about not knowing him."

"After the scare you put into him? That bit about finding just the right spot to shoot a man without killing him ... goddamned inspired, by the way."

"Thanks." Patrick allowed himself a brief smile. "I'm just glad he didn't call my bluff. So, Frankie was telling the truth, and the killer isn't in the rackets. What else?"

"If he's a regular at Cicero's, then he's got money or status in this town. If he can talk Lewis into getting directly involved, I'm guessing both."

Patrick drained his whiskey and reached for the bottle.

"So," he said as he topped off both glasses, "our man figures that Lewis is just the guy to handle Lundgren's murder discreetly, and Lewis chooses Daly to do the deed."

Mac nodded as he picked up his glass. Patrick set the whiskey back down on the table, then paused, looking at the bottle thoughtfully for a moment before he turned his attention to his friend once more.

"Why *Daly*?"

"What do you mean?"

"You said yourself that Brian Daly wouldn't have been the first person you'd have thought of when it came to murder."

"Well, obviously I was wrong about that, wasn't I?"

"Maybe, but Frankie said the only work Daly ever did for Lewis was moving booze, and apparently he couldn't even be trusted to do that. So why trust him with something like killing Carl?"

"He was made to order, wasn't he? He'd probably have been willing to do it for next to nothing since he hated the old man."

Patrick nodded, smiling grimly. "And how would Lewis have known that?"

"Didn't you say Daly threatened Lundgren?"

"Outside of Carl's office, at the factory. I doubt that would have been public knowledge, especially in Lewis's circle. But our mystery man shows up with a business proposal and Lewis coincidently chooses the one man in Portland who has a grudge against their target."

Mac leaned forward with an intense look in his eyes. "So you're saying Lewis didn't pick Daly. Our killer did, because somehow he knew about Daly's fight with Carl, and the threats."

"That's the only way it makes sense. And if our guy knew Daly, then Daly probably knew him as well. That would explain why he brought Lewis in to act as the middleman."

"You do know that might put our man right inside the company, don't you?"

"Damn it, Mac, I have to let Julia know that she's in danger."

"That should be an interesting conversation. 'You don't know me from Adam, but believe me when I tell you that your father was actually murdered by someone you probably know and trust ...'"

"That isn't funny, Mac."

"It wasn't meant to be," his friend said. "Whatever you do, you're going to have to think it through carefully. If the Lundgren girl doesn't believe you, then you lose any chance of being able to stay close enough to help her. And let's say you do convince her and she figures out who had her father killed. What then? You don't have any evidence that the D.A. will look at. What does our man do when he realizes that Julia knows about him?"

"I don't know," Patrick admitted. "Maybe he backs off, leaves town. Why stick around when someone knows you've committed murder?"

"Maybe, but if the picture we've painted of him is accurate—a man with money and status—would he give all that up without a fight? Paint him into that kind of a corner and you might just make him desperate enough to kill Miss Lundgren the way he killed her father."

"He has to have her to get his hands on the company," Patrick pointed out.

"Maybe, but losing out on a business deal is still better than being hanged for murder, isn't it?"

Patrick considered that for a moment. "So what's my next step, then?"

Mac offered a tight smile. "Don't think you're going to like it, but I need you to lay low for a couple of days."

"What the hell are you talking about?"

"I know, I know," the Scot said in a soft, firm voice, "but you poked a hornet's nest tonight, and Pellizotti probably has guys out looking for you right now. The last thing we need is for you to end up with a bullet in the back of your head. Give me a couple of days and I'll see what the word is on the street."

"And what about Julia? What if she doesn't *have* a couple of days?"

"I wouldn't start worrying too much just yet. If the company is what they really want, then they have no reason to go after her unless she refuses to sell. And they're not likely to even approach her about it until her father is in the ground, are they?"

Patrick nodded in reluctant agreement. Mac reached across the table and gripped his friend's shoulder, reassuringly.

"Give me those two days, and let's see where we're at, all right?"

"And what am I supposed to do while I'm cowering at the Campbell?"

"Well, you might give Lizzie a tumble," Mac said with a smirk. He motioned toward the waitress who was wiping down a table near the bar. "As I hear it, she might even be open to a little *room service* where you're concerned."

"Mac," Patrick said with a sigh, "you're truly a disreputable human being."

"I'm wounded, deeply."

"Somehow I doubt that. Anyway, I'm spoken for."

Mac arched an eyebrow. "The faithful type, are we? So, you've got a little lady back home. Home's a long way away."

"Home *is* a long way away, but Rachel's not the kind of woman you forget easily."

Mac studied him in silence for several moments, then grabbed the bottle and topped off their glasses once more.

"Then here's to you for the decent man you are," he said with a gentle smile as they lifted their glasses, "and here's to doing right by this Rachel of yours."

Two hours later they climbed the stairs toward Patrick's floor, Mac more than a little unsteady on his feet. They'd polished off most of the bottle of Jameson's before Patrick had announced that it was time to turn in. Mac— who appeared to be the farthest gone of the two of them—

had nevertheless insisted on making sure that his friend made it safely upstairs.

"And how are you going to get back to your own room?" Patrick pointed out in amusement.

"I am steady as a rock," the Scot pronounced, even as he staggered into the wall. "There isn't an Irishman alive who can out-drink me."

"No doubt," Patrick chuckled, pulling his room key from his pocket. As he unlocked the door, Mac reached out and grasped his arm.

"O'Connell," he said, his eyes misty, "you're a *damned* fine man, and I'm glad to have met you."

Patrick smiled at the obvious sincerity of the sentiment. "Thank you. The feeling is mutual."

"No, I mean it." His friend shook his head slowly, "I mean it. Just wish to god Maggie had met someone like you ... instead of that damned Brian Daly ... that goddamned Irish *prick* ..." Mac looked up at that, an embarrassed grin on his face.

"Sorry about that ... didn't mean that the way it sounded." He looked puzzled for a moment, as though his thoughts had gone one way and his words the other.

"You never met Maggie, did you?" he managed at last.

Patrick shook his head.

"She's ..." Mac paused a moment, "she *was* ... she was ... a lovely thing. Too lovely to have something like this happen, you know? "

Patrick nodded, the memory of her murder unshakeable.

"I ever find the bastard that did that to her ..." Mac's words came more and more slowly. Tears ran down his face, glistening in the graying stubble on his chin.

"I ever find him ..." he said again, almost inaudibly.

Patrick put an arm around his friend. "We'll find him, Mac, I promise. We'll make him pay."

The Scot smiled like a child at that, then turned to make his way down the hall.

"You and me, Patrick," he called over his shoulder in a voice too loud for the time of night. "You and me ..."

With that Mac turned and disappeared down the stairs, his footsteps echoing in the otherwise silent hotel corridor.

"You and me, Mac," Patrick said with a smile as he thanked the gods for the gift of friendship.

Payment for his night of drinking came the next morning in the form of a throbbing headache and a stomach that rolled and lurched like a rowboat on Lake Superior. Eating held no great appeal, but Patrick forced himself to go downstairs anyway, reasoning that one of the hotel's breakfasts would at least give his digestive system something of substance to wrestle with.

Mindful of the dull roar already going on between his ears, he settled in at a table near the door to the street, and as far from the clattering of pots and pans as he could manage. His location also removed him from the dark looks Mac's sister-in-law had cast in his direction when he'd entered. She seemed to be in a foul temper, judging by the wide berth the staff gave her.

Elizabeth hurried over to bring Patrick his usual cup of coffee and take his breakfast order, her typically friendly grin replaced that morning with a tight-lipped, nervous smile.

"Good morning, Mr. O'Connell."

"Elizabeth, I think you can call me Patrick by now."

Her smile warmed a little at that, but only a little. She glanced toward the kitchen. Seeing that Mrs. McKenzie was nowhere to be seen, she relaxed visibly and turned her attention back to him.

"I can't let the boss hear me call you by your first name. Any customer, really, but *especially* you."

"Oh? And why am I so special?"

"Because she thinks you're a bad influence on Mr. McKenzie, keeping him up half the night drinking like that."

He couldn't help but laugh, although his aching head caused him to instantly regret it. "She thinks that *I* put him up to that? Has she even *met* her brother-in-law?"

"I know, I know, but there's no convincing her. The truth is," Elizabeth added, lowering her tone conspiratorially, "I think she's a little sweet on him, not that she'll ever let on. Now, what can I get for you this morning?"

"Eggs, potatoes, and toast. And, Elizabeth, could you keep the coffee coming?"

"Sure thing, Mr. O'Connell. How do you want those eggs, over easy?"

"Runny yolks, the way I'm feeling?" Patrick could practically feel himself go green at the thought.

Elizabeth smiled knowingly. "I'll tell the boss to turn 'em over and step on 'em."

She hurried off with his order, leaving Patrick to sip his coffee. Through trial and error he found if he kept his head fairly still and eye lids half-closed to the light, his headache only registered a four on the Richter Scale.

He could only imagine how Mac was feeling.

"I'd say you're looking a bit the worse for wear this morning."

Patrick looked up to see Jim O'Halloron, resplendent in his black fireman's uniform.

"Mind if I join you?" the captain asked, even as he settled onto a chair.

"Glad for the company, as long as you promise to keep your voice down to a dull roar."

The big Irishman chuckled. "So it's one of those mornings, is it? Then I'll do my best to curb my charmingly boisterous nature."

"I can't tell you how much I appreciate that. To what do I owe the pleasure of your company?"

"I was just finishing up my breakfast at the counter when I saw you sit down, so I thought I'd say hello and see if you've had any luck with that problem you told me about."

"I've had a fair amount of luck. Not all of it good. Mac's been a great help, though, and he thinks that we're making progress."

"Glad to hear it. He's a good man, 'though I'd never say as much to his face. Where is he, anyway? He usually joins me for breakfast."

"Judging by the amount of whiskey he put away last night, I'm guessing that he's feeling even less inclined to face the morning than I was."

"Oh, that's what you're thinking, is it?" O'Halloron grinned, nodding in the direction of the door.

Patrick turned to see Mac hurrying in from the street, a broad smile on his face and—as far as Patrick was concerned, at least—an obscene bounce to his step. He spotted his friends almost immediately and took a seat beside O'Halloron.

"Good to see you, Jim," he said, cheerfully. "Sorry about missing breakfast, but I had to run a few errands bright and early today." He turned his attention to Patrick, a roguish look in his eye. "And how are you, this fine morning?"

"The jury is still out. Good lord, man, you must have the constitution of a horse. It was all I could do to crawl out of bed."

"Nothing that a little 'hair of the dog' couldn't cure. I'm sure that I could be prevailed upon to procure a little something for you as well ... purely for medicinal purposes, of course."

Patrick shook his head as vigorously as he could manage. "It will be awhile before I let you anywhere near me with a bottle in your hand."

"That's a resolution that no true Irishman can hold to. Perhaps a bit of good news will put me back into your good graces. I was speaking with one of my pals down at the precinct this morning, trying to find out what the word is out on the street ..."

"So, exactly how many mobsters are looking to kill me this morning?"

O'Halloron gave Mac a look of alarm. "I thought you said Patrick wasn't involved in that sort of business."

His friend grinned. "Oh, our Mr. O'Connell is no racketeer, but he is a dangerous man in his own right, as well as a damned fine actor. He played out a scene in the alley behind Cicero's that would have done Doug Fairbanks proud. And, in the process, he threw a hell of a scare into one Carlo Pellizotti."

"And just who is Carlo Pellizotti?" O'Halloron asked, obviously frustrated by being on the outside of the story.

"Pellizotti is a little weasel of a man with aspirations of becoming Portland's own Al Capone, but it turns out he doesn't quite have the stomach for it."

Patrick leaned forward, his headache forgotten. "What are you talking about?"

Mac ignored his question—clearly enjoying the role of story teller—and continued to bring O'Halloron up to date. Patrick settled back with a sigh, trying to wait patiently for his friend to get to the point.

"It turns out that the man causing problems for Patrick's lady friend was connected to "Black Dan" Lewis."

"The one they pulled out of the tunnels?"

"The same. And Pellizotti, Black Dan's right-hand man ..."

"Nice alliteration," Patrick pointed out with a chuckle.

"I do have a way with words, don't I? Anyway, with Dan out of the way, Pellizotti wasted no time in trying to take over the operation. So, last night Patrick and I headed down to Cicero's to see if we could shake loose a little information from Lewis's old bodyguard."

"And what did you find out?"

"From the bodyguard? Just bits and pieces. Enough to keep moving forward, at least. But my god, Jim, you should have seen Patrick dismantle that poor man. The guy was twice his size—four hundred pounds of muscle and bad intentions—and Patrick had him crawling on all fours and pleading for mercy."

"Stop embellishing," Patrick said in exasperation. "Just get to the point about Pellizotti, would you?"

"Best way to ruin a story is to hurry it," Mac said, sullenly. Apparently realizing that his friend's patience had run its course, he told O'Halloron, "The bodyguard spilled what little he knew, and then he asked our friend here how he's supposed to explain to Pellizotti why he got his ass handed to him."

"What did you tell him?" Jim asked Patrick.

"I kind of felt sorry for the guy, having to go back in and face his boss, so I suggested that he make up a story about being ambushed in the alley by guys with guns ..."

"Guys with guns, and an eye on Pellizotti's racket," Mac added, wresting the conversation back to his side of the table.

"I just figured that, if the weasel thought that he was in danger, he might go a little easier on his bodyguard."

"Well, whatever Frankie said to his boss, it worked. My pal downtown tells me that Pellizotti and four of his boys—including Frankie, by the way—boarded the first train for Seattle this morning. Left his sister's kid in charge of Cicero's, told him he'd be away indefinitely on business."

"So, they're not looking for me? At all?"

Mac grinned and shook his head. "My guess is, Pellizotti figures you were small fry compared to whoever is gunning for his operation. The boys downtown think he'll lay low up north until he finds out what he's up against."

"I'd love to see his face when he realizes that no one is actually moving in on his territory," Jim said with a chuckle.

"Don't kid yourself. If there isn't someone today, there will be tomorrow. Word gets out that the tough guy picked up his skirts and ran at the first sign of trouble, every mobster with an ounce of ambition will be looking to take him down."

"Great," Patrick said, "so now I've started a gang war."

"I wouldn't worry about it. Odds are, the little coward will never show his face in Portland again once things start heating up for real."

"So, what's our next move?"

Mac looked thoughtful for a moment, then turned to O'Halloron.

"Jim, I think that it might be best if you weren't in on the rest of this." He held up his hand, silencing his friend's protest. "Truth is, we don't know who we're dealing with, or how well-connected he—or they—are. What we do know is that four people have already died."

"All the more reason for me to help."

"No, you've got Delores and the kids to worry about. And, believe me, I do *not* want to face that woman's wrath if something happens to you."

Jim laughed. "She is a holy terror, isn't she? All right, I'll be leaving then, but I want you both to promise that you'll call if there's something I can do."

Both Patrick and Mac agreed, and O'Halloron said his goodbyes.

"If God had to curse me with Irishmen for company, I'm just glad he chose the two of you," Mac said as the door closed behind his friend.

"I suppose we could have done worse, ourselves, for that matter. So, do we have any idea what we should be doing next?"

Mac rubbed a calloused finger across the graying stubble on his chin. "Did that wardrobe of yours come with a dark suit?" he asked.

"It did. Why?"

"Because you and I are going to a funeral."

–10–

Patrick sat in the passenger seat of Mac's car, watching the scenery pass by as they drove south out of the city along Barbur Boulevard. Within minutes of leaving downtown Portland, the dense collection of homes and businesses that surrounded the city had transitioned into a forest of evergreens, dotted with small neighborhoods and the occasional service station or eatery.

Ahead of them, a long procession of cars followed the hearse carrying Carl Lundgren's body as it worked its way down the hillside in the direction of Riverview Cemetery.

"If we're right about our killer being someone who knew Lundgren well," Mac said, "then he'd almost have to be there at the service today. Hell, even if he wasn't as close to the family as we think, there's a good chance he'll show up anyway."

"Why is that?"

"Happens more often than you'd think. I worked on two different cases where the murderer attended the funeral, even though they'd never met the victims before. I don't know, maybe they got a thrill watching the pain they'd caused, like a guy who torches a building and then sticks around to watch it burn."

"So we'll just mingle with the rest of the mourners and look for a large man with a scar and a slight limp?"

Mac shook his head as they turned onto Terwilliger. "Better if we watch from a distance. We'll see more that way, and we're less likely to tip our hand to him."

Judging by the impressive obelisks, ornate statues and markers, Riverview Cemetery had clearly been serving the prominent citizens of Portland for a very long time. A few of the names carved into marble and granite—like Couch, Failing, and Terwilliger—would be familiar to anyone who had spent much time looking at street signs around Portland.

They followed the narrow lane as it curved to the right through the cemetery, easing by the automobiles already parked along the shoulder and the mourners making their way down the gentle slope to the grave site. Mac continued up the hill and away from the gathering. When he finally pulled the Buick over to a stop, they were at least two hundred yards from the funeral party.

Patrick pulled on his wool suit coat and gray felt fedora—contemporary fashion statements that lost a great deal of their appeal on a hot summer afternoon—while Mac grabbed a pair of binoculars from behind the driver's seat. Then they headed back toward the service.

As they walked, Patrick noticed that Mac seemed to be scrutinizing the headstones around them.

"Looking for someone in particular?"

"Someone told me that Virgil Earp was buried around here."

"As in Virgil '*Shootout at the OK Corral*' Earp? I didn't know that he lived in Portland."

"He didn't, but his daughter did. When he died, she had his body shipped out from Nevada so he could be buried close by. I'm big on western history, so I figured that as long as we're here ..."

Normally, Patrick would have been more than happy to help with the search, but they had a funeral to get to. He led the way, with Mac lagging behind only a little.

They took up position beside a tall marble monument, about sixty yards or so from the large crowd of mourners. The hillside below them teemed with people, a testament to the kind of man that Julia's father must have been.

Two rows of chairs had been set up on the far side of the open grave and polished casket. Several older men and women were seated in the front row, on either side of a slender woman in a black dress and hat. Her face was obscured by a veil, but Patrick knew that he was looking at the woman whose life he had become inextricably linked with.

"Do you see anyone who looks like our guy?" Mac asked.

"From this distance it's kind of hard to tell," Patrick said as he surveyed the crowd.

"Well, they're all pretty absorbed with what's going on down there. It should be safe enough to use these," his friend said, handing the binoculars over to Patrick.

He focused first on those closest to the grave side, in part because the open area afforded him the best look at their faces, but also because a man with the social status that they supposed their killer to have would probably be more prominently placed in the crowd. He scanned each candidate carefully before moving on to the next.

He paused when Julia come into view, his heart sinking as he watched her head drop forward. Her shoulders shook from the heavy sobs that consumed her. The people seated beside her—a distinguished silver-haired gentleman and a round-faced little woman—cradled Julia between them, offering as much comfort as they could.

The man directly behind them leaned forward to squeeze Julia's shoulder, briefly. He whispered something to her—although there was no indication that she'd heard what he'd said—and then settled back into his chair.

Patrick forced himself to move the glasses off of Julia and study the person behind her more closely. The angle the man was sitting at obscured the left side of his face from view, so Patrick couldn't see if he had a scar or not, but ...

"Something?" Mac asked.

"I'm not sure." Patrick handed the glasses back to his friend. "Take a look at the man seated just behind and to the right of Julia Lundgren."

"Too far away to see if he has that scar that Frankie was talking about. And there's no way to see if he's got a gimpy leg as long as he's sitting down."

"I know, but check out the expression on his face. Does he look like a man who has come to mourn?"

Even now, while others around the man were listening to the minister speak, he was staring off in apparent boredom.

"There are a lot of people down there who would rather be somewhere else."

"Maybe you're right, but there's something about him that bothers me, something that I can't put my finger on," he insisted as Mac returned the binoculars.

The Scott nodded. "That's good enough for me. You stay up here and keep on looking for anyone else who might be our man, and I'll go down and see what I can find out."

Patrick watched as Mac made his way down to the mourners below, following him with the glasses until he disappeared into the throng. Once he'd lost sight of his friend, he once again surveyed the crowd for anyone else who might fit the description of Maggie's murderer. Somehow, he always came back to the well-dressed man behind Julia.

Fifteen minutes later, Carl Lundgren's casket was lowered into the ground. People started moving toward the line of cars parked on the lane directly below Patrick's position, so he slipped the binoculars under his jacket and waited patiently for Mac to return.

It was another ten minutes before he saw his friend walking toward him. Patrick tried in vain to read his expression.

"What did you find out?" he asked as Mac drew near.

Rather than answering, Mac continued on, motioning with a tilt of the head for Patrick to follow. Only when they were well out of ear-shot of others did he slow a little, allowing Patrick to draw alongside.

"The guy you zeroed in on is Leon Brent," Mac said as they walked. "He's an attorney, but I'm not sure what his connection is to the Lundgrens. He's apparently a big shot in the legal community, judging from what I was told. Not exactly the kind of person you'd figure to be involved in four murders."

"He could still be our guy," Patrick insisted. "How close were you able to get to him?"

Mac came to a stop and looked at Patrick, his face expressionless.

"Close enough to see him limping back to his car," he said at last, a smile beginning to form. "Close enough to convince me that he might just be the son of a bitch that we're looking for."

"I hope Lundgren's house is big enough to hold this crowd," Mac said as he pulled the Buick into line behind the parade of cars heading back into the city.

"What do you mean?"

"There's a reception at her father's home after the funeral. From what I heard, most of the people who were there today were planning on stopping by."

"I'm guessing that includes Leon Brent."

Mac looked over at Patrick. "If you're thinking of making an appearance, I'd recommend against it. Give me a day or two to do some digging and find out a little more about him before you go charging in half-cocked."

"Maybe that would be the smart thing to do in a police investigation, Mac, but time is not on our side here. This guy has already killed four people, and until he convinces Julia to sell the factory, he still doesn't have what he's after. Worst of all, if Brent *is* the man behind all of this, then he's well-positioned and we're still on the outside looking in.

"Besides," he added as he watched the scenery go by, "I'm tired of playing catch-up."

Mac drove in silence as he considered Patrick's argument. Finally he nodded.

"All right, I guess it does make sense to approach this from two sides, as long as we're careful. After I drop you off at Lundgren's I'll start making some calls. Do you have a plan?"

"Other than getting close to Brent? Well, for one thing I think it's time that I finally introduce myself to Miss Lundgren."

Patrick watched guests drift by like leaves on a slow-moving stream, collecting in small groups just long enough to offer their sympathies before the current swept them off to the next clutch of mourners, the next hand to shake or shoulder to clasp. People were arriving at a steady pace, and it seemed only a matter of time before both the dining room and parlor would overflow to fill into the entryway.

Occasionally, someone would introduce themselves to Patrick and ask how he'd known Carl, but, for the most part, people sought solace among familiar faces.

Leon Brent stood in the dining room, talking to a small group of well-dressed men. Patrick had decided to keep his distance until more people arrived to screen his interest, so he occupied himself by observing the other mourners, some of whom he recognized from the funeral. For example, the stout little woman who had been seated to Julia's left at graveside had positioned herself at the top of the stairs, quietly shooing away anyone who ventured up. And the gentleman who had been seated on the other side had assumed the role of host, greeting people as they entered.

Patrick watched in amusement as one of the newcomers—a wiry old gent dressed in an ancient-looking suit—unceremoniously deposited a vase of daffodils into the man's hands before disappearing into the parlor, ignoring his sputtering objections.

"Can I offer some assistance?" Patrick asked, stepping up as the host glanced about in vain for a place to set the flowers. The silver-haired man smiled with gratitude.

"Thank you so much, Mr ...?" The sentence trailed off into a question as he handed the vase over.

"Patrick O'Connell." He reached out with his free hand. "And you are?"

"John Ingersol," the man replied as they shook.

"It's very nice to meet you." Patrick lifted the flowers up. "Where would you like me to take these?"

"To the kitchen, if you wouldn't mind. Do you know where it is?"

"I'm sure I can find my way."

He carried the arrangement through the dining room, past Brent and his companions. As he reached the door leading to the kitchen, he turned back to chance a quick look at the attorney.

The scar along the man's left temple was an ugly one, pale white and almost an inch and a half long, disappearing just above the ear.

Got you, you son of a bitch.

Whether by chance or instinct, at that instant Brent turned his head in Patrick's direction. Their eyes met briefly, and Patrick offered a brief nod as he backed through the swinging door and vanished into the kitchen.

He's here.

Leon hadn't seen him since that afternoon, outside of the Rosemont, but there was no doubt in his mind. And the way he'd looked, nodding his fucking head as if he didn't give a good goddamn whether Leon knew he was there or not.

Like a hunter staring down a rabbit from the business end of a rifle.

"Are you alright, Leon?" Judge Mitchner asked, studying him with curiosity.

"What? Oh, no, I'm fine, judge," Leon lied, forcing himself to calm down. "I was just trying to remember where I've seen that man with the flowers before. I don't suppose any of you know who he is? No? Well, I'm sure it will come to me sooner or later."

Patrick set the vase down on the nearest counter and considered the possibility that coming here had been a tactical error after all. Brent had clearly recognized him, but how? *Did he see me watching the funeral, or sitting in the diner across the street from Daily's apartment?*

And then he remembered what Mac had said the night of Maggie's murder, about the police finding the bloody overcoat and gloves just around the corner from the alley.

The bastard was watching me the whole time, while I was standing in the street looking like an idiot.

Strangely, the fact that he was no longer completely anonymous—and most likely hadn't been for some time—felt liberating. The risks had increased exponentially, true, but so had his options. For the first time, Patrick could start being on the offensive.

The mind latches onto the strangest of things. Small details etch themselves into memory forever; the words that were spoken, but not the voices of the people who said them, or the scent of someone's perfume or cologne, but not the face of the person who wore it every day.

On one of the most significant days of Julia's life, she knew she wouldn't remember anything more clearly than the sticky heat of the afternoon, and the droning of bees in the garden below as they struggled through the thick summer air. Time crawled by as though it, like she, had an appointment it didn't really want to keep.

Below her bedroom window a steady line of automobiles inched along Thurman Street, engines clattering as their drivers searched in vain for an empty stretch of curb to park along. How many had come? Probably more than the house could manage, she guessed. Certainly more than her father would have dreamed possible.

Julia stood slowly and took a moment to smooth the wrinkles from her simple black dress. She knew it was time to go downstairs. Past time, really. Opening her bedroom door, she nearly collided with Louise Ingersol—"Aunt" Louise—a stout dumpling of a woman who had stationed herself outside Julia's bedroom, determined that no one should disturb her until she was prepared to come down.

"Are you ready to see your guests?" Louise asked. A sad, gentle smile spread across the older woman's broad features.

"I suppose I should," Julia answered, resigned to her fate.

The two of them moved side by side to the top of the staircase where Louise held back, gently nudging Julia forward.

"I think perhaps we should go one at a time," the older woman whispered, patting her plump figure. "Too many years of fattigmann and lefsa, I'm afraid."

Julia nodded and started down. Almost at once a hush rippled out through those gathered below. Face after anxious face turned to look as the women descended the stairs. She faltered for an instant, momentarily overwhelmed by emotion and the awful finality of the moment.

"You must be strong," Louise whispered, snapping Julia back to the present. "It is who we are at times like these."

Julia willed her feet to move and the two women continued down the stairs to the people waiting below.

Rather than go back through the dining room, Patrick rejoined the reception through the kitchen door that led to the hallway outside of Carl's library.

The growing collection of people, gathered in the heat of the afternoon, had driven the temperature in the house to uncomfortable levels. Anyone who complained about missing the "good old days" had obviously forgotten the wonderful aroma of pre-deodorant society on a hot summer day.

The conversations around him died away suddenly, as though someone had thrown a switch. Julia had started down the stairs.

It was Patrick's first close look at her since he'd arrived in 1929, and he felt his breath catch in his throat as she approached. His mind went to Rachel, remembering some advice his dad had once given him; "If you want to know how a woman is going to age," he'd said, "take a look at the mother." With a little luck, the same rule applied to grandmothers as well.

And with a great deal of luck, I may even have an opportunity to find out for myself.

He watched as she made her way through the mourners. Soon she disappeared into the parlor, adrift in a sea of reminiscences and kind words. Patrick was content to observe from a distance, opting instead to keep watch on Brent, who had trailed her into the other room. The attorney stood near the entrance to the parlor, talking to a very tall, broad-shouldered man in a slightly rumpled suit, but he always seemed to have one eye on Julia.

And the other on Patrick.

Julia began to move back toward the entryway, the guests closest to her stepping aside to clear a path. Out of the corner of his eye, Patrick saw Brent work his way through the room as though he were going to intercept her. Instead, he veered off toward the outer edge of the gathering, apparently content to watch as she passed.

Julia moved slowly through the well-wishers, pausing briefly to accept their subdued, tearful words of sympathy. "He was such a good man ..." Again and again people said that, as though she—or any of those gathered—needed to be reminded. Their words began to run together in Julia's head, like a somber melody playing in some other room.

She didn't hear them, not really, but she was touched by the depth of the sadness in the eyes of her father's friends.

That was real.

That had meaning for her.

And when she found herself offering her own reassurances and condolences, Julia realized that these people may have come to comfort her, but more often than not it was her strength that they were drawing from, not the other way around.

"It is who we are at times like these," Louise had told her. For the first time, Julia understood that she played more than a passive role in the event. Somehow that made the painful ordeal bearable.

It was an unusual mix of people. Employees from the factory mingled awkwardly with leading members of the city's business aristocracy, all shuffled together like so many cards from mismatched decks.

"I'm truly sorry for your loss, Miss Julia."

The words, almost a whisper, drifted down and brought her back to the moment. She turned slightly and found herself looking up, then even farther up, into the tearful eyes of the biggest man she had ever seen. He towered above her and everyone else in the room by a good six inches.

"You're very kind." She recognized him now as one of her father's employees, although she couldn't quite attach a name to the face. The big man fiddled nervously with the well-worn black bowler hat he held between his sausage-like fingers.

"Your father was the finest man I've ever known," he offered, a hint of a Scandinavian accent in his soft voice.

He seemed on the verge of saying something else, so Julia gave an encouraging smile.

Standing a few feet away from Julia, Patrick watched the big man Brent had been speaking to mumble his condolences, emotion in his voice.

"Your father was the finest man I've ever known," he said softly. Then he paused, and Patrick saw him glance briefly over the heads of the other guests toward the far end of the room.

Then he looked back down at Julia. "I was wondering what will become of the company," he asked, "after it's sold, I mean."

Julia looked up at him with a stunned expression. The other conversations going on around them dropped to hushed whispers. At that moment, John Ingersol stepped up quickly from behind her.

"Now, Oscar," he said as he reached up and placed his hand on the big man's shoulder, "this is hardly the time or place to talk about selling the company, is it?"

Oscar looked once again toward the back of the room. Patrick followed his gaze to see Leon Brent watching events unfold, his expression impassive. There was little doubt where the seed of this rumor had come from.

When Patrick turned back, Oscar had lowered his head in obvious embarrassment.

"No, Mr. Ingersol, you're right," he admitted, his voice almost a whisper. "I hope you can forgive me, Miss Julia."

Julia managed a gentle smile, and Oscar brightened like a man just granted a reprieve. Without another word he turned and left the room, a giant wading chest deep through a pool of humanity. He left a ripple of whispered conversations in his wake.

"Don't let that bother you," Ingersol said. "He's just naturally a little concerned about what the future might hold."

She nodded, but Patrick could see the anxiety in her expression. Obviously shaken, she excused herself from the room.

He wandered after her, leaving the parlor just in time to see her hurry down the hallway. Weighing the pros and cons of following her, it wasn't a hard decision to make. He was Julia's friend—even though only he knew that at the moment—and she looked to be in desperate need of a friend.

Julia escaped quietly to the kitchen, where she found Mrs. Westbrook—the factory manager's wife—making coffee. Two other women, whose names escaped Julia at the moment, stood at the sink washing and drying dishes. All three turned toward Julia as she entered, their expressions mirror images of concern.

"I need a moment to myself," Julia told them. "Would that be all right?"

Mrs. Westbrook nodded. "Of course, dear. Take as long as you'd like."

Julia moved across the room to stand by the sink as they scurried out. The tile countertop was cool and soothing under her palms as she leaned against the cabinets and looked through the window to the back yard, unchanged since she had played there as a child. It didn't feel as though that were so long ago, really, and yet she couldn't for the life of her remember what it had felt like to be that child.

Julia heard the gentle rocking sound of the kitchen door, swinging on its hinges. She turned, suddenly grateful for the distraction.

Patrick entered the kitchen to find Julia standing alone at the window. She studied him for a moment, as though trying in vain to attach a name to the face.

"I hope I'm not intruding," he told her. "I was about to leave, but I wanted to offer my condolences."

"Thank you." She looked at him once more, obviously puzzled. "I don't believe we've met. Mister ...?"

"O'Connell."

"How did you know my father, Mr. O'Connell?"

"Sadly, I didn't. Your brother and I both served in the Fifth Division. I'm staying at the Campbell Hotel for a few days and I read about your father's funeral, so I thought I should pay my respects."

"That's very kind of you."

An awkward silence fell between them before Julia seemed to realize that she was still staring at him. A light blush rose in her cheeks as she glanced away quickly. In an effort to save her further embarrassment, Patrick turned his attention to the tea service sitting nearby on the counter.

"Ah, tea!" Patrick said, perhaps with a little more enthusiasm than was necessary.

He tested the pot with the backs of his fingers. Satisfied that it was still hot, he poured the amber liquid into a delicate cup and offered it, balanced carefully on a matching saucer, to Julia. She accepted with a grateful smile and moved to sit at the small table at the far end of the kitchen. Then he poured a second cup for himself and joined her.

"I find a cup of tea very soothing in difficult times. My father always says tea is 'a moment of peace in a world of chaos.'"

"He sounds like a wise man," Julia managed before her voice began to tremble with emotion. He saw tears well up, and pulled his handkerchief from his pocket. Julia shook her head, brushing her tears away with the back of her hand.

"So ... silly," she muttered under her breath as she struggled to control her emotions.

"Drink your tea," he urged, gently. Then he turned his attention to the yard beyond the window, allowing her a few moments to pull herself together.

He risked a glance when he heard her take a deep breath, then let it out in a slow, steady exhale. She sniffled a little, and offered a half-hearted smile of apology as she raised her teacup to her lips and took a small sip.

"What will you do now?" he asked. She seemed vaguely disconcerted at the question, as though no one had thought to ask her that before.

"I haven't given it much thought. I'm sure everyone out there wants me to sell my father's business."

"The question is," Patrick said with a smile, "what does *Julia* want?"

"It would probably be for the best. I'm a teacher, not a business woman."

"That doesn't sound like the Julia Lundgren I've heard about. 'An independent streak a mile wide,' I believe was how you were described. From the stories I've heard, I'd say you could accomplish almost anything you set your mind to."

She cocked her head a little to one side and studied him intently. Patrick held her gaze, his smile never dimming because—for the first time—he could see some of the strength, the real essence of Julia looking back at him. He had challenged her and the wheels inside her head were shaking off the rust of her despair.

"It seems you know me better than I do myself." She managed a smile. "What would you suggest that I do?"

"I don't think it's my place to give you advice."

"Well, you're undoubtedly the only man here honest enough to make *that* statement. Frankly, I can use some of that kind of honesty at the moment."

He wrestled with the answer, unsure of what he could—or *should*—tell her.

"Listening to your father's friends today," he said after a moment, "he didn't seem the type of man who would build a business for money alone."

"What other reason is there?"

"To create a legacy, and to provide for those he cared most about. For you, and for those employees out there who clearly thought the world of him."

Julia leaned back in her chair.

"You really think that I could take his place? I wouldn't know where to begin."

Patrick smiled. "I suspect that you know what you're capable of. On that note," he added, rising to his feet, "I'm afraid I really must be going."

Julia stood with him, and together they walked toward the kitchen door.

"How long will you be in Portland?" she asked.

"I'm not entirely sure." He paused as an idea formed. "Perhaps long enough to impose upon you for a tour of the famous Lundgren factory one day, if it wouldn't be too much trouble."

"I'd like that." Julia told him, rewarding him with her warmest smile of the afternoon.

For the briefest of moments he saw Rachel's reflection smiling at him from across the years.

As he left the kitchen, Patrick spotted Brent standing near the large oak table. Judging from the mound of food already on his plate, spreading rumors worked up an appetite.

Time to take a closer measure of the enemy, he decided, stepping up alongside the attorney.

"Good afternoon, counselor."

Brent looked up, his expression darkening as he realized who had spoken to him. "I don't believe we've met," he said, his tone impressively calm.

"That's true, we haven't. Yet." Patrick smiled. Brent's voice might be calm, but Patrick could see concern in his eyes. "This has been a very difficult week for you, hasn't it, Mr. Brent?"

"I'm not sure I know what you mean."

"First Mr. Lundgren's terrible ... accident, and then losing our friend, Mr. Lewis." The attorney's face tightened visibly. "Of course, a lot of us were upset when Dan passed."

"I'm afraid that I don't know any Mr. Lewis," Brent said, flatly.

"Really? He told me so much about *you*, and the project you were working on together." Patrick let his smile fade, returning Brent's hard stare. Doubt flickered in the other man's eyes. "Isn't that strange? But then, a lot of strange things have been happening lately."

The two men looked at each other in cold silence for several seconds before Patrick's smile returned.

"Well, if you'll excuse me," he said, "I have some business to attend to."

"And what kind of business are you in, Mr ...?"

"At the moment, buying and selling real estate," Patrick answered lightly as he walked away.

"I wish that I could have seen the bastard's face when you told him that," Mac said, grinning.

"Me, too, but I thought turning around and watching his expression would have diminished the effect, somewhat."

They sat in the Campbell's dining room, waiting for the last of the dinner customers to finish up so that the nighttime operations could begin. Elizabeth swung by their table to top off their coffee cups. She looked about done in; understandable given the fact that she had probably been serving since the breakfast rush.

"Mac, you're working this poor girl to death." Patrick gave the pretty waitress a wink. "Let her have a night off from time to time."

"I've tried, but she says she needs the hours. Isn't that right, Lizzie?"

"A girl's got to make ends meet."

"Besides," Mac added with a grin, "what *else* is she going to do with her evenings if you won't give her a tumble?"

A moment later he was bent over, trying to massage his leg under the table.

"Sorry, Mac," Elizabeth said, sweetly. "My foot must have slipped."

"Count yourself lucky," Patrick added. "She beat me to it."

"Christ, try to play cupid and this is the thanks I get. From now on, you two are on your own."

"Promises, promises," Elizabeth muttered as she moved on to another table.

"Can we get back to business now?" Patrick asked, trying unsuccessfully to hide his grin. "What, if anything, were you able to dig up on Leon Brent?"

"Not as much as I'd hoped, but I've still got a couple of calls to make." Mac pulled a small notepad from his shirt pocket and flipped it open. He thumbed through several pages before he found what he was looking for.

"Leon A. Brent, aged fifty-one ... Consensus of opinion seems to be that the A stands for Asshole. Apparently, Brent can be ruthless, both in and out of court. Of course, the same could probably be said of any lawyer who wants to win. And he does win, most of the time."

"What kind of law does he practice?"

"Officially? Business law. He's worked for some of the bigger companies in Portland over the last five years or so, frequently on the kind of cases where the clients were looking for—as one of my contacts put it—a 'gunslinger,' willing to get a little dirty."

"You said, 'Officially.' What about unofficially?"

Mac smiled. "Nothing concrete, but my friends on the Detective Squad have heard rumors for some time that Brent has been providing legal counsel to the city's more prominent criminal element, including ..."

"Let me guess. "Black Dan" Lewis."

"That's the word downtown, at least."

"What's his connection to Julia and her father?"

Mac referred back to his notes. "Brent moved to Portland from Chicago just after the war. For the first three or four years his entire client list seems to have consisted of two companies, Ingersol Tool and Die and Lundgren Furniture."

"I met someone named Ingersol at the reception this afternoon."

"That would probably be John Ingersol. He owns the tool and die company. I met him a few times when this was my beat. He always struck me as a good man."

"So what is he doing with a 'gunslinger' attorney like Leon Brent?"

"If you want to be successful in business, you don't choose your lawyer from the society pages. Besides, Brent served under him in France, so my guess is, Ingersol was trying to help a war buddy land on his feet."

"Where does all of this leave us?"

"With a lot of pieces that *we* know fit together, but no way to prove any of it. Brent knew Lundgren, but there's no apparent motive for wanting him dead. He *might* have known Brian Daly in his capacity as Lundgren's attorney. He might also have been giving legal advice to Dan Lewis. But as far as the police are still concerned, Daly and Lewis killed each other down in the tunnels.

"And Maggie ..." Mac paused, anger and frustration getting the better of him for a moment. "Maggie Daly was murdered in retaliation for what her husband did. Gangland retribution."

Patrick watched his friend take a deep, slow breath. When he spoke again, he seemed once more the professional detective reviewing the case.

"Lundgren's murder is the linchpin to this whole thing," he said quietly. "If we can prove that Brent had Carl killed, then I think we can tie him to the rest of the murders pretty easily. But as long as the ruling stands at accidental death ..."

"You said you had a couple of calls to make?" Patrick asked.

"I want to check into Brent's background a little more. So far, I haven't found anything to indicate that he's so much as jaywalked since he came to Portland. I'm betting that someone, somewhere, knew our boy before the mask of respectability went on."

"What do you know about his past?"

"Like I said, he came here from Chicago, where he graduated from the University of Chicago School of Law in 1911. Apparently he plays it close to the vest when it comes to his life before Portland. Even the few people who felt that they knew him reasonably well couldn't shed much light. I've got the names of a detective in Chicago who might be of some help. It's a long shot, but I'm running out of ideas."

Mac looked around at the now empty dining room.

"You ready for a drink?" he asked.

Patrick shook his head. "You just about did me in last night, Mac. I think I'll give it a rest this evening."

"I still say you're no Irishman with an attitude like that. All right, go and get some sleep. I'll see you all the earlier in the morning."

A half empty bottle of single-malt Scotch sat on the desk in Leon Brent's study. Beside it, his fully-loaded Colt revolver gleamed dully in the light from the banker's lamp. An interesting juxtaposition, he thought; the expensive whisky a symbol of how far he'd come in life, and the pistol a reminder of what it had taken to get himself there.

All of that dirty work should have been behind him at this point. Leon had arrived. Everyone—even the many who resented him for his courtroom tactics—considered him an unqualified success as an attorney, and he had a growing list of prestigious clients to prove it. True, most only came knocking when their backs were against the wall, but they were willing to pay all the more for his services because of that. When all was said and done, none of Leon's clients ever questioned his methods, or wondered why so many key witnesses seemed to fall apart on the stand. Leon was like a magician in the courtroom, and the audience enjoying the show never wanted to know the truth behind the illusion.

In return for Leon's legal advice—and a percentage of the fees he collected for the cases—Lewis's organization had applied pressure in the right places, whether it was blackmailing an expert witness who had a penchant for prostitutes, or reminding a plaintiff of just how dangerous the world could be for his wife and children.

Sacrificing Lewis had been a hard decision, but Leon really believed that Pellizotti would fit the bill just as well, and probably be easier to manipulate in the bargain. Of course, that was before someone had scared the little weasel out of town.

Leon had been so fucking proud of himself, the chess master planning his moves in intricate detail. He'd been sure that Lewis would keep their arrangement private from his own organization for a big enough share in the rewards. And turning Daly's anger at Carl into a willingness to commit murder had taken nothing more than nudging the small-timer in the right direction with the promise of a few hundred dollars.

But then the goddamned mick got greedy and decided to keep the money in the packet as well. Maybe Leon should have anticipated that, but he'd assumed that Daly would be too afraid to cross Lewis.

And Lewis had shot his mouth off about the whole fucking plan to that arrogant bastard from the funeral, no doubt about that. How else could anyone have connected Leon to any of this, or known about the arrangement to buy out Lundgren Furniture? Now it looked as though the little shit was planning on grabbing the whole deal for himself.

He reached out and ran his fingers along the barrel of the Colt, feeling the once-familiar coolness of the metal against his skin.

Compared to people, guns are so uncomplicated, he realized. *You just point, pull the trigger, and your problems go away.*

−11−

Patrick slept well and woke early, both firsts since checking in to the Campbell. He headed downstairs to the hotel entrance for a brisk walk before breakfast, although he would have preferred a long run in the nearby West Hills to shake some of the rust off. In this day and age, however, the only people who ran in the streets were probably either thieves or the police chasing them. Besides, the era of comfortable jogging shoes was a very long way off.

He turned north at 24th, unconsciously retracing the path he'd taken in the darkness the night he'd arrived. Engine House 17 stood quiet, its bay open and empty. Patrick found himself wondering whether O'Halloron's beautiful little fire station had still been standing in 1991. More than ever, he wished that he'd wandered these streets in his own time, so that the historian in him could have a better sense of how much the city would change over the decades.

Then it struck him that he might well witness those changes first hand if the portal that had brought him there had closed. How interesting would it be to watch the major events of history unfold when you already knew the outcomes, like a Nostradamus in a Brooks Brothers suit?

If nothing else, he realized with a smile, *I'll make some damned good money betting on prize fights and presidential elections. Truman's win over Dewey alone will make me a small fortune. And all that it will cost me is my own future.*

And Rachel.

Patrick's smile faded, and he shivered a little in spite of the morning's warmth.

By the time he returned to the hotel an hour later, his bleak outlook had been replaced by hunger. He entered the restaurant through the Hoyt Street door, rather than from the lobby above, but Mac still managed to spot him almost immediately.

"There you are," Mac said as he approached. "I sent Jimmy up for you fifteen minutes ago. I was a little worried when he said you didn't answer your door."

"I just went out for a morning walk." Patrick surveyed the crowded dining room. "I had no idea you did this kind of business at breakfast."

"That's because we haven't been able to drag your ass out of bed before eight-thirty since you got here."

"The tables look full up. I can sit at the counter," Patrick offered, ignoring the comment.

His friend grinned as he shook his head.

"Oh, no. Not this morning. *Special* arrangements have been made for you today."

With that he turned and started walking toward the far corner of the restaurant. Dutifully, Patrick trailed along behind, narrowly avoiding a collision when Mac stopped short just a few feet farther on.

"I told you we'd find him," the Scot said as he stepped aside.

"Thank you, Mr. McKenzie." Julia Lundgren smiled up at the innkeeper, then turned to Patrick. "I hope you don't mind, Mr. O'Connell, but I remembered you mentioning that you were staying here, and as I was planning on stopping by for breakfast, I thought ..."

Patrick opened his mouth to say something just as Mac's heavy hand guided him into the chair opposite hers.

"I'm sure he's delighted, Miss Lundgren. Aren't you?"

"Absolutely," Patrick managed.

"There, you see? Now, you two talk and I'll send someone over with the coffee." The last words floated back to them from over his shoulder as he moved toward the kitchen.

"I take it Mr. McKenzie is a friend of yours," Julia observed.

"For better or worse." Patrick took a moment to study her. Julia looked tired, he thought, and her eyes still held a certain sadness, but less so than when he'd met her at the reception the day before.

Elizabeth appeared beside their table, coffee pot and cups in hand. She appraised Julia for a moment before setting the cups down in front of them.

"Coffee, Miss?" she asked. Julia nodded. Elizabeth filled her cup, leaving room for cream and sugar. Then she turned to Patrick, smiling mischievously.

"And I know *just* how you like it," she said, sweetly, as she filled Patrick's cup to the brim.

Julia glanced quickly from the waitress to Patrick before turning her attention to the cream she was stirring into her coffee. She almost—but not quite—managed to suppress a knowing smile.

Patrick scowled at Elizabeth, who merely winked at him and took their breakfast orders. Then, coffee pot in hand, she sauntered off toward the kitchen. Patrick could swear that she put a little extra swish in her walk for their benefit.

Julia caught him watching. "Are you sure that you don't mind my asking you to join me?"

Patrick looked at her for a moment in puzzlement before understanding dawned.

"Oh, no. No, no, no. There's nothing going on here besides a waitress having a little fun at my expense." *And seriously jeopardizing her tip*, he added silently.

"Ah, so *that's* what that was all about." She sounded more amused than convinced.

"How often do you come here for breakfast?" he asked in an attempt to navigate to less awkward waters.

"Well, if you include this morning ... this is my first time." She flashed an embarrassed smile. "I've actually been intending to eat here for some time. I live just down the street, and everyone says that the food is delicious."

"So, when you said you were planning on stopping by for breakfast ..."

"I might have remembered that you were staying here, and *then* planned on stopping by." Her cheeks went slightly pink, but her eyes held that confidence that he'd come to know so well in the elder Julia, and in her granddaughter.

"I'm flattered, if a bit surprised."

"Oh, you needn't be. Surprised, I mean. As I said yesterday, your honesty was refreshing. You treated me like an adult, rather than a fragile child, and I can use all of that I can get right now."

"I wouldn't be too hard on the people at the reception. It's always difficult to find the right words to say at times like that."

"I know. And I appreciated their being there, honestly. It's obvious that my father meant a great deal to a great many people. It seems he cast a much larger shadow than even I realized."

"Worried that you might not be able to live up to what he accomplished?"

Julia looked up, surprised. "How did you know?"

Patrick smiled reassuringly. "We all measure ourselves against our parents, in one way or another. I think that's human nature. But I doubt that anyone expects you to be your father, Julia."

"Because I'm a *woman*?" Her tone was level, but he caught the flash behind those brown eyes.

"No, because you're your own person, with your own strengths and weaknesses. Make no mistake, some people will undoubtedly discount your abilities because you're a woman." His smile never wavered. "Imagine how satisfying it will be when you prove them wrong."

Before Julia could respond, Elizabeth arrived with a plate of fresh-baked biscuits. She looked as though she might have some new tease to offer, but one look at Patrick's expression and she scurried off to another table.

"I think you frightened the poor girl," Julia said with a grin as she spooned a little strawberry jam onto half a biscuit. She took a bite and her eyes widened. "These are delicious! If all of the food here is this good then I think I'm going to become a regular customer."

"I'm sure Mac will be very happy to hear that."

He watched as she finished the flakey delicacy, obviously savoring every bite. She grinned again and reached for the other half of the biscuit.

"If you're going to watch me eat, Mr. O'Connell, the least you can do is fill the conversational void."

"Call me Patrick, please. Anything in particular you'd like me to talk about?"

"I'd like to know a little more about the person I'm dining with. For instance, what brings you to Portland?"

"I'm here to take care of a personal matter for a friend. If all goes well, I'll be able to wrap everything up within a few days." He hoped he sounded more optimistic than he felt. To date very little had, to his mind at least, gone well.

"And then?"

"That's hard to say. Home, hopefully."

"And where is home?"

"Madison, Wisconsin." It was marginally the truth, or would be in a few decades. "I taught history at the University of Wisconsin."

"Really? I wouldn't have taken you for a history professor. But, you said 'taught.' What do you do now?"

"Well, I've come into a bit of money, so I suppose for the moment that makes me a man of leisure," he told her with a laugh.

The rest of their order arrived, matching plates of eggs, bacon and potatoes in generous portions. Julia eyed her meal warily, as though trying to visualize how she could possibly put away so much food.

Patrick grinned. "Daunting, isn't it?"

"You might have warned me," she said, reproachfully.

"Where would the fun have been in that?"

Despite her misgivings, Julia made a healthy dent in the mound of food before her. Patrick wondered how long it had been since she'd allowed herself a proper meal.

When at last she showed signs of slowing, she caught his amused look.

"I suppose I was a little hungrier than I thought," she said with a chuckle. "I see you've managed pretty well, yourself."

"Mac's sister-in-law is an excellent cook." He used his fork to organize the last few bites on his plate. "If I stay here too much longer I won't be able to fit through the doors."

"Well, before that happens ..."

"Yes?"

"You mentioned yesterday that you'd like to take a tour of Papa's factory before you left town. I need to attend to a few things at his office this morning, so I thought that perhaps we might take that tour together. After all, I should probably become more familiar with day-to-day operations."

"Does that mean that you've decided not to sell the factory after all?"

"Let's just say that I'm trying to keep an open mind," she said, softly, her voice so much like another young woman's.

"I'm glad to hear that." He was surprised at the slight tightness in his voice. Being around Julia would prove damned difficult if she kept casting Rachel's shadow.

He looked up to see Julia, watching him closely.

"Is something the matter?"

"You reminded me of someone, just then. It caught me a little off-guard. But I'm fine, really," he added, seeing the doubt in her eyes. "And I would be honored to accompany you to the factory."

They agreed to meet in front of the Campbell at half past nine, which gave Patrick more than enough time to bathe and change.

He had just finished buttoning his shirt when he heard footsteps stop just outside in the hallway.

"Come on in, Mac," he called out. In the mirror's reflection, Patrick saw his friend peaking sheepishly from around the door.

"What made you so sure it was me?" he asked as he closed the door behind him.

"Because you're a nosey son of a bitch who can't wait to find out what went on at breakfast," Patrick replied, straight-faced, as he pulled a tie out of the top dresser drawer.

"Fair enough," the Scot said with a laugh. "So, how did you get on with Miss Lundgren?"

"Just a friendly conversation over coffee and biscuits." Patrick fiddled with the strip of fabric around his neck. Even with a week's practice, he still struggled with the thin, short, neckties of the era.

"Good god, you need to hire yourself a valet to help you dress." Mac said. He had settled on the bed to enjoy Patrick's sartorial struggles. "Looks to me like you've made plans for the day."

"Julia offered to give me a tour of the factory this morning."

"So it's 'Julia' already? You don't waste any time, do you?"

"Believe me, time is one thing that I don't take for granted anymore." Patrick pulled the knot tight under his collar before looking at Mac again. "This whole thing revolves around Lundgren Furniture. Leon Brent is already on the inside. I need to be there, too."

"Maybe so, but Brent knows you now. You're going to have to watch your back from this point on."

"You worried, Mac?"

The Scot just shrugged in response.

"Look, maybe it's time I found someplace else to stay," Patrick said, quietly, giving voice to something he'd been considering for awhile. "I have no intention of putting your family at risk, and if Brent is as dangerous as we think ...."

His friend smiled as the sentence faded, a half-smile filled with affection. He stood and handed Patrick the coat draped over the foot of the bed.

"That won't be necessary," he said as he helped Patrick on with the jacket. "I'll just worry even more if I don't know what's going on. Besides, if you leave now I'll have to give back the rest of your money, and you know *that's* never going to happen."

The sound of saws and lathes running at high speed washed over Patrick and Julia as they entered through the south doors of the factory. The air was heavy with the smell of freshly-cut wood and machine oil, of glue and varnish.

They hadn't been on the floor long before they were met by the factory manager, a stocky, white-haired gentleman about Patrick's height, whose broad face radiated genuine warmth as he approached them.

"Mr. Westbrook," Julia said, by way of introduction, "this is Mr. O'Connell. Sid Westbrook has worked for my father as the manager since the factory opened."

"A pleasure to meet you," the older man said as he shook Patrick's hand. "Do you represent the people who are buying Lundgren Furniture?"

Before Patrick could answer, Julia stepped in.

"Mr. Westbrook, I don't know where this ridiculous rumor started, but I'm not aware of so much as a single offer to buy my father's company."

"Oh, there have been *several* bids over the last few years," Mr. Westbrook assured her as he guided them into his cramped little office. "Point of fact, just a few weeks ago some outfit named Peregrine Industries offered Mr. Lundgren quite a bit of money to sell out."

"Is Peregrine another furniture manufacturer?" Patrick asked.

"Not that I've heard of. But you know how it is these days; with big companies buying out little ones all the time, it's getting so you can't tell the players without a scorecard. Anyway, this Peregrine Industries offered Mr. Lundgren a load of cash to sell. I guess maybe this offer was too good to pass up."

"Who told you about this?" Patrick thought he already knew the answer, but he wanted Julia to hear the name from someone else.

"Mr. Lundgren's attorney, Leon Brent."

"No offense, Mr. Westbrook," Julia said, a hint of anger in her eyes, "but why would Mr. Brent share that kind of confidential information with you?"

The manager's smile faded.

"He just happened to mention it at your house yesterday." Westbrook looked down at the blotter on his desk and fiddled nervously with his pen. "Mr. Brent said your father had decided to take Peregrine up on their offer, and wondered if I knew anything about it."

Julia glanced over at Patrick, then back to Westbrook. After a few awkward moments of silence she rose, absently brushing the wrinkles from her black dress. Patrick started to get up as well, but she motioned for him to sit.

"Mr. Westbrook, if my father was entertaining the idea of selling this company, he would have mentioned it to me. Now, if you'll excuse me, I have business to attend to ..." She paused, looking once more at Patrick. "In *my* office," she added firmly.

Patrick couldn't hide his smile. Neither, he noted with satisfaction, could Westbrook.

"Now then, Mr. Westbrook, I have a favor to ask of you." The iron-hard tone in her voice had softened noticeably.

"Anything you need, Miss Lundgren."

"First of all, since it looks as though we're going to be working closely together for some time to come, I want you to call me Julia." The manager happily nodded agreement. "Secondly, I promised Mr. O'Connell a tour of the factory. Could you arrange that for me?"

"I'll see to it myself," he assured her, but she shook her head with a smile.

"I'm afraid that you'll be too busy pulling information together. I have a lot to learn about running a successful furniture company, and I'm relying on you to teach me what I need to know." She turned to Patrick. "It will probably take me a couple of hours to finish my work. Do you have other plans this morning, or would you be willing to wait for me?"

"No other plans," he assured her, flattered by the look of relief in her eyes. "I'll come up to your office after my tour."

Westbrook and Patrick sat in silence for a moment after the door closed behind Julia.

"Her father's daughter," the factory manager said at last. "I'd say she's going to be just fine."

Patrick laughed. "Sid, you can take that to the bank."

The two men grinned at each other.

"Now, for that tour. Let's find someone to show you around."

Patrick had a sudden inspiration. "Julia mentioned a foreman named Otis."

The manager nodded, a troubled look on his face. "Otis Loring, but, he's ..."

"I'm sure that he would do nicely. Unless you have some objection?"

"None whatsoever." Westbrook pushed himself away from his desk. "Let's go track him down."

They found Otis in the lathe area, moving between the workers at their noisy machines with a watchful eye.

"Otis!" Sid raised his voice to a shout so that he could be heard over the whirring of the motors. "Come on over here."

The foreman looked up, a startled look on his face when he saw Patrick standing beside the manager. Patrick shook his head, hoping the big man would take the hint and not let on that they'd already met. Otis took a moment to brush some of the wood shavings from his dark blue coveralls before stepping away from his crew.

"Otis," Sid Westbrook said, "this is a friend of Miss Lundgren's, Mr. O'Connell. I want you to take him on a tour of the factory, show him the sights."

"There anything in particular you want Mr. O'Connell to see?"

"Nope. Just give him the nickel tour, then take him up to Mr. Lundgren's office. Miss Lundgren will be waiting there for him." Westbrook turned to Patrick. "You're in good hands. Now I'd better get back to my office and gather up all that information Julia was talking about."

"So, you a friend of Miss Julia's?" Otis said quietly as the manager walked away. "Guess I missed that part last time we talked."

"Acquaintance would be more accurate. We met yesterday at the memorial service. I looked for you there, by the way."

A troubled look clouded the big man's expression.

"We sent flowers, my wife and me, but not too many people would have wanted to see us there."

"I'm sorry. That hadn't even occurred to me." The omnipresent racism of the twenties was something Patrick doubted that he would ever be able to get used to.

Otis shrugged. "Most times I don't let it bother me much, but I would have liked to pay my respects."

He guided Patrick up a narrow flight of wooden stairs that led to a railed catwalk high above the factory floor.

"I figure this is about the safest place for us to talk," the foreman told him when they reached the top. Indeed, there was no one else up there with them, and the cacophony of machine noises below made it impossible to be overheard.

Otis stood back against the wall, his massive arms crossed. "I'm guessing that you didn't come for no tour, so why you really here? You come to see me?"

Rather than reply, Patrick leaned tentatively against the wooden railing and watched the activity below.

"I came at Julia's invitation," he said at last, without looking at the foreman. "But I saw an opportunity to talk to you, so I took it."

"I read in the newspaper that Daly's wife got herself killed," Otis told him. "Seems like that happened about the time I told you where you could find Brian."

Patrick turned and met Otis's stare. "If you saw that in the newspaper, then you read the description of the person who killed her. Did that sound like me?"

"Couldn't say one way or the other. But you could have been there."

"I was, Otis." The big man's eyes widened, but he said nothing. "I was the one who kicked the door open and found Maggie Daly bleeding out in the kitchen. And I'm the one who has to live with the fact that I was too late to save her, and too late to catch the bastard who killed her."

Patrick's look never wavered as he added, "But I can still save Julia. And I'm going to."

Otis studied Patrick for a few moments. Then he took a deep breath and uncrossed his arms.

"Say I believe you. Don't know for sure that I do, but let's say I do for now. How can I help? I don't know nothing more than what I already told you."

"I think you might know something without realizing it. Who else was there the day Carl fired Daly, and Brian threatened to get even?"

The foreman ran his thick fingers through his salt-and-pepper hair as he thought about the question.

"I don't remember for sure. I know Miss Langseth—that's Mr. Lundgren's secretary—she was there. And one of the other foremen, Smitty, he was there with me outside of Mr. Lundgren's office. Don't think there was nobody else."

"What about inside Carl's office?"

"Might have been, but I just don't know." Otis gave Patrick a helpless look. "I'm sorry. I want to help Miss Julia, but that's all I remember."

"That's all right, Otis." Patrick reached out and gave the foreman's muscled arm a reassuring squeeze. "I'm still staying at the Campbell if you do think of anything else."

Julia closed the cover on the check ledger and locked the heavy binder back in the top drawer of the big oak desk. A glance at the clock on the wall told her that she'd been in her father's office for almost two and a half hours, looking at purchase orders, taking care of payments to suppliers, and signing the mid-month paychecks for one hundred forty seven employees. Most of them with families to support, and all of them looking to her to keep food on the table and a roof over their heads.

Well, she thought, *at least the company seems to be doing well enough at the moment.*

According to Mr. Talbot, the company's bookkeeper, Lundgren Furniture had turned a profit to the tune of about seventy-five thousand through the first six months of the year, with orders still to fill totaling another sixteen thousand. All this heading into fall, traditionally the busiest production time of the year.

"This should easily be the company's most profitable year to date," Talbot had told her.

Unless I manage to run it into the ground, she'd found herself thinking, dourly. Of course she kept her misgivings to herself, but she couldn't help but wonder if the same thought hadn't been running through the accountant's mind as well.

She looked at the silver-framed photograph on the corner of the desk, the picture of herself and her father that had been taken on their trip to New York just before her twenty-first birthday. The last four years had passed far too quickly. They had talked so often about planning another trip together—Europe, perhaps, or even sailing to the Hawaiian Islands—but something had always come up that forced them to wait a while longer.

"There's always next year," her father had said, time and time again.

Until there were no more next years.

"I guess we never make the best of the days we have, do we?" Julia whispered as she reached for the little calendar beside the photo.

The date still showed Friday, August 2, the last day that her father had been at his desk. *One week ago, today.* She idly ran her fingers over the engagements that he'd written there, smiling at his tidy, flowing script. Then, with a sigh, she turned the pages ahead a week. Her father had written only one entry for today, she noticed.

Baseball game, Saturday, with Julia

She felt like smiling and crying all at once. Baseball had been the first American tradition Julia's father had embraced when her grandparents immigrated to the United States, and his passion for the sport had never wavered. Ever since Julia could remember, her father had taken her to every Saturday home game to see the Portland club play. They'd arrive an hour before the ballpark opened to hand tickets out to the neighborhood kids who couldn't afford the ten cent admission. Then they would take their seats—always along the first base line—where they'd spend the afternoon dining on hot dogs and cheering for their favorite players.

The realization that she had no one left to share that tradition with seemed as heartbreaking to Julia as any aspect of her father's death. Apparently the little things, the most mundane threads that weave their way through a person's life, take on unrealized significance when they are gone.

Julia took a slow, deep breath to clear her emotions a bit. There were still tears to be cried, she knew, but this was neither the time nor the place for them. As she gathered herself, the intercom on the desk buzzed briefly. Julia flipped the little switch at the base of the small wooden box.

"Yes, Miss Langseth," she said, thankful that her voice sounded calm.

"Otis is here, Miss Lundgren, with a Mr. O'Connell. Mr. Westbrook said that Otis was to bring him to your office."

"Thank you, Miss Langseth. Please show them both in."

A moment later, Patrick walked through the doorway, followed, hesitantly, by Otis. Before the door had closed behind them, Julia greeted the foreman with a ferocious hug. Patrick looked on in obvious amusement while Otis stood there uncomfortably, arms at his side.

"Thank you for the flowers you and your wife sent yesterday," she said, softly. Otis looked down at her with an expression of embarrassment.

"Is something wrong?" she asked, stepping back.

"No, Miss Julia ... Miss Lundgren."

"Otis Loring, I've known you for most of my life. Don't you dare call me Miss Lundgren. Miss Julia, if you must, or better yet, simply Julia."

Otis looked shocked at the suggestion. "That wouldn't be proper. People might think that I'm ..."

"That you're what?"

Otis couldn't seem to find the right words. Julia saw him glance desperately at Patrick for guidance.

"I think what Otis is trying to say is that people might feel that he was forgetting himself."

"Well, I think that's ridiculous."

"Completely," Patrick agreed, "but it's also the way the world is, right now."

"Then the world needs to change," she said, matter-of-factly. Julia could see the foreman seemed uncomfortable with the entire line of conversation, so she let the matter go. "Anyway, thank you for delivering Mr. O'Connell to me safe and sound."

"You're welcome, Miss Julia." Otis turned to Patrick and held out his enormous right hand, a hint of a smile on his face as they shook. "It's been a real pleasure, Mr. O'Connell. I should be getting back to the floor. If there's anything I can do, Miss Julia, you just let me know."

"As a matter of fact, there is," Julia said with a smile. "It's been awhile since you've brought me any new Louis Armstrong records."

The foreman laughed. "I think I got a couple new ones for you. Bring 'em in on Monday, if you'll be here."

"I'll be here. After all, this company isn't going to run itself, is it?"

"No ma'am," Otis agreed with a grin.

Julia leaned back against her father's desk as the office door closed behind the foreman. She smiled broadly at Patrick.

"What?" he asked, self-consciously.

"That must have been some tour you took. The only other person around here I've seen Otis that comfortable with was Papa."

"I guess I just have a way with people." He held her gaze for a moment, then broke into a smile of his own. "So, did you get a lot accomplished this morning?"

"Payroll is finished, and the suppliers have been satisfied for the time being," Julia told him as she moved back around to the other side of the desk. "But I have a great deal to learn if I'm going to fill Papa's shoes."

"You'll do fine."

"Really? What makes you so confident?"

Patrick chuckled. "My crystal ball tells me so. That, and the way you set Mr. Westbrook straight earlier. You have ..." he paused for a moment, searching for the right word.

"Moxie," he said at last. "That's the word, moxie."

Julia laughed. "I need to keep you around. You do wonders for my confidence."

"I'm happy to be of service for as long as I'm in town."

The reminder that Patrick would only be in Portland for a short time chased away a little of Julia's lightheartedness, but she held her smile.

"Then I'm just going to have to come up with reasons for you to stay," she told him, firmly.

Patrick grinned back at Julia from across their table at Besaws, where he'd offered to buy lunch.

"How does it feel to be a prominent business woman?"

She paused, the last bite of potato salad perched precariously on the end of her fork, and managed a timid smile. "A little daunting to be honest," she admitted. "I'm beginning to wonder what you've gotten me into."

"I don't see how you can accuse *me* of getting you into anything."

"It's all that optimism you keep dishing out about how I can accomplish anything I put my mind to. Next thing I know, I'm neck-deep in invoices." Her fork started up towards her mouth, then stopped once more.

"Thank you for that, by the way. Having you believe in me means a great deal right now."

Patrick simply smiled. His own plate had already been cleared away, so he watched in silence as she ate the last of her meal. All the while he noted the similarities between this Julia and the one he knew so well—the tilt of her head when she smiled, and the humming noise she made when she ate something tasty, for instance—all traits that she would carry for the rest of her life.

"You have that distracted look in your eyes again," Julia said. "This morning you told me it was because I reminded you of someone else. That's not very flattering, by the way," she added with a smile.

"If you met the young woman in question, you would know just what a compliment that was."

"And were you thinking of her again, just now, while you were watching me?"

"No. Her *grandmother*, actually."

"Even more flattering," she laughed.

"Rachel's grandmother is the single most remarkable woman I've ever met, and the strongest. I see the same things in you."

Julia lowered her chin, looking down at her plate, but not before he saw the color in her cheeks.

"I feel anything but remarkable, or strong." Her voice had a soft, almost childlike hush to it. She looked up at him once more. "If it weren't for you ..."

"I can't make you believe in yourself, Julia. No one can do that but you."

"When most men talk like that, I suspect their motives. Somehow, from you, it feels genuine. Are you always so earnest?"

Patrick laughed. "Only with people I earnestly care about."

The blush in her cheeks returned once more, but she continued to meet his gaze. "And does that list include this Rachel woman?"

"More than I care to admit."

Julia nodded, her expression unreadable.

"Have you told *her* that?" Patrick's smile faded as he shook his head. "Why not?"

"At first, I didn't want to feel that way about her, or anyone else for that matter." He saw the doubt in her eyes. "I was married once before, and it didn't take."

"You mean you're divorced." She smiled. "This is 1929, Patrick. Being divorced doesn't carry quite the stigma it once did."

Patrick laughed. "True, but that doesn't mean I wanted to jump back into the fire right away, either. I did my best to resist, but Rachel's will was just a little stronger than my own, I guess … Well, a lot stronger, actually. By the time I'd accepted how I felt, I found out that I was coming here, so I decided to wait."

"You should never wait to say how you feel," she told him, seriously. "You never know what might happen between now and then. What are you doing for dinner this evening?"

"That might be the most abrupt conversational shift I've heard in quite awhile," he said with a chuckle. "Why do you ask?"

"I'm having dinner with a couple of dear friends, and I thought that it might be nice if you could join us. Unless you think that *Rachel* might object," she added, coyly.

"I think she'd understand," he said, although he wasn't entirely convinced that would be true if Rachel could see her grandmother as a formidable, and very attractive, twenty-five year old.

"Good. Meet us in the lobby of the Benson Hotel, say around 6:30."

"So, now its dinner, is it?" Mac shot Patrick a sly smile while he watched his friend button his vest. "And here I thought you were pining for the girl back home."

"Julia knows all about Rachel, for your information."

"Knowing and *caring* are very different things, my friend. But at least you've found a way to stay close to her. Did you learn anything during your tour of the factory?"

Patrick frowned and shook his head. "I would have bet money that Brent was in the office the day Carl fired

Daly, but if he was, Otis didn't see him. How about you? Did you dig up any more information on Brent from your Chicago contact?"

"Quite a bit, actually." Mac fished his little notebook out of his pocket. He flipped through a few dog-eared pages before he came to the entry he was looking for. "First of all, Brent was born Leo Henry Schneider. Had his name changed legally about the time he enrolled in the University of Chicago Law School. Before that, he worked for 'Diamond Jim' Colosimo's organization. He started out as a bag man, but apparently he moved his way up pretty quickly until he became one of Colosimo's fair-haired boys."

"How did he manage that?"

Mac smiled tightly. "By doing just about any dirty job that came along, and doing them well, according to the guy I talked to. Detective Yox said they could never pin anything on him, though. Either they had no evidence, or their witnesses suddenly clammed up on the stand. Or they disappeared altogether."

"What kinds of activities are we talking about?"

"Extortion and prostitution, mostly. Colosimo ran the White Slave Ring in Chicago, kidnapping and selling young immigrant girls off to pimps in other cities. Word on the street had Leo involved, but no one seems to know whether he was picking them up, dropping them off, or ... Well, let's just say those poor women were broken in before they were shipped out."

Patrick could practically feel the color drain from his face. "How does a monster like Schneider even get into law school?"

"Money talks, especially in Chicago. Colosimo recognized that Schneider was as smart as he was cold blooded, just the kinds of traits a guy in his line of work wants in an attorney. Besides, Leo stepped up in a big way when 'Diamond Jim' needed him to. You remember all of that Black Hand stuff in Chicago before the war?"

"Vaguely." Organized crime had never been an area of American history that had captured Patrick's interest, until now.

"Well, Jim Cosmano and the Black Hand tried the extortion routine, figuring on tapping some of that prostitution money 'Diamond Jim' had rolling in. So Colosimo imported Johnny Torrio from New York to take care of the problem. When the Black Hand showed up for their money, Torrio and a couple of local boys cut them down."

"And one of the local boys was Leo Schneider?"

Mac smiled darkly. "Rob Yox was sure of it, but the cops could never prove he was even in the neighborhood, or that he was involved in the assassination attempt on Cosmano a few months later. There were lots of rumors, but no hard evidence. All Yox knows for sure is that, after the attempt on Cosmano, one of the judges in 'Diamond Jim's' pocket approved Leo Schneider's name change to Leon Brent, and pushed for the university to accept him into law school."

"So that explains Leon Brent, Attorney at Law," Patrick muttered, as much to himself as to Mac. "But how did he end up here, working for a decent man like Lundgren?"

"Well, Leo may have been careful where the police were concerned, but not so much with women. In 1917,

Johnny Torrio's girl—a woman named Addie Sinclair—let it slip that she and Brent had been at it hot and heavy in some hotel in Joliet. The next thing anyone knows, Addie turns up dead in an alley on the Eastside. Torrio was out for blood when he found out, but by then, Leon Brent was long gone. Apparently, that's when he enlisted to fight the Kaiser for Uncle Sam. And that's how he met Ingersol."

"Does any of this information actually help us?"

"Well, we probably have enough circumstantial evidence and innuendo here to ruin his career in Portland, but nothing that will put his neck in the noose. On the other hand, every new detail about him gives us another needle to stick him with. He's spent most of the last twenty years hiding behind this mask of respectability. When we threaten to tear it off, he's going to get worried and desperate."

Patrick nodded. "And desperate people make mistakes."

"They usually do, but they can also become more dangerous. Want to take a guess as to how they found Torrio's girlfriend in that alley, back in Joliet?"

"Like Maggie." Based on Mac's expression, it was hardly a guess.

Mac nodded. "Just like Maggie. With her throat cut from ear to ear."

–12–

The Benson Hotel—a French-inspired architectural gem on Broadway—was clearly a showcase for the city's fashionable and elite. Patrick felt a little underdressed surrounded by men in black tie and tails. He could only hope that they were all there for some formal event to which he hadn't been invited.

As he eyed the crowd uncomfortably, someone slid their arm under his. He turned to see Julia smiling up at him from beneath a fitted, bell-shaped hat. To his relief, she wore a stylish—but far from formal—black dress, accented with a single strand of pearls.

"Patrick, you look worried. Were you afraid that I'd stand you up?"

"No, but I was beginning to feel like a stowaway around all of these tuxedos."

"Well, I think you look very handsome," she assured him with a wink. "Now, come and meet my friends."

She guided Patrick toward the restaurant, where a couple watched their approach with interest. Neither person could be described as imposing, yet they made an immediate impression. The young man, perhaps in his late twenties or early thirties, had a high forehead, a broad nose, and inquisitive eyes that seemed to take the whole room in at once. Though not a large man by any means, he still towered over his companion—an attractive redhead who couldn't have stood much more than five feet tall—by a good six inches.

"Mr. O'Connell," Julia said as they drew near, "I'd like you to meet two of my dearest friends, Jill and Ernest Haycox. Jill, Ernest, this is Patrick O'Connell."

The young man grinned warmly and shook Patrick's hand with enthusiasm. "Please, call me Erny."

"With a *y*!" Jill and Julia called out, in perfect chorus. Haycox gave them both a look of reproach.

"With a y?" Patrick asked, confused.

"I prefer to end my name with a y, rather than an *ie*." Erny explained, his good-natured smile returning.

"I like it. Sadly, my name doesn't lend itself well to creativity."

"You could always use Pat," Julia offered.

"Pat would be my grandfather, and my family tree is confusing enough as it is without trying to work through any Little Pat and Big Pat nonsense."

"Confusing in what way?" Erny asked.

"The first-born males in my family have been named, alternately, Patrick James or James Patrick for several generations. My father calls it tradition. I think we simply lack originality."

They all laughed. The restaurant's host appeared at that moment, subtly positioning himself so that Haycox would notice him.

"Is our table ready, then?" Erny asked.

The host nodded, then to the rest of the group he said, "If you will all follow me, please." With that, he began walking toward the dining room, Erny falling in step behind him.

"So, when you have a son, will he be James Patrick, after your father?" Jill asked as they tagged along behind. "Or do you plan on breaking with tradition?"

"I don't know. When, or if, I have a son, I suspect that his mother might want some say in the matter as well."

"Finally," Julia said, "a man who is willing to listen to a woman's opinion."

"Whatever you do, don't let Erny hear you say that," Jill warned. "He's already made it clear that our first boy will be named Ernest, after him. Honestly," she added, softly, "I wouldn't have it any other way."

"They're so much in love, it's positively sappy," Julia whispered.

"Julia!" her friend exclaimed, blushing. She did not, however, deny the accusation.

The dining room resonated with soft conversation and the clink of silverware against fine china. In the far corner of the restaurant, a string quartet provided quiet background music for the meal. Waiters glided almost silently from table to table, refilling water glasses and taking orders.

Erny had taken the liberty of asking the chef, Henry Thiele, to prepare a special meal for the evening, promising Patrick that he was in for a real epicurean treat.

"Henry is perhaps the best chef on the entire west coast," Erny said with certainty. "I don't think I've eaten finer meals anywhere."

"Not even when you were living in New York?" Julia asked.

Both Erny and Jill laughed. "In those days we couldn't have afforded the first course in a restaurant such as this," Erny confided. "The life of a starving artist."

"What do you do for a living now?" Patrick asked.

Before Haycox could answer, Julia said, "Ernest is Portland's most famous writer."

The young man waved the suggestion off. "I'm hardly very famous. I write short stories and novellas. Western fiction, mostly, with a few tales of the American Revolution thrown in to keep me from getting stale."

"And now a novel," Jill reminded him.

"Time will tell if that was a wise decision or not," Erny chuckled.

"How do you and Julia know each other?" Patrick asked.

"Her brother Jacob and I were best friends at Lincoln High School. We were both planning on enrolling at Oregon Agriculture after graduation."

"What happened?"

"I got restless," Erny admitted. "I suppose I found life more interesting than classes back then. I spent some time in San Francisco working odd jobs, even tried my hand as a peanut butcher on a train line that ran between Oakland and Sacramento."

"Peanut butcher?" Julia looked as puzzled by the term as Patrick was.

"A vendor, selling peanuts to the passengers. That's where I learned how to short-change customers," he added with a laugh.

"Erny!" His wife managed a look of both shock and amusement.

"All grist for the writer's mill," he told her, unapologetically. "Julia tells us that you're in Portland on personal business, Patrick. How long will you be staying?"

Patrick glanced at Julia, who seemed to be taking an inordinate amount of interest in the appetizer on her plate.

"I'm not entirely sure. My business is complicated, but I hope that I'm close to wrapping things up."

"And then what?" Julia asked. She looked at him with a quiet intensity, but he held her gaze.

"I imagine that I'll be going home ... back to Wisconsin," he added, for the Haycox's benefit.

"What line of business are you in?" Jill asked.

"Mr. O'Connell is an independent man of means," Julia answered. "That's why he can stay here indefinitely ... until his personal matter is taken care of. Isn't that right, Patrick?"

An awkward silence fell around them for a moment as Julia continued to study Patrick from across the table. He knew the look she was giving him all too well.

"Unfortunately, being independent doesn't mean that I don't have responsibilities of my own to attend to," he pointed out. "And people to see, of course."

"That's right, I almost forgot. *Rachel*," Julia said softly. She sat back in her chair, casting an embarrassed half-smile toward Jill and Erny, who watched her with vaguely worried expressions.

"Would you excuse me for a moment?" she asked as she rose from her chair. "I need to go powder my nose."

"I'll go with you," Jill insisted.

Patrick and Erny watched in silence as the ladies made their way through the dining room. When, at last, Julia and Jill had disappeared from sight, Erny leaned back in his chair and looked at Patrick.

"If you don't mind my saying so, Patrick, I think that you have a problem on your hands."

"So it would seem."

"And how do you propose to handle it?"

"As carefully as possible," Patrick assured him. "As carefully as possible."

"Julia Lundgren, what has gotten into you?" Jill whispered as they passed through the lobby toward the ladies lounge. "You are positively pushing yourself on that poor man."

Julia stopped walking and turned to her friend. "And what if I am?"

Jill seemed startled, her mouth open, her jaw twitching slightly as though she were trying to form words that refused to come out.

"It isn't proper," she managed, at last. "And besides, your father died less than a week ago."

"Well, I am still *very* much alive. And life is too uncertain to waste any of it worrying about being conventional."

The last word came out as though Julia considered the concept profane.

Jill studied her friend for a moment, then glanced around as if she were expecting everyone in the lobby to be listening. Satisfied that no one was paying them the slightest attention, she leaned closer to Julia and whispered, "But Patrick is so *old*."

"He's not *that* old. Tell me that you don't find him at least a little attractive."

"Julia, I'm a married woman. I don't look at other men that way."

"Liar," Julia said with a grin. Her friend's cheeks reddened. "Anyway, *I* find him attractive. And I feel good around him. I feel better than anyone has made me feel in longer than I'd care to admit."

Her friend was watching her with interest now. "How long have you known each other?"

Julia smiled in embarrassment. "An entire day," she admitted with a little laugh. "I know, it sounds crazy, doesn't it?"

Now it was Jill's turn to smile. "Erny and I met on the train to New York. He claims that he knew we were meant for each other before the first afternoon was over. Don't tell him, but I knew even sooner than that."

Her expression turned serious once more.

"Just be careful, Julia. You're been through a lot, and I don't want you to get hurt."

"I'll go slowly. I promise."

"Now who's lying?" Jill said, grinning.

They were almost across the lobby when Julia heard someone call her name. She turned to see her father's attorney, Leon Brent, dressed to the nines in a tuxedo. He'd separated himself from a large, formally attired, group and hurried toward them. She managed a tight smile, despite the unease that she'd always felt around him, and waited for him.

"Julia! What a surprise to find you here."

He stood just a little closer than necessary, forcing the two women to tip their heads back to make eye contact. It was one of the many things that Julia detested about the man, the way he always used his size to intimidate others.

"I'm having dinner with some friends. May I introduce Mrs. Ernest Haycox?" she said, trying to sound as stiff and uninviting as possible. "Mrs. Haycox, this is my father's attorney, Mr. Brent."

"Did you say Mrs. *Ernest* Haycox?" He took the tiny woman's hand in his. "This *is* a pleasure. I've been an avid reader of your husband's stories for many years now. In fact, I have a copy of *Free Grass* on my nightstand at home. His first novel, isn't it?"

"First of many to come, we hope." Jill looked uncomfortable as she tried to pull away from his grip.

"Julia, I never realized that you knew Ernest Haycox." Brent sounded almost reproachful, as though she had intentionally slighted him by withholding the information. "You must introduce me."

"Some other time, perhaps," Julia told him firmly, bringing a flicker of surprise to his eyes.

"Of course," he said in a quiet, slightly dark voice. "I wouldn't want to intrude on your dinner party."

"I appreciate that. It was very good to see you, Mr. Brent. Please don't let us keep you from your friends."

Her clear dismissal brought a scowl to the lawyer's face for a moment. Perhaps unconsciously, Jill took a step backward. Julia held her ground, however, looking up into

Brent's eyes. She could see him trying to compose himself in the face of her challenge. At last he nodded, the scowl replaced by a thin, insincere smile.

"Again, it was a pleasure." He turned to leave, then swung back around. "Julia, I almost forgot the reason I came over. Your father had scheduled an appointment on Monday with a representative from the law firm of Bishop and Goldmark to finalize some papers that he'd signed."

"What kind of papers?"

"I'm not entirely sure. Whatever it is, I'll be happy to deal with it for you. You have enough on your plate as it is."

"That won't be necessary. If it involves my company, then it involves me."

Once again she saw the brief, unmistakable, look of genuine surprise flash in his eyes. *He's not used to having people stand up to him*, she realized with satisfaction.

"I am very glad to hear that you feel that way." His tone said otherwise. "The appointment is at ten thirty, Monday morning, at your father's office."

"At *my* office, not my father's."

"Of course, Julia, at your office." He smiled down at her like an indulgent parent. "I'll see you there."

As the attorney wandered back to his own gathering, Jill let out a sigh of relief.

"Well, that was awkward," she said, softly. "I hope you won't have to work with Mr. Brent too often."

"Only until I can find a replacement for him," Julia vowed.

Patrick and Erny rose from their seats to pull the ladies' chairs away from the table as the women returned, whispering to each other. Julia looked at Patrick and sighed.

"Why do you men insist upon doing that?" she asked irritably as she sat down. "We're perfectly capable of seating ourselves."

Patrick managed to stifle a laugh, well aware that it would probably earn him a heated glare from his companion, or worse.

"Well," Jill said, rising to their defense, "I appreciate a little gallantry now and then."

Erny reached over and squeezed her hand fondly. "Thank you, dear. Are you two all right? You seem a bit flustered."

"We just had an encounter in the lobby with Julia's lawyer. He's really very unpleasant, even if he is apparently one of your most ardent readers, Erny."

Patrick leaned forward, his expression suddenly serious. "Leon Brent is here?"

Julia looked at him in surprise. "Do you know him?"

"I met him yesterday afternoon at your house, during the reception. I also found him to be ... unpleasant. Then, this morning, Mr. Westbrook mentioned that Brent was the one who told him about Peregrine Industries offer to buy the factory."

Julia's eyes widened at the mention of the deal.

"What did he want?" Patrick asked.

"He said that Papa had scheduled a meeting on Monday with a representative from Bishop and ..." she paused, trying to recall the rest.

"Goldmark?" Erny offered. Julia nodded. "I know that firm. They handled Frank Doernbecher's estate and charitable trust a few years back."

"Do you think this is about Peregrine Industries?" Julia asked Patrick, anxiously.

"It might be. What did he say, exactly?"

"Just that Papa scheduled this meeting to finalize some papers that he'd signed. Maybe he really *was* going to sell the factory," she said, a look of uncertainty in her eyes.

"I can't believe your father would have ever considered letting Lundgren Furniture go," Erny told her. "The Doernbechers tried to buy the company on two or three occasions—for top dollar, too—but they couldn't get anywhere with Carl."

"Doernbecher ... Why is that name so familiar?" Patrick wondered aloud.

"You've probably heard of the Doernbecher Memorial Hospital for Children that the family founded here in Portland," Jill suggested. "The Doernbechers owned the largest furniture factory in the city, out in Sullivan's Gulch. In fact, Erny is distantly related to them."

"And don't think for a moment that your father ever let me forget that, either. 'Fraternizing with the enemy,' he used to joke," Erny told Julia with a smile. Seeing the shaken look in her eyes, he reached out and took her hand. "Julia, we both know that Carl would never have sold the company, and certainly not without talking to you first. There has to be another explanation."

"I suppose I'll find out on Monday. I told Mr. Brent that I would be there."

"I'll be there, too." Patrick told her, firmly.

Julia looked up at him in surprise. "Are you sure? You have your friend's business to attend to."

He smiled. "*We're* friends, aren't we? I'm no legal expert, of course, but it couldn't hurt to have someone in your corner."

"And your father's attorney will be there, as well," Jill pointed out.

Julia frowned. "I'd almost feel better if he weren't. There is something about that man ..."

"Erny," Jill said, turning to her husband, "why don't you see if Ed might be available? Julia told me that she was going to replace Mr. Brent as soon as she can, and aren't you always telling me that Ed is one of the sharpest young men you know?"

"He is, dear, but Ed has been handling a case down in Salem this week. I share an office with a young attorney," Erny explained to the others. "By all accounts he's a crackerjack lawyer, and I'll be happy to introduce you to him, but I don't think that he'll be back in Portland until Monday, at the earliest."

Well then, Patrick thought, *Mac and I had better come up with a plan between now and then, because Leon Brent clearly isn't going to be backing down any time soon.*

Leon sat in the middle of the banquet room, only half-listening to Governor Patterson's speech. In truth, his mind was still on his encounter with Julia. The more he thought about the way she'd treated him, the angrier he became.

Refusing to introduce me to Haycox like that, acting like she's Queen of the fucking May. And insisting on attending the meeting with Bishop and Goldmark. As though she could even begin to understand contracts and business.

Goddamned spoiled little bitch.

She was threatening to throw yet another monkey wrench into his careful arrangements. And to think that he'd tried so hard to make sure she'd be well taken care of when the company sold.

Leon forced himself to calm down. Julia was the least of his worries, and probably the easiest to deal with. He still needed to focus on finding out who the bastard from the funeral was.

He'd stayed up half the night trying to figure out what this guy's play was. The only thing that made sense was that he'd gotten his hands on the forged contract and planned on a little blackmail. That's certainly what Leon would have done if he'd had that kind of leverage. *But if that's his scheme, what is he waiting for? Why the fucking game of cat and mouse?*

A round of applause marked the end of Governor Patterson's speech. Leon rose with the rest of the attendees and made his way out of the banquet room, making idle conversation with his colleagues along the way. He paused briefly near the door to shake the governor's hand, then pushed his way impatiently through the crowd to the lobby.

And stopped like a statue in mid-stride.

Julia and her party were just leaving the hotel. Mrs. Haycox was arm-in-arm with her husband—Leon recognized Ernest immediately from the newspaper photographs—while Julia walked alongside the man who had been haunting Leon's thoughts since the funeral.

"The only thing that could top a meal like that," Erny said as they stepped out onto the sidewalk, "would be a good cigar." He ignored the disapproving look from Jill and turned to the other couple. "How about you, Patrick? Are you a cigar smoker?"

"Only on special occasions."

Erny grinned. "How much more special does an occasion get than to be in the company of two lovely ladies?"

"And just what are those ladies to do while you're off smoking your cigars?" Jill asked.

"Point taken," her husband conceded. "Perhaps another time, Patrick, if you're in town long enough. May we drop you at your hotel?"

"I have a better idea," Julia said. "Why don't we all go to the Campbell and have a drink in the bar?"

"What makes you think that the Campbell *has* a bar?" Patrick asked with a laugh.

"Oh, it's a well-kept neighborhood secret. And I figure if their cocktails are as good as their breakfasts, we should be in for a treat."

"What I want to know is, when did *you* start drinking?" Erny asked.

"You were the one who suggested I go to Reed College for my degree," she pointed out with a wink.

Jill looked at her friend in surprise. "I'm beginning to think that I don't know you at all, Julia Lundgren."

"I'll let you in on a little secret," Julia told her with a sly smile. "I'm just beginning to learn a few things about myself, as well. What do you say, Patrick?" she added, taking him by the arm. "Will you do me the honor of escorting me into my first official speakeasy?"

"If your friends are game, then so am I. But you start dancing the Charleston on the table and I'm going to pretend we've never met."

"I prefer the Black Bottom," Julia said, "but, for you, I'll try to be on my best behavior. How about you, Jill? The night is young."

"I don't know. We really should be getting home. After all, we told Mrs. Norris that we'd be back to pick Mary Ann up before it got too late." She paused, looking at Julia's hopeful expression. "Oh, heavens, why not? Erny and I haven't done anything remotely scandalous in ages."

Leon smiled grimly as he settled into the chair behind his desk. New strategies had been forming in his mind since he'd left the Benson. *Time to starting putting them into motion*, he thought, reaching for his address book.

When he'd seen that man with Julia he'd experienced a moment—a rare moment—of panic, but now he realized the enemy was out in the open. Leon didn't know where the bastard had been hiding, but Julia was the key to finding him.

Unfortunately, the man he was after knew Leon by sight. As much as he wanted to avoid it, he was going to have to bring in some help. His first call was to Cicero's, but Pellizotti's nephew, Anthony De Campo, had already gone home to his wife and family. Leon looked at his watch; not even ten o'clock and the kid had already called it a night. Clearly De Campo wasn't cut out for running a gang, or a night club.

He returned to his address book, found the number Pellizotti had given him when he'd skipped town, and dialed.

"È tardi," the man on the other end answered gruffly. "Cosa vuoi?"

"I need to speak to Anthony," Leon told him.

"Oh yeah? And who the hell are you?"

"Tell him his uncle's attorney is calling."

There was a pause at the other end, then, "Mr. Brent?"

"That's right."

"This is Anthony, Mr. Brent. Sorry if I was short with you, but I wasn't expecting anyone to call this late. Have you heard from my uncle?"

The hopeful tone in the kid's voice confirmed that De Campo was less than thrilled to have been left holding the reins of Pellizotti's organization. Good. Leon was banking that Anthony would just as soon let others handle the dirty work.

"Not yet, I'm afraid. Listen, before your uncle left, he told me about a guy he wanted me to locate. I think I've found him. I need a couple of your boys—good ones—to take care of him."

Pellizotti's nephew was quiet for a moment, then, "What do you mean by 'take care of him?'"

"Do you really want the details?"

"No, not particularly."

"I didn't think so. Have your men at my office around noon, tomorrow, and I'll fill them in."

Leon hung up the telephone and stared into the darkness beyond his study. He wasn't too worried about explaining things to Pellizotti when, or if, the boss came back to town. After all, he was simply eliminating a threat to the organization, and protecting Anthony in the bargain. But if things went wrong, the trail now led directly back to Leon's doorstep.

That simply meant that nothing could be allowed to go wrong. This bastard would have to disappear so completely that it would take years just to find the pieces.

–13–

Given Erny's local celebrity, Patrick thought it best to find a private table in the back of the Campbell's dining room. Tucked behind strategically placed ferns, they were more or less hidden from the rest of the customers. Because of their placement, it took a few more minutes than usual to receive their drinks, but the conversation was good and the company even better.

As the waiter brought their order, Patrick asked, "Is Mr. McKenzie here this evening?" The server nodded. "Tell him that I'm here with guests, would you? Ask him to join us."

"For a man who's new in town, you certainly seem to have established yourself," Erny pointed out with a grin.

"Wherever I go, I make it a point to meet the best people. Present company included," he added. He raised his glass.

"To new friends and old," Erny called as he lifted his own glass. He paused, then glanced over at Julia before adding, "and to your father, one of the finest friends I've ever known."

Julia's smile was a little sad, but a smile nonetheless. She and Jill joined the toast.

"Do you know," Erny said, "some of my favorite moments with Carl were at the baseball games that he took us to. You should have seen him, Patrick. He loved to stand outside of the gate, distributing game tickets to the neighborhood children." He smiled at the memory. "I think to those kids, Carl was Santa Claus and the Easter Bunny rolled into one. I can't imagine what it will be like without him there."

Julia nodded. "I was looking at his calendar for today, and he'd written himself a reminder about taking me to tomorrow's game. It was all I could do to keep from crying when I saw it."

"You should go anyway," Jill said suddenly. Erny and Julia looked at her in surprise. "Well, you should. Carl would have wanted you to, wouldn't he? Go and hand out tickets and hold onto something your father loved just a little longer."

"I suppose we could all go ..." Julia said, hesitantly.

Erny started to nod, but Jill reached over and patted his hand before he could say anything.

"I'm afraid we can't, dear. I forgot to mention that we've been invited over to the Novotny's for lunch tomorrow. But I'm sure you two will manage to have a good time without us," she added, smiling sweetly at Julia and Patrick.

Patrick could almost swear he saw Jill throw in a quick wink for Julia's benefit.

"Jill, I don't know if that's appropriate," Erny said. "After all, they hardly know each other."

"Oh, pish!" She dismissed his objection with a theatrical wave of her hand. "It isn't as though they'll be off alone somewhere. There'll be dozens of people around them all of the time."

Julia seemed to be struggling to keep a smile from her face as she watched her friend. Finally, she turned to Patrick, an impish look in her eyes.

"What do you say, Patrick? You're not going to let me disappoint all of those children, are you?"

"You, young lady, do not play fair. And that goes for you, as well," he added, for Jill's benefit. "Under the circumstances, how can I possibly refuse?"

Jill leaned back in her chair with a self-satisfied smile and took a sip of her drink.

A moment later, Mac appeared, wiping his hands on the apron tied around his waist. The innkeeper smiled broadly when he saw Julia.

"Miss Lundgren! Twice in one day!" He nodded toward Patrick. "Don't tell me you're still in the company of this unsavory character."

"I'm not sure what to tell you, Mr. McKenzie. He's been following me around all day like a little lost puppy."

"I have the same problem," McKenzie confided with a sly grin. "He showed up on my doorstep and I haven't been able to get rid of him since. And that's quite enough of that *Mr. McKenzie* business. It's Mac to my friends."

"That always covered about half the town, as I recall."

Mac turned toward the voice, his eyes lighting up in recognition as his hand shot forward.

"Erny Haycox! I'll be ..." he glanced at the ladies in embarrassment before finishing with, *"blessed.* I'll be blessed," he repeated, a little more confidently as he pumped the young man's hand.

"I take it you know each other," Patrick said, pulling a chair up from a nearby table.

"When I was on the force, Erny here was the best police-beat reporter *The Oregonian* had. How long ago was that?"

"That would have been back in '23, not long before I met Jill. Mac, I'd like for you to meet the missus," Erny added, indicating the woman sitting to his left. "Jill, this is Detective Larry 'Mac' McKenzie."

"A pleasure. No doubt you're the muse behind all of these stories of Erny's that I've been reading." Mac turned to the writer. "I must say, you've made a name for yourself since the last time I saw you. Quite a change from your newspaper days, isn't it?"

"Not as dramatic a change as yours, certainly. I expected you to be a captain by now. How did you come to be a bartender?"

"It's worse than that. I'm part owner. My brother and sister-in-law and I bought the Campbell back in '25. When we lost Danny two years ago, I stepped in to help his wife run the place. The after-hour activities ... well, sad to say, this pays the lion's share of the bills around here.

"Speaking of which," he added, eyeing their nearly empty glasses, "why don't you let me get the next round?"

Erny shook his head as he rose from his chair. "I appreciate it, Mac, but we have a daughter to get home to. Julia, may we see you home?"

Jill stood as well, and gave her friend an encouraging smile.

"Thank you, Erny, but no," Julia said as she got up to give his wife a hug. "I only live two blocks from here, and I think that I'd like to take Mac up on that drink. Patrick can walk me home."

Erny glanced over at Patrick, who simply smiled and nodded. They were all standing now, and Erny shook hands with both men before guiding his wife away from the table.

They were almost to the door when Patrick caught up to them.

"I almost forgot," he said. "You said that your attorney friend would be out of town until Monday. How can I reach him when he gets back?"

"I believe that I have one of his cards." Erny pulled a worn, brown leather wallet from his inside coat pocket and extracted a business card.

"Thank you, Erny." Patrick shook his hand once more. "Jill, this evening has been a pleasure."

It was only after they had disappeared through the doorway that Patrick looked more closely at the card in his hand. It was all he could do to keep from laughing.

Edward Wirth

Attorney at Law

Well, he thought as he headed back to the table, *at least I can be confident that the legal side of things will be in good hands.*

Julia could feel herself beginning to fade as she sipped at her third Manhattan. Despite what she'd implied earlier, she'd never really been much of a drinker. The alcohol, combined with days of sleeplessness, had left her a little light-headed.

She looked over at Patrick sitting next to her, talking about the stock market with Mac. He was saying something about "buying on margin," and the collapse that was coming. Julia knew she should be paying attention, now that it fell to her to manage the investments she'd inherited from her father, but her focus kept drifting away from his words and back to the man himself.

Patrick always seemed so ... how had she described him at lunch? *Earnest. That's the word*, she remembered. Always seemed to say what he meant, and when he looked at someone ... at her ... she felt ... *What do I feel?*

Julia looked at Patrick, really looked at him. *It's the eyes*, she thought. *Mostly the eyes. Kind eyes ... genuine ... eyes you could get lost in ... definitely the eyes*, she decided.

She remembered what Jill had said earlier; "Patrick is so old," she'd said, as though he were tripping over a long grey beard or something.

But Jill didn't deny that he's attractive ... no, she didn't do that.

She realized that both Patrick and Mac were staring at her.

"Not the most interesting of conversations, I'm afraid," Patrick said, gently. "Perhaps it's time we called it a night."

"The night is still young," Julia protested, but he was already out of his chair.

"The night may be young, but I'm not," he told her as he helped her to her feet.

"So old," she said with a soft chuckle. "Patrick is *so* old."

Mac laughed at her comment, and she felt her cheeks go warm with embarrassment. But Patrick simply smiled down at her.

Nice smile, she thought. *Warm ... attractive smile.* Julia shook her head to clear her thoughts.

"Perhaps it is time to go," she acknowledged, reluctantly.

Mac followed them out to the street. To his obvious surprise—and to her own, for that matter—Julia gave him a hug as they said their goodbyes. Then she pointed Patrick in the direction of her bungalow.

Their footsteps echoed along an otherwise deserted Hoyt Street. Patrick stayed close, close enough to catch her if she lost her balance, she could tell, so Julia pretended to wobble a little and leaned up against him. After a moment's hesitation, he put his arm around her shoulder.

The Patricia Court Apartments came into view far too soon, and she guided him into the narrow courtyard. Julia hesitated on her doorstep, not wanting to open the door or cross the threshold, not wanting the evening to end.

"What we need here is a key," Patrick suggested at last, breaking the spell.

Julia sighed and pulled her keys from her beaded handbag. With only the slightest difficulty, she managed to fit the right key into the door and unlock it. She stepped forward, bracing herself against the frame, and looked up at him.

"Thank you, kind sir."

"M'lady," he said, matching her mock formality.

She smiled. Then, on impulse, she leaned forward and kissed his cheek, just as close to his lips as she dared, before hurrying inside. The door closed with a solid click behind her.

"You're a regular Valentino with the ladies, you know that?"

"I don't want to talk about it, Mac."

"Or maybe Svengali. I could call you *Sven*, for short."

Patrick sighed. After walking Julia home, he'd returned reluctantly to his friend at the bar, sure that Julia's behavior would almost certainly be the first topic of discussion. Seeing the sly grin on Mac's face when he entered the room, he knew that he'd been right.

"I'm serious, Mac," Patrick told him, firmly. "Julia's been through hell in the last few days. She's feeling alone and afraid, and confusing friendship for something else, that's all."

Mac nodded. "I'm sure you're right," his friend said, unconvincingly.

Patrick couldn't blame him; the truth was, Patrick wasn't very convinced himself. Julia kept showing very Rachel-like signs of being infatuated with him. As Yogi Berra would one day say, "It's like deja-vu, all over again." Patrick frowned at the thought, and decided to get to the real reason he'd come back to see Mac.

"Brent was at the Benson tonight," he announced to his friend.

"What the hell was *he* doing there?"

Patrick shrugged. "Apparently it was just a coincidence. He was attending some banquet and he happened to run into Julia by chance."

"Did he see you?"

"I doubt it. He never came in to the dining room. They talked for a few minutes out in the lobby."

"About?"

"Seems there's a meeting Monday morning with someone from the law firm of Bishop and Goldmark, to discuss some papers Carl signed."

"The Peregrine deal?"

"I think that's a pretty safe assumption. My guess is that Brent's trying to wrap this whole thing up as quickly as possible."

"What are you going to do?"

"I promised Julia that I'd be there with her, but that's as much of a plan as I have at this point. Frankly, the thought of going head to head with two attorneys is a little intimidating."

Mac smiled. "In a court of law, sure, but in the real world they're usually not that much harder to deal with than anyone else. You just have to figure out the chinks in their armor.

"I've had to deal with more lawyers than I'd care to admit over the years. Most of them are pretty decent guys, when it comes right down to it. But decent or not, there's something that's true of almost all of them: They'll do almost anything to protect their reputations, and the reputations of their clients.

"Now," he continued, warming to the subject, "I'd say the odds are good that Peregrine's lawyer doesn't know what Brent's really up to, or he wouldn't come within a hundred yards of this business, not with a hangman's noose waiting. So Brent has to set things up in such a way that Bishop and Goldmark are convinced Carl signed off on the sale, and that his death was nothing more than a tragic coincidence."

Patrick thought of the money in his room upstairs, the down payment that wasn't on Carl's desk when the police found Lundgren's body.

"As long as everything goes smoothly," Mac pointed out, "then their lawyer has no reason to worry or start asking questions. But if the going starts getting rocky enough, then maybe ... just maybe ... he starts asking questions that Brent doesn't have ready answers to."

Saturday mornings were the busiest of the week around the Campbell. In addition to the hotel guests, the neighborhood regulars saw to it that the restaurant stayed hopping from seven o'clock on. Mac's days started much earlier than that, of course. If he'd had his druthers, they would hire someone to come in and manage the dining room—especially given the fact that he had to close the bar every night—but there never seemed to be enough money to make that happen.

Besides, he admitted, Lucille kind of liked having him around all of the time.

Mac spotted Julia coming in through the street door. She gave a little wave and a smile when she saw him. He grinned in response as he headed her way.

"How are you this morning, Mr. McKenzie?"

"Never better, Julia, but I thought we settled all that *Mr. McKenzie* business. And how are you?"

"Famished," she confided, then, in a softer voice she added, "and a little embarrassed about last night, Mac. I think that last drink went straight to my head."

"That's the whole idea," he confided with a wink as he guided her to a table. "Dining with us two mornings in a row. You must really enjoy the food here. Or is it the company you come for?"

"Am I really that obvious?"

"Not really," Mac lied. "I'm just more observant than most. Blame it on my days as a detective."

"And what did you detect from Patrick while all of this was going on?"

Under other circumstances, Mac might have delighted in stoking the romantic fire just for the pure mischief of it. Then he remembered Brent—remembered what he'd done to Maggie, and to Julia's father—and the urge to play Cupid faded quickly.

"Patrick knows that you're going through a difficult time, and what you need most at the moment is a friend. You couldn't ask for a better one. Keep him close."

She grinned. "Oh, I intend to."

Well, Patrick, Mac thought as he walked away from the table to get Julia's coffee, *you can't say I didn't try.*

Ten minutes after Julia sat down, Patrick wandered in through the hotel entrance. She watched him glance around the dining room, and was relieved to see him smile when he spotted her. He stopped briefly to have a word with Mac, then headed over to her table. At least she hadn't frightened him away the night before with her forwardness.

Now would be a bad time to let that happen, regardless of how she'd begun to feel about him. Mac had been right about that much. She needed a friend, now more than ever. *As for the rest, well ...*

"You look deep in thought," Patrick noted as he settled in across the table from her. "Is everything all right?"

"Everything is just fine, although I think I might owe you a bit of an apology. I'm afraid that the alcohol last night made me a little daffy."

"I call that the McKenzie Effect." He smiled reassuringly. "I should have warned you. The same thing happens to me every time I drink with Mac."

"I'll be sure to take that into consideration the next time I suggest a nightcap. How are you this morning? Did you come back for another round after walking me home?"

"Two questions at once," he pointed out, "but I'll take them in order. I am well, in large part because I did *not* let Mac pour another for me when I got back. By the way, I'm looking forward to the ballgame this afternoon, assuming the offer still stands."

"To tell you the truth, I'd completely forgotten," Julia admitted with embarrassment.

"I see how you are." He feigned a hurt expression. "And after I've rearranged my entire schedule for the day."

She laughed. "Well, since I've put you to so much trouble, I suppose that the least I can do is suffer through an afternoon of baseball with you."

Leon heard the elevator kick into life just beyond his outer office door. The sound caught his attention because the building was virtually empty on Saturdays, and the elevator hadn't moved since he'd ridden it up to the sixth floor about an hour earlier. The cables hummed as the car descended back down toward the lobby.

That should be them, he thought. He checked his watch and saw that it showed almost half past twelve. "Better fucking be them," he muttered angrily to himself. *This meeting should have been over and done with by now.*

He heard the metallic clanking of the elevator doors opening and closing in the distance, then the whine of the motor hauling the car back up the shaft. After what seemed an interminable wait, the doors opened once more, this time on his floor. Through the opaque glass of his door, he could clearly make out the shadows of two men.

Leon waited patiently, the Colt in his hand beneath the desk.

One of the visitors rapped quietly on the glass, and he called for them to come in. When they entered, Leon felt himself relax. He recognized both men as being part of Lewis's organization from his visits to Cicero's, although he'd never spoken to either of them.

"Mr. Brent?" the taller of the two asked, tentatively. When the lawyer nodded, he said, "I'm Lanzo, and this is Mickey. Mr. De Campo said that you had a job."

"And did he also happen to mention that you were supposed to be here a half hour ago?" Leon eyed them coldly as he placed the pistol he'd been holding on top of his desk blotter.

Neither man seemed fazed by the sight of the Colt in front of the attorney. Lanzo simply shrugged and glanced at Mickey, who at least managed to look contrite.

"Sorry, Mr. Brent," he apologized. "My youngest boy, Tony, woke up sick last night, throwing up something awful. My wife and I spent most of the morning trying to clean up the mess." He paused, apparently waiting for some kind of response from Leon. When there was none, he added, "He's feeling much better, now."

"Frankly, I don't give a goddamn about your domestic issues," the attorney told Mickey in a soft, steely voice. "Now, get in here and close that door."

De Campo's boys shuffled inside. When the latch clicked shut behind them, Leon motioned for them to take a seat. He studied them for a few moments, letting the silence reinforce the fact that they were on his dime now.

Lanzo, the tallest of the two men, sat rigidly in the straight-backed chair and stared back at the lawyer without expression, waiting patiently. His thin face and lean frame stood in perfect counterpoint to his partner's squat, beefy physique.

For his part, Mickey leaned forward in his seat, thick hands fidgeting a little as he rested them on top of his knees. When Leon made eye contact with him, the little man shot him a goofy grin.

"So, what's this job?" he asked, pleasantly, breaking the silence.

"How much did De Campo tell you?" Leon asked.

"Just that you had a line on some guy that Mr. Pellizotti was looking for. He said you'd fill in the details. What's the guy's name?"

"I don't know yet. But he's been spotted with this woman." Leon slid a file across his desk.

Lanzo picked the manila folder up and opened it, holding the contents so that his partner could see from where he sat. Mickey reached over and pulled out a photograph, holding it carefully between his stubby fingers.

"Not too hard on the eyes," Lanzo observed. "What do you have on her?"

"Her name is Julia Lundgren. She lives in the Patricia Court bungalows. The address is on the back there."

Mickey flipped the photograph over, glancing at what Leon had written there.

"Memorize it," the lawyer directed, "because the picture stays here with me."

"Patricia Court, no problem. I take it you want us to watch the bungalow until our guy shows up, that it?"

"Julia's not the kind of woman to have men calling on her at her bungalow. No, you'll have to follow her until she leads you to him."

Lanzo took the photograph back from his partner and, after another quick look at Julia's picture, returned it to the file.

"And then what?" he asked as he handed the folder back to Leon. "Kill him?"

"No, you don't fucking kill him. I don't want you two to wipe your fucking *noses* without my say so, understand? You get in touch with me, and I'll tell you what to do next."

"Got it," Mickey nodded, undisturbed by the lawyer's tirade. "So what does this guy of ours look like?"

Leon described the man's general appearance. Lanzo and Mickey looked at each other, then back to the lawyer.

"Well, that narrows it down to about a thousand guys in Portland," Mickey said, unable—or unwilling—to completely mask his sarcasm. "That's the best you can do?"

"Just follow the girl," Leon snarled. "You'll find him. Now, get your asses moving and call me as soon as you come up with something." He wrote his private number down on the back of a business card and handed it to Lanzo.

"Sure thing, Mr. Brent," Mickey said as they stood and moved toward the door. He was just about to turn the knob when he paused.

"One more thing, though." He swung slowly back around to face the attorney. "We didn't discuss money."

"Money?" Leon glared at the two men. "I told you, this is for Pellizotti."

"That's right, you did." Mickey smiled thinly. "But since no one, including Mr. De Campo, has heard from him since he left town, we only have your word on that, don't we?"

His smile faded, and for the first time Leon could see the predator beneath the short man's exterior. "We get one hundred—each, per day—to locate this guy. Another grand if you're planning on having us make him disappear for good. If it turns out that Pellizotti is okay with this, then you can collect from him when he gets back."

"Fine. Just make it fast."

Mickey's smile returned. "Have a good day, counselor," he said as the door swung closed behind them.

"What do you think?" Lanzo asked his friend as they stepped out of the Dekum Building.

Instead of answering immediately, Mickey took a moment to adjust his hat, shading the midday sun out of his eyes. Satisfied, he looked at his partner and shrugged.

"I don't know. Maybe he's on the level about Pellizotti, or maybe he's just some jealous prick and this guy we're looking for is sniffing around his girlfriend. We get paid either way."

They started up Washington Street, toward the garage where they left their car.

"You know what I hate about our line of work?" Mickey said as they walked.

Lanzo shook his head. "No, Mick, what do you hate?"

"I hate how we never seem to get to knock off the guys I'd really like to see knocked off."

There it was, all laid out in black and white. The papers strewn across Leon's desk had revealed a solution to his problems. Perhaps even the *final* solution, if worse came to worst.

He'd had to go all the way back through the records to find what he'd been looking for, clear back to the earliest days of Lundgren's company.

In 1902, Carl had just begun to dabble in the furniture making business, but he lacked the capital to get started. His childhood friend, John Ingersol, convinced two other businessmen in the city—Julius Meier and C.S. Jackson—to help the fledgling company get off of the ground. Lundgren steadfastly refused to let the three men take the risk of investing in him, but he finally relented and accepted loans from each of them.

Within two years of Lundgren's successes at the Lewis and Clark Exposition, all three loans had been repaid, with interest. What Leon hadn't realized, not until he'd found the document sitting in front of him, was that the story hadn't ended there.

Leon allowed himself a smile. He put the Lundgren and Ingersol folders back in his filing cabinet and grabbed his hat off of the coat rack near the outer door. He felt like whistling.

In a simple act of generosity lay the seeds of his salvation. On the day that Carl had written the last check to pay off the loans, he'd also found a way to thank John Ingersol for the faith he'd shown; he'd given his good friend a twenty percent interest in Lundgren Furniture.

Julia was the last of the Lundgrens. When Carl died, she inherited everything as his sole living heir. But if Julia died as well, John Ingersol would have controlling interest in the factory.

If only I'd learned about that arrangement two months ago, he mused as he locked the office up behind him, *everything could have been resolved a lot sooner and with a great deal less fuss. After all, one big accident would have been so much easier to arrange than two small ones.*

–14–

Julia and Patrick jumped onto the No. 17 streetcar as it trundled north along 23rd Avenue. Judging from the snippets of conversation that Patrick could catch, most of the riders around them were also bound for the Vaughn Street ballpark. Outwardly, the passengers didn't resemble the baseball fans that Patrick had grown up with. The men wore slacks and ties, and light seersucker sports coats over button-down shirts. All of them wore hats, not team caps. Most favored straw "skimmers" with wide brims, like the one Mac had loaned Patrick for the game, to shade them from the August sun.

But close your eyes, Patrick thought, *and baseball fans sound the same in any era.* Only the players' nicknames lent a sepia-toned air to the conversations: There were "Raw Meat" Rodgers and "Junk" Walters for the Portland team, (the latter apparently catching or pitching for the home nine that afternoon, Patrick couldn't quite make out which); "Iron Horse" Lou Gehrig and "The Bambino," Babe Ruth, who had hit his 28th home run of the season against Philadelphia a few days earlier; "Bucketfoot" Al Simmons of those same Philadelphia Athletics, and the aptly-named "Hack" Wilson of Patrick's own Chicago Cubs.

The visiting team that afternoon would be, it seemed, the Sacramento Senators, but Patrick found himself more than a little confused about the identity of the Portland team. Some of the fans called them the Ducks, most referred to them as the Beavers, while one woman seated across from them seemed to be talking about the Rosebuds, although he'd probably misheard her.

"What *is* the name of your team?" he asked Julia, finally.

She simply grinned in response, while the gentleman standing in front of them laughed.

"Depends on who you're talking to," he said. "It's been the Beavers since oh-six, but for some reason the powers that be decided that name wasn't good enough this year and changed it to the Ducks. I guess they figured a new name might bring 'em more luck."

"Should have changed the players, then, instead of the name," someone said from the front of the streetcar, eliciting more than a few laughs and nods of agreement.

"Maybe Ducks seemed appropriate, given the number of eggs they've put up on the scoreboard this year," another man joked.

"Earlier in the season they called them the Rosebuds," Julia pointed out with a laugh. "Now there's a name that will strike fear in the hearts of your opponent."

"I liked the Rosebuds," protested the grey-haired woman across the aisle.

"Mother, you can't root for a team named after a flower," the elderly man seated next to her said. "It isn't right."

"What about our hockey team?" she pointed out. "The Portland Rosebuds played for the Stanley Cup in 1916."

"And are nowhere to be seen *now*, are they?" The elderly man replied, chuckling.

Julia nudged Patrick gently in the ribs, grinning up at him. "You see the can of worms you've opened? They'll be arguing about this all the way to the game."

"Then my work here is done," he told her, feigning a serious expression.

The streetcar emptied quickly in front of the Vaughn Street gate. Julia slipped her arm under Patrick's and guided him over to the ticket booth where a large group had already queued up to pay their admission. When their turn came at the window, the woman behind the counter looked up and smiled warmly.

"Miss Lundgren! I'm so happy to see you here. We were all terribly sorry to hear about your father."

"Thank you, Mae. I'm sure that would have meant a lot to him."

Mae looked from Julia to Patrick, then back again. "Two along the first base side?" she asked, her tone very nearly betraying none of her curiosity.

"Please, and twenty for the bleachers, as well," Julia added.

Mae smiled as she counted out the tickets and Julia's change.

"There will be a lot of very happy kids this afternoon," she said as she pushed the long strips of orange tickets across the well-worn wooden counter.

"I hope so," Julia said, clutching the paper strands in her hand. "That's what childhood is supposed to be about, isn't it?"

She turned and, with Patrick following close behind, walked west along Vaughn Street toward the far end of the ballpark. As he caught up with her, he saw the glistening of tears in her eyes. He fell a half-step behind so that she could have a moment to herself.

"I'd rather have you beside me." Julia reached back with her right hand and pulled him forward as he took hold of it. When he was alongside once more she gave his hand a quick squeeze, then released him to wipe the tears from her cheeks.

"Will it ever stop hurting?" she asked in a voice so soft she might have been speaking to herself.

In Patrick's mind he could see a much older Julia—silver-haired and dignified—a shadow of sadness drifting across her features as she talked about her father.

"Not completely."

Julia turned to face him, surprise at his candor obvious in her eyes.

"Oh, the pain you're feeling right now will fade, and life will find ways to fill the emptiness. Work, family ..."

"Friends," she offered, reaching out to take his hand in hers once more. Patrick smiled.

"And friends. You have a lot of people who care about you, and you always will. You, Miss Lundgren, will be much beloved."

Julia's cheeks reddened, and she looked away in embarrassment.

"But," he continued, "when someone important is taken away there's always some piece of them that's left behind. From time to time the memories are going to flare up, dull and aching, like an old wound."

With his free hand, Patrick gently touched her chin, turning her to face him.

"Believe it or not, you don't want to lose that. That's how we know they're still with us."

Tears welled up in her eyes, and he prepared himself for the flood of emotion that would surely follow. Instead, she simply dropped her chin until her forehead came to rest against his chest. He put his arms around her shoulders as she took deep, measured breaths to calm herself.

As he held her, he noticed a large group of young boys watching them intently from the corner.

"I think we have an audience."

Julia reluctantly stepped back and turned her head to look.

"Lundgren's Army," she told him, managing a small laugh as she wiped the last of her tears away.

"Lundgren's Army?"

"That's what Papa always called the boys he bought the tickets for." She looked down at the orange strips in her hand. "We'd better get these to them or they'll miss the first pitch."

Together, they walked toward the eagerly waiting kids gathered at the far corner of the ballpark fence. There were probably two dozen boys assembled there. The oldest looked perhaps fourteen or fifteen, and the youngest no more than seven, younger than Patrick would have expected to be running around the neighborhood without parents. Then again, this world probably still retained some of its innocence where childhood was concerned.

The kids jockeyed for position, nudging and pushing each other to move to the front of the pack. By the time Patrick and Julia arrived at the corner, the pecking order seemed to have been settled. The larger kids stood in front, while the smaller ones peeked sadly out from behind.

"Good morning, boys," Julia said. Patrick thought she sounded surprisingly chipper given the emotions she had churning inside.

"Good morning, Miss Lundgren," came the chorus of young voices.

She eyed the group like a general inspecting the troops. *Lundgren's Army, indeed.*

"You're all growing up so quickly," she said at last, affection evident in her voice. "But I'm surprised at you older boys. You remember my papa's rule."

"Yes, ma'am," the tallest one said, reluctantly. "The littler kids get the first tickets."

"That's right, Edgar." Julia rewarded his honesty with a warm smile.

At once the boys relegated to the back of the group flowed forward, like a wave surging through a picket fence. Julia handed one of the ticket strands to Patrick and they started passing them out to the eager children. Clutching their treasures, they raced off to the ballpark entrance as the next in line thrust his hand out anxiously.

In no time, all twenty of the passes had been doled out. Five boys still remained, looking hopeful.

"I'm sorry, boys," Julia told them. "The tickets went pretty quickly today."

"That's alright, Miss Lundgren," they said, almost in unison. Their disappointment was obvious. "Thank you anyway."

Julia smiled at their stoic display. After a moment's hesitation, she reached into the small beaded purse she carried and pulled out a leather coin purse. Undoing the clasp, she extracted five shiny dimes.

"Just this once," she told them as she placed a coin in each of their palms, "because you were all so polite."

The coins brought another round of appreciation from the boys. They all hurried off to purchase their tickets, all except for one towheaded boy—about nine or ten years old—who remained behind. Hands thrust deep into his overalls, he studied Julia and Patrick silently.

"Yes, Johnny?" she prompted, amusement written on her face.

"Who is he?" the boy asked, matter-of-factly.

"This is my friend, Mister O'Connell."

Johnny looked Patrick over as though he were about to pass judgment. "Did he make you cry?"

"No, Johnny, he didn't make me cry. He was comforting me."

"Then why were you crying?"

"John Michael Paveskovich! What would your mother say if she heard you asking a question like that?"

The boy flinched at the sound of his full name. "I'm sorry, Miss Lundgren," he said, earnestly.

"That's okay, Johnny," Julia told him. The boy smiled but stood his ground as he waited for an answer to his question. She sighed in resignation. "I was crying because I just lost my papa."

"Oh." A troubled look crossed the boy's face for a moment as he looked from Patrick back to Julia. "Then, is he your beau?"

She laughed as she reached out to tousle Johnny's blonde hair.

"No, Johnny, Mister O'Connell and I are just friends. *For the time being,*" she added in a voice so soft Patrick nearly missed it.

Apparently satisfied, Johnny grinned and ran off to catch up with his friends.

"You know that you have a secret admirer, don't you?" Patrick pointed out as they watched the boy scamper off.

"Johnny?" Julia laughed again and slid her arm under Patrick's. "That's not really much of a secret. Papa always said that the only thing in the world Johnny liked more than me was baseball. Confidentially, I don't think I run a close second in that contest."

"Paveskovich ... Is that Russian?"

"Croatian, I think. It took me awhile to learn how to pronounce it," Julia admitted. "Papa simply called him 'Little Pesky' for short. He said that was more appropriate for Johnny, anyway."

Baseball is the perfect game for time travelers, Patrick decided. *Regardless of the decade, four balls still earns a walk, three strikes an out.* Even more than the game's traditions, though, Patrick appreciated baseball for its unpredictability.

On any given afternoon the miraculous could, and often did, happen; a rookie pitcher throwing a no-hitter against the league's best offense, or a hobbled Kirk Gibson limping up to the plate to hit a pinch hit home run and win a World Series game. Every boy in the bleachers could picture himself a hero, every old man remember his own days on the diamond.

That afternoon, watching the Portland Ducks face off against the Senators of Sacramento, Patrick witnessed something he felt certain that he would never see in his own time. In the first game of the double-header, "Junk" Walters pitched a complete game for the home team, losing five to three on a throwing error in the top of the ninth that cost the Ducks two runs. The player responsible for the error was Walter's burly catcher, Ed Tomlin, who had otherwise played a stellar game.

To Patrick's amazement, in the second game of the afternoon the two men switched positions, with Walters settling in behind the plate to play backstop for Tomlin.

"They did that once before—Walters and Tomlin—in a double header last month," Julia told Patrick. "Called it the 'Reversible Battery.' The fans loved it. Of course, we won both games that day, so that might have something to do with why it was so popular."

Unfortunately for the home crowd, Sacramento had the Ducks' number this time around. Like Walters, Ed Tomlin threw a complete game—admittedly more the rule than the exception at this stage of baseball history, Patrick knew—but the Senators once again came up with ninth inning heroics to win, four to three. Even so, losing both ends of the double header seemed to do little to dampen the spirits of the Portland faithful.

"We haven't been very good for awhile now, so perhaps our expectations have just been lowered," Julia admitted as they joined the crowd making its way toward the gate. "I think I was ten the last time Portland took the pennant."

"I know how that feels. Growing up a Chicago Cubs fan in the Midwest traditionally means high hopes in spring and heartbreak by summer. The last time we won the World Series, in 1909, Taft was in the White House."

"You poor thing," Julia said with a grin. "Twenty years is a long time to wait, I'll grant you, but things are bound to turn around for the Cubs soon."

Patrick laughed. *Eighty one years and counting*, he thought to himself.

"I wouldn't want to put any money on that," he told her, simply.

By the time they reached the sidewalk outside of the ballpark, fans were already lined up six deep to board the next streetcar. Julia looked at the congestion, then turned to Patrick.

"You don't mind walking, do you?" she asked as she took his arm and guided him away from the steadily growing throng. Instead of heading east, toward 23rd, she led him west along Vaughn Street.

"I know I'm not from around these parts," he said as they strolled at a leisurely pace, "but aren't we going in the wrong direction?"

"All part of my clever plan to keep you around a little longer." Julia smiled slyly. "Actually, I want to show you something I think every visitor to this city should see."

They crossed the street and walked north to Upshur, where they turned west once more. Two blocks later Julia's tourist destination came into view. Patrick flattered himself that he was not easily impressed, but the structure in front of him—composed entirely of some of the most massive logs he'd ever seen—was nothing short of jaw-dropping.

"What do you think?"

"What do I think? It's incredible. I half expect to see Paul Bunyan and his blue ox coming around the corner. I'm guessing this is left over from the Lewis and Clark Exposition?"

She nodded. "Most of the buildings were meant to be torn down right after the fair closed. Even the lake they built everything around is gone now, drained to make way for factories and warehouses, so the old Forestry Building here is just about the last remaining vestige of the Exposition. As big as it is, it will probably still be around long after we're gone."

Except it wouldn't be, Patrick was sure. A building like this wasn't something he would have been likely to miss. Standing at least two hundred feet long and two storeys high—although in reality it looked more like three, even without the impressive gables at each end—the structure towered over the neighborhood.

Along the southern side of the building, eight majestic pillars of Douglas fir supported the awning high above the main entrance to the structure. No attempt had been made to remove the bark from the tree, no sanding or shaping of the wood into columns. It appeared for all the world as though these trees had been growing on the hill for centuries, simply waiting for the building to rise up around them.

But if the façade had seemed incredible, what waited inside was nothing short of awe-inspiring. The inner hall had been lined on either side by forty-four additional old-growth firs, nearly identical in diameter to one another—and to the columns that had greeted them out front—and, like those other columns, all still in their natural, unpeeled beauty.

"Anything like this back in Wisconsin?"

"Not that I've ever seen." Patrick could only imagine the herculean feat the builders had engaged in to create this miracle; first to locate so many trees of this stature, then to transport them from the forest to this site.

"Come with me." She took him by the hand. "There's something that I want you to see."

She led him past the exhibits of stuffed deer and elk, and glass cases containing logging artifacts from Oregon's pioneering days, to the far side of the hall and a long line of beautifully crafted wooden benches. A small brass plaque had been imbedded in the top rail of each bench, bearing the inscription, *Lundgren Furniture Makers Portland Oregon*.

"This is how Lundgren Furniture really started," Julia told him. "Papa made fifty of these, all total. They were scattered throughout the Exposition. I guess they cost him almost as much to make as the contract paid for them, but he thought it would be good publicity. Besides, he wanted to do something to contribute."

"Your father made furniture for some of the nearby hotels, as well, didn't he?"

She nodded. "He provided the furniture for the lobby of the American Inn, which was actually on the fairgrounds, and tables for the rooms at the Hotel Fairmont and the Outside Inn."

"All with these little plaques, no doubt."

"That was the key, Papa said. It worked, too. People from all over the country saw his benches at the Exposition each day, and his other pieces at the hotel each night. Before the year was over, we were receiving orders from coast to coast."

Patrick noted the *we* in that sentence with satisfaction; consciously or unconsciously, Julia had begun to think of Lundgren Furniture as her birthright.

"Pretty canny," he conceded. "And the rest, as they say, is history."

A troubled expression crossed her features. He turned her gently so that they were facing each other.

"You're worried that the rest might really *be* history, aren't you?"

She looked down at her feet. Patrick touched her chin, nudging it up so that he could see her eyes once more. There were no tears this time, he noted with relief, just a look of deep concern.

"Julia, you have to trust me on this. Lundgren Furniture will be around for a great many years to come, and you're going to be the reason. Your father left the family business in the best of all possible hands."

"You don't know that."

"Yes, I do," he said, firmly.

Now the tears started to well up in her eyes, and he instinctively pulled her close, holding her close against his chest. He waited for the dam to burst. But the waterworks never came, nor the sobs. Just deep, controlled breaths as—for the second time that afternoon—she managed to quickly bring her emotions into check. Still, she made no effort to pull away from his embrace.

A few people nearby were beginning to look their way, some scowling at the impropriety of such a public display, others with concern or amusement.

"If we're not careful, we might cause a scandal here," Patrick whispered to Julia.

"A little scandal is good for the soul," she replied, her voice muffled against his shirt. Nevertheless, she straightened and moved away, brushing the moisture from her eyes.

"Perhaps a little fresh air might do us both some good?" he suggested.

"As you say, Professor," she replied, unknowingly echoing her future granddaughter's nickname for him. She took his arm and guided him back toward the entrance.

"I still don't see why you have to inspect the damned place on a Saturday afternoon." Abner Cooper held his large key ring up, searching for the one that would open the Dekum Building's front doors. "I was about to go have a ... lemonade ... before you two showed up."

The fireman with the captain's bars nodded in understanding as the building super finally located the key he was looking for and slotted it into the lock.

"A cold one does sound fine on a hot afternoon," he agreed with a grin. "Believe me, I'll be having a beer or two myself as soon as we finish up here."

Cooper laughed at the captain's candor and pushed the door open, stepping aside to let the two firemen into the foyer. *It's a good fifteen degrees warmer in here than outside*, he thought, miserably. He pulled a stained rag from his back pocket and wiped the sweat from his brow. *Probably be even hotter upstairs.*

"How long is this going to take?"

"Well, that depends." The captain looked around, then down at the paperwork in his hand. "How many offices are there on the east side of the building?"

"About twenty, all total."

"Shouldn't take more than ten minutes for each one." The captain looked to the other fireman. "What do you think, Mac, done in three hours or so, give or take?"

His assistant nodded, wiping the sweat from his forehead with a handkerchief.

Cooper grunted in disappointment. *Three goddamned hours.* By the time he got out of there, Sadie would be home from her mother's with a list of things that she'd want him to do around the apartment. *Like I don't have enough to fix at work.*

"Well," he muttered, "that shoots getting a beer all to hell."

"Where do you usually go? Kelly's Olympian?" the captain asked.

"Sure. I've been there a time or two."

"I thought I'd seen you in there. Listen," the captain said, lowering his voice, "just because my boss saw fit to ruin my Saturday afternoon, there's no reason why you have to suffer as well. If you wanted to, you could leave us your keys and wait at Kelly's until we've finished. Hell, at that point I'll be ready to buy us all a round."

"Well, I'm not so sure." Cooper looked at the heavy ring in his hand. "I don't think the owner would like me handing these over ..."

Still, the cool basement at Kelly's sounded a damned sight more appealing than climbing up and down six flights of stairs in this heat. *Besides,* he reasoned, *these guys are firemen, for god's sake, not cops.*

In the end, the sweat trickling down his back made his decision for him.

"What the hell," he said, relinquishing the ring to the captain, "I suppose it won't hurt to stay out of your way while you do your job."

O'Halloron locked the door to the Dekum Building behind the maintenance man, then turned with a smug grin on his face. He twirled the heavy ring of keys on one finger like a gunslinger spinning his Colt.

"All right," Mac said with a laugh, "I admit it. It was a pretty damned good plan."

"Good? It was genius, pure and simple. And all it's going to cost you is the price of a few beers."

"Oh, no. I'm not parading around in this monkey suit any more than I have to."

"You've never looked better, boyo, though I'll grant you don't cut quite the figure that I do in that uniform."

"That's only because I can't puff my chest out as far as you," Mac told his friend, managing to suppress a smile. "Now, can we get on with this?" he asked, heading for the elevator.

"Fine, fine. But just so we're clear," Jim added, as he pulled the gate closed and pressed the button for the sixth floor, "you're still standing for a couple of rounds at Kelly's, right?"

The rumbling of the elevator car as it rose couldn't quite muffle Mac's laughter.

O'Halloron leaned against the wall beside Brent's office door, watching in amusement while Mac tried key after key unsuccessfully.

"I certainly hope that you were better at catching thieves than you are at being one." The Irishman's observation drew a scowl and an obscene gesture from his friend.

"If I were a thief, I'd just put my shoulder to the door and be done with it, but we don't want Brent, or anyone else, to know about this little visit, do we?"

"I suppose not, but getting inside sometime before the Second Coming would be nice."

"Don't worry. We'll finish in time for you to get that beer. Ahh ..." Mac let out a sigh of relief as the bolt slid back. "And in we go."

They entered Brent's outer office and closed the door behind them.

The reception area was almost Spartan in its décor. A row of plain wooden chairs lined one wall, facing the secretary's desk. Two tall oak filing cabinets sat along the wall opposite the windows. A glass-paneled door just beyond the cabinets led undoubtedly to Leon Brent's private office.

"Want me to take a look in the secretary's desk?"

Mac shook his head. "No point. We won't find what we're looking for there, or in these files," he added, pointing to the cabinets. "If we're going to find anything, I'm betting it'll be in Brent's office."

Everything they could have wanted to know about the man they were dealing with became clear from the furnishings of the lawyer's office. All of it—the ostentatious furniture, the expensively framed diploma and photos of Brent with the governor and mayor—every detail was designed to intimidate, pure and simple. Exactly what Mac would have expected, given what he'd already learned about the man.

"What a pompous prick," Jim muttered.

"In spades. Now let's find out exactly what this prick is up to. You start with that filing cabinet over there. Look for anything on Peregrine Industries or Lundgren Furniture. I'll take his desk."

The first two drawers Mac searched held nothing of value. In the next, however, he found Brent's ledger book. For the most part, the entries looked pretty standard; client names next to deposits, routine expenses in the debit column. But more than a few of the line items—most of them in fairly large amounts—were accompanied by decidedly vague entries. As Mac glanced through the pages, two deposits in particular caught his attention.

On July 15th, Brent deposited fifteen hundred dollars from "BG." On August 2nd, he'd deposited another twenty-five hundred from the same source. Could "BG" stand for Bishop and Goldmark, the law firm Julia was meeting with on Monday? Mac knew it was probably a long shot, but long shots paid off sometimes.

"Find anything interesting?" O'Halloron asked.

"Either Brent is a lousy bookkeeper, or there are details about his business he wants no record of. What about you? Making any headway over there?"

Jim grinned, holding a thick folder up in his right hand, and a much thinner one in his left.

"Lundgren, Carl," he said, nodding to the larger file. "Apparently, our attorney friend is as bad at filing as he is at accounting. I found it tucked away under *I* rather than the L."

"How about the other folder?"

"Peregrine Industries. Not much in this one, though."

Jim brought both over to Brent's desk. Mac opened the smaller file first.

At the front of the small collection of documents, he found a letter from the firm of—surprise, surprise—Bishop and Goldmark, dated August 2nd, the same day as one of the mystery deposits.

> *We have received in our offices the signed contract, finalizing the sale of Lundgren Furniture, Portland, OR to Peregrine Industries, Boston, MA. In accordance with the contract, and pursuant to our conversation of 26, July last, you will find enclosed a check made out to Mr. Lundgren in the amount of five thousand dollars, representing the agreed-upon down payment.*
>
> *My office will contact you early next week to complete the transfer of the Lundgren properties to our client.*
>
> *Your efforts to assist us in expediting this transaction are greatly appreciated.*
>
> *Yours,*
>
> *Stanley Goldmark*
>
> *Attorney at Law*

Beneath the letter, Mac found a copy of the purchase contract outlining the sale of Lundgren's company paper-clipped to another letter from Bishop and Goldmark, this one dated June 27th.

Mr. Brent,

I have tendered your counter-offer for the Lundgren properties to our client. They have approved a maximum purchase price of $185,000, contingent upon the completion of this transaction on or before 30 August, 1929.

I wish to emphasize that this represents my client's final offer. If for any reason these terms are not satisfactory to Mr. Lundgren, or the acquisition cannot be finalized by the date specified, Peregrine Industries will be forced to rescind their offers to purchase both Lundgren Furniture and Ingersol Tool & Die.

Please advise at your earliest convenience.

Like the first letter, this one was signed by Stanley Goldmark.

"Something?" Jim asked. Mac looked up slowly.

"You said that you found Lundgren's file with the *I's*," right?"

Jim nodded.

"Do me a favor, and see if you can find a file for John Ingersol. I-N-G ... It might be under Ingersol Tool and Die."

–15–

Northwest Portland lazed in the heat of the late afternoon sun. A few children played in their yards, or engaged in a lively game of stickball in the street, but for the most part the neighborhood seemed content to enjoy the quiet of a beautiful summer's day.

Julia and Patrick walked along Raleigh Street, past the grounds of Chapman Elementary School. A field of grass occupied the northwest corner of the lot where tennis courts would one day stand, but otherwise the schoolyard—and the school itself—were pretty much as he remembered from his own time.

"This is where you worked, isn't it?" he asked.

Julia looked at him in surprise.

"The newspaper article mentioned it," he explained.

"My first, and apparently last, year as a teacher," she answered with a sigh, looking up at the school wistfully. "Oh well, I had fun while it lasted. Hopefully, the factory will keep me too busy to dwell on it much. I *am* sad that I won't get to watch the little ones as they grow up, though."

"Oh, I'm sure you'll see them at the baseball games."

Julia looked puzzled.

"When they join the ranks of Lundgren's Army."

She laughed. "I'd better start stocking up on dimes, then, hadn't I?"

"How did you decide on teaching, anyway?"

"Papa was always very passionate about the power of education. 'Teachers yust have to plant the seeds,'" she quoted in her best Swedish accent, "'and Nature can grow miracles.' He even served on the school board for awhile, but he resigned a few years ago."

"I'm guessing the factory must have kept him pretty busy."

Julia laughed. "That man could fit twenty hours of work into a ten hour workday without batting an eye. No, he resigned out of protest. Not too far from Papa's house there's a home for—as Papa called them—'wayward women.' It was years before I figured out that meant unwed mothers," she added with a self-deprecating chuckle. "Anyway, some time back a couple of the mothers from the home tried to enroll their children at Chapman, much to the righteous indignation of more than a few of the *proper* parents in the community."

The way she spat out "proper" left no doubt how she felt about those particular parents.

"The school's principal sided with the parents and turned the girls away. When the board refused to intercede—much to Papa's outrage—he resigned on the spot."

Patrick smiled. "Somehow, from what I've heard about Carl, I doubt that was the end of the story."

Julia nodded. "Papa, and a few other more open-minded citizens around here, hired a teacher to come to the girls at the home. The factory even donated all of the chairs and desks they'd need for the classroom. Seeing those girls' faces ... it was like Christmas for them, they were so excited. And that's when I decided to become a teacher."

Her smile dimmed a little.

"Papa was so proud of me when I told him. I wonder what he'd say, now that I'm going to quit after just one year."

"Not being a teacher didn't seem to stop your father from having an impact on those girls' lives. There's a lot that a woman of influence can accomplish."

"Kind of putting the cart before the horse, aren't you? I have to figure out how to become a woman of business before I can even begin to think of becoming a woman of influence."

"You'll get there."

She accepted his assurance with a gratified, if skeptical, look.

"What about you?" she asked, redirecting the conversation. "How did you end up as a college professor? And of history, at that. You don't exactly look the part."

Patrick cast a bemused look her way.

"Not in a bad way," Julia added hastily, her cheeks reddening. "It's just that the history professors at Reed were stodgy gray beards. You're neither."

"Nice recovery," he said, chuckling. "I'm sure there's a compliment in there, somewhere."

He allowed her time to blush again before answering her question.

"The truth is," he admitted, "I just followed the path of least resistance. After the war, I had no idea what I wanted to do with my life, so I decided to go to college. I think I was hoping for some kind of epiphany, some divine inspiration ..."

"A little late in life for *that*, wasn't it?" she asked with a grin.

Patrick paused, momentarily confused. Then he realized that, when he'd returned from Vietnam, he'd only been twenty. In this timeline, he would have been at least thirty when World War I ended.

"I'm not the only soldier who came back with second thoughts about his life's goals. At any rate, I found myself a college student ... if an old one ..." he added, teasingly, "in search of a field of study. Somehow, I kept gravitating toward history, although my father was quick to point out that there wasn't any money to be made in education."

They turned onto a narrower walk, this one headed east through the school grounds.

"So, you became a teacher to spite your father?" Julia asked, coyly.

Patrick laughed. "I wouldn't put it past myself. But I also love history. I always have, as far back as I can remember."

"Why is that?"

"There are so many facets to history, so many lenses you can study the past through: political, economic, social, moral. I love the fact that there is no formula, no single right or wrong answer when you're looking at why people do the things they do."

"You almost make it sound interesting. *Almost*."

"Not a fan, I take it."

"Not really." She wrinkled her nose up in a disturbingly Rachel-like way. "At least you don't sound like the type of teacher who makes his students memorize a lot of useless names and dates. When was the last time the Alien and Sedition Acts was discussed at a social gathering, or the Compromise of 1854 ..."

"1850," Patrick corrected, earning himself a quick scowl for his trouble.

"Fine. The Compromise of 1850," she said, putting undue emphasis on the year. "When does anyone talk about *that* over lunch? What's past is past, isn't it?"

Not as much as you might believe, Patrick thought to himself.

"So, did you inherit this passion for history from your parents?" she asked as they reached the edge of the school grounds. They continued east on Quimby at an ambling pace.

"Only indirectly. When I was about ten years old, I came down with a bad case of the chicken pox and had to stay home from school for almost two weeks. There really wasn't much to do except lay in bed and read every book I could get my hands on.

"My mom and dad aren't much on reading, but somewhere along the line they ended up with a half dozen books on American history; the building of the Panama Canal, a biography of President McKinley, that sort of thing. I devoured them all in no time. And the rest, as they say ..."

"Is history," Julia finished along with him, with a chuckle. "You've already used that old chestnut, Professor O'Connell."

Their walk brought them at last to 23rd, where they joined the scattering of people wending their way through the small, cozy commercial area. Julia took Patrick's arm, and together they worked their way south along the avenue.

"So, how is that business with your friend going?" They had slowed to a stop in front of a shop window, Julia making a show of studying the dresses on display, rather than facing Patrick.

He turned her gently toward him.

"You're really wondering if I'm going to be leaving any time soon, aren't you?"

"You're right," she admitted, a hint of challenge in her expression, "that is exactly what I'm wondering."

"Then, for the record, I have no intention of leaving Portland until I know that things are settled with you and the company." Even as the words left his mouth he felt a pang of guilt, because his staying—or going—was completely beyond his control. Still, Julia needed some reassurance, not more uncertainty.

"So, you'll still be at the meeting on Monday?"

"I promised that I would be, didn't I? But you need more than the moral support of an old history professor when dealing with lawyers. If it's all right with you, I'm going to try and get in touch with Erny's friend, Ed Wirth, on Monday morning. It sounds as though you're going to be looking for a replacement for Leon Brent soon, anyway."

"As quickly as possible," Julia agreed. "I have never felt comfortable around that man."

"What do you know about him?"

"Why?"

"There's an old adage: 'know thy enemy.'"

Julia looked up at Patrick in surprise. "You think he might be my enemy?"

"Well, I'm not sure he's your friend," Patrick hedged. "And he's probably not going to be very happy when you let him go."

She considered that for a second. "Well, I can tell you that Papa never seemed to care for Mr. Brent any more than I do."

"Why did he keep him on, then?"

"Loyalty, I suppose. Mr. Brent served in the war under Uncle John ... Papa's best friend, John Ingersol."

Patrick nodded. "We met at the reception."

"Uncle John was a captain in the Army, and Mr. Brent was a sergeant or something like that. Anyway, in the last days of the war Mr. Brent was badly wounded. That's where that ugly scar on his head came from, I think. He was left for dead on the battlefield. Uncle John found him and managed to get him back to the aid station, even though he'd been wounded pretty badly himself.

"When Mr. Brent showed up in Portland after the war, Uncle John helped him establish a law office here in town, and asked Papa to become a client. I don't think he was ever very happy about the arrangement, but for Uncle John's sake, Papa stuck it out."

"Did your father ever say why he disliked Brent?"

Julia shook her head. "Not really. At least not to me. Papa always said he was a capable attorney, but I did hear him tell Uncle John once that Mr. Brent was overstepping, trying to get them to let him handle their investments as well as their legal matters, or something like that.

"Speaking of investments," she said as they stepped up onto the sidewalk in front of the Campbell, "I seem to recall that you and Mac were having an animated conversation about the stock market last night. Unfortunately, for some reason, that's about all that I remember."

Patrick laughed. "The dangers of socializing with an innkeeper. At least, *that* innkeeper," he added, nodding in the direction of the hotel's front steps, where Mac was smoking a cigarette.

The Scot stood and flicked the smoldering butt into the gutter, then started toward the corner where they stood. Even from a distance, Patrick could see his friend had a preoccupied look on his face.

"Well," Julia continued, watching Mac's approach, "I was hoping that you might give me some advice on what to do with the stocks Papa left to me. I'd welcome your thoughts as well, Mac," she offered as their friend joined them.

"My thoughts on ...?"

"The wonderful world of Wall Street," Patrick said.

"I think that I'll decline, then. The stock market and I are not on the best of terms at the moment."

"Then it falls to you," Julia said, nudging Patrick. "And in return, I'll buy your supper tonight."

Before Patrick could answer, Mac spoke up. "Actually, Julia, I was wondering if I could steal him away from you this evening. Something's come up, and I could use his help."

Patrick caught the look of disappointment in her eyes, but she recovered quickly.

"Of course, Mac. We can discuss business another time."

Mac smiled. "I'm sure he has nothing planned for tomorrow, do you?"

"Perhaps we could picnic somewhere," Julia suggested, before Patrick could even answer.

Mac clapped his beefy hands together. "That's a fine idea. I'll have my sister-in-law put something together for you. Let's say around one o'clock?"

"One would be fine," Julia said, "but you don't have to provide the food."

"I insist. It's the least I can do, since I'm depriving him of your company this evening. Besides," he added, lowering his voice conspiratorially, "this way I can charge it to his hotel bill."

Patrick laughed, raising his hands in surrender. "I don't stand a chance with the two of you working together, do I?" Julia and Mac simply looked at him, twin smirks on their faces. "It looks as though I'm going on a picnic."

Triumphant, Mac smiled at his friend. "There, that's settled. Patrick, why don't you see her home, and then we can get to work."

Julia shook her head. "That won't be necessary, Mac. You two have things to do."

"I'd feel better if one of us walked with you," the Scot insisted. He looked to Patrick for support.

"Stop worrying about me." She stepped up and gave Mac a brief hug. "You're a dear, really, but I'll be fine."

They watched as Julia disappeared around the corner, then Patrick turned to his friend.

"All right, Mac, what's going on?"

The Scot shook his head. "Later," he said, all lightness gone from his voice. He walked over to the corner, where he could see Julia as she walked down Hoyt.

"Are you planning on following her?"

"Just keeping an eye on her," Mac said. Together, they watched her in silence until she'd made the two blocks to her bungalow. Only then did Mac seem to relax a little. He turned to Patrick, seriousness etched into his features.

"Now, let's go have that talk."

The boredom is the worst part of the job, Mickey thought as he struggled to stay awake. With the late afternoon sun beating down, the car felt hot as a stove. Lanzo had already drifted off behind the wheel of the Durant, and who could blame him, sitting in a parked automobile for hours waiting for the girl they'd been sent to keep an eye out for. It was enough to make a guy start thinking about another line of employment.

Of course, the money they'd made working for Lewis had made up for a lot of these little inconveniences. Hopefully, they could expect more of the same under Pellizotti, or De Campo, or whoever the hell finally came out on top of the organization. *As long as it isn't Leon Brent,* Mickey decided, *I'll probably make out just fine.*

Any way you sliced it, Brent was, as Mickey's father would say, un grande stronzo ... a major asshole.

After leaving the attorney's office downtown, he and Lanzo had driven to the address that had been written on the back of Julia Lundgren's photograph. They found a parking spot under the shade of an old oak tree, half a block away from the Patricia Court bungalows. From there, they had a clear view of anyone coming and going. Mickey had wandered up to a nearby drugstore to find a phone booth so that he could call Floriana to check on how his son was feeling, and let his wife know not to expect him anytime soon.

That hadn't gone over well, Mickey could tell, but Flor knew better than to argue. He'd just have to find a way to make it up to her later.

They'd been camped there for almost three hours now. So far, no one in the neighborhood had shown any interest in them. In another hour or so they would move the car somewhere else to avoid suspicion, and so on, and so on, until their guy showed up.

He was just about to get out of the car and stretch when he spotted the young woman from the photograph walking toward them on the other side of the street.

"Hey, Lanzo." He nudged his dozing partner gently in the ribs to get his attention. "Here comes our chicken."

His friend grunted and yawned.

"Ahhh ... Gustosa," Lanzo observed, admiringly. "Wouldn't mind keeping a *real* close eye on that one."

"Do I need to have a talk with your wife?"

Lanzo laughed. "Why do you have to be such a fucking choir boy, Mickey? Besides, I need to have something to talk about during confession."

"Like you've ever had trouble coming up with something to confess."

"Any sign of our guy?"

Mickey shook his head. "Just the girl."

They watched as she turned right and disappeared from view through the wrought-iron entrance to Patricia Court.

"Now what?" Lanzo asked.

"Now we wait some more. Either this guy Brent wants shows up, or we follow the girl when she leaves and find him that way."

"Or this whole business is a complete fucking waste of time."

"Or that," Mickey conceded. "Whatever happens, we get paid."

Patrick took a few moments to look around Mac's quarters. There were framed photographs scattered around the room, most from his days on the force: Mac in a patrolman's uniform; a group picture in front of the Third Precinct; Mac, in street clothes, holding up a copy of a newspaper with the headline, *Warren Killer Arrested After Shootout*.

The more personal photos were on the wall over the dresser. Using his own deductive powers, Patrick surmised that the older couple in the center photograph were probably Mac's parents. It didn't hurt that Mac's father looked like an older version of his son. To the left of that picture, the same couple—perhaps thirty years younger—stood on either side of two young boys. Undoubtedly Mac and his kid brother.

The last photo showed a very fit Mac, dressed in dark swimming trunks. He was at the beach with a woman Patrick recognized at once as Mac's sister-in-law, Lucille. She was grinning up at the second man in the picture.

"That's Danny," Mac told him. "We sailed down to Bayocean for the week. A month later, he was gone from a heart attack. Thirty-eight goddamned years old."

He looked at the picture once more, then turned to sit on the end of the bed. Patrick took the chair near the window.

"I went through a few of Brent's files today," the Scot told him.

"His files? How the hell did you get a hold of his files?"

Mac arched an eyebrow. "That isn't important, but what I found just might be." He pulling the now-familiar notebook from his pocket and flipped it open. "Take a look."

Mac handed the pad over to Patrick.

"Is this in English?"

The Scot grinned, sheepishly, and took the notebook back. "So, handwriting isn't my strong suit. Here's what I found, in a nutshell. Some shady financial transactions; money coming in, money going out, but no details. There were two large deposits, by the way, totaling four thousand, from someone identified only as 'BG.'"

"Bishop and Goldmark."

"Probably, but we'll play hell proving it. There were also two letters from Stanley Goldmark to Brent, regarding Peregrine Industries' attempt to purchase Lundgren Furniture. The first one was dated ..." he checked the notebook, "June 27th. Peregrine had accepted a counter-offer for $185,000, as long as the deal was finalized by the end of August. The second one was dated about a month later; Lundgren had apparently signed the contract because they were enclosing a five thousand dollar check for Carl, to cover the down payment."

"What does all that mean, exactly?"

"My guess? I'd say that Bishop and Goldmark—or, at least, Stanley Goldmark—paid Brent to grease the wheels for the transaction. It also sounds like they thought the sale was legitimate, aside from Brent's conflict of interest. That should give you a little more leverage on Monday. Goldmark isn't going to want his firm dragged through the mud. But there's more. Lundgren Furniture wasn't the only company Peregrine was after."

Mac thumbed through a couple of pages, then handed the notebook back to his friend. This name Patrick could make out

Ingersol Tool and Die.

"You're kidding, right?"

Mac shook his head. "John Ingersol signed the contract with Peregrine on the twenty-fourth of June. The deal won't be finalized, though, until Lundgren Furniture is in the bag. It's all or nothing as far as Peregrine is concerned."

"You don't think that Ingersol is somehow involved in Carl's murder, do you?"

The Scot looked uncomfortable with the question.

"I'd say he's involved. I'm just not sure that he *knows* he's involved. There's one more thing. Did Carl have any other family besides Julia?"

"I don't think so. Why?"

"Because, back in the early days, Carl gave John Ingersol a twenty percent interest in Lundgren Furniture.

That means if Julia dies—and she has no heirs—Ingersol gains control of the company. The Peregrine deal goes through."

Patrick got up and wandered over to the window. Down below, on Hoyt, an old Model A chugged east, in the general direction of Julia's bungalow.

"What's the play, Mac?"

His friend rubbed a knuckle across the graying stubble on his chin as he thought about the question.

"With any luck," he said, "you'll be able to create enough doubt where Bishop and Goldmark are concerned to kill any chances of completing the deal. Then Brent won't have any incentive to go after Julia."

"And if I don't scare them off?"

"Playing devil's advocate here ... whatever Brent arranges for Julia, it will have to look like an accident, and a damned convincing one at that. Two deaths in the family over such a short time would be bound to raise suspicion. You'll just have to find a way to keep her close after that meeting on Monday.

"I don't think she'll object to that," he added, managing a sly smile.

After Patrick went back to his own room, Mac pulled out the drawer of his nightstand and removed the folder he'd stolen from Brent's office. He felt guilty about keeping information from his friend, but he didn't want anyone else to know about O'Halloron's part in breaking into the attorney's office. And showing Patrick the contents of the file he'd found in Brent's desk would only have caused more worry for his friend.

Mac opened the folder and studied the photograph of Julia. She was stepping out of a milliner's shop—Louella's Hats, on 23rd—unaware that someone was taking her picture at that moment. Even from a distance, the cameraman had managed to get a good enough shot of her face that anyone with a trained eye would be able to pick her out of a crowd.

Mac had run across photos like this before. Back in '22 a hood named Atcheson had gone into the blackmail business, cobbling together a group of small-timers to act as his eyes. Using pictures like these to identify their marks, Atcheson's operatives followed their would-be victims, hoping to catch them doing something that they wouldn't want their wives or husbands to know about. The scam had worked pretty well, too, until they tried it on someone who wouldn't back down. When Atcheson showed up to collect his money, Mac and his partner had been there to close him down for good.

Maybe that was all that Brent had in mind, find something on Julia that he could use to shame her into selling the company. Given the number of cases Brent had won because of witnesses who changed their testimony at the last minute, Mac was willing to bet that the bastard had been successful at that strategy more than a few times in the past.

Still, he couldn't completely ignore the possibility that Brent might be putting the wheels in motion for that accident Mac had warned Patrick about.

He closed the file and slipped it back into the drawer.

He still believed that nothing was going to happen until after the meeting with Peregrine's attorney. In the meantime, he needed to find out what John Ingersol's part was in all of this, if only for his own peace of mind.

–16–

The young woman in the mirror looked back at Julia with an amused expression for the umpteenth time that day.

"This is silly," she scolded herself as she battled with a strand of hair that had fallen out of place. "It's just a picnic with a friend."

But just because I'm making a strategic withdrawal, doesn't mean I have to concede the war.

Satisfied that the errant lock had been tamed, she applied a little lip rouge and studied the effect for a moment. *Not so bad*, she decided.

Her father's LaSalle sat at the curb outside of her bungalow, its dark green paint sparkling in the bright sunshine. Julia adored the car. She'd learned how to drive in the LaSalle during a weeklong trip along the Jeff Davis Highway to Seattle. The fact that Papa had trusted her enough to risk his new automobile and—early in the learning process, at least—his own life and limb, made the vacation one of her most special memories.

She opened the driver's side door, rolling the window down to let the summer heat escape from the closed automobile. Then she moved around to the passenger door and cranked the window down on that side as well. When she settled in behind the wheel and turned the starter, the LaSalle rumbled gently beneath her.

Lanzo tapped the dashboard to get his friend's attention. "She's leaving."

Mickey started the Durant up.

"Good," he said. "I could use a change of scenery."

The woman pulled away from the curb in a newer sedan and headed east down Hoyt. Mickey swung the Durant in behind her, easing back a little so that she wouldn't feel like they were riding up her tailpipe. The LaSalle turned right onto 21st Avenue, then right again one block later at Glisan. Mickey backed off a little bit more, confident that they could keep an eye on her from a distance.

She drove west for two blocks, turning right again onto 23rd.

"What, is she going in a fucking circle?" Lanzo muttered.

Mickey ignored the comment. The LaSalle had pulled over to the curb in front of the Campbell Hotel. He drove past and found a parking spot the next block down. Lanzo twisted around in his seat so that he could see out the back of the sedan.

"She's going inside."

Finally, Mickey thought. *Maybe now we're getting somewhere.*

Julia Lundgren came out of the hotel a few minutes later, in the company of a man. He wore a light seersucker suit and a skimmer, and carried a picnic basket. Lanzo watched as the couple settled the large basket in the back of the LaSalle.

"Think that's our guy?"

"Fits the description pretty neatly," Mickey admitted.

"So, now what?"

"After they pull away, you go see what you can find out about him. I'll stick with the lovebirds."

Lanzo nodded and climbed out of the Durant just as the other automobile nudged its way out into traffic. Mickey dropped in two cars behind them, heading north.

Lucille McKenzie placed her Sunday dress carefully on its hanger and tucked it away in the chifferobe where it would stay until next week's church services. Not what some might deem a devout woman, she nevertheless rode the trolley to Calvary Presbyterian every Sunday, except for those rare occasions when her brother-in-law let her ride in style in his automobile. Usually that only happened on Easter, and around Christmas. The rest of the year, Mac masked his ambivalence toward religion by pointing out how much work there was to do around the hotel.

Well, Lucille couldn't begrudge him that. With Danny gone, Mac had held the business together. She knew that resigning from the police force had been an incredibly difficult decision, but he'd taken that step without any prodding from her, and she thanked God for that.

She heard footsteps on the tiled floor of the lobby, then the ding of the front desk bell. Lucille took a moment to brush the wrinkles from her dress and pat her hair, making sure that she looked presentable.

The bell clanked a second time.

Why must people be so impatient these days? she wondered, scowling as she hurried from her quarters. Her door opened directly onto the area behind the hotel's front desk. A tall, angular man stood on the other side of the heavy oak counter, hand poised over the button of the bell. He seemed reluctant to lower his arm when he saw her, as though making that annoying sound had been the highlight of his day.

"May I help you?" Lucille asked, trying to hide her irritation. She caught him eyeing her up and down, appraising her.

"I was supposed to deliver a message." His tone was as neutral as the expression on his face. "But the guy I was supposed to deliver it to just drove off with that young woman."

"Mr. O'Connell?"

"That's the fella. I don't suppose you know when he might be coming back?"

"I'm sorry, I don't, but I'd be happy to deliver your message when he returns."

He shook his head.

"Thanks, but it's kind of personal. You understand. I'll try to catch up to him later." The man turned and started toward the steps and the door, then stopped and swung back around. "You don't have any idea when he might be checking out, do you?"

"I'm not at liberty to discuss the plans of our guests. You'll have to take that up with Patrick when you speak with him."

"Fair enough," the tall man said, the hint of a smile starting to show on his otherwise expressionless features. "That's just what I'll do. Thanks again, sugar. You've been a lot of help."

Sugar? Lucille scowled as the doors swung closed behind the man. *If that's the kind of rude company O'Connell keeps, then there's one more reason I won't be sorry to see him check out.*

"Where are we going for this picnic of yours?"

Julia smiled as she signaled for a left turn onto Thurman.

"A nice, quiet little spot out in the country. I hope it won't take too long to get there, because lunch smells delicious."

Mac's sister-in-law had packed the wicker basket with a small roasted chicken that already had Julia's mouth watering. Mac had hinted at other treats as well, including a little something extra hidden somewhere in the bottom of the carrier. Knowing him, that meant alcohol.

Julia glanced in Patrick's direction and wondered if getting him a little ossified might break that wall of respectability down enough to make some headway.

Lanzo headed for the payphone at Northwest Pharmacy, two blocks from the hotel. All in all, things were percolating pretty nicely. One day into the job and they had both an address and a name for Brent's mystery man.

He bought a pack of Lucky Strikes from the druggist, then made his way to the back of the narrow shop. The phone booth was tucked into an alcove at the end of the small lunch counter. Lanzo ducked inside and fished in his pocket for a nickel. He was about to drop the coin into the slot when he realized that the attorney's business card was currently sitting in Mickey's coat pocket, whereabouts unknown. He lit a cigarette and considered his options.

He could head back to the Campbell and find a spot to camp out until this O'Connell bird made an appearance. *Of course,* Lanzo thought, *if it were me picnicking with that hot little number, we wouldn't be back for hours. There's no way I'm sitting on my ass waiting for Brent's girl and her beau to come wandering home.*

He reached into his pocket and pulled out the small, leather-bound book he kept there. Running his thumbnail down the phone numbers, he quickly found the entry he was looking for. His nickel dropped into the slot with a satisfying clunk. A moment later the phone at the other end of the line was picked up.

"Hazel? It's me, Lanzo. How's my favorite little cuddler?"

"Lanzo? Where are you?"

"About three blocks away, and I find myself with a couple of hours to kill. Interested?"

"Are you going to make it worth my while?"

Lanzo laughed. "Don't I always, sweetness?"

Julia guided the LaSalle up the hill along Thurman, past her father's house and around the next curve.

"Leif Erikson Drive," Patrick said, softly.

She looked at him in surprise.

"How did you know that?"

"Someone told me about this road," he answered, vaguely. "The trees are beautiful this time of year."

"I love it up here. On summer evenings, this road is a veritable lovers' lane. You should see it sometime."

Patrick glanced her way, an amused expression on his face. Apparently, he decided to let her subtle innuendo go unanswered.

They drove along at a leisurely pace. Occasionally, Julia caught sight of a car in her rearview mirror—the only one they'd seen in awhile—but the driver appeared to be in no more of a hurry than they were. After a time, she paid it no further mind.

For his part, Patrick seemed content to watch the forest roll by slowly. The quiet weighed more heavily on Julia, like a void in need of filling.

"I'm glad you decided to come, today," she told him.

"The way you and Mac had me outmaneuvered, how could I refuse?"

"I'd rather you were here because you wanted to be."

He turned to her and flashed that absurdly charming, slightly amused grin of his. "I can't think of anywhere else I'd rather be on a beautiful day like today. As long as you don't have ulterior motives," he added, with a chuckle.

Julia laughed. "Oh, but I do. The worst kind of motive. Money."

He arched an eyebrow.

"Not yours, of course. My own. Papa left me quite a lot of investments, but when it comes to the stock market, I'm even more at a loss than I am at running a company."

"What makes you think that I'm any kind of an expert?"

"Believe it or not, I do remember a *few* things from Friday night. You said something about the market being a 'house of cards,' and you had that sincere, heartfelt tone that you get in your voice that makes what you say sound very convincing. Unfortunately," she grinned, sheepishly, "thanks to the 'McKenzie Effect,' that's about *all* I remember. So, care to enlighten me?"

Patrick considered the question for a moment before answering. Then, his mind apparently made up, he turned in his seat to face her.

"There are a lot of reasons why Wall Street's bubble is going to burst, and soon ..." he paused, then added, "At least, that's how *I* see it."

"Aren't you being a little pessimistic? Everything that I've been reading says business has never been better. Everyone is investing these days."

"That's part of the problem. Everyone is gambling on stocks, *including* the banks. What do you know about buying on margin?"

"Not much."

"Well, for the past few years, that's how most people have been purchasing stock. They put up ten or twenty percent of their own money, and borrow the rest—the margin—from a broker who, in most cases, turns around and borrows from the bank. The more people buy, the higher the stock prices go. Everything looks great on paper. But that paper is really only worth what Wall Street thinks its worth.

"Some of the bigger players in the market are getting wise. Stock prices dropped on Friday because foreign investors sold off their stocks in large quantities. They looked at what's really going on with the economy, like declines in steel production and consumer spending—not to mention the massive increase in personal debt from all that borrowing—and they wanted out.

Julia considered that as the LaSalle negotiated a tight curve. "But if the market is so bullish, won't someone just buy up all of those shares?" she asked.

"This time, probably. But those same warning signs that have the foreign investors jumping ship are going to start making other people nervous, too. As more and more start to sell off their stock, the prices will begin to fall. Brokers will have to call in the money they've loaned to all of those small investors, but the only way most of those people will be able to raise that kind of money will be to sell off their stocks."

"Which will make the prices fall again." Julia could see where Patrick was leading her.

"That's what I meant by a 'house of cards.' Eventually, stocks will be worth pennies on the dollar. What is today's date, anyway?"

"The eleventh."

"Of *August* ..." he seemed to be reassuring himself of the fact.

Julia nodded. She found it odd that Patrick could sound so confident and convincing about what was going to happen in the distant future, and yet sometimes seem completely out of step with the here and now.

"Two months, at the most, and it's going to start falling apart," he said, firmly.

Julia stole a glance at him. The look in his eyes told her that he, at least, was convinced he was right.

Somehow, she was too.

At the end of Leif Erikson, Julia turned west onto Germantown Road. The narrow, winding drive led them farther up into the West Hills. In several places, the going was so steep that the LaSalle barely managed ten miles an hour, especially where the road wound back and forth in hairpin curves.

At the crest of the ridge, they crossed over Skyline Boulevard and continued along Germantown, which snaked its way down the hillside, a narrow asphalt stream flowing into the valley below. Eventually the road straightened some as it ran along the edge of the gently undulating hills. Here and there, they passed the occasional farmhouse or ancient barn, but most of the land had been devoted to fruit orchards and fields of spring wheat ready for threshing.

Julia spotted the landmark she'd been watching for, the simple whitewashed steeple of Bethany Methodist Church. A hundred yards beyond, she turned right onto a narrow dirt road and parked beneath the shade of an ancient-looking oak tree. Farther along the private lane, a large orchard covered the hillside like a blanket, branches laden with beautiful red apples waiting to be picked.

"Where are we?" Patrick asked as Julia opened her door and stepped out onto the uneven ground.

"This farm belongs to friends of my family. I've been coming out here to picnic ever since I can remember. The Baxters used to send Papa home with bushel baskets full of apples this time of year."

"That's a lot of apple pies."

"No, that's a lot of hard cider," she disclosed with a wink. "Papa had his own press. He'd put Jacob and me to work turning the handle when we were children, and as a reward he'd set some of the fresh cider aside for us."

"Too bad Prohibition came along and shut him down before you were old enough to try the good stuff."

Julia laughed. "You're kidding, right? I think Papa made enough cider last year to have half the neighborhood feeling no pain. Pretty sure there's still some hidden away in the cellar, if you're interested."

Patrick pulled the picnic basket out from behind his seat while Julia grabbed the blanket she'd stowed away earlier. As they walked to a small clearing near the edge of the orchard, a dark blue sedan rounded the curve, slowing a little as it drew near. The driver glanced briefly in their direction before turning his attention back to the road in front of him. A moment later, both vehicle and driver had vanished down the lane.

"Apparently, we're not the only ones who wanted to go for a Sunday drive," Julia said as she spread the checkered blanket out on a level patch of ground. She couldn't be sure, but she thought that might have been the same car she'd seen from a distance back on Leif Erikson.

"Well, it is a beautiful day for it. Let's see what Mrs. McKenzie prepared for us this afternoon."

The wicker basket held wondrous things, enough to feed twice their number. There were a dozen pieces of chicken, fried to a golden brown and double-wrapped in butcher paper. A porcelain bowl filled with potato salad sat at the opposite end, nestled between two large slices of peach pie. Mac's sister-in-law had also included plates and silverware from the hotel's dining room, and pressed linen napkins, along with two drinking glasses. A small towel had been laid out to cushion the contents during the ride.

"We have glasses," Julia pointed out, "but nothing to drink."

Patrick grinned slyly, picking up the towel. Beneath, Julia spotted two holes cut into either end of the wooden bottom. He inserted a finger into each hole and lifted, pulling the false bottom up to reveal a bottle of wine cradled in yet another towel. A cork pull lay alongside.

"Your friend thinks of everything, doesn't he?"

Patrick laughed, holding the bottle up to the sunlight. Inside the clear glass, the wine fairly glowed with a deep red color.

"Always. The question is, where does he find this stuff?"

"Oh, wine isn't hard to come by. After all, grape juice wasn't outlawed by Congress, was it? And the grape producers have very thoughtfully published detailed warnings about all of the things people need to do to keep the juice from fermenting."

The cork pulled free with a satisfying pop. Patrick poured a generous amount into each glass.

"Then let's drink a toast," he said, "to American ingenuity ..."

She touched her glass to his.

"And to the teetotalers who have made scofflaws of us all," she added with a wink.

This is a hell of a way to spend a Sunday afternoon, Mickey thought to himself, *sitting on my ass in the tall weeds, watching these two work their way through lunch and a bottle of vino.*

He'd parked the Durant about a quarter mile down the road, and made his way back through the orchard to a spot where he could see the action without much risk of being seen himself. Not that there was much action to watch with these two.

So what the hell is this about, anyway? Mickey had figured this guy was making time with Brent's girl and the lawyer wanted to scare him out of the picture, but these birds weren't exactly throwing sparks. True, the lady showed some signs of interest. She'd laugh at most everything the man said, and she reached out frequently to touch his wrist or arm when she spoke; Floriana did things like that when Mickey had started courting her, little things to keep him coming back. But whatever signals this lady thought she was sending, the gent sure as hell wasn't receiving them.

This whole job feels squirrelly. Like that crap about Pellizotti asking Brent to track this guy down. Since when do we need some ambulance chaser to do our leg work?

He'd bet dollars to donuts Pellizotti didn't have clue one about what was going on, and wouldn't be happy about having one of his guys trailing a lovesick kitten and her reluctant beau all over the countryside.

Screw it, he thought as he stood up and brushed a few blades of dry grass from his trousers in disgust. He'd head back into town, see what Lanzo had dug up at the hotel, and then he was going home to his wife and kid for the rest of the night.

Patrick lay on his back beside Julia, his skimmer tipped forward to shield his eyes from the late afternoon sun. She couldn't tell if he was sleeping, or simply resting. He was, at the very least, thoroughly relaxed. Still, a little company would be nice.

"Patrick? Are you awake?"

"Mm-mm."

"Can I ask you a question?"

"Mm-mm."

She laughed. "Is that all you can manage to say?"

"Mm-mm." A smile appeared beneath the broad brim of his hat. "What's your question?"

Julia reached out and plucked a tall stalk of grass from the ground, rolling it between her thumb and fingers.

"What was France like?" she asked, quietly.

Patrick rolled over, propping himself up on one elbow to look at her. "France, or the war?"

"The war, I guess."

"What did Jacob tell you when he came home?"

"He never talked about it. At least, not to me."

"Why do you think that was?"

"I suppose because it was pretty horrible."

"War always is," Patrick assured her, as he lay back down.

"Have you ever talked to Rachel about the war?"

Beneath the hat, he shook his head. "She's never asked."

"What about your wife?"

Patrick sighed, rolling over to face Julia once more.

"Not with her either. I don't think she wanted to know the details. Dealing with my nightmares was enough for her. What's this all about?"

Julia shrugged, turning her attention once again to the blade of grass in her hand. She touched the tip of the feathery stalk to her nose.

"I miss Jacob. I can't help but think that he should have been the one to run the business."

"Worried about the meeting tomorrow?"

She nodded. "Do you think my father was really selling the company?"

He smiled. "No. I don't, and neither do you. Everything is going to be all right."

"As long as you're around."

"Everything is going to be all right," he repeated, "whether I'm around or not."

"Where the hell have you been?" Mickey could hear the irritation in his own voice.

He'd parked the Durant on 22nd, just around the corner from the girl's bungalow. Lanzo showed up a half hour later, wearing a sly grin and looking far too relaxed for Mickey's taste. He knew from experience that usually meant that his friend had gotten a little something on the side.

He didn't approve of infidelity, could never even imagine cheating on Floriana, but he'd broken enough other commandments in his time to know he was in no position to judge.

"How was your picnic?" Lanzo asked, dodging the question.

Mickey scowled.

"That good, huh?"

"Total fucking waste of time. You do any better?"

"I'd have to say, yeah, I did just fine." He let the innuendo hang until he realized that Mickey wasn't going to take the bait. "Our boy is, indeed, checked in at the Campbell, under the name Patrick O'Connell."

"You call Brent and tell him?"

"I was going to, but no dice. You had Brent's card in your pocket. I figured we'd call it in when you got back."

"Tomorrow's soon enough. That way we can squeeze a couple hundred more out of the prick."

"Works for me. So what do we do now?"

"No point hanging around here anymore. I'm going home to my family. I don't even *want* to know what you're planning on doing."

Lanzo grinned. "I bet Hazel could dig up a girlfriend for you."

"Pass. Meet me at the bar tomorrow morning around nine. We'll make our call to Brent then."

Lanzo shrugged and climbed out of the automobile.

"Suit yourself," he said. The door closed as he squatted to look back at his friend. "But I still say you need to learn to enjoy life a little."

The day had drifted away from Julia and Patrick. By the time they'd loaded the picnic basket into the LaSalle, afternoon had begun to nudge its way into evening.

Julia was in no hurry to get Patrick back to the hotel, even though she hadn't seemed to make any progress in working past the man's defenses.

She turned onto Leif Erikson, following the meandering lane along the side of the ridge. The sun, which had begun its journey toward the Pacific, cast dancing shadows upon the road in front of them. To their left, through the occasional break in the trees, she could see Mt. Hood jutting high above the eastern horizon. Off of its shoulder, the moon hung low in the sky. Small and pale, it looked like a thumbprint smudge on a vast azure canvas.

"This is why I love living here," Julia said softly.

"You'll get no argument from me."

"What's it like where you grew up?" Other than his war service, and his work at the University of Wisconsin, Julia realized that she really knew very little about him.

"Moline?" Patrick chuckled. "So flat, your West Hills would be considered a major mountain range."

"Moline ... that's in Illinois, isn't it?"

He nodded. "On the banks of the mighty Mississippi, and home of the John Deere tractor. It's funny ... when I was in high school I couldn't wait to get out of that town, but looking back now, it doesn't seem such a bad place to grow up." He smiled, a little wistfully. "I'm certainly a long way from home these days."

"Does your family still live there?"

He nodded. "Probably always will. Dad's been at John Deere almost forty years, since the Army."

Rounding a curve, they saw an old Ford—coming from the opposite direction—pull off of the road onto a grassy viewpoint. As the LaSalle drew near, Julia caught a glimpse of a young couple in the front seat looking furtively in their direction.

She laughed.

"Did I miss something?" Patrick asked.

"Do you remember my telling you that this road becomes a lovers' lane at night? Well, it looks like those two are already staking their claim to the best seat in the house."

"Smart kids."

Julia shot him a playful look. "Don't tell me that the good professor approves of such behavior."

"I was known to engage in a little parking and petting in my youth."

"I didn't realize that they even *had* automobiles that long ago," she teased, "or did you borrow your father's horse and buggy?"

"Very funny. And just what do *you* know about these things?"

"Not as much as my brother did, I'm sure. Jacob had more girls than an Arab sheik. I imagine he probably did very well with those French Mademoiselles during the war." Julia winked at Patrick. "I bet you did, as well."

"I hate to disappoint you, but I was already spoken for by the time I shipped out."

"The former Mrs. O'Connell?"

"The same."

"And look where your noble restraint got you in the end. If there's one thing the war should have taught you,

Patrick, it's to enjoy life when opportunities present themselves."

He smiled. "I don't think that Rachel would necessarily agree with you, under the circumstances."

They found a parking spot just a half block from her bungalow and unloaded the LaSalle. Together, they walked up the path to Julia's steps, Patrick carrying the picnic basket while she cradled the blanket under her arm.

"Can I hold that for you while you find your key?" he asked.

"I usually lock it only at night." To prove her point, she reached out and opened the door.

He looked past her into the dimly lit front room with obvious concern.

"I never took you for a worrier," she laughed. "Would you feel better if you came in and looked around?"

To her great surprise he nodded, and moved past her. She watched him with curiosity as he checked the dining room and kitchen, then followed him down the short hallway that led to the rest of the bungalow.

"My bedroom is on the right," she said with a chuckle, "if you'd care to investigate."

Julia had been certain that would get a reaction from him. Instead, he moved into the room and looked about. Julia wasn't sure if she should be embarrassed or worried. Patrick's whole demeanor had changed.

"What is this all about?" she asked, finally, as he turned at last and walked back toward the front room.

"It really isn't safe to leave your door unlocked," he said, simply.

"Don't be silly. This is Portland, not Chicago or New York."

"Bad things still happen to good people ... even here. Promise me that you'll lock the door after I leave."

"Don't start treating me like a child," she bristled. She knew her reaction stemmed more from the nerves she'd started to feel than from anything he'd done.

"I'm not. I'm asking you to promise because I care about you."

There it was, that damned earnestness that made him so compelling. She nodded.

"I promise, but only because you've managed to give me a bad case of the heebie-jeebies."

He smiled. "How about if I make it up to you by treating you to breakfast in the morning, before we go to the factory?"

"Well," Julia said, allowing herself a smile, "that's a start, at least."

"Around eight? Afterward, we can strategize before the meeting starts."

"Eight it is," she agreed.

He picked the picnic basket up from where he'd set it and started back down the walk. Julia watched him disappear from sight. Only then did she close the door.

And lock it.

Mrs. McKenzie glanced up from the register when Patrick opened the hotel's main doors. She seemed less than thrilled to see her prize guest. Apparently, he hadn't made it out of the doghouse for leading Mac astray.

He held up the picnic basket as he approached.

"Miss Lundgren asked me to tell you that lunch was magnificent. Thank you again, Mrs. McKenzie."

"Did all of my dishes make it back in one piece?"

"I believe they did," he assured her, "but if anything is broken, I will be happy to make it right."

"I'm *sure* you will. I don't suppose you'd mind taking that down to the kitchen. Mac will do an inventory."

She turned her attention back to the register. Recognizing a dismissal when he heard one, Patrick started for the dining room.

"By the way, Mr. O'Connell, did your *friend* ever find you?"

Patrick stopped in his tracks, his stomach tightening. He turned to see Mrs. McKenzie scowling at him.

"Someone was asking for me?"

"A very rude man stopped by just after you left with Miss Lundgren this afternoon."

"Was he about my size? With a limp?"

The innkeeper looked vaguely disconcerted by the urgency in Patrick's voice.

"No, he was taller than you by a good three inches, and much thinner. He told me that he had a message for you."

"What was the message?"

"If he'd *left* it, Mr. O'Connell, I would have given it to you already. He said that he'd catch up with you later. Frankly, if that's the kind of person you associate with, it might be best if you find another hotel."

"I think perhaps you're right, Mrs. McKenzie. I'm sorry that my ... friend ... upset you. I'll be checking out tomorrow."

—17—

"Like *hell* you're moving out," Mac growled.

"I made a promise to you when I arrived," Patrick reminded him. "None of this was going to come back on your family. The only people who might have tracked me down here are Brent, or Pellizotti's men. Either way, it's time I found somewhere else to stay."

"We'll talk about that after your meeting tomorrow. I can handle Lucille in the meantime. Right now, we have more important things to discuss."

They sat at a table near the back of the bar, far removed from the few customers who had come in so far. A bottle of Jameson sat between them, unopened. Neither of them felt much like drinking.

"What have you found out?" Patrick asked.

"My contacts mentioned that Ingersol and Brent are members at the Aero Club, downtown. Carl, too, as it turns out. So I got in touch with one of my old buddies from the precinct. Tommy took a job at the club as a bartender, after he retired.

"The thing about bartenders is that the good ones are pretty much invisible to the customers." Mac smiled. "If I told you half the things I've heard around here, you wouldn't believe me. Anyway, I wanted to see if he'd picked up on anything between Brent and John Ingersol. Plenty, as it turns out."

"Please tell me that Ingersol isn't involved. He's all the family Julia has left."

"He's not," Mac said, firmly, "not directly, not *knowingly*. About two months ago, Tommy overheard Brent and Ingersol having a heated conversation about some money they'd lost. Seems Brent made bad investments on Ingersol's behalf, serious money investments that had dried up. Brent kept saying that he'd find a way to make it back, somehow."

"What did Ingersol say?"

"Not much of anything. But, according to Tommy, he changed after that. He was never much of a drinker, but now he comes in most every night ... sometimes with Brent or Lundgren, but just as often he sits at the bar all by himself, talking about how he had let his wife down, how he was going to have to sell his company just to keep a roof over her head.

"Funny thing is, even though Brent lost the money, Ingersol still blames himself. And he's never asked for a dime from any of the other members at the club, so far as Tommy knows. Hell, Carl offered to give his friend the money to get back on his feet, but Ingersol wouldn't accept. Said he'd made his own bad decisions, and he would have to make it right.

"They also talked about the Peregrine deal that night," Mac added.

"Was Brent there?"

Mac shook his head. "It was just the two of them. And this is where it gets *really* interesting. Carl told Ingersol that he would sell his company so that the deal for the Tool & Die would go through."

Patrick leaned back in his seat, unable to conceal his shock. "Are you *sure*?"

"Absolutely. But Ingersol refused. In fact, he made Carl promise not to sell, said that he could never live with himself if his stupidity cost Carl his company. That he would rather put a bullet in his brain than let that happen. So Carl promised not to sell."

"None of this makes any sense."

"Oddly enough," Mac said, "I think it does. The one person in the world that Brent seems to feel any loyalty for, besides his own pitiful ass, is John Ingersol. The guy walked through fire to save Brent during the war, helped him start his practice here, and the little prick went and lost all of his money for him.

"Then the Peregrine deal comes along. I don't know whether Brent engineered it from the start, or it just fell into his lap, but it's a way to save the man he owes his life to. Probably didn't hurt that Brent could make a few bucks in the bargain.

"When Carl refused to go along, I'm guessing he never mentioned his promise to John. Brent must have assumed Lundgren was just being pig-headed, willing to let his best friend go bankrupt rather than sell his precious company. So, Brent arranged a little accident, figuring that Julia would be easier to manipulate."

Patrick sat in silence for a few moments. "That's a pretty damned good theory," he said at last.

"Problem is, that's all we have ... a theory. It isn't worth a damn when it comes to nailing this son of a bitch."

23rd Avenue buzzed with Monday morning traffic. Streetcars were filled to capacity with workers heading for the factories to the north, and businessmen going south toward their offices downtown.

It would be nice to be able to disappear into the crowd like the rest of them, Patrick mused, *to be caught up again in little, day-to-day dramas where lives aren't at stake.*

Locking his door behind him, he moved down the stairs toward the lobby. Much to his relief, the part-time clerk, Nelson, was manning the front desk instead of Lucille McKenzie.

"Good morning, Mr. O'Connell. I understand that you're leaving us today."

Patrick nodded. Regardless of Mac's feelings on the matter, he was not going to put his friend's family in danger any longer.

"That's the plan. I have some business to attend to this morning, and then I'll be settling my bill."

"I'm sorry to hear that. It's been a pleasure having you here. "

Tell that to Mrs. McKenzie, Patrick thought.

"Please, let me know if there's anything that I can do for you," Nelson added, sincerely.

"Actually, there is something." Patrick pulled some cash out of his pocket and held a twenty out to the clerk. "I'm going to need a large suitcase. Could you arrange for something, not too expensive?"

Nelson nodded. "Is noon early enough?"

"That would be fine. And, Nelson ..."

"Yes, Mr. O'Connell?"

"If you can keep Mac in the dark about my checking out today, the change is yours."

The clerk nodded again, but the look on his face said that he was weighing the possibility of a financial windfall against incurring the wrath of his employer. As Patrick stepped out onto the sidewalk, he wondered which way the decision would go.

Julia appeared on the second knock, looking nervous and tired, but relieved to see Patrick standing on her doorstep.

"Did you get any sleep last night?"

She shook her head.

"Hardly any." She stepped back inside and pulled a hat from the coat rack. It took a few adjustments to get it to sit properly on her head.

"I'm a wreck," she told her reflection.

"No, you're not."

She turned and scowled at him. "I have bags under my eyes, and my stomach is doing somersaults."

"The bags are barely noticeable, and your stomach will feel much better when we get some breakfast into you."

"I couldn't possibly eat a bite."

"You don't want me to eat my last meal at the Campbell alone, do you?"

Julia's eyes widened. "What do you mean, your last meal? You're leaving?"

"I'm just moving to another hotel. Mac's sister-in-law is not my greatest admirer, and I don't want to create any more problems. By the way, I haven't said anything to Mac about leaving. Probably best if we keep this between ourselves."

Mac found a clean table for them near the front door, and sent Elizabeth over with coffee.

"I hear you are checking out," the waitress whispered as she filled Patrick's cup.

"Obviously a well-kept secret," Julia observed, a thin, joyless smile on her face.

"I don't care who else knows," Patrick told them, "as long as Mac doesn't find out for awhile."

When their meals arrived, they ate slowly and in silence. Patrick knew that Julia was watching him, probably looking for some reassurance that the meeting ahead of them was going to turn out all right. And, of course, he knew that Julia *would* come out on top. But what happened to Mac and everyone else he'd drawn into the story, or even to *himself* ... that was still a complete mystery.

He closed his eyes and felt himself sliding into combat mode, that peculiar state of mind he'd experienced in the hours before a mission. The world slowed down around him, just a little, just enough to bring everything into greater focus. The white noise of self-doubt and uncertainty faded into the recesses of his mind.

Brent loses, and Julia wins. Whatever I have to do to ensure that, whatever it costs ...

"Patrick, you're frightening me a little."

He opened his eyes to find Julia watching him. He smiled, apologetically.

"Sorry. I get a little intense sometimes when I'm preparing for ... things like this," he ended, vaguely.

"I don't think I'm ready for this meeting."

"You'll be fine. No matter what the attorneys say, or what proof they say they have that your father was going to sell the company, you and I both know that it's not true. That's what you hold on to."

Patrick smiled again. He could hear the certainty in his own voice, and he knew that Julia could as well. Still, she looked troubled.

"Are you saying that they might falsify documents?"

"There would have to be some documentation, like your father's signature on a contract, to compel you to hand over the company."

"How can they get away with something like that?" Her eyes flashed with outrage.

This was the tricky part. He needed Julia to hold it together until the meeting was over. If she knew how long Brent had been planning this, she'd realize that her father's death had to have been part of the plan. Patrick wasn't sure she could handle that right now.

"Mac and I don't think that Peregrine Industries or their lawyers are involved," he told her.

"I don't understand. Who else could it be?"

"Leon Brent." He could see her confusion. "Mac did some digging, and found out that Brent is in trouble financially. Peregrine's lawyers were willing to reward him if the deal went through. Your father's death gave him the opportunity to make that happen."

"That *bastard!*" Julia's eyes widened as the words slipped out of her mouth. She looked around to see if anyone else had heard.

"I'm so sorry," she apologized, but the fire still smoldered behind her eyes.

Patrick chuckled in spite of himself.

"Under the circumstances, I'd say you're allowed. But keep that under control during the meeting. We can't let Brent know that we've figured things out until we have enough evidence to hang him."

Patrick paused while Elizabeth refilled their cups and cleared away the plates. When they were alone once again, he continued.

"I haven't been able to reach Erny's attorney friend yet. We can try again after breakfast, but it's probably too late to get him to the meeting this morning, anyway. So it's just you and me for the time being, Kiddo.

"Do you trust me?" he asked with a smile. He was gratified to see her nod without hesitation.

Ed Wirth settled into the chair behind his desk, thumbing through the mail that had collected while he'd been in Salem: a couple of bills, and a check from the Ingrams, accompanied by a very nice thank-you note for winning their lawsuit. Nothing else of importance.

On the bottom of the short stack, he found a letter from the local Republican chair asking for his support of George Baker, the mayoral incumbent in the next election. As a lifelong member of the Grand Old Party, there was no question that Ed would stand behind their candidate. He just wished that the mayor would be a little more selective about the company he kept. Old pictures of Baker with hooded Klansmen still circulated from time to time, and had almost certainly cost him in the 1924 primary, when he'd run for the Senate.

A good man held back by poorly chosen associates. There's a lesson to be learned there for any man entering politics, Ed realized.

The phone in the outer office rang, and he heard Abigail pick it up. He waited to see if the call was for him or for Erny. Sharing the office—and the cost of a secretary—with the writer had worked out well. If nothing else, the arrangement helped keep expenses down while Ed established his law practice.

"Phone call for you, Mr. Wirth," Abby yelled through the open doorway.

One of these days I'm going to have to invest in an intercom, the lawyer thought as he picked up the receiver on his desk.

"Ed Wirth."

"Mr. Wirth, my name is Patrick O'Connell. I'm calling on behalf of Miss Julia Lundgren."

Ed recognized that name immediately. Her father's unfortunate accident had made it into the Salem paper a few days earlier. Ed had actually met Carl Lundgren and his daughter a year or so before, at a party. Julia had made an impression, although he doubted that she would say the same of him.

"One moment, Mr. O'Connell." Ed set the receiver down on the desk blotter. He hurried over to close his office door, then returned to the phone. "I'm sorry for the delay. You said that you were calling on behalf of Miss Lundgren?"

"That's right. Erny Haycox thought that you could help with a legal matter that's come up regarding her company."

Ed leaned back in his chair. Securing a client like Lundgren Furniture would be quite a coup, if he was up to the task. Still, he was puzzled as to why they would come to him, even at Erny's suggestion.

"Doesn't the company already have representation?"

"Leon Brent is currently under retainer, but that relationship will be ending before the day is out. We were hoping your firm might be available to represent both Miss Lundgren and her company."

My firm of one, Ed thought with a frown. *Still, you have to start somewhere, don't you?*

"May I ask the nature of the legal matter?"

"Another company claims that Julia's father agreed to sell Lundgren Furniture just before he died. Julia is disputing that claim."

"And what does Mr. Brent say?"

After a moment's pause, Mr. O'Connell said, "We believe that Brent is engineering the purchase for his own benefit. We would like for you to make sure that Julia's company isn't stolen from her."

"And if Mr. Lundgren did, indeed, agree to sell?"

"Then you can help facilitate the deal and protect her interests. However, I can assure you that it won't come to that."

Ed had to admit that this Mr. O'Connell had no lack of confidence.

"We're meeting with Peregrine Industries' attorney, Stan Goldmark, in Julia's office at ten-thirty this morning," O'Connell added. "I don't suppose you'd be available to join us?"

Ed looked at his desk calendar. "I'm afraid that I have an appointment at ten, and it would be impossible to cancel on such short notice. Can you postpone at your end?"

"I don't think so. Any advice?"

Ed thought for a moment. "Insist on a court hearing to review the contracts," he advised. "That will give me enough time to familiarize myself with the details. Can Miss Lundgren come to my office this afternoon, around two o'clock?"

"We'll be there."

When O'Connell dropped off of the other end of the line, Ed rocked back in his chair, wondering exactly what he had just gotten himself into. Leon Brent had a reputation as a shark, someone you certainly did not want to cross if you could help it. Based on some of the stories Ed had heard, he could almost believe Brent capable of anything, including manipulating the sale of Lundgren's company. Still, both Brent and Stan Goldmark were well-placed in the state's Republican organization.

You can forget any political aspirations if you take them on and fall short, he reasoned as he stood and walked to the outer office. *Then again, what's life without a little risk?*

Ed crossed the tiny waiting room to Erny's door and knocked. He entered at his friend's request.

"Ed! Welcome back. How was Salem?"

"The case went well, Erny. Thanks for asking. Listen, I was wondering if you could do a favor for me."

The writer nodded. "Ask away."

"What can you tell me about Julia Lundgren?"

−18−

Leon fidgeted as the Dekum Building's elevator climbed slowly through the first five floors. He checked his watch again. A couple more hours and he could put this whole fucking mess behind him. Hopefully, Julia would see reason and walk away from Lundgren Furniture without a fight. If not ... well, he hoped a more permanent solution wouldn't be necessary. He'd taken enough chances already.

The car stopped at the sixth floor. Leon pulled the gate back and walked over to the public door to his office. His secretary, Miss Wilson, looked up as he entered.

"Good morning, Mr. Brent," she said, softly.

He ignored the greeting, amused at how nervous she still was around him after working there for almost six months. But she was damned good at her job. She was also easy on the eyes. One of these days he'd have to check out the whole package.

"I'm just here to pick up the Lundgren files for my meeting," he told her, brusquely. "I should be back by twelve-thirty. Have a copy of the Norwood deposition on my desk for review. Have there been any calls?"

"Not this morning, Mr. Brent."

He scowled. He'd expected to hear from Pellizotti's boys by now. *How hard is it to find one fucking guy, anyway?*

Leon pulled the door to his private office closed behind him and opened the cabinet drawer where he'd put Lundgren's file. Or, at least, where he *thought* he'd put the file. It should have been just behind Ingersol Tool and Die. He thumbed through the folders in front of, and behind, Ingersol's, but the file just wasn't there.

Anxiously, he bent down and opened the next drawer down. There, filed alphabetically, was Lundgren's file.

"Miss Wilson, get in here!" he growled angrily.

A moment later his secretary appeared in the doorway, a worried expression on her face.

"How many times have I told you to stay out of my private files?"

"Bu ... But, I *haven't* ... I mean, I've never ..." she stammered. She looked terrified, too terrified to be lying to him.

"Has anyone else been in here?" He'd lowered his voice, but his tone was still icy.

"No one has been in all morning."

"All right, go back to work, and close the door behind you."

He sat down at his desk and glared at the offending filing cabinet. Someone had been in the office, *his* fucking office, going through his own personal fucking files. Leon didn't need two guesses to figure out who had to be behind this.

He flipped open the folder and thumbed through its contents. Everything seemed to be there. So they may have stumbled across Lundgren's file but, chances were, they'd had no clue as to what they were looking at. But, if they saw the letters from Goldmark, including the one that linked Ingersol Tool and Die to the sale.

Shit.

He pulled John Ingersol's file, satisfying himself that nothing had gone missing there, either. Apparently they hadn't taken anything.

Is this bastard just fucking with me? Just letting me know I'm vulnerable?

Leon turned in his chair, banging his knee painfully on an open drawer in the process. A drawer that *should* have been closed. With a sinking feeling, he looked inside.

The folder with Julia's photograph was gone. In its place sat a note addressed to Brent. He unfolded it, irritated to see that his hand trembled ever so slightly as he did so. It took a moment to read what had been written, so poor was the handwriting, but the message was clear:

> *You slit Maggie Daly's throat just like Addie Sinclair's, back in Joliet*
>
> *Johnny T will be happy to know where you've been hiding.*

Leon closed his eyes and leaned back in his chair, the note dangling from his fingertips.

Addie Fucking Sinclair, Johnny Torrio's little whore, after all of these years.

He knew Torrio had come back from his self-imposed exile in Sicily, but he was still a continent away in New York. He couldn't possibly have anything to do with this. That would change, though, when he got word of where Leon was. Torrio had a long memory, and a longer reach.

Addie Sinclair had been a nobody, a cheap doxy who probably hadn't meant all that much to Johnny in the first place. But, in the gangs, hurting girlfriends and wives went against the unspoken rule.

Even if Addie didn't matter to Johnny, rules did.

They mattered a lot.

Leon looked around his office. A decade to build up a life, and a practice, and now it was crumbling around him. A week from now—a month at the outside—someone would show up to put a bullet in the back of his head.

But I sure as hell won't be here. I'll be setting up shop somewhere else, in Montana maybe, or Alaska, somewhere so remote that no one will ever find me again.

He looked at the picture of his wife and children on his desk. Evelyn had become an anchor around his neck, and he'd already more or less decided to do something about her, anyway. But the kids ... well, he'd miss the kids.

He slipped the Lundgren file into his briefcase and left by his private door. By the end of the week Leon Brent would have vanished forever, along with the contents of his bank accounts. In the meantime, he had some business to finish, and accounts to settle.

Mickey waved Lanzo over to the bar where he was working his way through yet another cup of coffee.

"Where have you been? It's almost ten o'clock."

Lanzo grinned. "Hard to get out of bed this morning. Besides, what's the rush?"

"I just want to get this job over and done with."

Mickey reached across the mahogany counter and set the telephone on the bar next to Brent's business card. Lifting the receiver, he flicked the cradle a couple of times to get the operator.

"Madison four-oh-six-five," he said, then waited while she connected him to the attorney's office. "Leon Brent, please."

Lanzo leaned against the bar, looking around the empty speakeasy. Cicero's was kind of a dump when the houselights were up, he decided. Then again, everything looks better after a drink or two.

"Any idea when he'll be back?" Mickey rolled his eyes in irritation. "Well, do you know where he is now? I have some information for him, and he said he wanted it right away. Lundgren Furniture? No, thanks, I know where it is."

"How'd she sound?" Lanzo asked as Mickey hung the receiver back onto the cradle.

His partner looked at him. "What do you mean, how'd she sound?"

"Young? Old? Pretty?"

"She sounded nervous, is how she sounded. Jesus, would you give your dick a rest for ten minutes? Grab your hat and let's go."

"Where to?" Lanzo asked as he fell into step behind his friend.

"Brent's going to a meeting at Lundgren Furniture. We'll catch up to him there."

"Don't you think he's going to get pretty annoyed, us showing up at his meeting?"

Mickey grinned. "He's the one who told us *anytime*, isn't he?"

"Yeah, but I'm pretty sure he meant call."

"Six of one, half dozen of another."

Sid Westbrook looked up over the top of his glasses to see Miss Lundgren's attorney standing in his doorway.

"Mr. Brent, something I can do for you?"

"I need you to pull together a complete equipment inventory, along with the maintenance logs for the past six months."

"Is that so? Why?"

The attorney looked agitated, which improved Sid's mood somewhat.

"Because I told you to. The new owners want to review the records as soon as possible."

"Which new owners are these?"

"Peregrine Industries. We're starting the transfer proceedings today."

Sid took his glasses off and leaned back in his chair. "The boss know about this?"

"The boss?" Brent looked puzzled for a moment. "You mean, Julia?"

Sid nodded.

"She will in about fifteen minutes."

"That's what I thought." The manager put his glasses back on and turned his attention to the paperwork in front of him.

"Are you going to get me those records, or aren't you?"

Without looking up, Sid said, "You'll have to take it up with my boss."

There was a long, uncomfortable silence.

"Westbrook," the attorney said in a steely voice, "this deal is going through, and when it does, I'll see to it that *you* are out on your ass."

Sid looked up again and smiled. "I'll believe that when it happens. Now, counselor, get the hell out of my office. I have work to do."

Brent stalked through the factory, heading for the stairs that would take him up to Julia's office. He could feel the rage rising within him with every step.

Lost in thought, he almost missed his name being shouted over the whine of the lathes. He turned toward the source and swore. Pellizotti's men. The shorter one—Mickey, Brent remembered—tapped his lanky friend on the shoulder, nodding in Brent's direction, but neither seemed inclined to come over to where the attorney stood.

Brent closed the gap between them quickly.

"What the fuck are you doing here?" he demanded. "You were supposed to *call* when you found something."

"I did call," Mickey told him. "Your secretary said you were here. Do you want to know what we came up with, or not?"

"Make it fast. I have a meeting in ten minutes."

Mickey looked to his friend, who said, "The guy's name is Patrick O'Connell. He's staying at the Campbell on 23rd."

O'Connell. The name meant nothing to Brent. "You sure he's the man I'm looking for?"

Mickey shrugged. "Matches the description you gave us, that's all we know. And he's hanging around with your girlfriend."

"She's not my goddamned ..." Brent caught himself. His voice had risen enough to catch the attention of a few of the workers. He waited until Lundgren's colored foreman got them back to work before he continued.

"You say he's at the Campbell? For how long?'

"How the hell are we supposed to know that?" Mickey asked with a laugh.

Brent glared at him, but that only seemed to fuel the man's amusement.

"All right, fine. Go back to the hotel and wait for him. I don't care how you do it, but pick him up. I need answers."

"Sure thing, but that's going to cost you," Mickey said, amiably.

"How much?"

"Five hundred, each. Cash. In advance."

"You think I just carry that kind of money around? Besides, I told you that this is for Pellizotti."

"Maybe, but Pellizotti isn't here. When can you have our money?"

Nothing good going on over there, Otis decided. He was too far away now to hear what those men talking with Mr. Lundgren's lawyer were up to, but he knew trouble when he saw it. The lawyer was mad enough to spit nails about something, and the other two ... well, they just looked hard, the kind of men you steered clear of if you wanted to stay healthy.

But even if he couldn't catch what they were planning exactly, Otis had heard enough before he'd moved out of earshot to know who they were talking about.

"Miss Lundgren is with someone at the moment," the woman behind the desk told Stan Goldmark. "Please, have a seat. She'll be with you shortly."

The attorney pulled his gold pocket watch out and checked the time. Not quite ten-thirty. He had hoped they might get an early start and wrap things up quickly so that he could hit the links, but apparently golf would have to wait.

He thanked the secretary and settled into a seat on the other side of the room. The chair seemed well made—walnut, and beautifully finished—and was surprisingly comfortable.

"Excuse me, were these chairs made here at this factory?"

The petite secretary looked up from her paperwork and nodded.

"I'll have to buy some for my own office," Stan said, running his palm appreciatively across the curved arm of the chair.

"I'm sure that can be arranged," she told him with a smile.

The door from the hallway swung back abruptly and Leon Brent stepped into the room. Stan exhaled involuntarily at the sight of the other attorney. Brent was not his favorite person, to be sure, but in the legal profession you don't always get to choose the company you keep. He stood and clasped the other man's hand.

"Leon, it's good to see you. I thought you were in with Miss Lundgren already."

"No, I was just detained for a few minutes." He turned to the secretary. "Miss Langseth, tell Julia that we're ready."

"Yes, Mr. Brent," she said, quietly.

"Miss Lundgren, Mr. Brent and Mr. Goldmark are here."

"Thank you." Julia looked up at Patrick, who smiled reassuringly. She took a deep breath and exhaled slowly to calm her nerves a bit, then pressed the intercom key again. "Please tell them to come in."

Brent came bustling through the door, briefcase in hand. When he saw Patrick standing near the desk he stopped so suddenly that the man who followed—a lean, well-dressed man with silver hair—nearly collided with him. Brent recovered quickly and continued on into the room, but the look he shot Patrick was pure venom.

"Julia," he said, "this is Mr. Goldmark, of Bishop and Goldmark. Stan, this is Julia Lundgren. And this, I believe," he added, turning toward Patrick, "is Mr. O'Connell."

As he spoke Patrick's name, a faint smirk appeared on his face, as though he expected to score a blow with the knowledge. The expression faded into uncertainty, however, when Patrick merely smiled and extended his hand to Mr. Goldmark.

"A pleasure," he told the other attorney.

"Mr. O'Connell is here at my request," Julia informed them.

A shadow crossed Brent's features. "Julia, we have important business matters to discuss."

"And Patrick will be here to protect my interests."

"That's what you pay *me* for," Brent pointed out.

"No, that was what my father paid you for. As of this morning, your services are no longer required." Her voice was surprisingly calm. "Miss Langseth has a copy of my formal written notification in the other room. I'll send someone to collect our files this afternoon. Please have them ready."

Brent's neck muscles tightened visibly beneath his starched collar. Perhaps instinctively, Goldmark put some distance between himself and his colleague.

"This is absurd. Julia, I don't know what this man has been telling you ..."

"I'd be happy to discuss that," Patrick offered. "I'm sure that Mr. Goldmark would find it all very interesting."

Brent was silent for a moment, the anger in his eyes slowly replaced with a cold darkness.

"Not today," Brent said, at last, moving to the door. "We all have more important business to attend to. I'll leave you to yours."

Goldmark looked like a deer caught in the headlights of an oncoming car as Brent slammed the door behind him.

"I apologize for that," Julia told her guest. "Please, have a seat."

"No need for apologies," the attorney assured her as he took his chair. "I thought that you handled that very capably, by the way," he added with a slight smile. "I do hope that this won't delay our business, however."

"That depends on the nature of the business."

"I'm not sure I understand." The attorney looked genuinely confused. "Prior to his death, your father agreed to sell Lundgren Furniture to Peregrine Industries for the sum of one hundred eighty-five thousand dollars."

"I'm afraid you're mistaken," Julia said, flatly.

The attorney blinked. "I assure you that he did, Miss Lundgren. I have a copy of the agreement right here in my briefcase, along with a cancelled check for the advance he received. Five thousand dollars."

He pulled the file from his satchel and extracted a document. Patrick recognized it as the counterpart to the contract he'd found near Carl's body. Julia took the paper from the attorney and studied it. The document quivered a little in her hand.

"That *is* your father's signature, isn't it?" Goldmark asked.

"I don't believe that it is," she said, quietly but firmly. She handed the contract back to the attorney.

Goldmark leaned forward in his chair. "I appreciate that this must come as a shock after everything that has happened, but I assure you that *is* Carl Lundgren's signature. As is this signature, on the back of the check," he added, pulling the cancelled draft from the file.

Patrick took the check from him. Drawn on the account of Bishop and Goldmark in the amount of five thousand dollars, the memo stated clearly that it was an advance for the sale of Lundgren Furniture. On the back someone had stamped *Bank of Kenton* just below Carl's signature.

"Mr. Goldmark, when was this check cashed?" he asked.

"The date is there on the back ... August 2nd."

Patrick caught the look of surprise on Julia's face, but somehow she held her tongue.

"Julia, did your father make any large deposits on that day?"

She shook her head. "I've been through both his personal account and the company's books. There were no deposits on that day, or for several days before."

"Did you, or the police, find any large sums of money at his house or here in the office?"

She shook her head once more.

"Which bank did your father use?"

"United States Bank. He never banked anywhere else. Why?"

Patrick looked to Julia. "Can you think of *any* reason why your father would go to the Bank of Kenton?"

"None at all. Kenton is miles from here, almost to the Washington border."

The attorney sat in silence for several moments.

"What would you have me do, Miss Lundgren?" he asked, at last. "My client entered into this agreement in good faith. We have a legal contract bearing your father's signature. We have a check, endorsed by your father, in the amount of the advance outlined in the terms of that agreement. And you ..." he smiled, ruefully, "you have wishful thinking and hunches. Hunches which *imply*, by the way, that the firm of Bishop and Goldmark may be complicit in unethical, perhaps even illegal, practices."

"I assure you," Patrick told the attorney, "we don't believe that your firm is involved in any wrongdoing. But given Miss Lundgren's concerns, and the timing of her father's death, I would think it's in everyone's best interest to have these signatures verified before we move forward. Wouldn't you agree?"

Goldmark considered the request for a moment. Then, with a sigh, he placed the contract and cancelled check back inside his briefcase.

"Under the circumstances, that seems reasonable," he conceded as he stood. "I'll advise my clients of the situation." He pulled a business card from his pocket, placing it on the desk between Julia and Patrick. "Reach me at that number. If I need to get in touch, should I contact you or Mr. O'Connell?"

"Miss Lundgren's new attorney is Ed Wirth," Patrick said, sliding over the business card Erny had given him. "He's the one you'll want to talk to."

–19–

"Mr. Brent? You in there?"

Leon sat behind his desk, the Colt revolver at the ready on his lap. "Come in."

Mickey and his friend entered from the outer office.

"There was no girl at the desk out front," Mickey pointed out as he closed the connecting door behind him.

"That's because I fired her."

"Why'd you do *that*?" This from the tall, lean one. What the hell was his name? Brent thought it was something that ended with an *o*, but that didn't narrow the possibilities down much when you were dealing with Italians.

"For telling you where you could find me this morning, that's why," he told them, flatly.

Mickey looked none too pleased to hear the news, but he kept his objections to himself.

"You got our money?" he asked.

Brent nodded toward an envelope sitting at the front of the desk. Mickey reached out and picked it up, sliding it into his coat pocket.

"Aren't you going to count it?"

"If it's not all there, you'll be hearing from us. So what's the plan?"

"There's an address in the envelope, a little farm I own out in Dundee. Let me know when you have O'Connell there."

"You want us to kill this guy, that's another five hundred, each."

Brent smiled coldly. "If I need any help with that, I'll let you know."

"I like that guy less and less every time we see him."

Mickey nodded but didn't answer. He and Lanzo walked the remaining block and a half to their car in silence while he reevaluated his original assessment of Leon Brent. The arrogant, condescending counselor had revealed a side of himself that Mickey hadn't expected. There was no doubt in his mind that Brent could, and would, kill O'Connell when the time came.

They climbed into the Durant. Mickey started the motor, but made no move to pull into traffic.

"What's cooking in that head of yours, Mick?"

He looked at his watch. Pellizotti's nephew should be at Cicero's by now. He put the automobile into gear and pulled away from the curb.

"I think it's time that we talked to De Campo," he told his friend. "Something just isn't adding up."

Ed Wirth appeared to be every bit as fastidious and precise as Rachel had said he was. A young man—by Patrick's standards, at least—of perhaps thirty, the attorney had round, Germanic features and hair that rose in a pronounced wave above his forehead. He dressed professionally, but not expensively, in a grey pinstriped suit and a crisp white shirt. His emerald green tie formed a perfect knot at his throat.

He sat behind a simple oak desk. The surface was clear of all clutter, adorned only by a leather desk blotter, an appointment book, a fountain pen and ink well, and a green-shaded bankers' lamp. Behind the desk, in a gilded frame, hung Wirth's degree from the University of Missouri–Kansas City School of Law.

The attorney had maintained an almost expressionless façade throughout the meeting, except for the warm smile he'd flashed Julia when they'd first arrived, and the brief look of disappointment in his eyes when she'd admitted that she didn't remember having met him before.

Wirth looked up from the notepad he'd been studying, a slight frown creasing his brow.

"Based upon the facts at hand, I would have to agree with Mr. Goldmark's assessment. They appear to have ample evidence that your father agreed to this sale."

Julia, who had been nearly silent since their meeting with the Peregrine attorney, nodded and rose from her chair. "Patrick, we should go. We're clearly wasting Mr. Wirth's time," she said quietly.

The attorney allowed himself a brief smile. "Please sit down, Miss Lundgren, I haven't finished." He waited until she had once again taken her seat before continuing. "Mr. O'Connell said that you were convinced that your father didn't cash that check the Friday before he died. How can you be so certain?"

Julia looked at Wirth, defiantly. "Firstly, because he never banked anywhere other than at the United States Bank in Portland. Secondly, he would have had no reason to be in Kenton that day ..."

"Could he have had business in the area?"

"If he were there on business, there would have been an entry on his calendar." Julia's voice was firm, her gaze unflinching. "I went back two months and found nothing.

No one at the company could think of any business there, either. And finally, there were no deposits made that day. My father never carried more than fifty dollars in cash at any given time. More than that was simply inviting trouble, as far as he was concerned."

Ed rocked back in his chair a little as he thought about what she'd said. Then he got up and walked to his door. "Abigail, could you please put a call through to the manager of the Bank of Kenton. I would like to speak with him as soon as possible."

"Yes, Mr. Wirth."

He looked at his guests. "I took the liberty of speaking with Erny about your father earlier. He, too, assured me that Carl Lundgren would never have considered selling his company, and certainly not without discussing the matter with you. Now that I've met you, Julia, I can understand why.

"We'll hire experts to compare your father's known signature with the endorsement on the bank draft, as well as the one on the contract. With your permission, I'd also like to hire a detective to look into your father's movements on the day in question."

Julia nodded.

"Of course, we'll need time to investigate, so I'll petition the court to grant a temporary injunction preventing the completion of the sale for sixty days. Given your father's standing, and the timing of his death, I'm sure they'll grant us that. Sixty days might just be long enough to cause Peregrine Industries to voluntarily terminate the deal, regardless of our findings. Either way, I promise we'll make life as difficult as possible for them."

Patrick glanced over at Julia as she pulled out into traffic. "So, what did you think of Mr. Wirth?"

Julia shrugged. "I admit that I could do worse than someone like that for an attorney. He seems a bit stodgy and pedantic, but capable."

She caught him smirking out of the corner of her eye.

"Is there something that you're not telling me?"

He shook his head, but a hint of a smile stayed firmly in place. "I suspect that you two will get along very well together," he told her, simply.

She pulled the La Salle over to the side of the road and turned off the motor, her hands trembling. After several moments, she looked at Patrick.

"If Brent forged that check and cashed it Friday," she said, hesitantly, "then he must have known that Papa wouldn't be around to contest the signature."

Patrick said nothing.

"He murdered my father." It wasn't a question.

Patrick nodded. "*Had* him murdered, yes. Mac and I just haven't been able to prove it. I know that's it's hard to believe ..."

"No, I saw the look in Brent's eyes this morning. He'll kill *you* if he has the chance," she said, tears welling in her eyes.

"After this morning, I don't think either one of us is very safe. That's why I'm changing hotels, and you're finding somewhere else to stay for awhile."

Julia slid across the seat and grabbed Patrick, hugging him tightly as she broke down, heavy sobs wracking her body. Minutes passed before she had herself under control once more. She pulled away, her eyes red from crying, and looked down in embarrassment.

"This is becoming a very bad habit," she said, wiping the tears away. "I don't know if I'm strong enough for this."

He leaned over and kissed her forehead tenderly.

"You're going to be fine. I promise. Now, let's find someplace for you to go."

–20–

As Anthony De Campo listened to his Uncle Carlo's men filling him in on Brent's plans, a dull ache started in, just behind his left eye. *I'm not cut out for this shit,* he realized yet again. *Running a restaurant, easy, but the rackets are a giant pain in my ass.*

"Mickey," he said, wearily, "you're a smart guy. Just tell me what you fucking think."

"I think we're being played, boss. Whatever this asshole is up to, I don't think it has shit to do with Pellizotti."

Eyes closed, Anthony stroked his temples gently in thought.

"All right," he said at last, "you two keep an eye on this O'Connell, but you do nothing ..." he emphasized his words by jabbing his finger at them. "I repeat ... you do *nothing* ... until I speak with Uncle Carlo. Check in with me every hour. And don't tip your fucking hand to him. We may need this guy."

As the door closed behind Lanzo and Mickey, Anthony reached for the telephone.

"Bergonian Hotel, Seattle," he told the operator. As Anthony waited, he tried to think of what he was going to say to Uncle Carlo.

Julia packed while Patrick kept watch in the hallway outside of her bedroom. She looked around, wondering if she'd ever feel safe here again. Or anywhere.

"How are you doing?"

"Almost done," she told him as she placed the last of her clothes in the grip.

She'd decided to stay at her father's house. Patrick had argued against it, initially, until she'd pointed out that the last place Brent would probably look was the house where her father had just died.

"All set." Her whispered voice sounded painfully loud in the otherwise silent bungalow.

"Good. I'll get you settled in, then go back to the hotel and check out. I'm sure Mac's sister-in-law will be glad to see the last of me."

"Do you know where you're going to stay?"

"When I do, you'll be the first to know." He smiled, reassuringly. "I promise."

Once inside Carl's house, Patrick made a tour of the downstairs, checking the windows and doors. Satisfied that everything was secure, he returned to the entryway.

"Wait here," he told her. "I want to take a quick look upstairs."

He checked Julia's room first, then the next room down; Jacob's room, judging by the sports pennants on the walls. Patrick paused a moment to look at the line of framed photographs on the dresser, studio portraits of young, attractive women. "More girls than an Arab sheik," Julia had said of her brother, and here was the evidence to support her claim.

Satisfied that the room was clear, Patrick moved on to Carl's bedroom. As soon as he touched the doorknob, an all-too-familiar tingle ran up his arm and through his body.

Every muscle in his body contracted painfully, and he felt as though he were moving at incredible speed, yet the world around him remained static.

Not yet, he prayed. *Please God, not yet.*

The sensation began to pass. He forced himself to relax, taking in slow, measured breaths. His hand still clutched the doorknob.

Reluctantly, he opened the door to the room, thankful to see Carl's things on the dresser and night stand rather than his own. But time was clearly growing short.

He made his way downstairs to find Julia waiting for him in the parlor.

"Are you all right?" she asked, looking at him with concern. "You look pale."

"I'm fine. It's just been a long day. I should be going."

"I can drive you," she offered.

"No, you need to stay put. I'll catch the streetcar back."

She followed him to the front door. As he went to unlock it, she came up behind him and wrapped her arms around him. Patrick laid his arm across hers, reassuringly.

"I'll call you when I know where I'm staying," he promised her. Still she held him, unwilling to let him leave. "Everything is going to be all right, Julia."

At last she relented. He stepped out onto the front porch, closing the door behind himself.

Mickey was dozing behind the wheel of the Durant when Lanzo nudged him through the open car window.

"Here's our boy," he said, stabbing his cigarette in O'Connell's direction. They watched as O'Connell climbed the steps to the hotel entrance. Mickey looked at his watch. They weren't due to check in with De Campo for almost an hour. So far, there'd been no word from Pellizotti. All they could do at this point was watch and wait.

"All right," he said with a yawn. "Wake me up when it's time to call in, or O'Connell takes off, whichever comes first."

Patrick pushed the door to his room open, jumping noticeably when he saw his friend at the end of his bed, next to the new suitcase.

"Looks like you're planning on going somewhere."

"Dammit, Mac, you scared the crap out of me," Patrick said, closing the door behind him. "I know what you're going to say, but I'm not putting either you or your family into any more danger."

"Fine. I know better than to argue with an Irishman."

Patrick eyed him, skeptically. "Since when?"

Mac ignored the jab. "Before you leave, though, you have to fill me in on what's been going on."

"The long version, or the short one?"

Mac smiled. "The long, of course. But not now. I have to open up the bar in fifteen minutes. Come down and you can tell me everything over a farewell drink."

"All right," Patrick agreed. "But just the one."

"Of course, just the one. That is, unless you're buying."

The setting sun cast long shadows across the floor of Leon's study. He sat in his armchair, cradling a half-empty glass of Scotch in one hand as he looked around the room.

A stack of folders—the confidential files that would be of the most interest to the police after he was gone—lay on the floor beside the fireplace, their contents already ashes in the grate. When Leon Brent disappeared from the world, his indiscretions would disappear with him.

There were just a couple of lingering problems to take care of first.

Julia sat in the growing darkness of her old room, watching the sun disappear beyond the West Hills. The house seemed deathly still.

With a sigh, Julia rose from the window seat and wandered down the hall to the bathroom to splash some water on her face. She looked in the mirror above the sink. Her eyes were still red from crying. *Thank goodness Patrick isn't here to see me like this*, she thought.

Feeling a little more collected, she decided to go make some tea. As she neared the landing, she noticed that the door to her father's room was ajar. Pushing the door open, she stepped inside, the first time she'd been able to bring herself to go into that room since his death.

In truth, she'd never gone in there very often, even when her father was alive. This had been his sanctuary, the room he retreated to when he needed to be alone. It was where he'd grieved after Jacob and Mama had passed. Late at night she would sit on the other side of his bedroom door and listen to him sob in the darkness, and she would cry with him.

And *for* him.

She lay down on the bed and buried her face in her father's pillow, searching for his familiar scent, hoping it would bring him alive for her again, if only for a moment. Only a faint trace remained.

Frustrated, she rolled onto her side and looked at the gilt-framed photograph of her parents on the nightstand. She'd almost forgotten how beautiful her mother was, and how tiny. The top of her head came only to her Papa's chest.

She was about to get up when she noticed the small locket beside the picture and smiled. The locket had once belonged to her mother, but since she'd never actually used it, Julia had appropriated it as a birthday present to her father that March. Inside, she'd placed a small photo of herself, and had the opposite side of the oval case engraved with the words, *With love, Julia.*

"It's beautiful, child," he'd told her, hugging her close, "but men don't wear lockets."

Still, he'd gone out and purchased a new chain to hang it from. She grinned at the thought that her father might have carried the piece of jewelry around like a secret treasure. Then again, that was a very Lundgren thing to do.

As a child she'd had her own small collection of treasures, she remembered; souvenirs from family trips mostly, and a few personal mementos that her brother had felt important enough to hold on to. She'd rescued one of her father's old cigar boxes from the dust bin, placed the keepsakes inside, and taken the box up to the attic. A time capsule, to remind her of life before the world had turned upside-down.

Julia dangled the silver locket from its chain, studying the way the light from the hallway reflected off of the jewelry's polished surface. Papa's treasure should take its place alongside her own, she decided.

She climbed the stairs to the garret, thankful that the dusk still provided enough light to see by. Negotiating the room with care, trying not to disturb some of the more precariously placed heirlooms along her path, she spotted the small box still tucked away in the rafters near the window.

As she pulled her time capsule from its resting place, a cloth bundle sitting next to it on the beam fell to the floor with a thump. Julia picked it up to find a pair of men's trousers, rolled up around an odd looking shirt. The pale light from the window glinted off of the emerald-green leaves of a shamrock pin, set in silver.

Intrigued, she carried the clothes and the cigar box back downstairs.

–21–

"Hey, Mick. Wake up." Lanzo nudged his sleeping friend. "Take a look."

His friend blinked, drowsily, and pushed his fedora up from the bridge of his nose. "O'Connell on the move?"

"No, look over there." Lanzo pointed to the other side of the street. "Isn't that the nigger we saw at the factory this morning?"

Mickey shot a scathing look his partner's way.

"What?" Lanzo asked.

"How would you like it if someone went around calling you dago or wop?"

"I'd cut their fucking tongue out and feed it to them," Lanzo told him. His friend nodded. "Oh, for fuck's sake. Fine. Isn't that the *colored* boy from the factory?"

The big man had drawn even with their automobile. He stood at the corner of 23rd and Hoyt, across from the Campbell, waiting for traffic to pass.

"Looks like him," Mickey agreed.

"What do you think he's doing around here? This ain't exactly his neighborhood."

"Only one way to find out." Mickey started to climb out of the car, but Lanzo put a hand on his shoulder.

"What are you doing? De Campo told us not to tip O'Connell off."

"Yeah, well ... I have a feeling that buck over there is planning on doing that for us."

Mac went to pour a little more whiskey into Patrick's glass, but his friend shook his head.

"If you're thinking that you can keep me here by getting me drunk, it isn't going to work."

"Can't fault me for trying, can you?" The Scot turned serious. "I still say you're just as safe here as you'll be anywhere else, if not safer. Besides, it'll be that much harder for me to help you if you leave."

"I might be safer, but your family isn't." He raised his hand to silence Mac's protest. "You've been more help than I can begin to tell you, but I have to take it from here.

"Besides," Patrick continued, managing a smile. "There's no reason for Brent to go after Julia anymore. The Peregrine deal is all but dead. After all of the questions we raised this morning, I'd be surprised if Stan Goldmark hasn't already advised them to walk away. And Julia is in good hands with Ed Wirth from here on out."

"Yeah, that explains why you moved her out of her bungalow. I'm not buying. And I'm not prepared to let that son of a bitch get away with murder."

Patrick nodded. "All right, we both know the only way this ends for sure is if Brent is *permanently* out of the picture. But you're not going to be the one to do it."

"The problem is, pal of mine, you're no killer."

"You'd be surprised what I'm capable of, when I have to be. Besides, I have the least to lose if things don't work out."

His friend looked at him skeptically. "Is that so? I think your Rachel might have something to say about that. Julia, too, for that matter."

"Julia isn't going to find out about this," Patrick said, firmly. "And Rachel ... Well, as you once pointed out, Rachel is a long way away. This isn't a debate, Mac. The decision has been made."

Mac studied Patrick in silence. Then, with a heavy sigh of resignation, he went to top off both of their glasses. This time, Patrick made no effort to stop him.

Otis sensed someone coming up behind him, even before he heard their footsteps. He forced himself to look back slowly. He was a big man in the wrong part of town. Sudden movements were a very bad idea. When he saw Mr. Brent's friends from the factory, he realized that he was in trouble no matter what he did.

"Something we can help you with, boy? You look a little lost." This from the shorter of the two. His tone was friendly enough, but there wasn't much kindness behind his eyes. Otis spotted the edge of a shoulder holster under the stocky man's jacket.

"No sir. I was just delivering a message to someone here at the hotel."

"A message for Mr. O'Connell?" the taller one asked. Realizing it was pointless to deny that much, Otis nodded. "All right, then. Why don't you give it to us? He's a friend of ours."

"I was supposed to deliver it to him, personal."

The tall man darkened, but the other just smiled.

"Sure, I get it. Of course, you can't go in through the front door. That wouldn't be right, would it? You can go in through the alleyway. Down there," he indicated, pointing along Hoyt. "We'll show you."

Otis didn't have much choice but to agree. He turned and started down past the hotel.

The alley, at the rear of the building, ran no farther back from the street than the far corner of the building. Otis had gone in about twenty feet or so when he heard one of the men behind him say, "That's far enough. Now turn around."

They both held pistols. The tallest of the men stepped forward, his gun hand out in front of him, grinning like he intended to enjoy what was coming.

"Now, what did you have to say to O'Connell that was so damned important you'd come around here, alone, this time of night?"

Otis didn't say a word. Instead, he straightened up slowly. Ignoring the gun barrel hovering inches from his chest, he looked his attacker in the eyes. The gunman flared at the challenge.

"I said, give me the fucking message." The grin had vanished, the man's voice transformed into a harsh growl.

"No, sir," Otis said, quietly. "I don't believe I can."

The thug studied him for a moment, then turned to his friend standing near the entrance to the alley.

"Do you believe this guy? He don't want to talk to us."

When he spun back around, he slammed the butt of his pistol hard against the side of Otis's head.

Mac looked up to see his dishwasher, Len, hurrying over to their table with a worried look on his face.

"You better hurry, Mr. McKenzie. There are two white men beating a colored boy out back."

Before Mac could say anything, Patrick had already leapt up from his chair and headed for the side door.

Lanzo couldn't believe that the big man was still on his feet. A blow like that would have sent most guys to their knees. The Negro looked dazed and uncertain, and a heavy stream of blood—crimson against his ebony skin—flowed down the left side of his face to disappear beneath the worn collar of his shirt. But he was still standing.

"Are you going to talk now, or am I going to have to hit you again?"

The man wavered for a moment, then shot Lanzo a clear look of defiance and shook his head, slowly.

Lanzo raised the gun high once more. Either this guy was going to talk to them, or he wasn't talking to anybody.

As he braced himself for the next blow to fall, Otis saw the man nearest the street go flying, his pistol clattering into the dustbins behind the hotel. At the sound of the gun hitting the pavement, the thug in front of Otis glanced back over his shoulder.

In all of his fifty-five years, Otis had never hit a white man before.

He hit this one with every bit of strength he had left.

Lanzo crumpled against the hotel wall and dropped to one knee. His jaw felt like someone had tried to shove it back up into his head. As he wiped away the blood trickling down from the right corner of his mouth, it took him a moment to realize that the hand he was using still held the pistol. Getting unsteadily to his feet, he turned to face the man who had clocked him. The nigger looked about done in, down on hands and knees, barely able to hold himself up.

Lanzo aimed the pistol at the man's head.

"Put the gun down, Lanzo."

He knew the voice, but in his daze he couldn't quite place it.

"Goddamn it, I said, put it down."

Lanzo turned and tried to make sense of what he saw. Mickey sat on the ground, looking up at O'Connell. Nearby stood an all-too-familiar figure, leveling a revolver in Lanzo's direction.

"McKenzie? What the hell are you doing here? You ain't a cop no more."

"I'm not going to tell you again, Lanzo. Put the goddamned gun down."

Lanzo did as he was told. He was still feeling so wobbly from the punch, he doubted if he could manage to aim straight, anyway.

"Now, kick it behind you."

"You shouldn't be nosing in, McKenzie." The handgun skittered noisily across the pavement. "This doesn't concern you."

"You let me worry about that. I have to say, I'm surprised you guys are running errands for a shit like Brent, after what he did to your old boss." The former detective must have caught the look on Lanzo's face. "You didn't know Brent killed Lewis, did you? What about you, Mickey? Did you have any idea you guys were being played?"

Lanzo's friend looked up, sullenly. "So you say."

"We go back a long way, you and me. How many times did I run you in, over the years?"

"Too many for my taste," Mick admitted with a begrudging smile.

"But I always played straight with you, didn't I?" Mickey nodded. "So you know me, and you know Brent. Who do *you* think you can trust?"

Mick looked over at his friend, then back up at McKenzie. "Let's hear your side of it, then."

"Why don't you go help Lanzo, first? He looks like he's about to fall over."

Julia had been sitting behind the wheel of the La Salle for several minutes, eyeing the entrance to the Campbell. Finally, reluctantly, she climbed out of the automobile and made her way around the corner of the building, toward the after-hours entrance.

If she could get Mac alone for a few minutes, she hoped, maybe she could get some answers to her questions. Maybe he could help her make some sense of what Patrick was up to.

As she neared the side door, Julia heard voices in the alleyway behind the building. One of them was Mac's.

The Negro was still on his hands and knees near the back of the alley. Even from this distance, Mac could see blood streaming down the side of the big man's face onto the ground below.

"So, let's have it," Mickey said, his left shoulder up under Lanzo's arm as he half-carried his partner back toward the street.

"Brent needed Lewis and Daly to help him pull off a deal," Mac said, "When he was done with them, he killed them to cover his steps. Made it look like they'd had a falling out. He murdered Daly's wife, too."

"Why?"

Mac shrugged. "My guess is, so that it would look like you boys were out to make an example of her."

"Yeah, that's the angle the cops were trying to push, all right." Lanzo spat a gob of blood, grimacing at the effort. "Like we go around killing women."

"You don't, but Brent does. Maggie wasn't his first."

"Where does *she* fit in?" Mickey asked, nodding past the Scot's shoulder.

Patrick and Mac turned to see Julia, staring wide-eyed at the scene before her.

"What are you doing here?" Patrick asked, anxiously. She barely glanced in his direction.

"Mac," she said, her voice tense, "what's going on? Who are these men?"

Before he could answer, she spotted the figure on the ground behind them.

"Oh, God, *Otis!*" she cried, rushing past them all to help him.

A fleeting look of guilt passed over Mickey's face. Lanzo merely spat once more, his blood staining the ground by his feet.

Mac nodded to Patrick, who hurried after her.

"Listen," the Scot told Lanzo and Mickey, quietly, "bring De Campo around to the bar in about an hour and I'll fill you in on everything. There's something he and Pellizotti should know about Leon Brent."

"What about our guns?" Lanzo asked.

Mac smiled. "I'll give them to you when you get back ... As long as you're not planning on shooting up my bar, of course."

Otis had managed to sit down with his legs in front of him by the time Julia reached his side. She knelt and inspected the gash along the side of his head. It didn't look too deep, thank God, but blood still flowed from it. What frightened her most was the unfocused look in her friend's eyes.

"Otis, can you hear me?"

He nodded, sluggishly.

"Let me take a look," Patrick said, firmly.

Julia moved to one side to let him examine the side of Otis's head.

"There's some swelling ..." He glanced at Julia and smiled, reassuringly. "Swelling isn't a bad thing. That means the pressure has some place to go. We need to get a towel and some ice."

"I'll get it," Mac said.

Julia looked up to see him leaning over her shoulder. There was no sign of the two men he'd been talking with.

"Call an ambulance," Patrick told his friend. "We've got to get Otis to a hospital."

Mac looked at him in surprise. "There aren't any colored hospitals in Portland. We'll have a hell of a time even finding a doctor who will treat him."

Julia watched Patrick's face and neck muscles tighten in outrage. "You have got to be *fucking* kidding me. How is that even possible?"

"I don't make the rules," Mac said, defensively. "And, for what it's worth, I'm not too happy about it, either. I'll go get the ice."

"I don't believe this," Patrick growled as he turned his attention back to Otis. "*Colored* hospital ..."

The word "colored" sounded foreign and foul-tasting, the way he said it. Julia saw him take a deep breath to collect himself. Then he shook his head and looked over at her.

"I'm sorry about that. I kind of lost it there, didn't I?"

"I thought that you'd be gone by now," she said, after a moment.

"I'm all packed and ready to go. Mac talked me into sticking around for a farewell drink."

"I'm glad that he did."

Mac came back with the ice, wrapped in a towel. Patrick applied the towel to the swelling.

"How's he doing?" his friend asked.

"Little better," Otis mumbled. "Thanks for helping."

Mac nodded, showing a hint of a smile. "You're welcome, but try not to make a habit of this. Why did you come here, anyway?"

"I came to warn Mr. O'Connell about those two men." Otis shifted his eyes to look at Patrick. "Guess that didn't work out so well."

"You did just fine," Mac assured him. "I've got Len setting up a cot in the storage room, then we'll see about getting you a doctor."

"Miss Julia, could you get a hold of Callie? She'll be worried sick if I don't come home soon."

"Of course. Mac, may I use your telephone?"

"You don't even need to ask. Just tell Len I said it was okay."

Len guided her to the telephone—in a back room just off of the kitchen—and she asked the operator to connect her to the number that Otis had given her. His landlord answered, and hurried off to find Otis's wife.

While she waited, Julia took a deep breath and gathered her thoughts. This day felt like the longest of her life.

Callie Loring came on the line with a tentative, "Hello?"

"Callie, this is Julia Lundgren. Otis asked me to telephone you and let you know that he's been hurt. He's going to be fine, though."

Please, God, let me sound more confident of that than I feel.

"Where is he at? I want to see him."

Julia eyed the small cot that Mac's employee had set up along the far wall of the room, trying to imagine how Otis could possibly fit on it.

"Miss Lundgren?"

"I'm sorry, Callie. Otis is going to be staying at my father's house." The words were out of her mouth before she'd even given the idea much thought. "Once we get him settled we'll find a doctor, just to make sure that's he's going to be fine."

"I can try to reach Dr. Unthank, if that would be all right with you."

"If Dr. Unthank will come, why wouldn't it be all right?"

There was brief silence on the other end, then, "Well, he's a colored doctor, Miss Lundgren."

Julia hadn't even known that Portland had a colored doctor. "Find him, Callie. Have him come to this address as soon as possible ..."

When Julia came back from her phone call, Patrick and Mac were carefully helping Otis to his feet.

"I talked to Callie," she said. "I told her you were injured, but that you should be all right. She's sending for Dr. Unthank, and he'll meet us at my father's house."

"Julia, I don't think that's a very good idea," Mac said.

"Well, he can't very well stay in your back room. At least at the house he won't be dangling his legs off the end of a cot."

"I'm not sure he'll even be able to make it up the front steps," Patrick pointed out.

"That's why you're coming with us. Now, wait here while I bring the car around."

Five minutes later, Otis lay in the back of the La Salle while Julia drove down 23rd. Traffic was light, thankfully. There was no telling how long it might take for Dr. Unthank to get to her father's house, but in the meantime, they could get Otis into a bed and make him as comfortable as possible.

Out of the corner of her eye, Julia saw Patrick watching her.

"You still haven't told me why you were at the hotel tonight," he said. "I thought you were supposed to stay put for awhile."

Julia glanced at the back seat. Otis's eyes were closed, but she couldn't be certain whether he was asleep or awake.

"There was something I needed to talk to Mac about," she said, simply. "It's not important right now."

Navigating the steps leading up the hill to Carl's house turned out to be easier than Patrick had expected. Otis managed under his own power, requiring only a little support along the way.

Julia unlocked the front door and ushered them in.

"We'll put him in my father's room. It has the biggest bed."

Otis looked horrified. "Miss Julia, It wouldn't be right for me to stay in Mr. Lundgren's bed."

"Otis, hush. I don't think Papa would have had it any other way. Now, do you need to rest, or are you up to a few more stairs?"

Patrick couldn't help but smile. When Julia took that tone, he knew from personal experience, there was little point in arguing. The big man shuffled over to the staircase.

The climb took quite a bit out of Otis. Patrick braced himself against the foreman, providing as much support as he could while Julia opened the door to Carl's bedroom. She hurried over and turned on the small lamp at the nightstand, then pulled the covers back. Patrick guided Otis over to sit on the edge of the mattress. While Patrick held him in place, Julia removed the injured man's shoes. Together, they eased him onto the bed.

The cut on the side of Otis's head had stopped bleeding. The swelling looked as though it had gone down a little, as well. If he were a betting man, Patrick would lay odds that the big man had nothing more serious than a mild concussion.

"How is it?" Julia asked, watching him closely.

"He's going to be fine." Patrick turned to look at her. "How are you doing? It's been quite a day."

She gave him a curious look. "It's been that, in spades, but I'm coming to expect that when you're around. By the way, I took the liberty of having Len put your grip in the back of the car."

"Now why would you do that?"

"It's not as though you have anywhere else to go, do you? Besides, I'll need your help with Otis. Why don't you go get your bag while I put on a pot of tea?"

"Best do as she says," Otis whispered. His eyes were closed, but there was a faint, knowing smile on his face. "There ain't no arguing with this woman."

–22–

De Campo sat across the table from Mac, a cup of coffee in front of him. Mickey and Lanzo, looking a little the worse for wear, were stationed nearby to keep an eye on things.

So far, the meeting had gone well. De Campo seemed to be a reasonable young man, and neither of his gunmen appeared to hold a grudge about what had happened in the alley.

Of course, Mac knew that could change in a hurry. That's why he had closed the bar and sent Len upstairs to watch the front desk for awhile. If things turned ugly, he didn't want anyone else involved.

"So, this is all about some fucking real estate deal." De Campo looked none too happy.

Mac nodded. "There's something else that you and your uncle should know about Leon," he added, "something that happened back in Chicago before the war."

When he'd finished laying it all out, Pellizotti's nephew sat in silence for a few seconds. Then he got up and went over to Mickey. They huddled together in conference for a moment before De Campo came back to the table.

"Mickey tells me you're all right, but you know I'm going to have to check all this out," he said, at last. "I'm not taking your word on something like this."

"I wouldn't expect you to."

De Campo nodded. "You have a telephone that I can use? I'll reverse the charges," he added with a smile.

"Don't bother. If this will take care of Brent, I'll spring for the call."

Julia had just poured the tea when the front bell rang. She started for the door but Patrick stopped her.

"Stay here until we know who it is," he told her as he left the kitchen.

Moving quietly through the darkened dining room, he edged toward the entryway. Through the window, he saw a black man holding a medical bag. He opened the door to find the doctor standing beside a stout, worried looking woman he assumed to be Otis's wife.

"Doctor, I'm glad you could come so quickly," he said, extending his hand. The other man looked a little surprised, but showed no hesitation in shaking Patrick's hand.

Patrick turned to the woman next to him. "And you must be Callie," he said, warmly. "Please, come in."

He stood aside to let them enter, then locked the door behind them as Julia hurried into the room. She immediately embraced the older woman.

"Callie, I'm so sorry," she whispered. "But Otis is going to be just fine. He's been in good hands," she added, looking to Patrick.

"Thank you, Miss Lundgren."

Julia stepped back and looked Otis's wife in the eyes.

"No more of that. It's Julia." She turned to the doctor and held out her hand. "I'm Julia Lundgren. And this is my friend, Patrick O'Connell. Thank you so much for coming."

"DeNorval Unthank. It's very nice to meet you both." The doctor glanced toward the parlor. "Is my patient in there?"

"No, we put him in my father's room, upstairs. Patrick, why don't you show Dr. Unthank the way while we wait down here?"

Callie started to protest, but Unthank patted her shoulder reassuringly.

"It will be easier for me to examine him that way. It won't take long, I promise."

"He took a pretty hard blow to the head, on the left side," Patrick explained as he led the doctor upstairs. "I don't think that he lost consciousness, and there didn't appear to be any nausea or slurred speech. His pupils were a little dilated when I first looked at him," he added as they entered Carl's bedroom.

Otis was sleeping. Dr. Unthank found the switch near the door and turned the ceiling light on so that he could better examine his patient. Otis stirred, but didn't wake. The doctor moved around to the far side of the room and placed his bag gently on the foot of the bed.

"Anything else you can tell me?" he asked.

"He has a cut, just above the hairline on the left side of his head. Not very deep, but there was a lot of bleeding. And there was some swelling. We applied an ice pack, and I think that its' gone down a bit."

"That's very thorough," Unthank said as he pulled his stethoscope out. "Have you had medical training, Mr. O'Connell?"

"Just some basic first aid during the war."

"That would be the place to learn it, I suppose."

The doctor listened to Otis's heartbeat and breathing, and took his pulse. Then Unthank performed a cursory examination of the wound before taking a seat on the edge of the bed.

"Otis," he said, softly. "Otis, wake up. This is Dr. Unthank. Can you hear me?"

The big man's eyes fluttered opened, only to squeeze shut against the assault of the ceiling light.

"Mr. O'Connell," the doctor said, using his hand to help shield Otis's face. "I think we might dispense with that light now."

When the room was darker, Unthank lowered his hand, resting it on his patient's chest.

"Try to open your eyes now."

Otis raised his eyelids cautiously. Even the light from the bedside lamp seemed to bother him, but he managed to keep them open. Dr. Unthank leaned in close and examined Otis's pupils.

"The good news is that, even though they're still dilated, they're equal. That's promising. Otis, can you tell me what day this is?"

"Monday." His voice wasn't strong, but he sounded clear and confident.

"That's right. And do you know where you are?"

"Mister Lundgren's house."

"Very good. Now, can you tell me what happened?"

"Two men, in an alley ... one of them hit me with his pistol. If Patrick and his friend hadn't come along ..."

"Do you have any idea who these men were?" he asked, but Otis's eyelids had closed as if he were drifting back into sleep. The doctor looked from his patient back up to Patrick. He managed a thin smile as he put his stethoscope away.

"It seems we're done here," he said as he stood. "Why don't we let the ladies know that they can come up?"

Well, Mac thought, *it's out of my hands now.*

He looked up to see Len coming into the otherwise-empty bar.

"Is everything all right?" the young man asked, eyeing the bottle of Scotch and half-full glass in front of his boss.

"As right as they can be, I hope. You lock the front doors before you came down?"

"Yep. I'm going to head home now, unless there's something else that you need me to take care of."

Mac shook his head. "Have a good night. We'll see you tomorrow."

"Good night, Mr. McKenzie." Len started to turn away, then stopped and reached into his coat pocket, pulling out a thick envelope. "I almost forgot. When that lady asked me to fetch Mr. O'Connell's grip from upstairs, I found this on the nightstand. It's got your name on it."

Mac waited until he was alone once more before turning the envelope over to open it. He paused, reading the note his friend had written beneath the flap.

I can't possibly thank you enough for all that you've done, or for your friendship, but this is a start. Give my best to O'Halloron, and take care of that family of yours.

Mac lifted the flap and looked inside. He studied the contents for a moment, then reached for the bottle in front of him, his hand shaking just a little.

Patrick poured a cup of tea for Dr. Unthank, then took a seat on the other side of the little kitchen table. The doctor poured a little cream into the amber liquid. Then he added two lumps of sugar, methodically stirring the mixture until the cubes had dissolved completely. Satisfied, he raised the cup to his lips and took a sip.

"How is it?" Patrick asked.

"I'm not usually much of a tea drinker, but this is very nice." He took another sip before placing his cup back on its saucer. "It sounds as though Otis is fortunate that you came along when you did. Where did this happen?"

"Not far from the factory," Fortunately, *far* was a relative term so, at most, Patrick was just stretching the truth a little.

"May I ask how you ended up bringing him here?"

"That was Julia's idea. I wanted to get him to a hospital, but I've been informed that there aren't any hospitals in this city that would take him in."

Unthank frowned as he nodded. "That's true. In fact, I'm no more welcome than my patients."

"How can you sound so calm about that? I'd be so angry I'd want to throttle someone."

The doctor smiled. "Of course I'm angry. And I've met more than a few men who could probably use a good throttling. But if things are ever going to change, my people need to show the best of what we are, not the worst of we can be."

Patrick nodded, a little ashamed of his outburst.

"Good men building bridges faster than bigots can tear them down," he said.

"Something like that," Unthank agreed with a smile.

"You're right. That's exactly what changes the world."

"Then we have something to look forward to," Julia said, softly.

The men looked to find the two women standing in the doorway. Patrick couldn't help but notice that Julia wore an odd, unreadable expression. Callie, on the other hand, looked much more relaxed now that she had seen her husband.

"Otis is sleeping," she told them.

"Callie needs to get home to Sarah and the baby, doctor," Julia added. "I can drive her, if you'd like."

"No need. I have another patient in her neighborhood, anyway." Unthank rose. "I don't think that Otis is in any danger, but if you need to reach me, here are my home and office numbers."

Patrick took the doctor's card and followed the other three to the door.

"I'd like to look in on Otis in the morning, if that would be all right," the doctor said.

"You're welcome any time," Julia assured him.

"Then I will see you both tomorrow."

Julia glanced at Patrick for a moment. "I hope so, Doctor," she said, earnestly.

–23–

The lock to Julia's front door unlatched with a soft click. Apparently, Leon hadn't lost any of the skills he'd learned in his youth. He pushed the door open and stepped inside. The bungalow was empty, but he'd assumed as much when night had fallen and no lights had come on.

He turned his flashlight on, taking care to keep the beam away from any windows, and moved down the hallway to the bedroom in search of a place to wait. He only needed to buy himself a few seconds before she spotted him. Just enough time to keep her from screaming.

Using a knife was out of the question, tonight. He couldn't risk anything that might tie Julia back to the way that Daly's wife had died. But Julia was a small woman. He could squeeze the life out of her, perhaps even snap her neck with a little effort. Not as tidy as an accident, but by the time he was done, the police would have no doubt that the pretty girl's murder was the result of an assault gone wrong.

He was going to enjoy that.

The bedroom door hinged on the right, hard against the wall, so it provided no real cover. That left the closet. Less than ideal, unless that was where she kept her nightclothes. He scanned the space with the flashlight. Strangely, it was almost empty; there were a couple of robes hanging there, but no dresses or jackets, except those too heavy for summer wear.

Suddenly anxious, he turned to the bedroom, casting his light across the dresser at the foot of the bed. Two of the drawers were partially pulled out, as though someone had been in too great a hurry to close them. He checked to find them emptied of their contents.

He cursed under his breath and looked in the closet again, and under the bed, anywhere Julia might keep a suitcase. Nothing.

Damn her to hell, she's moved out of reach, he realized, angrily. Killing her had been his last chance to save John Ingersol, and there was no time to find her now. Not with the specter of Johnny Torrio looming.

Frustrated, he slipped back out of the bungalow. All that was left for him now was to go home and wait for Pellizotti's boys to call when they had that fucking Irishman, O'Connell.

At least he still had that much to look forward to.

Julia stood at the kitchen sink. She lifted her head at the sound of the doors swinging on their hinges when Patrick entered the room, but didn't look around.

"I've put a fresh cup of tea on the table for you," she said in a tired voice. "You'd better drink it before it grows cold."

He took his seat at the small table, and Julia joined him a moment later. As she set her own cup and saucer down, Patrick saw the hand that held them tremble a little.

"Are you holding up okay?" he asked, gently. "You've had quite a ride, today."

She looked down at the cup in front of her. "What was it that your father says about tea? 'A moment of peace ...'"

"'In a world of chaos,'" he finished for her, smiling.

She nodded, closing her eyes. He watched her breath slowly, deliberately, as he'd seen her do before when she was composing herself.

"Julia?" he asked, tentatively.

"When was your father born, Patrick?"

"I'm sorry?"

She looked at him, her brown eyes holding his unflinchingly.

"Your father. What year was he born, Patrick? For that matter, what year were *you* born?" When he didn't answer, she smiled. "That's all right. I already know."

Julia lifted her left hand, the one she had been resting in her lap. She held a small card between her thumb and finger. His driver's license, he saw at once.

"I found this up in the attic." She looked up at him, suspicion in her eyes. "This says that you were born on March 21st, *1950*. How old does that make you? Thirty nine? Forty?"

"Forty," he admitted, calmly. He knew he wasn't creative enough to come up with a more plausible explanation, anyway. "No ... actually, I'll be forty one in four days, if I make it home."

She pushed herself back in her chair. "Am I supposed to believe that you're here from *1991*?"

Patrick shrugged. "I can't think of a single reason why you would, Julia. I had a difficult time of it, myself."

"This isn't possible," she whispered to herself. "How can any of this be possible? You've been lying to me this entire time," she said, accusingly.

"Only through omission."

"You told me that you knew my brother."

He smiled at that. "I think I said we were in the same division in the Army, which is true. We just served in very different wars."

She scowled, as though she wanted to argue the point but couldn't.

"Explain how you supposedly managed to travel through time, then," she challenged.

"I'm not sure myself. The only theory that I have came from your friend, Max Templeton."

She leaned forward, confused. "*Who* did you say?"

"Doctor Max Templeton. He's a physics professor at the college I teach at." Patrick smiled. "Nice guy. You're going to like him. Anyway, he theorized that a wormhole somehow connected my present to yours."

"Templeton," she muttered, "Max Templeton? I don't believe ..." She shook her head as though trying to clear her thoughts. "What did you call it? A *wormhole*? What in the world is a wormhole?"

"Some kind of shortcut through space, or time ... something like that. In truth, I only understood about half of what he was talking about."

"What were your things doing in the attic?"

"This is where I started from ... the night your father was murdered. I was here."

"You saw my father being murdered?" Julia's voice quavered as she struggled to control her emotions.

"No, I arrived too late to stop that, but I saw his murderer."

"Brent," Julia whispered.

Patrick shook his head. "One of your father's former employees, a man named Brian Daly. But Brent paid him to do it. I figured out who Daly was the next day, but by then he was already dead."

"Daly ... Mac was talking about his wife in the alley tonight." The skepticism in her voice seemed to have faded, at least a little.

Patrick nodded. "I was too late to stop Maggie Daly's death, too, but I got a decent look at her killer. When I saw Brent at your father's funeral, I was pretty sure he was the guy. Mac helped me prove it."

"So that's why you came here after the service," she said, as she fit the pieces together. "And that's the reason that you've been following me around."

He smiled. "You came to *me*, remember? You were the one sitting at my table at the Campbell that morning." She reddened as he added, "And I'm glad you did. You're a remarkable woman, Julia. Then again, I knew that before I came here."

Julia smiled, in spite of her best efforts not to. "So we know each other, where you come from?"

"When I moved ... *move* ... to Portland to teach at the university, you hire me to be a live-in caretaker for this house. And you land on my list of favorite people very quickly," he confessed.

"In 1991 I'll be eighty-six." She laughed softly. "And to think Jill Haycox warned that you were too old for *me*."

Julia stared down at her tea in silence. Patrick could only imagine the questions and doubts running through her mind at that moment.

"Julia, I realize that this is impossible for you to believe right now ..."

She looked up, a faint, sad smile on her face. "I don't understand any of this, but I *do* believe you." She tapped her finger on the driver's license in front of her. "After all, why would anyone go to this much trouble to promote such an absurd story? Do you know everything that's going to happen, then?"

He shrugged. "Generally, if I haven't changed something by being here."

"What happens now?"

"The Peregrine deal doesn't go through. I think we've raised enough doubts to make sure of that, at least. Brent won't have any reason to hurt you."

"Other than revenge. But that wasn't what I was really asking. What happens to *you*? Do you go back?"

He frowned. "I don't know, but the portal is still open. I felt it this afternoon."

"Do you *have* to go?' she asked, softly. "You could stay here."

"I don't think I'd be strong enough to resist the temptation to change the future. Not where *you're* concerned." Her cheeks flushed as the meaning of his words registered. "Now, why don't you get some sleep? I'll stay up so that I can check in on Otis from time to time."

"No," Julia said, firmly. "I don't think I'll be able to sleep, anyway. I've made the bed up in Jacob's room for you."

"All right, if you're sure." He stood and took his cup and saucer to the sink, then made his way toward the door.

"Patrick," Julia called out as he was almost to the dining room. He turned back to face her. "Who is Rachel?"

"She may be the great love of my life." He smiled. "And she's more like her grandmother than I could ever have imagined."

The phone, ringing on the nightstand, jolted Leon awake from what had been a fitful sleep. He rolled over and flicked the lamp on, muttering darkly as he checked the alarm clock. *Twelve thirty in the fucking morning.* He lifted the receiver from its cradle, hoping that one of Pellizotti's boys would be on the line.

"Leon?" The woman on the other end sounded distraught. It took him a moment to recognize Louise Ingersol's voice. "I'm sorry to call so late, but with Carl gone, I didn't know who else to turn to."

"It's all right, Louise. What's wrong? Has something happened to John?"

"He hasn't come home tonight." She sounded as though she were on the verge of tears. "I called the Aero Club and they said that he was there. He's been drinking heavily, again. Leon, I've never seen him like this."

"Don't worry, Louise, Everything is going to be all right." He swung his legs out from under the covers, using his bare feet to feel for his slippers. "I'll be at the club in twenty minutes."

He hung the receiver up and sat on the edge of the bed, pressing the palms of his hands against his temples in frustration and anger. Frustration that John would fall apart like this. Anger at the ones who had made it impossible for Leon to make things right; at Lundgren and his bitch daughter for being so goddamned selfish and stubborn, and at O'Connell for finding a way to beat him.

There would be no end to the agony he was going to inflict on that fucking Irishman, he decided as he dressed.

Ten minutes later, Leon stepped off of the elevator and strode quickly through the lobby of the Ludlow Apartments. Sal, the night doorman, hurried to open the heavy, brass-framed door to Salmon Street. The attorney stalked past him without comment—taking the steps to the sidewalk two at a time—and headed for 21st Avenue, where he'd left the Packard.

He moved between the front of his car and the old Dodge he'd parked behind, pausing to check for oncoming traffic. A large automobile had just pulled away from the curb, its headlights temporarily blinding him as they approached. He waited for it to pass before stepping into the street.

Instead, the sedan pulled up alongside Leon's car and came to a stop. Inside, Mickey grinned up at him from the front passenger's seat.

"Evening, counselor. A little late to be going out, isn't it?"

"What are you doing here?" Leon kept his tone calm, much calmer than he felt.

"You told us to come get you when we had O'Connell."

"I said to let me know when you had him, not come to my apartment."

Mickey merely shrugged. "We were in the neighborhood. Why don't you get in, and we'll take you to him."

The alarms went off inside of Leon's head as he heard the words he himself had used more than once in another life back in Chicago. Cautiously, he peered into the sedan. There were only two men inside; Mickey, and the driver. Leon recognized him as Lewis's bodyguard from the club. The big man seemed indifferent to the whole conversation, his eyes scanning the street around them.

Leon felt the comforting weight of his pistol in its leather holster under his coat.

"I have someplace I need to be right now," Leon told Pellizotti's men, stalling for a little more time. "I'll meet you out at the farm in the morning."

Mickey started to open the passenger door. "Just get into the car, counselor," he ordered, the smile gone from his face.

Leon snatched at the opportunity. He brought his right hand up under his coat, fingers grasping for his Colt. Mickey—caught halfway out of the automobile—made no move for his own weapon. The driver hadn't moved either.

Too fucking easy, Leon thought as he began to pull the pistol free. Then the world exploded inside of his brain. He was only dimly aware of the pain radiating from the back of his skull as the pavement drifted up slowly to meet him.

A moment later, he stopped being aware of anything at all.

–24–

The lights of a thousand houses glowed like tiny stars in the valley below, a constellation of normalcy in a universe that had stopped making sense to Julia. Sitting at the window seat in her bedroom, knees tucked under her chin, Julia looked out over the distant neighborhoods in silent envy.

It must be nice to think of the future in terms of weeks rather than decades, years rather than a lifetime. To be able to hold on to someone you love.

Patrick's wallet sat on the cushion in front of her, its contents arranged neatly around it. Strange, thick cards, embossed with numbers and issued by banks she'd never heard of, and money dating sixty years into the future. The driver's license, stiff like celluloid, bearing Patrick's photograph and an all too familiar address. All of it irrefutable evidence of what she wanted so badly not to believe.

And then there was that bit about Max. She'd almost laughed when he'd told her the most absurd element of the story, and the most convincing.

Julia returned the items to the wallet, doing her best to put everything back as she'd found them. Then, with a deep sigh of resignation, she stood and pulled a light robe on over her thin cotton night dress, slipping the wallet into her pocket.

She made her way quietly across the hall to her father's room. Taking care not to make too much noise, she looked in on Otis, listening to her friend's slow, labored breathing as he slept.

How did you become involved in all of this, she wondered.

Satisfied that he was resting comfortably, Julia stepped back into the hallway and made her way to Jacob's room. Nervously, she turned the knob and pushed the door open.

The room was dark, and she could just see Patrick's sleeping form under the sheet. He lay on his back, his left arm stretched out to the side, his head turned away from the door.

Once her eyes had adjusted more fully, Julia spotted the clothes that she'd laid out on the bed for him—the ones she'd discovered in the attic—folded neatly on the chair next to the closet. She pulled the wallet from her robe and walked across the room, her footsteps barely a whisper on the cool wooden floor, and placed the billfold gently atop the clothes. Then she turned to the bed once more.

Patrick's eyes were still closed in relaxed sleep. The sheet, draped across his body just below his bare chest, rose and fell slowly with each breath. Julia studied him in the darkness.

He couldn't stay with me if he wanted to, she realized, sadly. And some part of him did want to stay. He'd as much as said so.

Well, he's here now, and this may be the only moment I have with him.

She removed her robe and set it carefully over the back of the chair above his clothes. Then she eased herself onto the bed until her body pressed gently against his, separated only by a sheet and the thin cotton of her night dress.

As she laid her head on his shoulder Patrick shifted in his sleep, pulling his arm down to cradle her closer.

–25–

It felt as though someone had removed the back of Leon's head with a dull axe. He grimaced and tried to raise a hand to check the damage, but his arms were tied firmly behind his back. He pulled at the cords, felt them cut deeply into his wrists. Each movement caused his head to throb, and gained him nothing. He gave it up as a lost cause and opened his eyes, squinting against the glare.

Morning sunlight streamed through the dust-streaked window in front of him. Mickey, sitting nearby at a small wooden table, smiled when he saw Leon was awake.

"Look who is back among the living. Good morning, counselor."

Details from the night before formed slowly in Leon's aching brain ... the car outside of his apartment building ... Mickey and the driver and ... someone had sapped Leon from behind.

He forced himself to fight through the pain and turn his head. The tall, thin Italian—*why the hell can't I ever remember his name,* Leon wondered, vaguely—stood near the sink, watching him coldly. The left side of the man's face was heavily bruised.

"Thanks for suggesting this farm, counselor." Mickey was speaking again. "Nobody around for half a mile. The perfect place to conduct our business, isn't it, Lanzo?"

"Couldn't be better."

Leon eyed his captors in sullen silence.

"Nothing to say, counselor?" Mickey's smile faded. "Not even going to try to sway the jury? Then again, you already know the verdict, don't you? From what I've heard, you were in this racket back when Lanzo was still sticking up crippled newsies for nickels and dimes. You were big time, running with Johnny Torrio and Big Al Capone back in the day, weren't you?"

At the mention of Torrio's name, the last vestige of hope faded from Leon's mind.

"Johnny T asked us to pass along a long-overdue present, counselor. But first, we have a couple of presents of our own for you. Hold him down, Frankie."

Two enormous hands pressed down heavily on Leon's shoulders from behind, sausage-like fingers digging painfully into his muscles. Lanzo stepped into sight, cradling a crowbar in his hands. Panic finally cut through Leon's fog as he realized death wasn't going to come quickly.

"First one is for killing Dan Lewis," Mickey said, his voice icily calm, "and sticking us with Pellizotti."

Leon heard the iron bar crush his left knee a moment before the pain registered. He threw his head back and howled in agony. The hands holding him down left his shoulders long enough to grip his jaw and forehead, forcing his mouth open while someone rammed a foul-tasting rag or towel inside, effectively muffling his screams.

"Don't want to wake the neighbors," he heard Mickey say.

Leon opened his tear-filled eyes to see the gunman standing close, even as he felt himself slipping into unconsciousness. A stinging backhand across his face brought him back from the brink.

"Not yet, counselor. We've just started to have fun here. This next one is for conning De Campo into having us clean up your little mess."

Leon closed his eyes, bracing himself for the next blow. Instead, he felt hot breath against his ear as Mickey leaned close and whispered, "But mostly, this is for the way you butchered the Daly woman, you fucking coward."

This time, the sound of bones shattering and the excruciating pain hit as one.

–26–

Patrick opened his eyes, unsure at first where—or when—he was. When he felt the body nestled close against him, his first thought was of Rachel. Then the faint scent of lavender washed over him and he realized that his arm was around Julia. Her head rested on his shoulder, her left arm stretched across his bare chest. Reluctantly, he eased himself gently away from her and slipped out of bed.

She sighed and rolled over, still asleep. Taking care not to wake her, Patrick pulled the light comforter at the foot of the bed gently up over Julia. Then he gathered his clothes up from the chair and left the room.

Ed Wirth hung the receiver up and looked over his notes, his mind wrestling with what to do about the information he'd just received. Finally, he reached for the phone again and dialed the number Mr. O'Connell had given him the day before.

Stan Goldmark answered on the second ring.

"Mr. Goldmark, this is Ed Wirth. I'm representing Lundgren Furniture."

"So I was told. I've heard good things about you, Mr. Wirth."

Ed wasn't sure whether to be flattered, or concerned that Goldmark had apparently been asking around about him.

"I'm assuming that you've had a chance to familiarize yourself with the details of the Peregrine deal," Goldmark continued. "Hopefully, you can help your client understand how useless it would be to drag this through civil court."

"Actually, Mr. Goldmark, that's why I wanted to speak with you ... before I contact the police."

There was a moment of silence at the other end of the line.

"The police?" Goldmark said at last, his voice impressively even. "I hope that you're not implying that my firm is involved in anything illegal."

"Not at all. I believe that you and your client are as much victims in this as Miss Lundgren is."

"The contract and the endorsement *are* forgeries, then." It was more statement than question, the way Goldmark said it.

"Without a doubt. But I'm afraid this goes well beyond forgery. I just spoke with the manager of the Bank of Kenton, where Lundgren allegedly cashed your check. At my request, he went through the books for the day in question. The transaction was handled by a teller named ..." Ed checked his notes, "Samuel Lederer."

"And did you speak with Mr. Lederer?"

"I'm afraid that's impossible, Mr. Goldmark. Sam Lederer's body washed up in the Columbia River two days after the check was cashed. At the moment, the police haven't ruled whether his death was the result of an accident or suicide. But the timing of his death, and Mr. Lundgren's accident ..."

Ed let the attorney consider the obvious implications.

"I would like to keep Peregrine Industries and my firm out of any inquiries, if possible," Goldmark said, at last. "Understand, I'm not asking you to withhold evidence from the police."

"At this point, I have no evidence, only concerns relating to a disputed business arrangement between your client and my own."

"And if that arrangement was no longer a concern for your client?"

"There would be no further need to pursue this matter from our end," Ed said, pragmatically. As sickening as he found the possibility of Leon Brent getting away with two murders, he doubted the police would find enough evidence to convict him.

"You understand," Goldmark said, "I will need to confirm your information with the bank manager."

"Of course."

"I'll be in touch with you as soon as I've spoken with my client. And, Ed, thank you for calling," the attorney added. "I think I may owe you one."

The morning sun fell across Julia's closed eyes, nudging her out of her sleep. She blinked against the light, sighed, and rolled over. Then she remembered where she was and her eyes flew open. She sat up in bed, clutching the comforter to her chest, and looked around Jacob's bedroom.

Patrick was gone, his clothes missing from the chair.

Julia slipped out from under the covers and hurried out into the hallway. Looking to her right and seeing that the bath was empty, she went over to her father's room and quietly opened the door. She could hear someone snoring softly from the other side.

"Patrick?" she whispered, peeking her head around the edge of the door. Otis stirred slightly in bed, but didn't wake. There was no one else in the room.

Anxiety bordering on panic rose in her chest. She almost ran down the stairs, a feeling of hopelessness taking hold of her.

"Patrick!" she called out frantically as she neared the last step. *He can't have gone back. Not yet.*

"I'm in here, Julia," he called from the parlor.

She rounded the corner to find him waiting for her, a faint smile on his face. She wrapped her arms around him and held on tightly, her face pressed against his chest. He put his left arm around her while he gently stroked her hair with his other hand. After a few moments, she forced herself to relax her grip and stepped back, brushing the tears from her eyes.

Patrick had dressed in the clothes she'd found in the attic. To her embarrassment, the front of his shirt was wet where her face had been pressed. He looked down at himself and grinned.

"Fortunately, it's Wash-and-Wear," he laughed.

Julia looked up at him, puzzled.

"Wash-and-Wear. It's a ... thing," he finished, lamely. "Not important. Anyway, I'm sorry that I had you worried. I came downstairs to see about making coffee and something for breakfast, but there doesn't seem to be any food in the icebox and, frankly, I couldn't figure out how to work the percolator. It's a little different than my Mr. Coffee."

Julia laughed. "*Mr. Coffee*? You must be joking."

"Just think of what you have to look forward to."

"I can't wait," she said, unenthusiastically. "In the meantime, allow me to show you how it's done."

Fifteen minutes later, the comforting aroma of freshly-brewed coffee filled the kitchen. Patrick waited patiently for the pot to stop percolating before pouring a cup. In the meantime, Julia dialed the number for a local grocer and ordered enough food to last for at least a couple of days. The shopkeeper promised to have the supplies delivered within the hour.

"Now, that's a service I wish had survived the years," Patrick told her. "Going to the supermarket is not my favorite pastime."

"Supermarket? Does everything have a ridiculous name where you come from?"

"More or less," he admitted, with a smile. "Blame advertising."

Julia settled into the chair across the table from him. "What else does my future hold, Patrick?"

He sighed, studying the serious glint in her eyes.

"I've already told you more than I probably should have. The rest you'll have to discover on your own."

"Will I be happy?" she persisted.

"I think so. I know that you'll be loved."

She looked away, her cheeks flush from embarrassment.

"Why don't you pour us both a cup of coffee," he suggested, gently, "while I go look in on our patient."

As the door swung closed behind him, Julia looked back on the last few days and the glimpses he'd offered of her future. She'd been so quick to dismiss them all as kind words and platitudes.

Lundgren Furniture survives, perhaps even thrives. From the sounds of it, I might just do the same. But, be happy?

At the moment, that hardly seemed possible.

The sound of the telephone, ringing in her father's office, snapped her out of her gloom. Thinking it might be Dr. Unthank calling to check in on Otis, she hurried to pick up.

"Lundgren residence."

"Julia? It's Mac. I need to speak with Patrick."

"Is everything okay, Mac?" she asked, hearing the tension in his voice. The line was silent for a moment.

"Everything is fine," he said at last. "Brent won't be bothering you anymore."

"Mac, you didn't ..." she couldn't form the rest of the question.

"No, I didn't. Not that the thought didn't cross my mind. Is Patrick there, Julia? I really need to talk with him."

"He went upstairs to check on Otis. Let me get him."

Mac sat at the end of his bed, waiting. Patrick's envelope full of twenties sat beside him. Four thousand dollars—he knew, because he'd counted the money twice—neat little stacks held together by Bank of Kenton bands. The same bank that Brent had used to cash the forged check for nearly the same amount.

Coincidences like that made Mac uncomfortable. He didn't for a moment doubt his instincts about Patrick, or his friend's motives, but the questions raised by all of that cash needed some answers.

At last he heard someone at the other end of the receiver.

"Patrick?"

"He's gone, Mac." Julia's voice was thick with emotion. "Patrick is gone."

–27–

Patrick rested his shoulder against the door frame, waiting for the last surge to ebb around him. He knew instinctively that, when he could bring himself to open his eyes, the world would have shifted around him once more. He risked a glance, relieved to see Carl's bedroom door in front of him. That was encouraging. At least he knew the *where*, if not the when.

"Patrick?" he heard Julia call out, her words carrying up to him from the entryway. Hearing her voice at that instant felt like the answer to an unspoken prayer.

He struggled to his feet. To his left, above the staircase, he could see the gilded portrait of the Julia he'd just left, the woman from a lifetime ago. A moment later the other Julia came into view. She climbed the steps slowly, grasping the rail for support. For a moment the two women—young and old—were juxtaposed, the contrast between the images almost too painful for Patrick to contemplate.

Then she paused on the stairway and turned to him, a worried half-smile on her face. She looked at him, questioningly, and he nodded, even managed a weak smile of his own.

She hurried the rest of the way up to him. Patrick wrapped his arms around her, feeling the wetness of still more tears through his clothes.

"I think we've played this scene before, haven't we?" he whispered, hugging her gently. "At this rate my shirt is never going to dry out."

She laughed, tipping her head back to look up at him.

"I swore that I wasn't going to cry. It's your fault though," she added as she pressed herself against him again, "disappearing like that without even saying goodbye."

"I won't let it happen again." Then he stepped back and looked at his friend. "It *doesn't*, does it? Happen again, I mean."

Julia shook her head.

"Is everything all right up there?"

Patrick's head snapped up at the sound of Rachel's voice. Julia eased out of his arms with a sigh.

"Go on, then," she said, her smile a little sad. "You have a bad habit of making the women of this family wait."

Besaw's Café

March 23, 1991

Patrick looked at the menu and chuckled, thinking back to the last time he and Julia had eaten lunch at this restaurant. Meatloaf sandwiches and hamburgers were still on the bill of fare, but a cup of coffee now cost as much as his entire meal had sixty years earlier. He ordered a glass of Pinot—something definitely not on the menu in 1929—and settled in to wait.

Julia arrived fifteen minutes later. She shook the Portland rain from her umbrella and looked around the café. Spotting Patrick, she beamed and waved. Behind her, Max Templeton, a large envelope in his hand, flashed a grin so wide it threatened to split his face in two.

They made their way back through the tables to where Patrick now stood. Julia stretched up to plant a gentle kiss on his cheek. Templeton waited until she had taken a seat before reaching out to pump Patrick's hand enthusiastically.

"Dr. Templeton, this is a pleasant surprise," Patrick admitted as they took their own seats. Max set the envelope he'd been carrying on the table in front of him.

"I hope you don't mind," Julia said, "but when I heard that Rachel wouldn't be able to join us, I took the liberty of inviting him along."

"What is Rachel up to today, anyway?" Max asked.

"Packing," Patrick explained. "She's supposed to be out of her apartment by the end of the month ..."

Templeton's surprise was evident. "Rachel's moving?"

Julia grinned at Patrick, who laughed.

"She's moving in with me. I'm still not sure how it all happened so fast."

"*I* am," her grandmother said, taking his hand between her own. "She is, after all, a Lundgren."

Patrick smiled at that. "Yes, she is," he admitted, fondly. "Anyway, I offered to help her, but she told me that I'd just be in the way. So, I thought that this might be a good opportunity to ... catch up on old times ... with Julia."

"That's why I invited Max. He's been waiting for years for this moment."

"In fact," Templeton added with a wink, "you're the reason I went into physics in the first place. I grew up listening to stories about you from Julia and my grandfather."

"Your grandfather?" They must have seen the puzzled look on Patrick's face, judging by their amused expressions.

"Otis Loring was my grandfather."

"And the only other person I ever shared my secret with," Julia said. "I had to tell him something. Apparently, you put on quite a light show when you disappeared. Besides, I needed to confide in someone."

"He was a fine man," Patrick told Max. "I probably owed him my life."

Templeton smiled. "He always said the same of you. How are you doing after your ordeal?"

"I have to tell you, it's an incredibly strange feeling to be only a week—and yet an entire lifetime—removed from everything that happened. There are so many questions running through my mind right now."

Julia reached over and picked up the large envelope Max had brought with him.

"I think this might fill in some of the gaps," she said, offering it to Patrick with a smile.

Inside, he found a small stack of newspaper articles, photographs and papers, much of it yellowed with age. With the reverence of a historian, he carefully pulled them free of the envelope and set them down on the table in front of him.

The headline of the clipping on top caught Patrick's attention immediately.

Body of Prominent Portland Attorney Found on Dundee Farm

Evidence Suggests Gangland Execution

The body of Portland attorney Leon Brent was discovered by police late yesterday afternoon in the kitchen of a farm house near Dundee. The lawyer, gagged and tied to a chair, had been brutally beaten before dying of a single bullet to the back of the head. One detective indicated the killing had all the earmarks of a gangland slaying.

Brent was reported missing by his wife, Evelyn, who had been staying with her parents in Idaho. She had been unable to reach her husband at either their home or his office for several days.

An anonymous tip that Brent owned property outside of Portland eventually led detectives to the Dundee farm where the lawyer's body was found.

According to police, Brent had long been suspected of being involved with the city's underworld. A former detective familiar with the attorney indicated that Brent, whose real name may have been Leon Schneider, had ties to Chicago's gang violence dating back to before the war.

Patrick looked up from the clipping. "The men from the alley?" he asked.

Julia shrugged. "Mac wouldn't tell me for sure. In fact, he wouldn't talk about Brent, or what happened that night, at all. He never stopped asking about you, though."

"So, he's gone, then? I hope things worked out for him. I'm not sure what I would have done without him."

"He made out fine," she said, smiling. "In fact, I'm pretty sure there's a wedding invitation somewhere in that stack."

"His sister-in-law?"

Julia grinned.

"I'm glad to hear it," he said with a laugh. "If anyone could keep him in line, it was Louise."

He continued thumbing through the collection in front of him. In addition to more articles regarding Brent's murder he found one announcing, briefly, Peregrine Industries' decision not to build a new factory in Portland. Not surprisingly, the company offered no further explanation.

One clipping did catch him completely by surprise, however. Three days after Leon Brent's body had been discovered, John Ingersol committed suicide in his office at Ingersol Tool & Die. He'd left a note, citing financial problems and the loss of his friend, Carl Lundgren.

Patrick looked at Julia, who was watching him closely. "He didn't have anything to do with Brent's plan, you know," he told her, softly.

"I knew that. Uncle John loved Papa like a brother." She took his hand again, giving it a gentle squeeze. "You simply couldn't undo all of the damage Brent caused, Patrick."

He nodded and looked down at the pile in front of him. After everything that he'd been through—that *they'd* been through, he amended, looking at Julia—he should have known better than to hope for events to wrap themselves up in a tidy little package.

"I think that's enough for now," Julia said, as if she could read his thoughts. She gathered the papers and placed them carefully back into the envelope. "You can read the rest later. I hope that answered at least a few of your questions."

"Most of them," Patrick conceded. Then he caught a familiar glint in her eyes. "Unless there's something else that you're not sharing."

Julia looked from Patrick to Max, who was trying unsuccessfully to mask a grin, then back to Patrick once more.

"I have no idea what you're talking about," she told him, innocently. "Now, who's ready for lunch? My treat."

–28–

Moline, Illinois

March 23, 1950

In the annals of baby gifts, the box that Katie and Jim had just received took first prize for the most unusual, hands down.

There was a biography—*Memorial Life of William McKinley Our Martyred President*—dated 1901, and a recounting of the building of the Panama Canal published in 1915. There was a book on the Oregon Trail dating from the turn of the century, and another on the Compromise of 1850, from around the same period.

Beneath those, Jim found a western novel titled *Chaffee of Roaring Horse*, personally autographed by the author, Ernest Haycox. And, finally, a book title that he at least recognized: *The Time Machine*, by H. G. Wells.

"What in the world?" Jim looked to his wife for some kind of an explanation.

"I told you that it was a strange gift. Read the card that came with it."

She pointed to an envelope on the table. He pulled the card free and opened it. *Dear Mr. and Mrs. O'Connell*, he read ...

> *Congratulations on the birth of your son, Patrick. As bright as his future will no doubt be, I thought it appropriate to give him a gift of the past. I suspect, in time, that your son will come to enjoy many of these books as much as my father once did.*
>
> *With kindest regards, Julia Lundgren Wirth and Senator Ed Wirth.*

Jim's eyes widened in recognition. The senator and his wife had come to Moline the year before as members of a farm commission junket, and Jim had been selected to tour them around the plant. Only later did they learn that the Senator had specifically requested of Charles Deere Wiman, the president of John Deere, that Jim serve as their guide. Why a man he'd never met would have asked for him by name was still a mystery, but having the attention of Mr. Wiman certainly hadn't hurt at promotion time.

"I wonder how Mrs. Wirth found out that we'd had the baby," Katie mused.

"And why would she send us these?" Jim muttered, holding one of the books up. "Of all the useless ... For that matter, why would she send us anything at all? We hardly know the woman."

Katie smiled. "I have no idea, but not everything she sent was useless."

She pulled a folded piece of paper from her apron pocket, holding it up with trembling hands for Jim to read.

The check, drawn on a Portland, Oregon bank, had been made out in the amount of five thousand dollars. According to the memo Mrs. Wirth had written, it was intended for their son's college education.

Jim looked at the check in stunned silence. Five thousand dollars, a small fortune for a family like theirs, and from someone they scarcely knew. *Two days old and little Patrick's future has already taken a turn for the better.*

"Well," Jim said with a grin, pulling his Katie close, "under the circumstances, I suppose having a few history books around can't do any harm, can they?"

About the Author

Keith Tittle is a software trainer, a life-long history buff, and a native of the Pacific Northwest. He lives with his wife and family—and assorted cats—in Southwest Washington.

Twice a finalist in the Pacific Northwest Writers Association literary contest for short fiction, Drawn Back is his first novel.

Made in the USA
San Bernardino, CA
21 June 2014